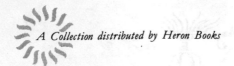 *A Collection distributed by Heron Books*

THE
GREATEST MASTERPIECES
OF
RUSSIAN LITERATURE

MAXIM GORKY

THE SPY

Introduction by
R. D. B. Thomson M.A. (Oxon) D.Phil. (Oxon)

Original Frontispiece by Jean-Pierre Chabrol

Original Illustrations by Anthony Colbert

Distributed by
HERON BOOKS

13 005 28 R

Maxim Gorky

INTRODUCTION

To appreciate the works of Maxim Gorky, the famous Russian writer, novelist and playwright, it is important to know something of his life and times. For Gorky's works are always about life as he knew it, and they are nearly always set in Russia and in his own life-time at that. Gorky depended very little on his imagination for the plots of his stories, in fact he himself claimed that he had hardly had to invent a single one. He was able to write straight out of the wealth of his own personal experience, recalling either some of the strange incidents that he had witnessed, or the extraordinary personalities that he had encountered. In the same way, the ideas behind Gorky's works represent the conclusions that Gorky himself had drawn from his unusual life.

Gorky's first memories were of the death of his father, followed by the death soon after birth of a younger brother. Then came a painful and bewildering estrangement from his mother, and a life of incomprehensible brutality in the home of his grandparents, whose family business, a dye-works, was slowly going downhill and dragging the family into bankruptcy. At the age of ten Gorky was sent out to work, to help support his penniless grandparents. Here an even more depressing picture met Gorky's eyes. Everywhere people seemed to be deceitful, malicious and unhappy, and this in turn led to yet more deceit and more suffering; there seemed to be no escape from this vicious circle. And if read from this angle Gorky's stories of his early life might seem to be utterly hopeless and gloomy. But here we must remember Gorky's own life and the all-important point that he for one did escape from this wretched existence; and not only that, but he lived to fight against it by his books and, to some extent, by his political activity. Gorky found in his own rise from the depths the proof that human cruelty and folly was not the only truth about human nature.

There were two decisive influences in Gorky's life that enabled him to get out of his situation and survey it from the outside. The first was his exceptionally wide reading. In books he discovered the existence of a new and better world, where the heroes were invariably courageous, heroines beautiful, and even the villains seemed noble by comparison with the squalid individuals he met in everyday life. Of course, Gorky realised that such characters contained a great deal of romantic exaggeration, but he knew too that writers could not have invented them without some justification in real life; and he could not fail to notice that such books tended to come from the West, whereas Russian literature was predominantly harsh and gloomy. Gorky deduced from this that life in Russia was not typical of life everywhere; that Russian conditions were in some way peculiarly unfavourable. But at this early stage Gorky's reading gave him no idea of how to change these conditions; instead they gave him an intense reverence for books and the vision of a better life that they provided. This was to be an important stage in his miraculous rise from his unpromising beginnings.

The second important influence in Gorky's life came during the years 1888-1892, which he spent in tramping all over Western Russia. Much of the time Gorky was simply looking for work, but at the same time he was looking for answers to the questions that plagued him about life in Russia. Gorky was not alone in his travels. Driven out of their homes by unemployment and a succession of bad harvests, hundreds of other Russians were tramping the roads of Russia at just this time. Gorky was brought into contact with a type of Russian quite different from the settled, unadventurous citizens of the towns where he had spent his childhood. What particularly impressed Gorky about these people was the fact that they had refused to conform to the standards of organised society, because this meant the loss of their individuality. Their self-reliance was matched by their physical strength and intellectual independence. When work meant long hours of degrading drudgery with only a pittance for wages, these men had chosen to live their own lives their own way. Some of them were content to live on charity, or to make do with occasional jobs which would bring in a bit of money and temporary security. Others, like the smuggler Chelkash, described in the story of the same name, took to crime. Gorky came to the conclusion that the good qualities of these men made them some of the finest people to be found in Russia of the time. The immense variety of their social backgrounds, aristocratic, intellectual, middle-class, artisan and peasant, indicated that these problems were felt by multitudes of other independent-minded Russians.

Gorky felt that there must be something wrong with a country which neglected the talents of so many of its citizens, and he spent much time and thought on this problem. At first he tended to see it as a universal situation, and he naturally romanticised the rebels and the outsiders in their protest, whether passive or active, against the deadening conformity of organised society. But gradually he came to believe that it was not just a problem of two types of psychology— the conformists and the rebels, but that it was a direct consequence of the defects of existing Russian society. The autocratic system of Imperial Russia and the feudal structure of its bureaucracy meant that only yes-men could get to the top under normal conditions. There was no place inside the system for originality or disagreement. Such men were disgraced, exiled or even executed.

Thus Gorky's thoughts about the tramps of Russia led him on inevitably to the idea of re-organising the whole of Russian society, and this deeper view of affairs led him by a natural process into sympathy with the Russian revolutionary movements. This evolution can be traced quite plainly in Gorky's early fiction. The romantic aura investing his early individualistic heroes is gradually stripped away. They are no longer rebel-heroes, showing men how they ought to live, but isolated and doomed protesters, as much victims of their society as the faceless conformists they so detested.

Thus, from about 1900 onwards Gorky's stories take on a more markedly political slant. His characters, whether strong or weak, are shown as helpless victims of their environment. But even here Gorky instinctively retained his sympathy for the strong; they might be doomed, but at least they fought to the last. He could discern elements of tragedy in such figures as Foma Gordeev (in the novel of the same name, written in 1899); but for the weak he felt nothing but con-tempt, and his novel The Spy *is an eloquent illustration of this prejudice.*

INTRODUCTION

But by 1907, when Gorky composed this novel, the political situation inside Russia had changed dramatically, and the author's views had crystallised into definite political ideas and an active sympathy for Lenin's party of the Bolsheviks. The crucial event of these years was the Russian Revolution of 1905, which was only finally subdued in 1907. Gorky himself played an active part in these events; indeed he was so active that he was arrested and thrown into prison by the Tsarist authorities. But after world-wide protests on his behalf (for the Tsarist Government was sensitive to world opinion) he was released on the understanding that he should leave the country immediately. So it came about that Gorky was to spend the next seven years in emigration, mainly in the Isle of Capri. But first he went to the United States, where he hoped to mobilise popular opinion and official policy against the Tsarist Government, which was then negotiating a loan to cover the serious financial losses incurred in the disastrous Russo-Japanese War of 1904-5. It was hoped too that he might be able instead to raise some money for the revolutionary cause.

These hopes, however, ended in utter fiasco when the Tsarist Embassy in America revealed to the Press that Gorky's travelling-companion, the famous actress Maria Andreeva, was not his legal wife. The American Press seized on the story, and the greater part of American society turned its back on the Russian writer. This rebuff was a terrible shock to Gorky, but it served only to strengthen his convictions, and he soon produced a series of vitriolic articles and other writings on bourgeois society, both Western and Russian: the pamphlet on New York, 'The City of the Yellow Devil', the play Enemies, and, best-known of all, the novel Mother. It is sometimes forgotten, however, that at the time of writing these works Gorky was still living in America in the house of a friend—one of the few who had not deserted him.

Mother is an account of the revolutionary movement among the workers of a small industrial town in Central Russia. It was in fact based on real incidents and real characters; but Gorky's feelings were running too high at the time for him to be fully objective in his attitude, and the book reads at times like a political tract. This led Gorky later to turn against the novel, and describe it as ' a bad book, written in a fit of irritation '. Lenin, however, welcomed the book just because of its propaganda value, and as a result it has always enjoyed a high reputation in Soviet Russia.

INTRODUCTION

The Spy *was Gorky's next novel, and in it he returns again to the same events of 1905, but this time he depicts them from another angle, that of the police. The central figure (one can hardly call him a hero), Evsey Klimkov is an agent provocateur working for the Tsarist police. It is easy to guess that Gorky's attitude to such a character was bound to be highly critical, if not actually contemptuous. However, the characterisation here is subtler than in* Mother, *and Gorky successfully resists the temptation to turn Evsey into a monster of iniquity. Instead he shows him as merely unintelligent and passive. He hardly understands what he is doing, and he makes little attempt to act or take decisions. He drifts into situations in which he betrays his closest friends and associates, rather than consciously planning their downfall. Although Gorky does not draw the reader's attention to this, the irony is none the less obvious and very effective.*

Evsey's feebleness does not mitigate his behaviour in Gorky's eyes. Just the opposite; he believed passionately that indecision and passivity were vices, just as harmful in their consequences as the crimes which are generally recognised as such, such as murder and treachery. Indeed, he tries to show in this novel that the former lead inevitably into the latter. In this he was of course influenced by the hardships and struggles of his own early life. He had learnt the hard way that men must take decisions and act if they are to achieve anything at all. He wished also to counter the religious teaching of Tolstoy and Dostoevsky, who advocated non-resistance to evil and a voluntary abnegation of self in all dealings with the outer world. Gorky, on the other hand, believed that these Christian attitudes were frequently hypocritical, and that they could be twisted to permit the grossest acquiescence in immoral actions, and a conscious turning of the blind eye. Thus the figure of Evsey Klimkov in The Spy *carries also a moral and philosophical argument. His first words in the book are: ' I don't know ' and Gorky time and again stresses his utter failure to understand what is going on, and even the implications and consequences of his own actions. From his childhood onwards he is known as ' old man ', because of his tired and flaccid character. He is perpetually afraid, and he tends to explain everything in terms of fear and suspicion. In all these details Gorky indicates his hatred of Evsey and those like him.*

So it is that Evsey drifts into working for the political police. He dislikes his work, but he lacks the character to do anything about it.

INTRODUCTION

He is even attracted by the revolutionaries whom he is supposed to observe. They are shown as young men, full of energy, and bursting with good health and gaiety. Their youth suggests that the future lies with them, and their ideas for reform are presented as elementary common-sense with which any reasonable person must agree. But Evsey is afraid of taking the plunge; he feels that work in the police is a protection from the insecurity of normal life, which he fears more than anything else, and above all from the prospect of social change for which he is utterly unprepared. Gorky would have been appalled if he had foreseen that the revolutionaries he depicted so sympathetically would set up their own police system, equally brutal and cynical, within a few weeks of their coming to power in 1917.

The type of the police spy was a common one in the last decades of Tsarist Russia, and during the years of the 1905 Revolution their numbers and influence reached extraordinary proportions. Most notorious of all was Evno Azef, who was at one and the same time an important official in the political police and the chief organiser of the terrorist activities of the Social-Revolutionary Party. By comparison with Azef Evsey is obviously only a small fish, but the widespread existence of this type in Russian life at the time explains the topical appeal of Gorky's novel, which is itself a revelation of the corrupt and divided state of Russian contemporary society. Not surprisingly, the Soviet regime has been rather cautious about using this particular novel of Gorky's for its propaganda value.

The Spy, *however, is an interesting novel, because it shows Gorky's interest in a different type and class of character from his usual heroes, and, although it stands outside the mainstream of his works, it provides a valuable sidelight on the complexities of his own character. A very similar situation re-appears again in his last novel, the unfinished* Life of Klim Samgin, *and several of his later short stories, ' The Tale of a Hero ' and ' Karamora ', deal with the peculiar psychology of the police-spy. Indeed the persistence of this theme in Gorky's work suggests a more than passing interest, and there may well have been some such experience in Gorky's own life. In his autobiographical* My Universities *he tells how he was tentatively approached by the Tsarist police in his youth; and the vividness with which he later described the fictional Klim Samgin's reactions to the same approach may well be based on his own memories; though*

Samgin rejects the offer he is surprised to discover that he is not particularly shocked; perhaps Gorky was afraid of these weaknesses in himself.

After the writing of The Spy *Gorky continued to keep up his political contacts with Lenin and the other Bolshevik leaders. He also tried to contribute to the education of the Russian working-classes by founding a school called Proletarian Culture in Capri. Lenin, however, disliked the idea; he suspected that Gorky intended to put the stress on culture, and not, as he would have liked, on revolutionary tactics. Accordingly, he took steps to undercut the success of the school, and it soon collapsed. As a result of this, relations between Gorky and Lenin became somewhat strained, and Gorky's revolutionary enthusiasms subsided. He continued to take a close interest in Russian affairs, but his exile effectively prevented him from playing any part in them. For one of Gorky's temperament this enforced inactivity was intolerable, and he consoled himself with more purely literary concerns.*

Gorky's chance to return to Russia came in 1913, when the 300th anniversary of the Romanov dynasty was made the occasion for a wide-ranging amnesty. Gorky took advantage of this opportunity, and soon after his return he set about opening a newspaper, called Chronicle, *which he used as a mouthpiece for his views. On the outbreak of the First World War he took a pacifist line, risking considerable unpopularity by this ' unpatriotic ' stand; he was even accused of being a German agent. But Gorky was not the man to trim his opinions to win easy favour, and he was doing his patriotic duty as he saw it. For he was convinced that the Great War constituted a terrible threat to the first timid steps, recently taken towards creating democratic institutions in Russia; and above all he was actuated by purely humanitarian motives. Subsequent history has illustrated all too clearly the correctness of Gorky's fears in both these respects.*

In the crisis of February-March 1917, which led to the abdication of Tsar Nicholas II, and the setting up of a revolutionary caretaker Government under Kerensky, pending full-scale democratic elections, Gorky's position was unequivocal. His newspaper gave unconditional support to the new Government, and he changed its name from Chronicle *to* New Life, *eloquent evidence of his enthusiasm for the revolution. Now that democracy seemed at last to have been established in Russia, and his lifelong dreams finally realised, Gorky was determined to protect this new popular government in every way he could. And so, paradoxically, he now advocated the continuation of the war, in the fear that the return of masses of disaffected troops from the front might upset the delicate balance of political power in the country, and throw it into anarchy. He now recommended stern measures against Lenin and the Bolsheviks, because they were hostile to Kerensky's Government, and were openly plotting its overthrow in the name of the Communist proletarian revolution. As the Bolsheviks stepped up their agitation, so Gorky attacked them ever more bitterly. And even after the Bolsheviks had achieved their ends by the coups of November 1917 and January 1918, he continued to attack them for having betrayed the cause of Russian democracy, just for the sake of personal power.* New Life *(its title now sounding wholly ironic) was finally forced to close down in the middle of 1918.*

Gorky continued to work with the Bolshevik leaders for a few more years, but his many disagreements on matters of principle led to increasing friction, and eventually Gorky had to emigrate once again, just as he had done under the Tsar sixteen years earlier. This spell of emigration was to prove even longer, for the Soviet authorities were at first hostile to Gorky and only gradually relented towards him. He returned to the Soviet Union for a brief visit in the summer of 1928, when he was greeted as a national hero, and he repeated these visits in subsequent years, finally settling in Russia in 1933; he remained there until his death in 1936.

Since his return Gorky's name has been a household word in Soviet Russia. His works are widely read and loved, and would-be writers are exhorted to follow his example. But it must be admitted that in this canonisation of Maxim Gorky, many of the complexities of his life and character have been ignored. His disputes with Lenin and the early Bolsheviks have been glossed over, the true reasons for his emigration have been played down, and even such works as The Spy *which do not fit in with the official account of Gorky have not received their just appreciation.*

R. D. B. Thomson

CHAPTER I

WHEN Yevsey Klimkov was four years old, his father was shot dead by the forester ; and when he was seven years old, his mother died. She died suddenly in the field at harvest time. And so strange was this that Yevsey was not even frightened by the sight of her dead body.

Uncle Piotr, a blacksmith, put his hand on the boy's head, and said :

"What are we going to do now ?"

Yevsey took a sidelong glance at the corner where his mother lay upon a bench, and answered in a low voice :

" I don't know."

The blacksmith wiped the sweat from his face with his shirt-sleeve, and after a long silence gently shoved his nephew aside.

" You're going to live with me," he said. " We'll send you to school, I suppose, so that you won't be in our way. Ah, you old man !"

From that day the boy was called Old Man. The nickname suited him very well. He was too small for his age, his movements were sluggish, and his voice

1

thin. A little bird-like nose stuck out sadly from a bony face, his round, colourless eyes blinked timorously, his hair was sparse and grew in tufts. The impression he made was of a puny, shrivelled-up little old fellow. The children in school laughed at him and beat him, his dull, oldish look and his owl-like face somehow irritating the healthier and livelier among them. He held himself aloof, and lived alone, silently, always in the shade, or in some corner or hole. Without winking his round eyes, he looked forth upon the people from his retirement, cautiously contracted like a snail in its shell. When his eyes grew tired he closed them, and for a long time sat sightless, gently swaying his thin body.

Yevsey endeavoured to escape observation even in his uncle's home ; but here it was difficult. He had to dine and sup in the company of the whole family, and when he sat at the table, Yashka, the uncle's eldest son, a lusty, red-faced youngster, tried every trick to tease him or make him laugh. He made faces, stuck out his tongue, kicked Yevsey's legs under the table, and pinched him. He never succeeded, however, in making the Old Man laugh, though he did succeed in producing quite the opposite result, for often Yevsey would start with pain, his yellow face would turn grey, his eyes open wide, and his spoon tremble in his hand.

" What is it ?" his Uncle Piotr sometimes asked.

" It's Yashka," the boy explained in an even voice, in which there was no note of complaint.

If Uncle Piotr gave Yashka a box on the ear, or pulled his hair, Aunt Agafya puckered up her lips and muttered angrily :

" Ugh, you tell-tale !"

And then Yashka found him somewhere, and pummelled him long and assiduously upon back, sides,

and stomach. Yevsey endured the drubbing as something inevitable. It would not have been profitable
to complain of Yashka, because if Uncle Piotr beat his
son, Aunt Agafya repayed the punishment with interest
upon her nephew, and her blows were more painful
than Yashka's. So when Yevsey saw that Yashka
wanted to attack him, he merely ran away, though he
was always overtaken. Then the Old Man dropped to
the ground, and pressed his body to the soil with all his
might, pulling up his knees to his stomach, covering
his face and his head with his hands, and silently yielding his sides and back to his cousin's fists. The more
patiently he bore the buffeting, the angrier grew
Yashka. Sometime Yashka even cried and shouted,
while he kicked his cousin's body :

" You nasty louse, you, scream !"

Once Yevsey found a horseshoe and gave it to the
little pugilist, because he knew Yashka would take it
from him, in any case. Mollified by the present, Yashka
asked :

" Did I hurt you very much when I beat you the last
time ?"

" Very much," answered Yevsey.

Yashka thought a while, scratched his head, and
said in embarrassment :

" It's nothing. It will pass away."

He left Yevsey, but somehow his words settled deep
in the Old Man's heart, and he repeated hopefully in an
undertone :

" It will pass away."

Once Yevsey saw some women pilgrims rubbing
their tired feet with nettles. He followed their example,
and applied the nettles to his bruised sides. It seemed
to him his pain was greatly assuaged. From that time

he religiously rubbed his wounds with the down of the noxious and despised weed.

He was poor at his lessons, because he came to school full of dread of being beaten, and he left school swelling with a sense of insult. His apparent apprehension of being wronged evoked in others the unconquerable desire to ply the Old Man with blows.

It turned out that Yevsey had a counter tenor, and the teacher took him to the church choir. After this he had to be at home less, but to compensate he met his schoolmates more frequently, at the rehearsals, and they all fought no less than Yashka.

The old frame church pleased Yevsey. He was always strongly drawn to peep into the snug, warm quiet of its many dark corners, expecting to find in one of them something uncommon and good, which would embrace him, press him tenderly to itself, and speak to him the way his mother used to. All the sacred images, black with many years of soot, with their good yet stern expression, recalled the dark-bearded face of Uncle Piotr.

At the church entrance was a picture, which depicted a saint who had caught the devil, and was beating him ; the saint a tall, dark, sinewy fellow with long hands, the devil a reddish, lean, wizened creature of stunted growth resembling a little goat. At first Yevsey did not look at the devil ; he had a desire to spit at him surreptitiously ; but then he began to pity the unfortunate little fiend, and when nobody was around he tenderly stroked the goat-like little chin, disfigured by dread and pain. Thus, for the first time, a sense of pity sprang up in the boy's heart.

Yevsey liked the church for another reason : here all the people, even the notorious ruffians, dropped their boisterousness, and conducted themselves quietly and submissively. For loud talk frightened Yevsey. He ran away from excited faces and shouts, and hid himself, owing to the fact that once on a market-day he had seen a brawl between a number of muzhiks, which began by their talking to one another in very loud voices. Then they shouted and pushed ; next someone seized a pole, waved it about, and struck another man. A terrible howl ensued ; many started to run. They knocked the Old Man off his feet, and he fell face downwards in a puddle. When he jumped up, he saw a huge muzhik coming toward him waving his hands, with a quivering, gory blotch instead of a face. This was so terrible that Yevsey yelled, and suddenly felt as if he were being precipitated into a black pit. He had to be sprinkled with water to bring him to his senses.

Yevsey was also afraid of drunken men. His mother had told him that a demon takes up his abode in the body of a drunkard. The Old Man imagined this demon prickly as a hedgehog and moist as a frog, with a reddish body and green eyes, who settles in a man's stomach, stirs about there, and turns the man into an evil fiend.

There were many other good things about the church. Besides the quiet and tender twilight, Yevsey liked the singing. When he sang without notes, he closed his eyes firmly, and letting his clear, plaintive soprano blend with the general chorus in order that it should not be heard above the others, he hid himself deliciously somewhere, as if overcome by a sweet sleep. In this drowsy state it seemed to him he was drifting away from life, approaching another gentle, peaceful existence.

5

THE SPY

A thought took shape in his mind, which he once expressed to his uncle in these words :

" Can a person live so that he can go everywhere and see everything, but be seen by nobody ?"

" Invisibly ?" asked the blacksmith, and thought a while. " I should suppose it would be impossible." He turned his black face to his nephew, and added seriously, " Yes, of course, it would be very nice if you could do it, Orphan."

From the moment that all the villagers began to call Yevsey " Old Man," Uncle Piotr used " Orphan " instead. A peculiar man in every respect, the blacksmith was not terrible even when drunk. He would merely remove his hat from his head and walk about the street waving it, singing in a high, doleful voice, smiling, and shaking his head. The tears would run down his face even more copiously than when he was sober.

His uncle seemed to Yevsey the very wisest and best muzhik in the whole village. He could talk with him about everything. Though he often smiled, he scarcely ever laughed ; he spoke without haste, in a quiet, serious tone. Either failing to notice his nephew, or forgetting about him—which especially pleased Yevsey—he would talk to himself in his shop, keeping up a constant dispute with some invisible opponent, and for ever admonishing him.

" Confound you," he would mumble, but without anger. " Greedy maw ! Don't I work ? There, I have scorched my eyes. I'll soon get blind. What else do you want ? A curse on this life ! Hard luck ! No beauty—no joy !"

His interjections sounded as if he were composing psalms, and Yevsey had the impression that his

6

uncle was actually facing the man he was addressing.

Once Yevsey asked :

" Whom are you talking to ?"

" Whom am I talking to ?" repeated the blacksmith, without looking at the boy. Then he smiled, and answered : " I'm talking to my stupidity."

But it was a rare thing for Yevsey to be able to speak with his guardian, for he was seldom alone. Yashka, round as a top, often spun about the place, drowning the blows of the hammer and the crackling of the coals in the furnace with his piercing shouts. In his presence Yevsey did not dare even to look at his uncle.

The smithy stood at the edge of a shallow ravine, at the bottom of which, among the osier bushes, Yevsey passed all his leisure time in spring, summer, and autumn. Here it was as peaceful as in the church. The birds warbled, the bees and drones hummed, and a fine, quiet song quivered in the air. The boy sat there, swaying his body, and brooding with tightly shut eyes ; or he roamed amid the bushes, listening to the noise in the blacksmith's shop. When he perceived his uncle was alone, he crept out and went up to him.

" What, you, Orphan ?" was the blacksmith's greeting, as he scrutinized the boy with his little eyes, wet with tears.

Once Yevsey asked :

" Is the evil power in the church at night ?"

The smith thought a while, and answered :

" Why should it not be ? It gets everywhere. That's easy for it."

The boy raised his shoulders, and, with his round eyes, searchingly examined the dark corners of the shop.

7

" Don't be afraid of the devils," the uncle advised.

Yevsey sighed, and answered quietly :

" I am not afraid."

" They won't hurt you," the blacksmith explained with assurance, wiping his eyes with his black fingers. Then Yevsey asked :

" And how about God ?"

" What about Him ?"

" Why does God let devils get into the church ?"

" What's that to Him ?   God isn't the keeper of the church."

" Doesn't He live there ?"

" Who ?   God ?   Why should He ?   His place, Orphan, is everywhere.   The churches are for the people."

" And the people—what are they for ?"

" The people—it seems they are—in general—for everything.   You can't get along without people."

" Are they for God ?"

The blacksmith looked askance at his nephew, and answered after a pause :

" Of course."   Wiping his hands on his apron and staring at the fire in the furnace, he added : " I don't know about this business, Orphan.   Why don't you ask the teacher or the priest ?"

Yevsey wiped his nose on his shirt-sleeve.

" I'm afraid of them."

" It would be better for you not to talk of such things," the uncle advised gravely.   " You are a little boy.   You should play out in the open air, and store up health.   If you want to live, you must be a healthy man.   If you are not strong, you can't work.   Then you can't live at all.   That's all *we* know, and what God needs is unknown to us."   He grew silent, and meditated without removing his eyes from the fire.   After a time he continued in a serious tone, speaking abruptly :

THE SPY

" On the one hand I know nothing, on the other hand I don't understand. They say all wisdom comes from Him. Yet it's evident that the thicker one's candle before God the more wolfish the heart." He looked around the shop, and his eyes fell on the boy in the corner. "Why are you squeezing yourself into that crack ? I told you to go out and play." As Yevsey crept out timidly, the smith added, " A spark will fall into your eye, and then you'll be one-eyed. Who wants a one-eyed fellow ?"

His mother had told Yevsey several stories on winter nights when the snowstorm, knocking against the walls of the hut, ran along the roof, touched everything as if groping for something in anguish, crept down the chimney, and whined there mournfully in different keys. The mother recited the tales quietly, drowsily. Her speech sometimes grew confused ; often she repeated the same words several times. It seemed to the boy she saw everything about which she spoke, but obscurely, as in the dark.

The neighbours reminded Yevsey of his mother's tales. The blacksmith, too, it seemed, saw in the furnace-fire both devils and God, and all the terrors of human life. That was why he continually wept. While Yevsey listened to his talk, which set his heart a-quiver with a dreadful tremor of expectation, the hope insensibly formulated itself that some day he would see something remarkable, not resembling the life in the village, the drunken muzhiks, the cantankerous women, the boisterous children—something quite different, without noise and confusion, without malice and quarrelling; something lovable and serious, like the church service.

One of the neighbours was a blind girl, with whom Yevsey became intimate. He took her to walk in the

9

village, carefully helped her down the ravine, and spoke to her in a low voice, opening wide his watery eyes in fear. This friendship did not escape the notice of the villagers, all of whom it pleased. But once the mother of the blind girl came to Uncle Piotr with a complaint. She declared Yevsey had frightened Tanya with his talk, and now she could not leave her daughter alone, because the girl cried and slept poorly, had disturbed dreams, and started out of her sleep screaming. What Yevsey had said to her it was impossible to make out. She kept babbling about devils, about the sky being black and having holes in it, about fires visible through the holes, and about devils who made sport in there, and teased people. What does it mean ? How can anyone tell a little girl such stuff ?

" Come here," said Uncle Piotr to his nephew.

When Yevsey quietly left his corner, the smith put his rough, heavy hand on his head and asked :

" Did you tell her all that ?"

" I did."

" Why ?"

" I don't know."

The blacksmith, without removing his hand, shoved back the boy's head, and looking into his eyes asked gravely :

" Why, is the sky black ?"

" What else is it if she can't see ?" Yevsey muttered.

" Who ?"

" Tanya."

" Yes," said the blacksmith. After a moment's reflection he asked : " And how about the fire being black ? Why did you invent that ?"

The boy dropped his eyes and was silent.

"Well, speak. Nobody is beating you. Why did you tell her all that nonsense, eh ?"

"I was sorry for her," whispered Yevsey.

The blacksmith pushed him aside lightly.

"You shan't talk to her any more, do you hear ? Never ! Don't worry, Aunt Praskovya, we'll put an end to this friendship."

"You ought to give him a whipping," said the mother. "My little girl lived quietly, she wasn't a bit of a bother to anybody, and now someone has to be with her all the time."

After Praskovya had left, the smith, without saying anything, led Yevsey by the hand into the yard.

"Now talk sensibly. Why did you frighten the little girl ?"

The uncle's voice was not loud, but it was stern. Yevsey became frightened, and quickly began to justify himself, stuttering over his words.

"I didn't frighten her—I did it just—just—she kept complaining—she said I see only black, but for you everything—so I began to tell her everything is black to keep her from being envious. I didn't mean to frighten her at all."

Yevsey broke into sobs, feeling himself wronged. Uncle Piotr smiled.

"You fool ! You should have remembered that she's been blind only three years. She wasn't born blind. She lost her sight after she had the smallpox. So she recollects what things are really bright. Oh, what a stupid fellow !"

"I'm not stupid. She believed me," Yevsey retorted, wiping his eyes.

"Well, all right. Only don't go with her any more. Do you hear ?"

11

THE SPY

" I won't."

" As to your crying, it's nothing. Let them think I gave you a beating." The blacksmith tapped Yevsey on the shoulder, and continued with a smile : " You and I, we're cheats, both of us."

The little fellow buried his head in his uncle's side, and asked tremulously :

" Why is everybody down on me ?"

" I don't know, Orphan," answered the uncle, after a moment's reflection.

The wrongs to which he was subjected now began to yield the boy a sort of bitter satisfaction. A dim conviction settled upon him that he was not like everybody else, and this was why all were down on him. He observed that all the people were malicious and worn out with ill-will. They lived, each deceiving his neighbour, abusing one another, and drinking. Everyone sought for mastery over his fellow, though over himself he was not master. Yevsey saw no man who was not in constant fear of something. The whole of life was filled with terror, and terror sundered the people one from another.

The village stood upon a low hill. On the other side of the river stretched a marsh. In the summer after a hot day it exhaled a stifling lilac-coloured mist, which breathed a putrid breath upon the village, and sent upon the people a swarm of mosquitoes. The people, angry and pitiful, scratched themselves until blood came. From behind the thin woods in the distance climbed a lowering reddish moon. Huge and round it looked through the haze like a dull sinister eye. Yevsey thought it was threatening him with all kinds of misery and dread. He feared its dirty, reddish face. When he saw it over the marsh he hid himself, and in his sleep he was tormented by heavy dreams. At night bluish, trembling lights strayed over the marsh, said to be the homeless spirits of sinners. The villagers sighed over them sorrowfully, pitying them. But for one another they had no pity.

It was possible for them, however, to have lived differently, in friendship and joy. An incident Yevsey once witnessed proved this to him.

One night the granary of the rich muzhik Veretennikov caught fire. The little boy ran into the garden, and climbed up a willow-tree to look at the conflagration.

It seemed to him that the many-winged, supple body of a horrible smoke-begrimed bird with a fiery jaw was circling in the sky. It inclined its red, blazing head to the ground, greedily tore the straw with its sharp, fiery teeth, gnawed at the wood, and licked it with its hundred yellow tongues. Its smoky body playfully coiled in the black sky, fell upon the village, crept along the roofs of the houses, and again raised itself aloft majestically and lightly, without removing its flaming red head from the ground. It snorted, scattering sheaves of sparks, whistling with joy in its evil work, singeing, puffing, and spreading its raging jaw wider and wider, embracing the wood more and more greedily with its red ribbons of flame.

In the presence of the fire the people turned small and black. They sprinkled water into its jaws, thrust long poles at it, and tore flaming sheaves from between its teeth. Then they trampled the sheaves. The people, too, coughed, sniffed, and sneezed, gasping for breath in the greasy smoke. They shouted and roared, their voices blending with the crackling and roaring of the fire. They approached nearer and nearer to the

13

great bird, surrounding its red head with a black, living ring, as if tightening a noose about its body. Here and there the noose broke, but they tied it again, and crowded about more firmly. The noose strangled the fire, which lay there savagely. It jumped up, and its body swelled, writhing like a snake, striving to free its head; but the people held it fast to the ground. Finally, enfeebled, exhausted, and sullen it fell upon the neighbouring granaries, crept along the gardens, and dwindled away, shattered and faint.

" All together !" shouted the villagers, encouraging one another.

"Water !" rang out the women's voices.

The women formed a chain from the fire to the river, strangers and kinsmen, friends and enemies all in a row. And the buckets of water were rapidly passed from hand to hand.

" Quick, women ! Quick, good women !"

It was pleasant and cheerful to look upon this good, friendly life in conflict with the fire. The people emboldened one another. They spoke words of praise for displays of dexterity and disputed in kindly jest. The shouts were free from malice. In the presence of the fire everybody seemed to see his neighbour as good, and each grew pleasant to the other. When at last the fire was vanquished, the villagers grew even jolly. They sang songs, laughed, boasted of the work, and joked. The older people got whisky to drink away their exhaustion, while the young folk remained in the streets amusing themselves almost until morning. And everything was as good as in a dream.

Yevsey heard not a single malicious shout, nor noticed a single angry face. During the entire time the fire was burning no one wept from pain or abuse; no one roared with the beastly roar of savage malice, ready for murder.

The next day Yevsey said to his uncle :

" How nice it was last night !"

" Yes, Orphan, it was nice. A little more, and the fire would have burned away half the village."

" I mean about the people," explained the boy. " How they joined together in a friendly way. If they would live like that all the time, if there were a fire all the time !"

The blacksmith reflected for an instant, then asked in surprise :

" You mean there should be fires all the time ?" He looked at Yevsey sternly, and shook his finger. " You wiseacre, you look out ! Don't think such sinful thoughts. Just see him ! He finds pleasure in fires !"

CHAPTER II

WHEN Yevsey completed the school course, the black-smith said to him :

"What shall we do with you now ? There's nothing for you here. You must go to the city. I have to get bellows there, and I'll take you along, Orphan."

"Will you yourself take me ?"

"Yes. Are you sorry to leave the village ?"

" No, but I am sorry on account of you."

The blacksmith put a piece of iron in the furnace, and adjusting the coals with the tongs, said thought-fully :

" There's no reason to be sorry on account of me. I am grown up. I am the muzhik I ought to be, like every other muzhik."

" You're better than everybody else," Yevsey said, in a low voice.

It seemed that Uncle Piotr did not hear the last remark, for he did not answer, but removed the glowing iron from the fire, screwed up his eyes, and begun to hammer, scattering the red sparks all about him. Then he suddenly stopped, slowly dropped the hand in which he held the hammer, and said, smiling :

" I ought to give you some advice—how to live and all such things."

Yevsey waited to hear the advice. The blacksmith,

however, apparently forgetful of his nephew, put the iron back into the fire, wiped the tears from his cheeks, and looked into the furnace. A muzhik entered, bringing a cracked tire. Yevsey went out to go to the ravine, where he crouched in the bushes until sunset, waiting for his uncle to be alone, which did not happen.

The day of his departure from the village was effaced from the boy's memory. He recalled only that when he rode out into the fields, it was dark and the air strangely oppressive. The waggon jolted horribly, and on both sides rose black, motionless trees. The further they advanced, the wider the space became and the brighter the atmosphere. The uncle was sullen the whole way, and reluctantly gave brief and unintelligible answers to Yevsey's questions.

They rode an entire day, stopping overnight in a little village. Yevsey heard the fine and protracted playing of an accordion, a woman weeping, and occasionally an angry voice crying out, "Shut up!" and swearing abusively.

The travellers continued on their way the same night. Two dogs accompanied them, running around the waggon and whining. As they left the village a bittern boomed sullenly and plaintively in the forest to the left of the road.

" God grant good luck !" mumbled the blacksmith.

Yevsey fell asleep, and awoke when his uncle lightly tapped him on his legs with the butt-end of the whip.

" Look, Orphan."

To the sleepy eyes of the boy the city appeared like a huge field of buckwheat. Thick and varicoloured, it stretched endlessly, with the golden church steeples standing out like yellow pimpinellas, and the dark bands of the streets looking like fences between the patches.

"Oh, how large!" said Yevsey. After another look, he asked his uncle cautiously: "Will you come to see me?"

"Certainly, whenever I come to the city. You will begin to make money, and I will ask you to give me some. 'Orphan,' I'll say, 'give your uncle about three rubles.'"

"I'll give you all my money."

"You mustn't give me all. You should give only as much as you won't be sorry to part with. To give less is shameful; to give more is unfair."

The city grew quickly and became more and more varied in colouring. It glittered green, red, and golden, reflecting the rays of the sun from the glass of the countless windows and from the gold of the church steeples. It seemed to make promises, kindling in the heart a confused curiosity, a dim expectation of something unusual. Kneeling in the waggon with his hand on his uncle's shoulder, Yevsey looked before him while the smith said:

"You live this way—do whatever is assigned to you; hold yourself aloof; beware of the bold men. One bold man out of ten succeeds, and nine go to pieces."

He spoke with indecision, as if he himself doubted whether he was saying what he ought to say, and he searched his thoughts for something else more important. Yevsey listened attentively and gravely, expecting to hear a special warning against the terrors and dangers of the new life. But the blacksmith drew a deep breath, and after a pause continued more firmly and with more assurance: "Once they came near giving me a lashing with switches in the district court.

18

THE SPY

I was betrothed then. I had to get married. Nevertheless they wanted to whip me. It was all the same to them. They don't mind about other people's affairs. I lodged a complaint with the governor, and for three and a half months they kept me in prison, not to speak of the blows. I got the worst beatings. I even spat blood. It's from that time that tears are always in my eyes. One policeman, a short, reddish fellow, always went for my head."

" Uncle," said Yevsey quietly, " don't speak of it."

" What else shall I speak to you about ?" cried Uncle Piotr, with a smile. " There is nothing else."

Yevsey's head drooped sadly.

One detached house after another seemed to step toward them, dirty and wrapped in heavy odours, with chimneys sticking from their red and green roofs, like warts. Bluish-grey smoke rose from them lazily. Some chimneys, monstrously tall and dirty, jutted straight up from the ground, and emitted thick black clouds of smoke. The ground was compactly trodden, and seemed to be steeped in black grease. Everywhere heavy alarming sounds penetrated the smoky atmosphere. Something growled, hummed, and whistled ; iron clanged angrily, and some huge creature breathed hoarsely and brokenly.

" When shall we get to the place ?" asked Yevsey.

Looking carefully in front of him, the uncle said :

" This isn't the city yet. These are factories in the suburb."

Finally they pulled into a broad street lined with old squat frame-houses painted various colours, which had a peaceful, homelike appearance. Especially fine were the clean, cheerful houses with gardens, which seemed to be tied about with green aprons.

"We'll soon be there," said the blacksmith, turning the horse into a narrow side-street. "Don't be afraid, Orphan."

He drew up at the open gate of a large house, jumped down, and walked into the yard. The house was old and bent. The joists protruded from under the small dim windows. In the large, dirty yard there were a number of carriages, and four muzhiks, talking loudly, stood about a white horse, tapping it with their hands. One of them, a round, bald-headed fellow with a large yellow beard and a rosy face, waved his hands wildly on seeing Piotr, and cried :

"Oh !"

They went to a narrow, dark room, where they sat down and drank tea. Uncle Piotr spoke about the village. The bald fellow laughed and shouted, so that the dishes rattled on the table. It was close in the room and smelt of hot bread. Yevsey wanted to sleep, and he kept looking into the corner where, behind dirty curtains, he could see a wide bed with several pillows. Large black flies buzzed about, knocking against his forehead, crawling over his face, and tickling his perspiring skin ; but he restrained himself from driving them away.

"We'll find a place for you !" the bald man shouted to him, nodding his head gaily. "In a minute ! Natalya, did you call for Matveyevich ?"

A full woman with dark lashes, a small mouth, and a high bust, answered calmly and clearly :

"How many times have you asked me already ?"

She held her head straight and proudly, and when she moved her hands, the rose-coloured chintz of her new jacket rustled sumptuously. Her whole being recalled some good dream or fairy-tale.

"Piotr, my friend, look at Natalya. What a Natalya! Droppings from the honeycomb!" shouted the bald man deafeningly.

Uncle Piotr laughed quietly, as if fearing to look at the woman, who pushed a hot rye-cake filled with curds toward Yevsey, and said :

"Eat, eat a lot. In the city people must eat a good deal."

A jar of preserves stood on the table; honey in a saucer, toasted cracknels sprinkled with aniseed, sausage, cucumber, and vodka. All this filled the air with a stong odour. Yevsey grew faint from the oppressive sensation of over-abundance, though he did not dare to decline, and submissively swallowed everything set before him. "Eat !" cried the bald man, then continued his talk with Uncle Piotr.

"I tell you, it's luck. It's only a week since the horse crushed the little boy. He went to the tavern for boiling water, when suddenly——"

Another man now made his entrance unnoticed by the others. He, too, was bald, but small and thin, with dark spectacles on a large nose, and a long tuft of grey hair on his chin.

"What is it, people ?" he asked in a low, indistinct voice.

The master jumped up from his chair, uttered a cry, and laughed aloud. Yevsey was suddenly seized with alarm.

The man addressed Piotr and his hosts as "people," by which he separated himself from them. He sat down at some distance from the table, then moved to one side, away from the blacksmith, and looked around, moving his thin dry neck slowly. On his head, a little above his forehead, over his right eye, was a large bump.

21

His little pointed ears clung closely to his skull, as if to hide themselves in the short fringe of his grey hair. He produced the impression of a quiet, grey, seedy person. Yevsey unsuccessfully tried to get a surreptitious peep at his eyes under the glasses. His failure disquieted him.

The host cried :

" Do you understand, Orphan ?"

" This is a trump," remarked the man with the bump.

He sat supporting his thin dark hands on his sharp knees, and spoke little. Occasionally Yevsey heard the men utter some peculiar words.

At last the newcomer said :

" And so it is settled."

Uncle Piotr moved heavily in his chair.

" Now, Orphan, you have a place. This is your master." He turned to the master.

" I want to tell you, sir, that the boy can read and write, and is not at all a stupid fellow. I am not saying this because I can't find a place for him, but because it is the truth. The boy is even very curious—— "

" I have no need for curiosity," said the master, shaking his head.

" He's a quiet sort. They call him Old Man in the village—that's the kind he is."

" We shall see," said the man with the bump on his forehead. He adjusted his glasses, scrutinized Yevsey's face closely, and added, " My name is Matvey Matveyevich."

Turning away, he took up a glass of tea, which he drank noiselessly. Then he rose, and with a silent nod walked out.

Yevsey and his uncle now went to the yard, where they seated themselves in the shade near the stable.

THE SPY

The blacksmith spoke to Yevsey cautiously, as if groping with his words for something unintelligible to him.

" You'll surely have a good time with him. He's a quiet little old man. He has run his course, and left all sorts of sins behind him. Now he lives for a bite and a sup, and he grumbles and purrs like an overfed tom-cat.'

" But isn't he a sorcerer ?" asked the boy.

" Why ? I should think there are no sorcerers in the cities." After reflecting a few moments, the blacksmith went on. " Anyway, it's all the same to you. A sorcerer is a man, too. But remember this, a city is a dangerous place. This is how it spoils people : the wife of a man goes away on a pilgrimage, and he immediately puts in her place some housemaid or other, and indulges himself. But the old man can't show you such an example. That's why I say you'll have it good with him. You will live with him as behind a bush, sitting and looking."

" And when he dies ?" Yevsey inquired warily.

" That probably won't be soon. Smear your head with oil to keep your hair from sticking out."

About noon the uncle made Yevsey bid farewell to their hosts, and, taking him firmly by the hand, led him to the city. They walked for a long time. It was sultry. Often they asked the passers-by how to get to the Circle. Yevsey regarded everything with his owl-like eyes, pressing close up to his uncle. The doors of shops slammed, pulleys squeaked, carriages rattled, waggons rumbled heavily, traders shouted, and feet scraped and tramped. All these sounds were inextricably jumbled together in the stifling, dusty atmosphere. The people walked quickly, and hurried across the streets under the horses' noses as if afraid of being too late for something. The bustle tired the boy's eyes. Now and then he closed them, whereupon he would stumble and say to his uncle :

" Come faster !"

Yevsey wanted to get to some place in a corner where it was not so stirring, not so noisy and hot. Finally they reached a little open place hemmed in by a narrow circle of old houses, which seemed to support one another solidly and firmly. In the centre of the Circle was a fountain, about which moist shadows hovered on the soil. It was calmer here, and the noise was subdued.

" Look," said Yevsey, " there are only houses, and no ground around them at all."

The blacksmith answered with a sigh :

" It's pretty crowded. Read the signs. Where is Raspopov's shop ?"

They walked to the centre of the Circle, and stopped at the fountain. There were many signs, which covered every house like the motley patches of a beggar's coat. When Yevsey saw the name his uncle had mentioned, a chill shiver ran through his body, and he examined it carefully without saying anything. The sign was small and eaten by rust, and was placed on the door of a dark basement. On either side the door there was an area between the pavement and the house, which was fenced in by a low iron railing. The house, a dirty yellow, with peeling plaster, was narrow, with four stories and three windows to each floor. It looked blind as a mole, crafty, and uncomfortable.

" Well," said the smith, " can't you see the sign ?"

" There it is," said the boy, indicating the place with a nod of his head.

" Let's cross ourselves and go."

They descended to the door at the bottom of five stone steps. The blacksmith raised his cap from his head, and looked cautiously into the shop.

" Come in," said a clear voice.

The master, wearing a black silk cap, was sitting at a table by the window, drinking tea.

" Take a chair, peasant, and have some tea. Boy, fetch a glass from the shelf."

The master pointed to the other end of the shop. Yevsey looked in the same direction, but saw no boy there. The master turned toward him.

" Well, what's the matter ? Aren't you the boy ?"

" He's not used to it yet," said Uncle Piotr quietly.

The old man again waved his hand.

" The second shelf on the right. A master must be understood when he says only half. That's the rule."

The blacksmith sighed. Yevsey groped for the glass in the dim light, and stumbled over a pile of books on the floor in his haste to hand it to the master.

" Put it on the table. And the saucer ?"

" Oh, you !" exclaimed Uncle Piotr. " What's the matter with you ? Get the saucer."

" It will take a long time to teach him," said the old man, with an imposing look at the blacksmith. " Now, boy, go around the shop, and fix in your memory the place where everything stands."

Yevsey felt as if something commanding had entered his body, which impelled him powerfully to move as it pleased. He shrank altogether, drew his head into his shoulders, and straining his eyes, began to look around the shop, all the time listening to the words of his master. It was cool, dusky, and quiet. The noise of the city entered reluctantly, like the muffled lapping of a stream. Narrow and long as a grave, the shop was closely lined with shelves holding books in compact rows. Large piles of books cluttered the floor and barricaded the rear wall, rising almost to the ceiling. Besides the books Yevsey found only a ladder, an umbrella, galoshes, and a white pot the handle of which was broken off. There was a great deal of dust, which probably accounted for the heavy odour.

" I'm a quiet man. I am all alone, and if he suits me, maybe I will make him perfectly happy."

" Of course, it lies with you," said Uncle Piotr.

" I am fifty-seven years old. I have lived an honest and straightforward life, and I will not excuse dishonesty. If I notice any such thing, I'll hand him over to the court. Nowadays they sentence minors too. They have founded a prison to frighten them called the Junior Colony of Criminals—for little thieves, you know."

His colourless, drawling words enveloped Yevsey tightly, evoking his timorous desire to soothe the old man and please him.

" Now, good-bye. The boy must get to work."

Uncle Piotr rose and sighed.

" Well, Orphan, so you live here now. Obey your master. He won't want to do you any harm. Why should he ? He is going to buy you city clothes. Now don't be downcast, will you ?"

" No," said Yevsey.

" You ought to say ' No, sir !' " corrected the master.

" No, sir," repeated Yevsey.

" Well, good-bye," said the blacksmith, putting his hand on the boy's shoulder ; and giving his nephew a little shake, he walked out as if suddenly grown alarmed.

Yevsey shivered, oppressed by a chill sorrow. He

went to the door, and fixed his round eyes question-
ingly on the yellow face of the master. The old man,
twirling the grey tuft on his chin, looked down upon the
boy. Yevsey thought he could discern large, dim
black eyes behind the glasses. As the two stood thus
for a few minutes, apparently expecting something
from each other, the boy's breast began to beat with
a vague terror ; but the old man merely took a book
from a shelf, and pointed to the cover.

" What number is this ?"

" 1873," replied Yevsey, lowering his head.

" That's it."

The master touched Yevsey's chin with his dry
finger.

" Look at me."

The boy straightened his neck and quickly mumbled,
closing his eyes :

" Little uncle, I shall always obey you. I don't need
beatings." His eyes grew dim, and his heart sank
within him.

" Come here."

The old man seated himself, resting his hands on his
knees. He removed his cap and wiped his bald spot
with his handkerchief. His spectacles slid to the end
of his nose, and he looked over them at Yevsey. Now
he seemed to have two pairs of eyes. The real eyes
were small, immobile, and dark grey with red lids.
Without the glasses the master's face looked thinner,
more wrinkled, and less stern. In fact, it wore an injured
and downcast expression, and there was nothing in the
least formidable in his eyes. The bump over his forehead got larger.

" Have you been beaten often ?"

" Yes, sir, often."

27

" Who beat you ?"

" The boys."

" Oh !"

The master drew his glasses close to his eyes and mumbled his lips.

" The boys fight a lot here, too," he said. " Don't have anything to do with them—do you hear ?"

" Yes, sir."

" Be on your guard against them. They are impudent rascals and thieves. I want you to know I am not going to teach you anything bad. Don't be afraid of me. I am a good man. You ought to get to love me. You will love me. You'll have a good time with me—you understand ?"

" Yes, sir. I will."

The master's face assumed its former expression. He rose, and taking Yevsey by the hand, led him to the further end of the shop.

" Here's work for you. You see these books ? On every book the date is marked. There are twelve books to each year. Arrange them in order. How are you going to do it ?"

Yevsey thought a while, and answered timidly :

" I don't know."

" Well, I am not going to tell you. You can read, and you ought to be able to find out by yourself. Come, get to work."

The old man's dry, even voice seemed to lash Yevsey, driving away the melancholy feeling of separation from his uncle, and replacing it with an anxious desire to begin to work quickly. Restraining his tears, the boy rapidly and quietly untied the packages. Each time a book dropped to the floor with a thud he started and looked round. The master was sitting at the table

28

writing with a pen that scratched slightly. As the people hastened past the door, their feet flashed, and their shadows jerked across the shop. Tears rolled from Yevsey's eyes one after the other. In fear lest they should be detected, he hurriedly wiped them from his face with dusty hands, and full of a vague dread, went on intently with his work of sorting the books.

At first it was difficult for him, but in a few minutes he was already immersed in that familiar state of thoughtlessness and emptiness which had taken powerful hold of him when, after beatings and insults, he sat himself down alone in some corner. His eye caught the date and the name of the month, his hand mechanically arranged the books in a row, while he sat on the floor, swinging his body regularly. He became more and more deeply plunged in the tranquil state of half-conscious negation of reality. As always at such times, the dim hope glowed in him of something different, unlike what he saw around him. Sometimes the all-comprehending, capacious phrase uttered by Yashka dimly glimmered in his memory :

" It will pass away."

The thought pressed his heart warmly and softly with a promise of something unusual. The boy's hands involuntarily began to move more quickly, and he ceased to notice the lapse of time.

" You see, you knew how to do it," said the master.

Yevsey, who had not heard the old man approach him, started from his reverie. Glancing at his work, he asked :

" Is it all right ?"

" Quite right. Do you want tea ?"

" No."

" You ought to say, ' No, thank you.'   Well, keep on
with your work."

He walked away.   Yevsey, looking after him, saw
a man carrying a cane enter the door.   He had neither
a beard nor moustache, and wore a round hat shoved
back on the nape of his neck.   He seated himself at
the table, at the same time putting upon it some small
black and white objects.   When Yevsey again started
to work, he every once in a while heard abrupt sounds
from his master and the new-comer.

" Castle."

" King."

" Soon."

The confused noise of the street penetrated the shop
wearily, with strange words quacking in it, like frogs
in a marsh.

" What are they doing ?" thought the boy, and
sighed.   He experienced a soft sensation, that from all
directions something unusual was coming upon him,
but not what he timidly awaited.   The dust settled
upon his face, tickled his nose and eyes, and set his
teeth on edge.   He recalled his uncle's words :

" You will live with him as behind a bush."

It grew dark.

" King and checkmate !" cried the guest in a thick
voice.   The master clucked his tongue, and called out :

" Boy, shut up the shop !"

The old man lived in two small rooms in the fourth
story of the same house.   In the first room, which had
one window, stood a large chest and a wardrobe.

" This is where you will sleep."

The two windows in the second room gave upon the
street, with a view over an endless vista of uneven
roofs and rosy sky.   In the corner, in front of the ikons,

flickered a little light in a blue glass lamp. In another corner stood a bed covered with a red blanket. On the walls hung gaudy portraits of the Czar and various generals. The room was close, and smelt like a church, but it was clean.

Yevsey remained at the door looking at his elderly master, who said :

" Mark the arrangement of everything here. I want it always to be the same as it is now."

Against the wall stood a broad black sofa, a round table, and about the table chairs, also black. This corner had a mournful, sinister aspect.

A tall, white-faced woman, with eyes like a sheep's, entered the room, and asked in a low, singing voice :

" Shall I serve supper ?"

" Bring it in, Bayisa Petrovna."

" A new boy ?"

" Yes, new. His name is Yevsey."

The woman walked out.

" Close the door," ordered the old man. Yevsey obeyed, and he continued in a lower voice : " She is the landlady. I rent the rooms from her, with dinner and supper. You understand ?"

" I understand."

" But you have one master—me. You under-stand ?"

" Yes."

" That is to say, you must listen only to me. Open the door, and go into the kitchen and wash yourself."

The master's voice echoed dryly in the boy's bosom, causing his alarmed heart to palpitate. The old man, it seemed to Yevsey, was hiding something dangerous behind this words, something of which he himself was afraid.

While washing in the kitchen, he surreptitiously tried to look at the mistress of the apartment. The woman was preparing the supper noiselessly but briskly. As she arranged plates, knives, and bread on an ample tray, her large round face seemed kind. Her smoothly-combed dark hair, her unwinking eyes with thin lashes, and her broad nose, made the boy think : " She looks like a gentle person."

Noticing that she, in her turn, was looking at him, the thin, red lips of her small mouth tightly compressed, he grew confused, and spilt some water on the floor.

" Wipe it," she said, without anger. " There's a cloth under the chair.'

When he returned, the old man looked at him, and asked.

" What did she tell you ?'

But Yevsey had no time to answer before the woman brought in the tray.

" Well, I'll go," she said, after setting it on the table.

" Very well," replied the master.

She raised her hand to smooth the hair over her temples—her fingers were long—and left.

The old man and the boy sat down to their supper. The master ate slowly, noisily munching his food, and at times sighing wearily. When they began to eat the finely-chopped roast meat, he said :

" You see what good food ! I always have only good food."

After supper he told Yevsey to carry the dishes into the kitchen, and showed him how to light the lamp.

" Now go to sleep. You will find a piece of padding in the wardrobe, and a pillow and a blanket. They belong to you. To-morrow I'll buy you new clothes, good clothes. Go, now."

When he was half asleep, the master came in to Yevsey.

" Are you comfortable ?"

Though the chest made a hard bed, Yevsey answered :
" Yes."

" If it is too hot, open the window."

The boy at once opened the window, which looked out upon the roof of the next house. He counted the chimneys. There were four, all alike. He looked at the stars with the dim gaze of a timid animal in a cage, but the stars said nothing to his heart. He flung himself on the chest again, drew the blanket over his head, and closed his eyes tightly. He began to feel stifled, thrust his head out, and without opening his eyes listened. In his master's room something rustled monotonously ; then Yevsey heard a dry, distinct voice :

" Behold, God is mine helper : the Lord is with them that uphold——"

Yevsey realized that the old man was reciting the Psalter, and, listening attentively to the familiar words of King David, which, however, he did not comprehend, the boy fell asleep.

CHAPTER III

Yevsey's life passed smoothly and evenly. He wanted
to please his master, even realized this would be of
advantage to him, and felt he would succeed, though
he behaved with watchful circumspection and no
warmth in his heart for the old man. The fear of
people engendered in him a desire to suit them, a
readiness for all kinds of services, in order to defend
himself against the possibility of attack. The constant expectation of danger developed a keen power
of observation, which still more deepened his mistrust.

He observed the strange life in the house without
understanding it. From basement to roof people lived
close packed, and every day, from morning until night,
they crawled about in the tenement like crabs in a
basket. Here they worked more than in the village,
and, it seemed, were imbued with even keener bitterness. They lived restlessly, noisily, and hurriedly, as
if to get through all the work as soon as possible in
preparation of a holiday, which they wanted to meet
as free people, washed, clean, peaceful, and tranquilly
joyous. The heart of the boy sank within him, and
the question constantly recurred :

" Will it pass away ? "

But the holiday never came. The people spurred
one another on, wrangled, and sometimes fought.

THE SPY

Scarcely a day passed on which they did not speak ill of one another.

In the mornings the master went down to the shop, while Yevsey remained in the apartment to put it in order. This accomplished, he washed himself, went to the tavern for boiling water, and then returned to the shop, where he drank the morning tea with his master. While breakfasting, the old man almost invariably asked him :

" Well, what now ?"

" Nothing."

" Nothing is little."

Once, however, Yevsey had a different answer.

" To-day the watchmaker told the furrier's cook that you receive stolen articles."

Yevsey said this unexpectedly to himself, and was instantly seized with a trembling fear. He bowed his head. The old man laughed quietly, and said in a drawling voice, without sincerity :

" The scoundrel !" His dark, dry lips quivered. " Thank you for telling me. Thank you. You see how the people don't love me."

From that time Yevsey began to pay close attention to the conversation of the tenants, and promptly repeated everything he heard to his master, speaking in a quiet, calm voice, and looking straight into his face. Several days later, while putting his master's room into order, he found a crumpled paper ruble on the floor ; and when at tea the old man asked him,

" Well, what now ?"

Yevsey replied : " Here, I have found a ruble."

" You found a ruble, did you ? I found a gold piece," said the master, laughing.

Another time Yevsey picked up a twenty-kopek

piece in the entrance to the shop, which he also gave to the master. The old man slid his glasses to the end of his nose, and, rubbing the coin with his fingers, looked into the boy's face for a few seconds without speaking.

"According to the law," he said thoughtfully, " a third of what you find, six kopeks, belongs to you." He was silent, sighed, and stuck the coin into his vest pocket. " But anyway you're a stupid boy." Yevsey did not get the six kopeks.

Quiet, unnoticed, and, when noticed, obliging, Yevsey Klimkov scarcely ever drew the attention of the people to himself, though he stubbornly followed them with the broad, empty gaze of his owl-like eyes, with the look that did not abide in the memory of those who met it.

From the first days the reticent, quiet Rayisa Petrovna interested him strongly. Every evening she put on a dark, rustling dress and a black hat, and sallied forth. In the morning, when he put the rooms in order, she was still asleep. He saw her only in the evening before supper, and that not every day. Her life seemed mysterious to him, and this silent being with, her white face and stationary eyes, roused in him vague suggestions of something peculiar. He persuaded himself that she lived better and knew more than everybody else. A kindly feeling which he did not understand sprang up in his heart for this woman. Every day she appeared to him more and more beautiful.

Once he awoke at daybreak, and walked into the kitchen for a drink. Suddenly he heard someone opening the door of the vestibule. He rushed to his room in fright, lay down, and covered himself with the blanket, trying to press himself to the chest as closely as possible. In a few minutes he stuck out his ear, and in the kitchen heard heavy steps, the rustle of a dress, and the voice of Rayisa Petrovna.

" Oh, oh, you——" she was saying.

Yevsey rose, walked to the door on tiptoe, and looked into the kitchen. The quiet woman was sitting at the window, taking off her hat. Her face seemed whiter than ever, and tears streamed from her eyes. Her large body swayed, her hands moved slowly.

" I know you !" she said, shaking her head. She rose to her feet, supporting herself on the window-sill.

The bed in the master's room creaked. Yevsey quickly jumped back on his chest, lay down, and wrapped himself up.

" They've done something bad to her," he thought, full of keen pity. At the same time, however, he was inwardly glad of her tears. They brought this woman, who lived a secret nocturnal existence, nearer to him.

The next moment someone seemed to be passing by him with sly steps. He raised his head, and suddenly jumped from the chest, as if burned by the thin angry shout :

" Ugh ! Go away !"

Then there was some hissing. The master in his nightgown hastily came out of the kitchen, stopped, and said to Yevsey in a whistling voice :

" Sleep, sleep ! What's the matter ? Sleep !"

The next morning in the shop the old man asked him :

" Were you frightened last night ?"

" Yes."

" She was in her cups. It happens to her sometimes."

THE SPY

Though the question trembled on his lips, Yevsey did not dare to ask what her occupation was. Some minutes later the old man asked :

" Do you like her ?"

" I do."

" Well," said the master sternly, " even if you do, you ought to know that she's an extremely shrewd woman. She is silent, but bad. She's a sinner. Yes, that's what she is. Do you know what she does ? She's a musician. She plays the piano." The old man accurately described a piano, and added didactically : " A person who plays the piano is called a pianist. And do you know what a house of ill-fame is ?"

From the talk of the furriers and glaziers in the yard, Yevsey already knew something about disreputable resorts ; but desiring to learn more, he answered :

" I don't know."

The old man gave him a lengthy explanation in words very intelligible to Yevsey. He spoke with heat, occasionally spitting and wrinkling up his face to express his disgust of the abomination. Yevsey regarded the old man with his watery eyes, and for some reason did not believe in his aversion.

" So, you see, every evening she plays in a house like that, and depraved women dance with drunken men to the accompaniment of her music. The men are all rogues, some of them, may be, even murderers." Raspopov sighed in exhaustion, and wiped his perspiring face. " Don't trust her. You understand ? I tell you, she's a cunning woman, and she's mean."

The boy believed everything the master told him about the piano and the house of ill-fame, but failed to be impressed by a single word regarding the woman. In fact, everything the old man said of her merely increased the cautious, ever-watchful feeling of mistrust with which Yevsey treated his master, and by colouring Rayisa Petrovna with a still deeper tinge of the unusual, made her seem even more beautiful in his eyes.

Another object of Yevsey's curiosity besides Rayisa was Anatol, apprentice to the glazier Kuzin, a thin, flat-nosed boy with ragged hair, dirty, always jolly, and always steeped in the odour of oil. He had a high, ringing voice, which Yevsey liked very much to hear when he shouted :

" Wi-i-ndow pa-anes."

He spoke to Yevsey first. Yevsey was sweeping the stairway, when he suddenly heard from below the loud question :

" Hullo ! kid, what government are you from ?"

" From this government," answered Yevsey.

" I am from the government of Kostrom. How old are you ?"

" Thirteen."

" I am, too. Come along with me."

" Where to ?"

" To the river, to go bathing."

" I have to stay in the shop."

" To-day is Sunday."

" That doesn't make any difference."

" Well, go to the devil."

The glazier's boy disappeared. Yevsey was not offended by his oath.

Anatol was off the whole day carrying a box of glass about in the city, and usually returned home just as the shop was being closed. Then almost the entire evening his indefatigable voice, his laughter, whistling, and singing, would rise from the yard. Everybody scolded him, yet all loved to meddle with him and laugh at his pranks. Yevsey was surprised at the boldness with which the ragged, snub-nosed boy behaved toward the grown-up folk, and he experienced a sense of envy when he saw the gold-embroidery girl run about the yard in chase of the jolly, insolent fellow. He was powerfully drawn to the glazier's boy, for whom he found a place in his vague fancies of a clean and quiet life.

Once, after supper, Yevsey asked the master :

" May I go down in the yard ?"

The old man consented reluctantly.

" Go, but don't stay long. Be sure not to stay long."

Another time when Yevsey put the same request the master added :

" No good will come of your being in the yard."

Yevsey ran down the stairway quickly, and seated himself in the shade to observe Anatol. The yard was small and hemmed in on all sides by the high houses. The tenants, working men and women, and servants, sat resting on the rubbish-heaps against the walls. In the centre of the ring Anatol was giving a performance.

" The furrier Zvorykin going to church !" he shouted.

To his astonishment, Yevsey saw the little stout furrier with hanging lower lip and eyes painfully screwed up. Thrusting out his abdomen and leaning his head to one side, Anatol struggled toward the gate with short steps, reluctance depicted in his walk. The people sitting around laughed and shouted approval.

" Zvorykin returning from the saloon !"

Now Anatol swayed through the yard, his feet dragging along feebly, his arms hanging limp, a dull look in his wide-open eyes, his mouth gaping hideously

THE SPY

yet comically. He stopped, tapped himself on the
chest, and said in a wheezy, pitiful voice :

" God—how satisfied I am with everything and
everybody ! Lord, how good and pleasant everything
is to Thy servant, Yakov Ivanich. But the glazier
Kuzin is a blackguard—a scamp before God, a jackass
before all the people—that's true, God——"

The audience roared, but Yevsey did not laugh. He
was oppressed by a twofold feeling of astonishment
and envy. The desire to see this boy frightened and
wronged mingled with the expectation of new pranks.
He felt vexed and unpleasant because the glazier's boy
did not show up men who inflicted hurt, but merely
funny men. Yevsey sat there with mouth agape and
a stupid expression on his face, his owlish eyes staring.

" Here goes glazier Kuzin !"

Before Yevsey appeared the gaunt red muzhik, always
half-drunk, the sleeves of his dirty shirt tucked up, his
right hand thrust in the breast of his apron, his left
hand deliberately stroking his beard—Kuzin had a
reddish, forked beard. He was frowning and surly,
and moved slowly, like a heavy cart-load. Looking
sidewise, he screeched in a cracked, hoarse voice :

" You are carrying on again, you heretic ? Am I
to listen to this nonsense for long ? You blasted,
confounded——"

" Skinflint Raspopov !" announced Anatol.

The smooth, sharp little figure of Yevsey's master
crept past him, moving his feet noiselessly. He worked
his nose as if smelling something, nodded his head
quickly, and kept tugging at the tuft on his chin with
his little hand. In this characterization something
loathsome, pitiful, and laughable became quite apparent
to Yevsey, whose vexation arose. He felt sure his

41

master was not such as the young glazier represented him to be.

Next, Anatol took to mimicking members of the audience. Inexhaustible, stimulated by the applause, he tinkled until late at night like a little bell, evoking kindly, cheerful laughter. Sometimes the man who was touched would rush to catch him, and a noisy chase about the yard would ensue.

Yevsey sighed. Anatol noticed him, and pulled him by the hand into the middle of the yard, where he introduced him to the audience.

"Here he is—sugar and soap. Skinflint Raspopov's little cousin."

Turning the boy's little figure in all directions, he poured forth a flowing stream of strange, comic words about his master, about Rayisa Petrovna, and about Yevsey himself.

"Let me go!" Yevsey quietly demanded, trying to tear his hand from Anatol's strong grip, in the meantime listening attentively in the endeavour to understand the hints, the filth of which he felt. Whenever Yevsey struggled hard to tear himself away, the audience, usually the women, said lazily to Anatol :

"Let him go."

For some reason their intercession was disagreeable to Yevsey. It exasperated Anatol, too, who began to push and pinch his victim, and challenge him to a fight. Some of the men urged the boys on.

"Well—fight ! See which will do the other up."

The women objected—

"A fight ! Thanks, we're not interested. Don't."

Yevsey again felt something unpleasant in these words.

Finally Anatol scornfully pushed Yevsey aside.

" Oh, you kid !"

The next morning Yevsey met Anatol outside the house carrying his box of glass, and suddenly, without desiring to do it, he said to him :

" Why do you make fun of me ?"

The glazier's boy looked at him.

" What of it ?"

Yevsey was unable to reply.

" Do you want to fight ?" asked Anatol again. " Come to our shed. I will wait for you until evening."

He spoke calmly and in a business-like way.

" No, I don't want to fight," replied Yevsey quietly.

" Then you needn't ! I'd lick you anyway," said the glazier, and added, with assurance : " I certainly would."

Yevsey sighed. He could not understand this boy, but he longed to understand him. So he asked a second time :

" I say, why do you make fun of me ?"

Anatol apparently felt awkward. He winked his lively eyes, smiled, and suddenly shouted in anger :

" Go to the devil ! What are you bothering me about ? I'll give it you so——"

Yevsey quickly ran into the shop, and for a whole day felt the itching of an undeserved insult. This did not put an end to his inclination for Anatol, but it forced him to leave the yard whenever Anatol noticed him, and he dismissed the glazier's boy from the sphere of his dreams.

CHAPTER IV

Soon after this unsuccessful attempt to draw near to a human being Yevsey was one evening awakened by talking in his master's room. He listened, and thought he distinguished Rayisa's voice. Desiring to convince himself of her presence there, he rose and quietly slipped over to the tightly closed door, and put his eyes to the keyhole.

His sleepy glance first perceived the light of the candle, which blinded him; then he saw the large, rotund body of the woman on the black sofa. She lay face upward, entirely naked. Her hair was spread over her breast, and her long fingers slowly weaved it into a braid. The light quivered on her fair body. Clean and bright, it seemed like a light cloud which rocked and breathed. It was very beautiful. She was saying something. Yevsey could not catch the words, but heard only the singing, tired, plaintive voice. The master was sitting in his nightgown upon a chair by the sofa, and was pouring wine into a glass with a trembling hand. The tuft of grey hair on his chin also trembled. He had removed his glasses, and his face was loathsome.

" Yes, yes, yes ! H'm ! what a woman you are !"

Yevsey moved away from the door, lay down on his bed, and thought :

" They have got married."

He pitied Rayisa Petrovna for having become the wife of a man who spoke ill of her, and he pitied her because it must have been very cold for her to lie naked on the leather sofa. An evil thought flashed through his mind, which confirmed the words of the old man about her, but Yevsey anxiously drove it away.

The evening of the next day Rayisa Petrovna brought in supper as always, and said in her usual voice :

" I am going."

The master, too, spoke to her in his usual voice, dry and careless.

Several days passed by. The relation between the master and Rayisa did not change, and Yevsey began to think he had seen the naked woman in a dream. He was very reluctant to believe his master's words about her.

Once his Uncle Piotr appeared unexpectedly and, so it seemed to Yevsey, needlessly. He had grown grey, wrinkled, and shorter.

" I am getting blind, Orphan," he said, sipping tea from a saucer noisily, and smiling with his wet eyes. " I cannot work any more, so I will have to go begging. Yashka is unmanageable. He wants to go to the city, and if I don't let him he will run away. That's the kind of a chap he is."

Everything the blacksmith said was wearisome, and difficult to listen to. He seemed to have grown duller. He looked guilty, and Yevsey felt awkward and ashamed for him in the presence of his master. When he got ready to go, Yevsey quietly thrust three rubles into his hand, and saw him out with pleasure.

THE SPY

Though Yevsey endeavoured as before to please his master in every way, he became afraid to agree with him. The bookshop after a time aroused a dim suspicion by its resemblance to a tomb tightly packed with dead books. They were all loose, dog's-eared, and stained, and emanated a mouldy, putrid odour. Few were sold, which did not surprise Yevsey. What stirred his curiosity was the attitude of the master to the purchasers and the books.

The old man would take a book in his hand, carefully turn over its musty pages, stroke the covers with his dark fingers, smile quietly, and nod his head. He seemed to fondle the book as though it were alive, to play with it as with a kitten or a puppy. While reading a book, he carried on with it a quiet, querulous conversation, like Uncle Piotr with the furnace-fire. His lips moved in good-humoured derision, his head kept nodding, and now and then he mumbled and laughed.

" So, so—yes—h'mm—see—what's that ? Ha, ha ! Ah, the impudence—I understand, I understand—it'll never come about—no-o-o—ha, ha !"

These strange exclamations, coming from the old man as if he were disputing with somebody, both astonished and frightened Yevsey, and pointed to the secret duplicity in his master's life.

" You don't read books," said the master to him once. " That's good. Books are always lechery, the child of a prostituted mind. They deal with everything, they excite the imagination, and create useless agitation and disturbance. Formerly we used to have good historical books, stories of quiet people about the past. But now every book wants to inspire you with hostility to life, and to lay bare man, who ought always to be covered up both in the flesh and in the spirit in order to defend him from the Devil, from curiosity, and from the imagination, which destroys faith. It's only in old age that books do no harm to a man, when he is guarded against their violence by his experience."

Though Yevsey did not understand these talks, he remembered them well ; and though they met with no response in him, they confirmed his sense of mystery— the mystery that invested all human life, as it were, in a hostile envelope.

When he sold a book, the old man regarded it with regret, and fairly smelled the purchaser, with whom he talked in an extremely loud and rapid voice. Sometimes, however, he lowered his voice to a whisper, when his dark glasses would fix themselves upon the face of the customer. Often, on seeing to the door a student who had bought a book, he followed him with a smile, and nodded his head queerly. Once he shook his finger at the back of a man who had just left—a short, handsome fellow, with fine black tendrils on a pale face. The largest number of customers were students, and people having a certain resemblance to them. Sometimes old men came. These rummaged long among the books, and haggled sharply over the prices.

An almost daily visitor was a man who wore a chimney-pot, and on his right hand a large gold ring set with a stone. He had a broad, pimply nose on a stout, flat, shaven face. When Dorimedont Lukin played chess with the master, he snuffled aloud and tugged at his ear with his left hand. He often brought books and paper parcels, over which the master nodded his head approvingly and smiled quietly. He would then hide them in the table, or in a corner on a shelf at the back. Yevsey did not see his master pay for these books, but he did see him sell them.

One of the students began to visit the shop more frequently than the others. He was a tall, blue-eyed young man, with a carrot-coloured moustache, and a cap stuck on the back of his head, leaving bare a large white forehead. He spoke in a thick voice, laughed aloud, and always bought many old journals.

Once the master pointed out a book to him that Dorimedont had brought, and while the student glanced through it the old man told him something in a quick whisper.

" Interesting ! " exclaimed the student, smiling amiably. " Ah, you old sinner, aren't you afraid, eh ? "

The master sighed, and answered :

" If you absolutely feel it's the truth, you ought to help it along in whatever little ways you can."

They whispered a long time. Finally, the student said aloud :

" Well, then, agreed ! Remember my address."

The old man took the address down on a piece of paper, and when Dorimedont came and asked, " Well, what's new, Matvey Matveyevich ? " the master handed him the address, and said with a smile :

" There's the new thing."

" S-so Nikodim Arkhangelsky," read Dorimedont. " That's business. We'll look up this Nikodim."

Some time after, upon sitting down to play chess, he announced to the master :

" That Nikodim turned out to be a fish with plenty of roe. We found something of pretty nearly everything in his place."

" Return the books to me," said the master.

" Certainly." And Dorimedont snuffled.

THE SPY

The blue-eyed student never appeared again. The short young man with the black moustache also vanished after the master had given Dorimedont his address. All this was strange. It fed the boy's suspicions, and indicated some mysterious and enigma.

Once, when the master was absent from the shop, Yevsey, while dusting the shelves, saw the books brought by Dorimedont. They were small, soiled, and ragged. He carefully and quickly put them back in the same order, scenting something dangerous in them. Books in general did not arouse his interest. He tried to read, but never succeeded in concentrating his mind, which, already burdened by a mass of observation, dwelt upon minutiæ. His thoughts drifted apart, and finally disappeared, evaporating like a thin stream of water upon a stone on a hot day. When he worked and moved about he was altogether incapable of thinking—the motion, as it were, tore the cobweb of his ideas. The boy did his work slowly and accurately, like an automaton, without putting anything of himself into it, and scarcely understanding its meaning.

When he was free and sat motionless, he was carried away by a pleasant sensation of flight in a transparent mist, which enveloped the whole of life and softened everything, changing the boisterous reality into a quiet, sweetly sounding half-slumber.

When Yevsey was in this mood, the days passed rapidly in a flight not to be stayed. His external life was monotonous. Thought-stirring events happened rarely, and his brain insensibly became clogged with the dust of the working day. He seldom went about in the city, for he did not like it. The ceaseless motion tired his eyes, the noise filled his head with heavy, dulling confusion. The endless city at first seemed like a monster in a fairy-tale, displaying a hundred greedy mouths, bellowing with hundreds of insatiable throats. But when Yevsey regarded the varied tumult of the street life, he saw in it merely painful and wearisome monotony.

In the morning, when he tidied his master's room, Yevsey put his head out of the window for several minutes, and looked down to the bottom of the deep, narrow street. Everywhere he saw the same people, and already knew what each of them would be doing in an hour or the next day. The cabmen drove in the same indolent fashion, and sat on the box each like the other; the shop-boys, all of whom he knew, were unpleasant. Their insolence was a source of danger. Every man seemed chained to his business like a dog to his kennel. Occasionally something new flashed by, or whispered to him, but it was difficult for him to see and understand it in the thick mass of all that was familiar, ordinary, and unpleasant.

Even the churches in the city did not please him. They were not cosy, nor bright, but close and penetrated by extremely powerful odours of incense, oil, and sweat. Yevsey could not bear strong smells. They made his head turn, and filled him with confused, anxious desires.

Sometimes on a holiday the master closed the shop, and took Yevsey through the city. They walked long and slowly. The old man pointed out the houses of the rich and eminent people, and told of their lives. His recitals were replete with accounts of women who ran away from their husbands, of dead people, and of funerals. He talked about them in a dry, solemn voice, criticizing and condemning everything. He

grew animated only when telling how and from what
this or that man died. In his opinion, apparently,
matters of disease and death were the most edifying
and interesting of earthly subjects.

At the end of every walk he treated Yevsey to tea
in a tavern, where musical machines played. Here
everybody knew the old man, and behaved toward him
with timid respect. Yevsey, grown tired, his brain
dizzied by the cloud of heavy odours, would fall into
drowsy silence under the rattle and din of the music.

Once, however, the master took him to a house
which contained numerous articles of gold and silver,
marvellous weapons, and garments of silk brocade.
Suddenly the mother's forgotten tales began to beat
in the boy's breast, and a winged hope trembled in
his heart. He walked silently through the rooms for
a long time, disconcertedly blinking his eyes, which
burned greedily.

When they returned home, he asked the master :

" Whose are they ?"

" They are public property—the Czar's,'' the old
man explained impressively.

The boy put more questions.

" Who wore such coats and sabres ?"

" Czars, boyars, and various imperial persons."

" There are no such people to-day ?"

" How so ? Of course there are. It would be impossible to be without them. Only now they dress
differently."

" Why differently ?"

" More cheaply. Formerly Russia was richer, but
now it has been robbed by various foreign people—
Jews, Poles, and Germans."

Raspopov talked for a long time about how nobody

loved Russia, how all rob it, and wish it every kind of harm. When he spoke much Yevsey ceased to believe him or understand him. Nevertheless, he asked :

" Am I an imperial person, too ?"

" In a sense. In our country all are imperial people, all are subjects of the Czar. The whole earth is God's, and the whole of Russia is the Czar's."

Before Yevsey's eyes handsome, stately personages in glittering garb circled in a bright, many-coloured round-dance. They belonged to another fabulous life, which remained with him after he had lain down to sleep. He saw himself in this life clad in a sky-blue robe embroidered with gold, with red boots of morocco leather on his feet. Rayisa was there, too, in brocade, and adorned with precious gems.

" So it will pass away," he thought.

To-day this thought gave rise not to hope in a different future, but to quiet regret for the past.

On the other side of the door he heard the dry, even voice of his master :

" Except the Lord build the house, they labour in vain——"

CHAPTER V

ONE day after closing the shop, Yevsey and his master went to the yard, where they were met by an anxious, ringing shout. It came from Anatol.

" I won't do it again, dear uncle. Never !"

Yevsey started, and instinctively exclaimed in quiet triumph :

" Aha !"

It was pleasant to hear the shouts of fear and pain coming from the breast of the cheerful boy, who was everybody's favourite.

" May I stay here in the yard ?" Yevsey asked the master.

" We must get our supper. But I'll stay here, too, and see how they punish a rascally good-for-nothing."

The people had gathered at the door of the brick shed behind the stairway. The sound of heavy blows and the wailing voice of Anatol issued from the shed.

" Little uncle, I didn't do it. Oh, God ! I won't do it, I won't ! Stop, for Christ's sake !"

" That's right ! Give it to him !" said watchmaker Yakubov, lighting a cigarette.

The squint-eyed embroiderer Zina upheld the tall, yellow-faced watchmaker :

" Perhaps we shall have peace after this. You couldn't have a single quiet moment in the yard."

Raspopov turned to Yevsey, and said :

" They say he's a wonder at imitating people."

" Of course," rejoined the furrier's cook. " Such a little devil ! He makes sport of everybody."

A dull scraping sound came from the shed, as if a sack filled with something soft were being dragged over the old boards of the floor. At the same time the people heard the panting, hoarse voice of Kuzin and Anatol's cries, which now grew feebler and less frequent.

" Forgive me ! Oh ! Help me—I won't do it again —oh, God !"

His words became indistinct, and flowed together into a thick choking groan. Yevsey trembled, remembering the pain of the beatings he used to receive. The talk of the onlookers stirred a confused feeling in him. It was fearful to stand among people who only the day before had willingly and gaily taken delight in the lively little fellow, and who now looked on with pleasure while he was being beaten. At this moment these half-sick people, surly and worn out with work, seemed more comprehensible to him. He believed that now none of them shammed, but were sincere in the curiosity with which they witnessed the torture of a human being. He felt a little sorry for Anatol, yet it was pleasant to hear his groans. The thought passed through his mind that now he would become quieter and more companionable.

Suddenly Nikolay the furrier appeared—a short, black, curly-headed man with long arms. As always, daring and respecting nobody, he thrust the people aside, walked into the shed, and from there his coarse voice was heard crying out twice :

" Stop ! Get away !"

Everybody suddenly moved back from the door.

THE SPY

Kuzin bolted out of the shed, seated himself on the ground, clutched his head with both hands, and opening his eyes wide, bawled hoarsely :

" Police !"

" Let's get away from evil, Yevsey," said the master, withdrawing to one side.

The boy retreated to a corner by the stairway, and stood there looking on.

Nikolay came out of the shed with the little trampled body of the glazier's boy hanging limply over his arm. The furrier laid him on the ground ; then he straightened himself, and shouted :

" Water ! Women, you rotten carrion !"

Zina and the cook ran off for water.

Kuzin, lolling his head back, snorted dully :

" Murder ! Police !"

Nikolay turned to him and gave him a kick on the breast which laid him flat on his back.

" You dirty dogs !" he shouted, the whites of his black eyes flashing. " You dirty dogs ! A child is being killed, and it's a show to you ! I'll smash every one of your ugly mugs !"

Oaths from all sides answered him, but nobody dared to approach him.

" Let's go," said the master, taking Yevsey by the hand.

As they walked away, they saw Kuzin run noiselessly in a stooping position to the gates.

" To call the police," the master explained to Yevsey.

When Yevsey was alone he felt that his jealousy of Anatol had left him. He strained his slow mind to explain to himself what he had seen. It merely *seemed* that the people liked Anatol, who amused them. In reality it was not so. All people enjoyed fighting, enjoyed looking on while others fought, enjoyed being cruel. Nikolay had interceded for Anatol because he liked to beat Kuzin, and actually did beat him on almost every holiday. Very bold and strong, he could thrash any man in the house. In his turn he was beaten by the police. So to sum up, whether you are quiet or daring, you'll be beaten and insulted all the same.

Several days passed. The tenants, talking in the yard, said that the glazier's boy, who had been taken to the hospital, had gone insane. Then Yevsey remembered how the boy's eyes had burned when he gave his performances, how vehement his gestures and motions had been, and how quickly the expression of his face had changed. He thought with dread that perhaps Anatol had always been insane. He soon forgot the glazier's boy.

CHAPTER VI

In the rainy nights of autumn, short broken sounds came from the roof under Yevsey's window. They disquieted him and prevented him from sleeping. On one such night he heard the angry exclamations of his master :

" You vile woman !"

Rayisa Petrovna answered, as always, in a low singing voice :

" I cannot permit you, Matvey Matveyevich."

" You low creature ! Look at the money I am paying you !"

The door to the master's room was open, and the voices came in clearly to Yevsey. The fine rain sang a tearful song outside the window. The wind crept over the roof, panting like a large homeless bird fatigued by the bad weather, and softly flapping its wet wings against the panes. The boy sat up in bed, put his hands around his knees, and listened, shivering.

" Give me back the twenty-five rubles, you thief !"

" I do not deny it. Dorimedont Lukin gave me the money."

" Aha ! You see, you hussy !"

" No, permit me—when you asked me to spy on the man—— "

" Hush ! What are you screaming for ?"

Now the door was closed, but even through the wall Yevsey could hear almost everything that was said.

"Remember, you vile woman, you, that you are in my hands," said the master, rapping his fingers on the table. "And if I notice that you've struck up relations with Dorimedont——"

The woman's voice was warm and flexible, like the supple movements of a kitten, and it stole in softly, coiled around the old man's malicious words, wiping them from Yevsey's memory.

The woman must be right. Her composure and the master's whole relation to her convinced the boy that she was. Yevsey was now in his fifteenth year, and his inclination for this gentle and beautiful woman began to be marked by a pleasant sense of agitation. Since he met Rayisa very rarely, and for only a minute at a time, he always looked into her face with a secret feeling of bashful joy. Her kindly way of speaking to him caused a grateful tumult in his breast, and drew him to her more and more powerfully.

While still in the village he had learned the hard truth of the relations between man and woman. The city bespattered this truth with mud, but it did not sully the boy himself. His being a timid nature, he did not dare to believe what was said about women, and such talk, instead of exciting any feeling of temptation, aroused painful aversion. Now, as he was sitting up in bed, Yevsey remembered Rayisa's amiable smile, her kind words, and carried away by the thought of them, he had no time to lie down before the door to the master's room opened, and she stood before him, half-dressed, with loose hair, her hand pressed to her breast. He grew frightened and faint. The woman wanted to open the door again to the old man's room, and had already put out her hand, but suddenly smiling, she withdrew it, and shook a threatening finger at Yevsey. Then she walked into her room. Yevsey fell asleep with a smile.

In the morning, as he was sweeping the kitchen floor, he saw Rayisa at the door of her room. He straightened himself up before her with the broom in his hands.

" Good-morning," she said. " Will you take coffee with me ? "

Rejoiced and embarrassed, the boy replied :

" I haven't washed yet. One minute."

In a few minutes he was sitting at the table in her room, seeing nothing but the fair face with the dark brows, and the good, moist eyes with the smile in them.

" Do you like me ? " she asked.

" Yes."

" Why ? "

" You are good and beautiful."

He answered as in a dream. It was strange to hear her questions. Her eyes, fixed upon him, vanquished him. They must know everything that went on in his soul.

" And do you like Matvey Matveyevich ? " Rayisa asked in a slow undertone.

" No," Yevsey answered simply.

" Is that so ? He loves you. He told me so himself."

" No," rejoined the boy.

Rayisa raised her brows, moved a little nearer to him, and asked :

" Don't you believe me ? "

" I believe you, but I don't believe my master, not a bit."

" Why ? Why ? " she asked, in a quick whisper,

59

moving still nearer to him. The warm gleam of her look penetrated the boy's heart, and stirred within him little thoughts never yet expressed to anybody. He quickly uttered them to this woman.

"I am afraid of him. I am afraid of everybody except you."

"Why are you afraid?"

"You know."

"What do I know?"

"You, too, are wronged, not by one master. I saw you cry. You were not crying then because you had been drinking. I understand. I understand much. Only I do not understand everything together. I see everything separately in its tiniest details, but side by side with them something different, not even resembling them. I understand this, too. But what is it all for? One thing is at variance with the other, and they do not go together. There is one kind of life and another besides."

"What are you talking about?" Rayisa asked in amazement.

"That's true."

For several moments they looked at each other in silence. The boy's heart beat quickly. His cheeks grew red with embarrassment.

"Well, now, go," said Rayisa, quietly arising. "Go, or else he will ask you why you stayed away so long. Don't tell him you were with me. You won't, will you?"

Yevsey walked away filled with the tender sound of the singing voice, and warmed by the sympathetic look. The woman's words rang in his memory enveloping his heart in quiet joy.

That day was strangely long. Over the roofs of the houses and the Circle hung a grey cloud. The day, weary and dull, seemed to have become entangled in its grey mass, and, like the cloud, to have halted over the city.   After dinner two customers entered the shop, one a stooping, lean man with a pretty, grizzled moustache, the other a man with a red beard and spectacles.   Both pottered about among the books long and minutely.   The lean man kept whistling softly through his quivering moustache, while the red-bearded man spoke with the master.

Yevsey knew beforehand just what the master would say, and how he would say it.   The boy was bored. He was impatient for the evening to come, and he tried to relieve the tedium by listening to the words of the old man Raspopov, and verifying his conjectures while he arranged in a row the books the customers had selected.

" You are buying these books for a library ?" the old man inquired affably.

" For the library of the Teachers' Association," replied the red-bearded man.   " Why ?"

" Now he'll praise them up," thought Yevsey, and he was not mistaken.

" You show extremely good judgment in your choice.   It is pleasant to see a correct estimate of books."

" Pleasant ?"

" Now he'll smile," thought Yevsey.

" Yes, indeed," said the old man, smiling graciously. " You get used to these books, so that you get to love them.   You see, they aren't dead wood, but products of the mind.   So when a customer also respects books, it is pleasant. Our average customer is a comical fellow.   He comes and asks : ' Have you any interesting books ?'   It's all the same to him.   He seeks amusement, play, but no benefit. But occasionally someone will suddenly ask for a prohibited book."

" How's that ? Prohibited ?" asked the man, screwing up his small eyes.

" Prohibited from libraries—published abroad, or secretly in Russia."

" Are such books for sale ?"

" Now he will speak very low." Again Yevsey was not mistaken.

Fixing his glasses upon the face of the red-bearded man, the master lowered his voice almost to a whisper.

" Why not ? Sometimes you buy a whole library, and you come across everything there—everything."

" Have you such books now ?"

" Several."

" Let me see them, please."

" Only I must ask you not to say anything about them. You see, it's not for the sake of profit, but as a courtesy. One likes to do favours now and then."

The stooping man stopped whistling, adjusted his spectacles, and looked attentively at the old man.

To-day the master was utterly loathsome to Yevsey, who kept looking at him with cold, gloomy malice. And now, when Raspopov went over to a corner of the shop to show the red-bearded man some books there, the boy suddenly and quite involuntarily said in a whisper to the stooping customer :

" Don't buy those books."

Yevsey trembled with fright the moment he had spoken. The man raised his glasses, and peered into the boy's face with his bright eyes.

" Why ?"

With a great effort Yevsey answered after a pause : " I don't know."

The customer readjusted his glasses, moved away from him, and began to whistle louder, looking sidewise at the old man. Then he raised his head, which made him straighter and taller, stroked his grey moustache, and without haste walked up to his companion, from whom he took the book. He looked it over, and dropped it on the table. Yevsey followed his movements, expecting some calamity to befall himself. But the stooping man merely touched his companion's arm, and said simply and calmly :

" Well, let's go."

" But the books ?" exclaimed the other.

" Let's go. I won't buy any books here."

The red-bearded man looked at him, then at the master, his small eyes winking rapidly. Then he walked to the door, and out into the street.

" You don't want the books ?" demanded Raspopov.

Yevsey realized by his tone that the old man was surprised.

" I don't," answered the customer, his eyes fixed upon the face of the master.

Raspopov shrank. He went to his chair, and suddenly said, with a wave of his hand in an unnaturally loud voice, which was new to Yevsey :

" As you please, of course. Still—excuse me, I don't understand."

" What don't you understand ?" asked the stooping man, smiling.

" You looked through the books for two hours or more, agreed on a price, and suddenly—— Why ?" cried the old man in excitement.

" Well, because I recollected your disgusting face. You haven't given up the ghost yet ? What a pity !"

The stooping man pronounced his words slowly—not

loud—and precisely. He left the shop deliberately, with a heavy tread.

For a minute the old man looked after him, then tore himself from where he was standing, and advanced upon Yevsey with short steps.

"Follow him. Find out where he lives," he said in a rapid whisper, clutching the boy's shoulder. "Go! Don't let him see you! You understand? Quick!"

Yevsey swayed from side to side, and would have fallen had the old man not held him firmly on his feet. He felt a void in his breast, and his master's words crackled there drily like peas in a rattle.

"What are you trembling about, you donkey? I tell you——"

When Yevsey felt his master's hand release his shoulder, he ran to the door.

"Stop, you fool!" Yevsey stood still. "Where are you going? Why, you won't be able—oh, my God! Get out of my sight!"

Yevsey darted into a corner. It was the first time he had seen his master so violent. He realized that his annoyance was tinged with much fear, a feeling very familiar to himself; and, notwithstanding the fact that his own soul was desolate with fear, it pleased him to see Raspopov's alarm.

The little dusty old man threw himself about in the shop like a rat in a trap. He ran to the door, thrust his head into the street, stretched his neck out, and again turned back into the shop. His hands groped over his body impotently, and he mumbled and hissed, shaking his head till his glasses jumped from his nose.

"Um—well, well—the dirty blackguard—the idea! The dirty blackguard! I'm alive—alive!" Several minutes later he shouted to Yevsey, "Close the shop!"

THE SPY

On entering his room the old man crossed himself. He drew a deep breath, and flung himself on the black sofa. Usually so sleek and smooth, he was now all ruffled. His face had grown wrinkled, his clothes had suddenly become too large for him, and hung in folds from his agitated body.

" Tell ·Rayisa to give me some peppered brandy—a large glassful." When Yevsey brought the brandy, the master rose, drank it down in one gulp, and, opening his mouth wide, looked a long time into Yevsey's face.

" Do you understand that he insulted me ?"

" Yes."

" And do you understand why ?"

" No."

The old man raised his hand, and silently shook his finger.

" I know him—I know a great deal," he said, in a broken voice.

Removing his black cap, he rubbed his bare skull with his hands, looked about the room, again touched his head with his hands, and lay down on the sofa.

Rayisa Petrovna brought in supper.

" Are you tired ?" she asked, as she set the table.

" It seems I am a little under the weather. Fever, I think. Give me another glass of brandy. Sit down with us. It's too early for you to go."

He talked rapidly. Rayisa sat down ; the old man raised his glasses, and scanned her suspiciously from head to foot. At supper he suddenly lifted his spoon and said :

" Impossible for me to eat. I'll tell you about something that happened." Bending over the plate, he was silent for some time, as if considering whether or not to speak of the incident. Then he began with a sigh. " Suppose a man has a wife, his own house—not a large house—a garden, and a vegetable garden, a cook—all acquired by hard labour without sparing himself. Then comes a young man, sickly, consumptive, who rents a room in the garret, and takes meals with the master and mistress."

Rayisa listened calmly and attentively. Yevsey felt bored. While looking into the woman's face, he stubbornly endeavoured to comprehend what had happened in the shop that day. He felt as if he had unexpectedly struck a match and set fire to something old and long dried, which began to burn alarmingly, and almost consumed him in its sudden malicious blaze.

" I must keep quiet," he thought.

" Were you the man ?" asked Rayisa.

Raspopov quickly raised his head.

" Why I ?" he asked. He struck his breast, and exclaimed with angry heat, " The question here is, not about the man, but about the law. Ought a man to uphold the law ? Yes, he ought. Without law it is impossible to live. You people are stupid, because man is in every respect like a beast. He is greedy, malicious, cruel."

The old man rose a little from his arm-chair, and shouted his words in Rayisa's face. His bald pate reddened. Yevsey listened to his exclamations without believing in their sincerity. He reflected on how people are bound together and enmeshed by some unseen threads, and how, if one thread is accidentally pulled, they twist and turn, rage and cry out. So he said to himself :

" I must be more careful."

The old man continued :

THE SPY

" Words bring no harm if you do not listen to them. But when the fellow in the garret began to trouble her heart with his ideas, she, a stupid young woman, and that friend of his who—who to-day—— " The old man suddenly came to a stop, and looked at Yevsey. " What are you thinking about ? " he asked in a low, suspicious tone.

Yevsey rose and answered in embarrassment :

" I am not thinking."

" Well, then, go. You've had your supper. So go. Clear the table."

Desiring to vex his master, Yevsey was intentionally slow in removing the dishes from the table.

" Go, I tell you ! " the old man screamed, in a squeaking voice. " Oh, what a fool you are ! "

Yevsey went to his room, and seated himself on the chest. Having left the door slightly ajar, he could hear his master's rapid talk.

" They came for him one night. She got frightened, began to shiver ; understood then on what road these people had put her. I told her—— "

" So it was you ? " Rayisa asked aloud.

The old man now began to speak in a low voice, almost a whisper. Then Yevsey heard Rayisa's clear voice :

" Did he die ? "

" Well, what of it ? " the old man shouted excitedly. " You can't cure a man of consumption. He would have died, at any rate."

Yevsey sat upon the chest, listening to the low rasping sound of his talk.

" What are you sitting there for ? "

The boy turned around, and saw the master's head thrust through the door.

" Lie down and sleep."

The master withdrew his head, and the door was tightly closed.

" Who died ?" Yevsey thought, as he lay in bed.

The dry words of the old man came fluttering down and fluttering down, like autumn leaves upon a grave. The boy felt more and more distinctly that he lived in a circle of dread mystery. Sometimes the old man grew angry, and shouted, which prevented the boy from thinking or sleeping. He was sorry for Rayisa, who kept peacefully silent in answer to his ejaculations. At last Yevsey heard her go to her own room. Perfect stillness then prevailed in the master's room for several minutes, after which Raspopov's voice sounded again, but now even as usual :

" Blessed is the man that walketh not in the counsel of the ungodly, nor standeth in the way of sinners, nor sit——"

With these reassuring words ringing in his ears, Yevsey fell asleep.

The next morning Rayisa again called him to her.

" What happened in the shop yesterday ?" she asked, with a smile, when he had seated himself.

Yevsey told her everything in detail, and she laughed contentedly and happily. She suddenly drew her brows together and asked in an undertone :

" Do you understand who he is ?"

" No."

" A spy," she whispered, her eyes growing wide with fright.

Yevsey was silent. She rose and went to him.

" What a tragic fellow you are !" she said thoughtfully and kindly, stroking his head. " You don't understand anything. You're so droll. What was

68

the stuff you told me the other day? What other life?"

The question animated him; he wanted very much to talk about it. Raising his head, and looking into her face with the fathomless stare of blind eyes, he began to speak rapidly.

"Of course, there's another life. From where else do the fairy-tales come? And not only the fairy-tales, but——"

The woman smiled, and rumpled his hair with her warm fingers.

"You little stupid! They'll seize you," she added seriously, even sternly. "They'll lead you wherever they want to, and do with you whatever they want to. That will be your life."

Yevsey nodded his head, silently assenting to Rayisa's words.

She sighed, and looked through the window upon the street. When she turned to Yevsey, her face surprised him. It was red, and her eyes had become smaller and darker.

"If you were smarter," she said, in an indolent, hollow voice, "or more alert, maybe I would tell you something. But you're such a queer fellow, there's no use telling you anything, and your master ought to be choked to death. There, now; go, tell him what I've said—you tell him everything."

Yevsey rose from the table, feeling as if a cold stream of insult had been poured over him. He inclined his head and mumbled:

"I'll never tell anything about you—to nobody. I love you very much, and—even if you choked him, I wouldn't tell anybody. That's how I love you."

He shuffled to the door, but the woman's hands caught him like warm white wings, and turned him back.

"Did I insult you?" he heard. "Well, excuse me. If you knew what a devil he is, how he tortures me, and how I hate him! Dear me!" She pressed his face tightly to her breast, and kissed him twice. "So you love me?"

"Yes," whispered Yevsey, feeling himself turning around lightly in a hot whirlpool of unknown bliss.

"How?"

"I don't know. I love you very much."

Laughing and fondling him, she said:

"You'll tell me about it. Ah, you little baby!"

Going down the stairs, he heard her satisfied laugh, and smiled in response. His head turned, his entire body was suffused with sweet lassitude. He walked quietly and cautiously, as if afraid of spilling the hot joy of his heart.

"Why have you been so long?" asked the master.

Yevsey looked at him, but saw only a confused, formless blur.

"I have a headache," he answered slowly.

"And I, too. What does it mean? Has Rayisa gotten up?"

"Yes."

"Did she speak to you?"

"Yes."

"What about?" the master asked hastily.

The question was like a slap in Yevsey's face. He recovered, however, and answered indifferently:

"She said I hadn't swept the kitchen clean."

A few moments later Yevsey heard the old man's low, dejected exclamation:

"That woman is a dangerous creature! Yes, yes.

70

She tries to find everything out, and makes you tell her whatever she wants."

Yevsey looked at him from a distance, and thought : " I wish you were dead."

The days passed rapidly, fused in a jumbled mass, as if joy were lying in wait ahead.   But every day grew more and more exciting.

CHAPTER VII

THE old man became sulky and taciturn. He peered around strangely, suddenly burst into a passion, shouted, and howled dismally, like a sick dog. He constantly complained of a pain in his head and nausea. At meals he smelt of the food suspiciously, crumbled the bread into small pieces with his shaking fingers, and held the tea and brandy up to the light. His nightly scoldings of Rayisa, in which he threatened to bring ruin upon her, became more and more frequent. But she answered all his outcries with soft composure.

Yevsey's love for the woman waxed stronger, and his sad, embittered heart was filled with hatred of his master.

"Don't I understand what you're up to, you low-down woman?" raged the old man. "What does my sickness come from? What are you poisoning me with?"

"What are you saying? What are you saying?" exclaimed the woman, her calm voice quivering. "You are sick from old age."

"You lie! You lie!"

"And from fright besides."

"You miserable creature, keep quiet!"

"You suffer from the weight of years."

"You lie!"

"And it's time you thought of death."

" Aha ! That's what you want ! You lie ! You
hope in vain ! I'm not the only one to know all about
you. I told Doriedmont Lukin about you." He burst
again into a loud, tearful whine. " I know he's your
paramour. It's he who talked you over into poisoning
me. You think you'll find it easier with him, don't
you ? You won't, you won't !"

One night, during a similar scene, Rayisa left the
old man's room with a candle in her hand, half-dressed,
white and voluptuous. She walked as in a dream,
swaying from side to side, and treading uncertainly with
her bare feet. Her eyes were half closed, the fingers
of her outstretched right hand clawed the air convulsively. The little smoky red tongue of the candle
inclined toward her breast, almost touching her
shirt. It illuminated her lips parted in exhaustion
and sickness, and set her teeth agleam.

After she had passed Yevsey without noticing him,
he instinctively followed her to the door of the kitchen,
where the sight that met his gaze numbed him with
horror. The woman was holding a large kitchen-knife
in her hand, testing its sharp edge with her finger. She
bent her head, and put her hand to her full neck near
the ear, where she sought something with her long
fingers. Then she drew a deep breath, and quietly
returned the knife to the table. Her hands fell at her
sides.

Yevsey clutched the doorpost. At the sound the
woman started and turned.

" What do you want ?" she demanded in an angry
whisper.

Yevsey answered breathlessly :

" He'll die soon. Why are you doing that to yourself ? Please don't do it. You mustn't."

" Hush !"

She put her hands on Yevsey as if for support, and walked back into the old man's room.

Soon the master became unable to leave his bed. His voice grew feeble, and frequently a rattle sounded in his throat. His face darkened, his weak neck failed to sustain his head, and the grey tuft on his chin stuck up oddly. The physician came every day. Each time Rayisa gave the sick man medicine, he groaned hoarsely :

" With poison, eh ? Oh, oh, you wicked thing !"

" If you don't take it, I'll throw it away."

" No, no ! Leave it ! and to-morrow I'll call the police. I'll ask them what you are poisoning me with."

Yevsey stood at the door, sticking first his eye, then his ear, to the chink. He was ready to cry out in amazement at Rayisa's patience. His pity for her rose in his breast more and more irrepressibly, and an ever keener desire for the death of the old man. It was difficult for him to breathe, as on a dry, icy-cold day.

The bed creaked. Yevsey heard the thin sounds of a spoon knocking against glass.

" Mix it ! mix it ! You carrion !" mumbled the master.

Once he ordered Rayisa to carry him to the sofa. She picked him up in her arms as if he were a baby. His yellow head lay upon her rosy shoulder, and his dark, shrivelled feet dangled limply in the folds of her white skirt.

" God !" wailed the old man, lolling back on the broad sofa. " God, why hast Thou given over Thy servant into the hands of the wicked ? Are my sins more grievous than their sins, O Lord ? And can it be that the hour of my death is come ?" He lost

breath and his throat rattled. " Get away !" he went
on in a wheezing voice. " You have poisoned one
man—I saved you from hard labour, and now you are
poisoning me—ugh, ugh, you lie !"

Rayisa slowly moved aside. Yevsey now could see
his master's little dry body. His stomach rose and
fell, his feet twitched, and his lips twisted spasmodically, as he opened and closed them, greedily gasping
for air, and licked them with his thin tongue, at the
same time displaying the black hollow of his mouth.
His forehead and cheeks glistened with sweat, his
little eyes, now looking large and deep, constantly
followed Rayisa.

" And I have nobody, no one near me on earth, no
true friend. Why, O Lord ?" The voice of the old
man wheezed and broke. " You wanton, swear before
the ikon that you are not poisoning me."

Rayisa turned to the corner, and crossed herself.

" I don't believe you ; I don't believe you !" he
muttered, clutching at the underwear on his breast
and at the back of the sofa, and digging his nails into
them.

" Drink your medicine. It will be better for you,"
Rayisa suddenly almost shrieked.

" It will be better," the old man repeated. " My
dear, my only one, I will give you everything, my own
Ray——"

He stretched his bony arm toward her, and beckoned
to her to draw near him, shaking his black fingers.

" Ah, I am sick of you, you detestable creature !"
Rayisa cried, in a stifled voice ; and snatching the pillow
from under his head, she flung it over the old man's face,
threw herself upon it, and held his thin arms, which
flashed in the air.

" You have made me sick of you !" she cried again.
" I can't stand you any more. Go to the devil ! Go,
go !"

Yevsey dropped to the floor. He heard the stifled
rattle, the low squeak, the hollow blows ; he understood
that Rayisa was choking and squeezing the old man,
and that his master kept beating his feet upon the sofa.
He felt neither pity nor fear. He merely desired
everything to be accomplished more quickly. So he
covered his eyes and ears with his hands.

The pain of a blow caused by the opening of the door
compelled him to jump to his feet. Before him stood
Rayisa arranging her hair, which hung over her
shoulders.

" Well, did you see it ?" she asked gruffly. Her face
was red, but now more calm. Her hands did not
tremble.

" I did," replied Yevsey, nodding his head. He
moved closer to Rayisa.

" Well, if you want to, you can inform the police."

She turned and walked into the room, leaving the
door open. Yevsey remained at the door, trying not
to look at the sofa.

" Is he dead, quite dead ?" he asked, in a whisper.

" Yes," answered the woman distinctly.

Then Yevsey turned his head, and regarded the little
body of his master with indifferent eyes. Flat and
dry, it lay upon the sofa as if glued there. He looked
at the corpse, then at Rayisa, and breathed a sigh of
relief.

In the corner near the bed the clock on the wall
softly and irresolutely struck one and two. The woman
started at each stroke. The last time she went up to
the clock, and stopped the halting pendulum with an

76

uncertain hand. Then she seated herself on the bed, putting her elbows on her knees, and pressing her head in her hands. Her hair, falling down, covered her face and hands as with a dense, dark veil.

Scarcely touching the floor with his toes, so as not to break the stern silence, Yevsey went over to Rayisa, and stationed himself at her side, dully looking at her white round shoulder. The woman's posture roused the desire to say something soothing to her.

" That's what he deserved," he uttered, in a low, grave voice.

The stillness round about was startled, but instantly settled down again, listening, expecting.

" Open the window," said Rayisa sternly. But when Yevsey walked away from her, she stopped him with a low question : " Are you afraid ?"

" No."

" Why not ? You are a timid boy."

" When you are near I'm not afraid."

" Are you sorry for him ?"

" No."

" Open the window."

The cold night wind streamed into the room, and blew out the lamp. The shadows quickly flickered on the wall and disappeared. The woman tossed her hair back and straightened herself to look at Yevsey with her large eyes.

" Why am I going to ruin ?" she asked in perplexity. " It has been this way all my life. From one pit to another, each deeper than the one before."

Yevsey again stationed himself beside her. They were silent for a long time. Finally she put her soft but cool hand around his waist, and pressing him to her, asked softly :

" Listen, will you tell ?"

" No," he answered, closing his eyes.

" You won't tell ? To nobody ? Never ?" the woman asked, in a mournful tone.

" Never !" he repeated quietly but firmly.

" Don't tell. I'll be helpful to you," she urged him, kindly stroking his cheek.

She rose, looked around, and spoke to him in a business-like way :

" Dress yourself. It's cold. And the room must be put in order a little. Go, get dressed."

When Yevsey returned, he saw the master's body completely covered with a blanket. Rayisa remained as she had been, half dressed with bare shoulders. This touched him. They set the room to rights, working without haste, and looking at each other now and then silently and gravely. The boy felt that this silent nocturnal activity in the close room bound him more firmly to the woman, who was just as solitary as himself, and, like him, knew terror. He tried to remain as near her as possible, and avoided looking at the master's body.

The day began to dawn. Rayisa listened to the sound of the waking house and city. She sighed, and beckoned to Yevsey.

" Now go ; lie down and sleep. I will wake you soon, and send you with a note to Dorimedont Lukin. Go !" She led him to the chest upon which he slept, and felt the bedding with her hand. " Oh, what a hard bed you have !"

When he had lain down, she seated herself beside him, and stroked his head and shoulders with her soft smooth hand, while she spoke in a gentle chant.

" Give him the note. And if he asks you how it

happened, tell him you don't know. Tell him you were asleep and didn't see anything."

She was silent, and knit her brows. Overcome by exhaustion, Yevsey, warmed by the woman's body and lulled by her even speech, began to drowse.

" No," she continued, " that's not right."

She gave her directions calmly and intelligently, and her caresses, warm and sweet, awakened memories of his mother. He felt good. He smiled.

" Dorimedont Lukin is a spy, too," he heard her lulling, even voice. " Be on your guard. Be careful. If he gets it out of you, I'll say you knew everything, and helped me. Then you'll be put in prison, too." Now she, too, smiled, and repeated : " In prison, and then hard labour. Do you understand ?"

" Yes," Yevsey answered happily, looking into her face with half-closed eyes.

" You are falling asleep. Well, sleep." Happy and grateful, he heard the words in his slumber. " Will you forget everything I told you ? What a weak, thin little fellow you are ! Sleep !"

Yevsey fell asleep, but soon a stern voice awoke him.

" Boy, get up ! Quick ! Boy !"

He rose with a start of his whole body, and stretched out his hand. At his bed stood Dorimedont Lukin, holding a cane.

" Why are you sleeping ? Your master died, yet you sleep."

" He's tired. We didn't sleep the whole night," said Rayisa, who was looking in from the kitchen with her hat on and her umbrella in her hand.

" Tired ? On the day of your benefactor's death you must weep, not sleep. Dress yourself."

The flat, pimply face of the spy was stern. His words compelled Yevsey imperiously, like reins steering a docile horse.

"Run to the police-station. Here's a note. Don't lose it."

In a half-fainting condition Yevsey dressed himself wearily, and went out in the street. He forced his eyes open as he ran over the pavement, bumping into everyone he met.

"I wish he would be buried soon," he thought disconnectedly. "Dorimedont will frighten her, and she'll tell him everything. Then I'll go to prison, too. But if I am there with her, I won't be afraid. She went after him herself, she didn't send me; she was sorry to wake me up—or maybe she was afraid—how am I going to live now?"

When he returned he found a black-bearded policeman and a grey old man in a long frock-coat sitting in the room. Dorimedont was speaking to the policeman in a commanding voice.

"Do you hear, Ivan Ivanovich, what the doctor says? So it was a cancer. Aha, there's the boy. Hey, boy; go, fetch half a dozen bottles of beer. Quick!"

Rayisa was preparing coffee and an omelette in the kitchen. Her sleeves were drawn up over her elbow, and her white hands darted about dexterously.

"When you come back, I'll give you coffee," she promised Yevsey, smiling.

Yevsey was kept running all day. He had no chance to observe what was happening in the house, but felt that everything was going well with Rayisa. She was more beautiful than ever. Everybody looked at her with satisfaction.

THE SPY

At night, when almost sick with exhaustion, Yevsey lay down in bed with an unpleasant sticky taste in his mouth, he heard Dorimedont say to Rayisa in an emphatic, authoritative tone :

" We mustn't let that boy out of our sight, you understand ? He's stupid."

Then he and Rayisa entered Yevsey's room. The spy put out his hand with an important air, and said, snuffling :

" Get up ! Tell us how you're going to live now."

" I don't know."

" If you don't know, who is to know ?" The spy's eyes bulged, his face and nose grew purple. He breathed hotly and noisily, resembling an overheated oven. " I know," he answered himself, raising the finger on which was the ring

" You will live with us—with me," said Rayisa kindly.

" Yes, you will live with us, and I will find a good place for you."

Yevsey was silent.

" Well, what's the matter with you ?"

" Nothing," said Yevsey, after a pause.

" You ought to thank me, you little fool !" Dorimedont exclaimed condescendingly.

Yevsey felt that the little grey eyes held him fast to something as if with nails.

" We'll be better to you than relatives," continued Dorimedont, walking away, and leaving behind the heavy odour of beer, sweat, and grease.

Yevsey opened the window and listened to the grumbling and stirring of the dark, exhausted city sinking into sleep. A sharp aching pain stole up from somewhere. Faintness seized the boy's body. A thin cord, as it were, cut at his heart, and made breathing difficult. He lay down and groaned, and peered into the darkness with frightened eyes. Wardrobes and trunks moved about in the obscurity, black dancing spots rocking to and fro. Walls, scarcely visible, turned and twisted. All this oppressed Yevsey with unconquerable fear, and pushed him into a stifling corner, from which it was impossible to escape.

In Rayisa's room the spy guffawed.

" M—m—m—my ! Ha, ha, ha ! It's nothing—it will pass away—ha, ha ! You'll get used—— "

Yevsey thrust his head under the pillow in order not to hear these irritating exclamations. A minute later, unable to catch his breath, he jumped from bed. The dry dark feet of his master flashed before him, his little red sickly eyes lighted up. Yevsey gave a little shriek, and ran to Rayisa's door with outstretched hands. He pushed against it, and cried :

" I'm afraid."

Two large bodies in the room bounded to their feet. Someone bawled in a startled, angry voice :

" Get out of there !"

Yevsey fell to his knees, and sank down on the floor at their feet like a frightened lizard.

" I'm afraid ! I'm afraid !" he squeaked.

The following days were taken up with preparations for the funeral and with the removal of Rayisa to Dorimedont's quarters. Yevsey flung himself about like a little bird in a cloud of dark fear. Only occasionally did the timid thought flicker in his mind like a will-o'-the-wisp, " What will become of me ?" It saddened his heart, and awoke the desire to run away and hide himself. But everywhere he met the eagle eyes of Dorimedont, and heard his dull voice :

" Boy, quick !"

The command resounded within Yevsey, and pushed him from side to side. He ran about for whole days at a time. In the evening he fell asleep, empty and exhausted, and his sleep was heavy and black and full of terrible dreams.

CHAPTER VIII

FROM this life Yevsey awoke in a dusky corner of a large room with a low ceiling. He sat holding a pen in his hand at a table covered with dirty green oilcloth, and before him lay a thick book in which there was writing, and a few pages of blank ruled paper. He did not understand what he had to do with all this apparatus, and looked around helplessly.

There were many tables in the room, with two or four persons at each. They sat there with a tired and vexed expression on their faces, moving their pens rapidly, smoking much, and now and then casting curt words at one another. The pungent blue smoke floated to the window casements, where it met the deafening noise that entered importunately from the street. Numberless flies buzzed about the occupants' heads, crawled over the tables and notices on the walls, and knocked against the panes. They resembled the people who filled this stifling, filthy cage with their bustle.

Gendarmes stood at the doors, officers came and went, various persons entered, exchanged greetings, smiled obsequiously, and sighed. Their rapid, plaintive talk, which kept up a constant seesaw, was broken and drowned by the stern calls of the clerks.

Yevsey sat in his corner with his neck stretched over the table, and his transparent eyes wide open, scruti-

84

nizing the different clerks in an attempt to remember their faces and figures. He wanted to find someone among them who would help him. The instinct of self-protection, now awakened in him, concentrated all his oppressed feelings, all his broken thoughts, into one clear endeavour to adapt himself to this place and these people, as soon as possible, in order to make himself unnoticed among them.

All the clerks, young and old, had something in common—a certain seedy and worn appearance. They were all equally dejected, but they easily grew excited, and shouted, gesticulating and showing their teeth. There were many elderly and bald-headed men among them, of whom several had red hair, and two grey hair. Of the two, one was a tall man who wore his hair long, and had a large moustache, whose beard had been shaven off. The other was a red-faced man with a huge beard and a bare skull. It was the last who had put Yevsey into a corner, set a book before him, and, tapping his finger upon it, had told him to copy certain parts of it.

Now an elderly woman all in black stood before this old man, and drawled in a plaintive tone :

" Little father, gracious sir."

" You disturb me in my work," shouted the old man, without looking at her.

And at the door, sitting upon a bench, a little thin young girl in a pink dress was sobbing and wiping her face with her white apron.

" I am not guilty."

" Who is whining there ?" asked a sharp voice.

The outsiders who came in did nothing but complain, make requests, and justify themselves. They spoke while standing, humbly and tearfully. The officials, on the other hand, remained seated, and shouted at them, now angrily, now in ridicule, and now wearily. Paper rustled and pens squeaked, and all this noise was penetrated by the steady weeping of the girl.

"Aleksey," the man with the grey beard called aloud, "take this woman away from here." His eyes were arrested by the sight of Klimkov. He walked up to him hastily, and asked gruffly, in astonishment: "What's the matter with you? Why aren't you writing?"

Yevsey dropped his head, and was silent.

"Hmm! another fool given a job," said the old man, shrugging his shoulders. "Hey, Zarubin!" he shouted, as he walked away.

A dry, thin boy, with a low forehead and restless eyes, and black curls on a small head, sat down beside Yevsey.

"What's the trouble?" he asked, nudging Yevsey's side with his elbow.

"I don't understand what to do," explained Klimkov in a frightened tone.

From somewhere within the youngster in the region of his stomach came a hollow, broken sound, "Ugh!"

"I'll teach you," he said, in a low voice, as if communicating some important secret. "I'll teach you, and you'll give me half a ruble. Got half a ruble?"

"No."

"When you get your pay? All right?"

"All right."

The boy seized the paper, and in the same mysterious tone continued:

"You see? The first names and the family names are marked in the book with red dots. Well, you must copy them on this paper. When you are done, call me, and I'll see whether you haven't put down a pack of lies. My name is Yakov Zarubin."

Again a sound seemed to break inside the boy's body and drop softly : " Ugh !" He glided nimbly between the tables, his elbows pressed to his sides, his wrists to his breast. He turned his small black head in all directions, and darted his narrow little eyes about the room. Yevsey looked after him, then reverently dipped pen in ink, and began to write. Soon he settled into that pleasant state of forgetfulness of his surroundings which had grown customary with him. He became absorbed in the work, which required no thought, and in it he lost his fear.

Yevsey quickly became accustomed to his new position. He did everything mechanically, and was ready to serve anyone at any time. In order the more immediately to get away from people, he subordinated himself submissively to everybody, and cleverly took refuge in his work from the cold curiosity and the cruel pranks of his fellow-clerks. Taciturn and reserved, he created for himself an unobserved existence in his corner. He lived like a nocturnal bird perched upon a dark post of observation without understanding the meaning of the noisy, motley days that passed before his round, fathomless eyes.

Every hour he heard complaints, groans, ejaculations of fright, the stern voices of the police officers, the irritated grumbling and angry fun of the clerks. Often people were beaten on their faces, and dragged out of the door by their necks. Not infrequently blood was drawn. Sometimes policemen brought in persons bound with ropes, bruised and bellowing with pain.

The thieves who were led in wore an embarrassed air, but smiled at everybody as with familiars. The street women also smiled ingratiatingly, and always arranged their dress with one and the same gesture. Those who had no passports observed a sullen or dejected silence, and looked askance at all with a hopeless gaze. The political offenders under police supervision came in proudly. They disputed and shouted, and never greeted anybody connected with the place. They behaved toward all there with tranquil contempt or pronounced hostility. This class of people was talked of a great deal in the chancery, almost always in fun, sometimes inimically. But under the ridicule and enmity Yevsey felt a hidden interest and something like reverent awe of these people who spoke so loudly and independently with everybody.

The greatest interest of the clerks was aroused by the political spies. These were men with indeterminate physiognomies, taciturn and severe. They were spoken of with keen envy. The clerks said they made huge sums of money, and related with terror how everything was known to them, everything open, and how immeasurable was their power over people's lives. They could fix every person, so that no matter where he moved he would inevitably land in prison.

The broad gaze of Klimkov lightly embraced everything moving about him. He imperceptibly gathered up experience, which his weak, uninformed mind was incapable of combining into a harmonious whole. But the numerous impressions heaping up one upon the other were forced into unity by the very weight of their mass, and aroused an unconscious greed for new observations. They sharpened his curiosity, unexpectedly pointed to conclusions, and secretly hinted at certain possibilities which sometimes frightened Yevsey by their boldness.

THE SPY

No one around him pitied anybody else. Neither was
Yevsey sorry for people. It began to seem to him that
all were feigning, even when they cried and groaned
from beatings. In all eyes he saw something concealed, something distrustful, and more than once
his ear caught the cry, threatening, though not uttered
aloud :

" Wait ; our turn will come some day, too."

In the evening, during those hours when he sat almost
alone in the large room and recalled the impressions of
the day, everything seemed superfluous and unreal ;
everything was unintelligible, a hindrance to people,
and caused them perplexity and vexation. All seemed
to know that they ought to live quietly, without malice,
but for some reason no one wanted to tell the others
his secret of a different life. No one trusted his neighbour, everybody lied, and made others lie. The irritation caused by this system of life was clearly apparent.
All complained aloud of its burdensomeness, each
looked upon the other as upon a dangerous enemy, and
dissatisfaction in life waged war with mistrust, cutting
the soul in two.

Klimkov did not dare to think in this wise, but he felt
more and more clearly the lack of order and the oppressive weight of everything that whirled around him. At
times he was seized by a heavy, debilitating sense of
boredom. His fingers grew languid ; he put the pen
aside, and rested his head on the table, looking long and
motionlessly into the murky twilight of the room. He
painstakingly endeavoured to find in the depths of his
soul that which was essential to him.

Then his chief, the long-nosed old man with the
shaven face and grey moustache, would shout to him :

" Klimkov, are you asleep ?"

Yevsey would seize the pen, and say to himself with a sigh :

" It will pass away."

But Yevsey could not make out whether he still believed in the phrase, or had already ceased to believe in it, and was merely saying it to himself for the sake of saying it.

CHAPTER IX

In the morning, Rayisa, half dressed, with a sallow face and dim eyes, gave Yevsey his coffee without speaking to him. Dorimedont coughed and spat in her room. Now his dull voice began to sound even louder and more authoritative than ever. At dinner and supper he munched noisily, licked his lips, thrust his thick tongue far out, bellowed, and looked at the food greedily before he began to eat. His red pimply face grew glossy, and his little grey eyes glided over Yevsey's face like two cold bugs, unpleasantly tickling his skin.

"I know how hard life is, brother," he said. "I know what's what. I know what a pound of good and what a pound of bad is worth to a man—yes, sir. And you had good luck to come to me at the start. Here I have placed you in a position, and I am going to push you farther and farther to the highest point possible—if you aren't a fool, of course."

He swung his bulky body as he spoke, and the chair under him groaned. Yevsey, as he listened to his talk, felt that this man could force him to do everything he wanted.

Sometimes the spy announced boastfully in self-applause :

"I received thanks again to-day from my chief, Philip Philippovich. He even gave me his hand."

91

THE SPY

Once at supper Dorimedont pulled Yevsey's ear, and began a recital :

" About two months ago I was sitting in a restaurant near a railroad-station, and I saw a man eating cutlets. He kept looking around and consulting his watch. You must know, Yevsey, that an honest man with an easy mind doesn't glance around in all directions. People do not interest him, and he always knows the time. The only persons who look about for people are the agents of the Department of Safety and criminals. Of course, I kept my eye on the gentleman. The suburban train pulled in ; another little gentleman comes into the restaurant—a dark fellow with a little beard, apparently a Jew. He wore two flowers in his buttonhole, a red and a white one—a sign. I see them greet each other with their eyes. ' Aha !' thinks I. The dark man ordered something to eat, drank a glass of seltzer, and walked out. The one who was in the restaurant first followed him without hurrying, and I after them."

Dorimedont puffed up his cheeks, and then blew a stream of air steeped with the odour of meat and beer into Yevsey's face. Yevsey ducked his head, and the spy burst out laughing. Then he belched noisily, and continued, raising his thick finger :

" For a month and twenty-three days I tracked the two men. Finally I reported them. I said I was on the track of suspicious people. They went away and came back again. Who are they ? The fair-haired fellow who had eaten the cutlet said : ' It's none of your business.' But the Jew gave his real name, and on inquiry it turned out we needed the man. Along with him we took a woman known to us—the third time she fell into our hands. We went to various other places, picked the people up like mushrooms. But we knew the whole gang. I was a good deal put out, when suddenly yesterday the fair-haired man gave us his name. He turned out to be an important fellow escaped from Siberia. Well, well, New Year I am to expect a reward."

Rayisa listened, looking over the spy's head, while she slowly chewed a crust of bread and bit off little pieces at a time.

" You catch them, and catch them, but they're not exterminated," she said lazily.

The spy smiled, and answered impressively :

" You don't understand politics. That's why you talk nonsense, my dear. We don't want to exterminate these people altogether. They serve as sparks to show us where the fire really begins. That's what Philip Philippovich says, and he himself was once a political —moreover, a Jew. Yes, yes. It's a very sharp game."

Yevsey's gaze wandered goomily about the contracted room. The walls, papered in yellow, were hung with portraits of Czars, generals, and naked women. These motley, obtrusive spots fairly cut the eyes, recalling sores and wounds on the body of a sick person. The furniture, smelling of whisky and warm, greasy food, pressed close against the walls, as if to withdraw from the people. The lamp burned under a green shade, and cast dead shadows upon the faces.

For some reason Yevsey recollected the old, sickly, flat-nosed beggar, with the restless eyes of a sharper, whom he met almost every day on his way to the office. The beggar pretended to be a jolly fellow, and would chant garrulously, as he stretched out his hand for alms :

THE SPY

"Stout of body, red of nose,
Pining for the want of booze;
Prithee, help God's pilgrim true,
Charity to whom 'tis due!
Help my burning thirst to slake.
Rum, oh rum, for the Lord's sake!"

The spy put his hand across the table, and pulled Yevsey's hair.

"When I speak, you must listen."

Dorimedont often beat Klimkov. Though his blows were not painful, they were particularly insulting, as if he struck not the face, but the soul. He was especially fond of hitting Yevsey on the head with the heavy ring he wore on his finger, when he would knock the boy's skull so that a strange, dry, cracking sound was emitted. Each time Yevsey was dealt a blow Rayisa would say indifferently, moving her brows:

"Stop, Dorimedont Lukin. Don't."

"Well, well, he won't be chopped to pieces. He has to be taught."

Rayisa grew thinner, blue circles appeared under her eyes, her gaze became still more immobile and dull. On evenings when the spy was away from home she sent Yevsey for whisky, which she gulped down in little glassfuls at a time. Then she spoke to him in an even voice. What she said was confused and unintelligible, and she frequently halted and sighed. Her large body grew flabby, she undid one button after the other, untied her ribbons, and, half dressed, spread herself on the arm-chair like sour dough.

"I am bored," she said, shaking her head. "Bored! If you were handsomer, or older, you might divert me in my gloom. Oh, how useless you are!"

94

Yevsey hung his head in silence. His heart was pricked with the burning cold of insult.

"Well, why are you staring at the floor?" he heard her sad complaining. "Others at your age would have started to love girls long ago; they live a living life, while you—oh, how irresponsive you are!"

Sometimes, after she had drunk whisky, she drew him to herself, and toyed with him. This awoke a complex feeling of fear, shame, and sharp, yet not bold, curiosity. He shut his eyes tightly, and yielded himself silently, involuntarily, to the power of her shameless, coarse hands. The weak, anæmic boy was oppressed by the debilitating premonition of something terrible.

"Go to bed, go! Oh, my God!" she exclaimed, pushing him away, dissatisfied and disgusted.

Yevsey left her to go to the anteroom in which he slept. Gradually losing the undefined, warm feeling he had had for her, he withdrew into himself more and more.

As he lay in bed filled with a sense of insult and sharp, disagreeable excitement, he heard Rayisa singing in a thick, cooing voice—always the same song—and heard the clink of the bottle against the glass.

But once on a dark night when fine streams of autumn rain lashed the window near his room with a howl, Rayisa succeeded in arousing in the youngster the feeling she needed.

"There, now," she said, smiling a drunken smile. "Now you are my paramour. You see how good it is? Eh?"

He stood at the bed also intoxicated of a sudden. His feet trembled, he was out of breath. He looked at her large, soft body, at her broad face spread in a smile. He was no longer ashamed, but his heart was seized with the grief of loss, and it sank within him outraged. For some reason he wanted to weep. But he was silent. This woman was a stranger to him, unnecessary and unpleasant. All the good, kind feelings he had cherished for her were at one gulp swallowed up by her greedy body, and disappeared into it without leaving a trace, like belated drops in a muddy pool.

" We'll live together, and we'll give Dorimedont the go-by, the pig !"

" But won't he find out ?" inquired Yevsey quietly.

" Oh, you little coward, come here !"

He did not dare to refuse, but now the woman was no longer able to overcome his enmity to her. She toyed with him a long time, and smiled with an air of having been offended. Then she roughly pushed his bony body from her, uttered an oath, and went away.

When Yevsey was left alone he thought in despair :

" Now she will ruin me. She'll store this up against me. I am lost."

He looked through the window. Something formless and frightened throbbed in the darkness. It wept, lashed the window with a doleful howl, scraped along the wall, jumped on the roof, and fell down into the street moaning and wailing. A cautious, seductive thought stole into his mind.

" Suppose I tell Kapiton Ivanovich to-morrow that she suffocated the old man."

The question frightened Yevsey, and for a long time he was unable to push it away.

" She will ruin me, one way or the other," he answered himself. Yet the question persistently stood before him, beckoning to him.

In the morning, however, it seemed that Rayisa had

forgotten about the tragic, violent incident of the night before. She gave him his bread and coffee lazily, and with an indifferent air. As always, she was half sick from the previous day's drinking. By neither word nor look did she hint of her changed relation to him.

He left for the office somewhat calmed, and from that day he began to remain in the office for night-work. He would walk home very slowly, so as to arrive as late as possible, because it was difficult for him to remain alone with the woman. He was afraid to speak to her, dreading lest she should remember that night when she had destroyed Yevsey's feeling for her. Feeble though it had been, it had yet been dear to him.

Yakov Zarubin and Yevsey's chief, Kapiton Ivano-vich, the man with the grey moustache, whom everybody called Smokestack behind his back, remained in the chancery with him for night-work more frequently than the others. The chief's shaven face was often covered with little red stubble, which glistened golden from afar, and at close range resembled tiny twigs. From under his grey lashes and the eyelids that drooped wearily, spiritless eyes gleamed angrily. He spoke in a grumbling growl, and incessantly smoked thick yellow cigarettes. The clouds of bluish smoke always hovering about his large white head distinguished him from all the other workers, and won him the nickname Smokestack.

"What a grave man he is!" Yevsey once said to Zarubin.

"He's cracked in the upper story," Zarubin answered, pointing to his head. "He spent almost a whole year in an insane asylum. But he's a quiet man."

Yevsey saw that sometimes the Smokestack took a small black book from the pocket of his long grey

jacket, brought it close to his face, and mumbled something through his moustache, which moved up and
down.

" Is that a prayer-book ?"

" I don't know."

Zarubin's swarthy face quivered spasmodically. His
little eyes bulged; he swung himself over toward Yevsey,
and whispered hotly :

" Do you go after the girls ?"

" No."

" Why ?"

Yevsey answered in embarrassment :

" I'm afraid."

" Ugh ! Come with me. All right ? We can get
it for nothing. We need only twenty-five kopeks for
beer. If we say we are from the Department of Police,
they'll let us in, and give us girls for nothing. They
are afraid of police officers. Everybody is afraid of
us." In a still lower voice, but with more fire and
appetite, he continued : " And what girls there *are !*
Stout, warm, like down-feather-beds ! They're the
best, by golly ! Some fondle you like your own mother,
stroke your head, and so you fall asleep. It's good !"

" Have you a mother ?"

" Yes, only I live with my aunt. My mother is a
sow. She's a lewd woman, and lives with a butcher
for her support. I don't go to her. The butcher won't
let me. Once I went there, and he kicked me on the
back. Ugh !"

Zarubin's little mouse ears quivered, his narrow eyes
rolled queerly, he tugged at the black down on his upper
lip with a convulsive movement of his fingers. He
throbbed all over with excitement.

" Why are you such a quiet fellow ? You ought to

be bolder, or else they'll crush you with work. I was afraid at first, too, so they rode over me. Come, let's be friends for the rest of our lives."

Though Yevsey did not like Zarubin, and was intimidated by his extreme agility, he replied :

" All right. Let's be friends."

" Your hand. There, it's done ! So to-morrow we'll go to the girls ?"

" No, I won't go."

They did not notice the Smokestack coming up to them.

" Well, Yakov, who will do what ?" he growled.

" We're not fighting," said Zarubin, sullenly and disrespectfully.

" You lie !" said the Smokestack. " Now, Klimkov, don't give in to him, do you hear ?"

" I do," said Yevsey, rising before him.

A feeling of reverent curiosity drew him to the man. Once, as usual unexpectedly to himself, he took courage to speak to the Smokestack.

" Kapiton Ivanovich."

" What is it ?"

" I want to ask you, if you please——"

Without looking at him, the Smokestack said :

" Pluck up ! Pluck up !"

" Why do people live so badly ?" Yevsey brought out with a great effort.

The old man raised his heavy brows.

" What business is it of yours ?" he rejoined, looking into Klimkov's face.

Yevsey was staggered. The old man's question was like a blow on the chest. It stood before him in all the power of its inexplicable simplicity.

" Aha !" said the old man quietly. Then he drew

his brows together, whipped a black book from his pocket, and, tapping it with his finger, said : " The New Testament. Have you read it ?"

" Yes."

" Did you understand it ?"

" No," answered Yevsey timidly.

" Read it again. Well, anyway——" Moving his moustache, the old man hid the book in his pocket. " I've been reading this book for three years—yes, three years. Nobody understands it. It's a book for children, for the pure in heart. No one can understand it."

He grumbled kindly, and Yevsey felt a desire to ask more questions. They did not formulate themselves, however. The old man lighted a cigarette, the smoke enveloped him, and he apparently forgot about his questioner. Klimkov glided off quietly. His attraction for the Smokestack had grown stronger, and he thought :

" It would be good for me to sit nearer to him."

Henceforth this became his dream, which, however, came into direct conflict with the dream of Yakov Zarubin.

" You know what ?" Zarubin said in a hot whisper. " Let's try to get into the Department of Safety, and become political spies. Then what a life we'll lead ! Ugh !"

Yevsey was silent. The political spies frightened him because of their stern eyes and the mystery surrounding their dark business and dark life.

CHAPTER X

AN accident happened at home. Dorimedont appeared
late at night in torn clothes, without hat or cane, his
face bruised and smeared with blood. His bulky body
shook, tears ran down his swollen cheeks. He sobbed,
and said in a hollow voice :

"It's all over ! I must go away—to another city—
the minute I can."

Rayisa silently, without haste, wiped his face with
a towel dipped in brandy and water. He started and
groaned.

"Not so roughly ! Not so roughly ! The beasts !
How they beat me—with clubs. To beat a man with
clubs! *Please* be more careful. Don't you understand?"

Yevsey handed the water, removed the spy's shoes,
and listened to his groans. He took secret satisfaction
in his tears and blood. Accustomed as he was to see
people beaten until blood was drawn, their outcries did
not touch him, even through he remembered the pain
of the pommellings he had received in his childhood.

"Who did it to you ?" asked Rayisa, when the spy
was settled in bed.

"They trapped me, surrounded me, in a suburb,
near a thread factory. Now I must go to another city.
I will ask for a transfer."

When Yevsey lay down to sleep, the spy and Rayisa
began to quarrel aloud.

THE SPY

" I won't go," said the woman, in a loud and unusually firm voice.

" Keep quiet ! Don't excite a sick man !" the spy exclaimed, with tears in his voice.

" I won't go !"

" I will make you."

In the morning Yevsey understood by Rayisa's stony face and the spy's angry excitement that the two did not agree. At supper they began to quarrel again. The spy, who had grown stronger during the day, cursed and swore. His swollen blue face was horrible to look upon, his right hand was in a sling, and he shook his left hand menacingly. Rayisa, pale and imperturbable, rolled her round eyes, and followed the swinging of his red hand.

" Never ! I'll never go !" she stubbornly repeated, scarcely varying her words.

" Why not ?"

" I don't want to."

" But you know I can ruin you."

" I don't care."

" No, you'll go."

" I won't."

" We shall see. Who are you, anyway ? Have you forgotten ?"

" It's all the same to me."

" All right."

After supper the spy wrapped his face in his scarf, and departed without saying anything. Rayisa sent Yevsey for whisky. When he had brought her a bottle of table whisky and another bottle of some dark liquid, she poured a portion of the contents of each into a cup, sipped the entire draught, and remained standing a long time with her eyes screwed up, and wiping her neck with the palm of her hand.

102

" Do you want some ?" she asked, nodding over the bottle. " No ? Take a drink. You'll begin to drink some time or other, anyway."

Yevsey looked at her high bosom, which had already begun to wither, at her little mouth, into her round, dimmed eyes, and remembering how she had been before, he pitied her with a melancholy pity. He felt heavy and gloomy in the presence of this woman.

" Ah, Yevsey," she said, " if one could only live his whole life with a clean conscience."

Her lips twitched spasmodically. She filled a cup and offered it to him.

" Drink !"

He shook his head in declination.

" You little coward !" she laughed quietly. " Life is hard for you—I understand. But why you live I don't understand. Why ? Tell me."

" Just so," answered Yevsey gloomily. " I live. What else is one to do ?"

Rayisa looked at him, and said tenderly :

" I think you will hang yourself."

Yevsey was aggrieved, and sighed. He settled himself more firmly in his chair.

Rayisa paced through the room, stepping lazily and inaudibly. She stopped before a mirror, and looked at her face long without winking. She felt her full white neck with her hands, her shoulders quivered, her hands dropped heavily, and she began again to pace the room, her lips moving up and down, up and down. She hummed without opening her mouth. Her voice was stifled like the groan of one who suffers from toothache.

A lamp covered with a green shade was burning on

the table. Through the window the round disc of the moon could be seen in the vacant heavens. The moon, too, looked green, as it hung there motionless, like the shadows in the room, and it augured ill.

" I am going to bed," said Yevsey, rising from his chair.

Rayisa did not answer, and did not look at him. Then he stepped to the door, and repeated in a lower voice :

" Good-night. I am going to sleep."

" Go ; I'm not keeping you. Go."

Yevsey understood that Rayisa felt nauseated. He wanted to tell her something.

" Can I do anything for you ?" he inquired, stopping at the door.

She looked into his face with her weary, sleepy eyes.

" No, nothing," she answered quietly, after a pause.

She walked up and down in the room for a long time. Yevsey heard the rustle of her skirt and the doleful sound of her song, and the clinking of the bottles. Occasionally she coughed dully.

Rayisa's composed words stood motionless in Yevsey's heart : " I think you will hang yourself." They lay upon him heavily, pressing like stones.

In the middle of the night the spy awoke Klimkov rudely.

" Where is Rayisa ?" he asked, in a loud whisper. " Where did she go ? Has she been gone long ? You don't know ? You fool !"

Dorimedont left the room hastily, then thrust his head through the door, and asked sternly :

" What was she doing ?"

" Nothing."

" Was she drinking ?"

" Yes."

" The pig !"

The spy pulled his ear and disappeared.

" Why did he speak in a whisper ?" Yevsey wondered.

The light in the lamp flickered and went out. The spy uttered an oath, then began to strike matches, which flared up, frightening the darkness, and went out. Finally a pale ray from the room reached Yevsey's bed. It quivered timidly, and seemed to seek something in the narrow anteroom. Dorimedont entered again. One of his eyes was closed from the swelling, the other, light and restless, quickly looked about the walls, and halted at Yevsey's face.

" Didn't Rayisa say anything to you ?"

" No."

" Such a stupid woman !"

Yevsey felt awkward to be lying down in the presence of the spy, and he raised himself.

" Stay where you are ! Stay where you are !" said Dorimedont hastily, and sat down on the bed at Yevsey's feet.

" If you were a year older," he began, in an unusually kind, quiet, and thoughtful tone, " I would get you into the Department of Safety as a political agent. It's a very good position. The salary is not large, but if you are successful, you get rewarded. And it's a free life. You can go wherever you want, have a good time—yes, indeed. Rayisa is a beautiful woman, isn't she ?"

" Yes, beautiful," agreed Yevsey.

" Yes, ahem !" said the spy, with a sigh and a strange smile. He kept stroking the bandage on his head with his left hand, and pinching his ear. " A woman you can never have enough of—the mother of temptation and sin—where did she go ? What do you think ?"

" I don't know," answered Yevsey quietly, beginning to be afraid of something.

" Of course. She has no paramour. No men came to her. Do you know what, Yevsey ? Don't be in a hurry with women. You have time enough for that. They cost dear, brother. Here am I, who have made thousands and thousands of rubles, and what's become of them ?"

Heavy, cumbersome, bound with rags, he shook before Yevsey's eyes, and seemed ready to fall to pieces. His dull voice sounded uneasy. His left hand constantly felt his head and his breast.

" Ah, I got mixed up with them a great deal !" he said, peering suspiciously around the dark corners of the room. " It's troublesome, but you can't get along without them. Nothing better in the world. Some say cards are better, but card-players can't get along without women either. Nor does hunting make you proof against women. Nothing does."

In the morning Klimkov saw the spy sleeping on the sofa with his clothes on. The room was filled with smoke and the smell of kerosene from the lamp, which had not been extinguished. Dorimedont was snoring, his large mouth wide open, his sound hand dangling over the floor. He was repulsive and pitiful.

It grew light, and a pale square piece of sky peeped into the little window. The flies awoke, and buzzed plaintively, darting about on the grey background of the window. Besides the smell of kerosene, the room was penetrated with some other odour, thick and irritating.

After putting out the lamp, Yevsey, for some reason, washed himself in a great hurry, dressed, and started for the office.

CHAPTER XI

At about noon Zarubin called out to Yevsey :

"Hey there, Klimkov; you know Rayisa Petrovna Fialkovskaya : she's your master Lukin's mistress, isn't she ?"

"Yes."

"There now !"

"What's the matter ?" asked Yevsey hastily.

"She has cut her throat."

Yevsey rose to his feet, stung in the back by a sharp blow of terror.

"She was just found in a store-room.   Let's go and look."

Zarubin ran off, announcing to the clerks on his way :

"I told you she was Dorimedont Lukin's mistress."

He shouted the word "mistress" with particular emphasis and zest.

Yevsey looked after him with wide-open eyes. Before him, in the air, hung Rayisa's head, her heavy, luxuriant hair flowed from it in streams, her face was pale green, her lips were tightly compressed, and instead of eyes there were deep, dark stains. Everything round about him was hidden behind the dead face, which Yevsey, numb with terror and pity, was unable to remove from his vision.

THE SPY

" Why don't you go to lunch ?" asked the Smokestack.

Scarcely anybody remained in the office. Yevsey
sighed, and answered :

" My mistress has cut her throat."

" Oh yes. Well, go to a café."

The Smokestack walked off, carefully picking his
steps. Yevsey jumped up and seized his hand :

" Take me."

" Come."

" No ; take me to stay with you altogether," Yevsey
besought him.

The Smokestack bent toward him.

" What do you mean by ' altogether '?"

" To your rooms—to live with you—for all the time."

" Aha ! Well, in the meantime let's get our lunch.
Come on."

In the café a canary-bird kept up a piercing song.
The old man silently ate fried potatoes. Yevsey was
unable to eat, and looked into his companion's face
inquiringly.

" So you want to live with me ? Well, come on."

When Yevsey heard these words he instantly felt that
they partitioned him off from the terrible life. Encouraged, he said gratefully :

" I will clean your shoes for you."

The Smokestack thrust his long foot, shod in a torn
boot, from under the table.

" You needn't clean this one. How about your mistress ? Was she a good woman ?"

The old man's eyes looked directly and kindly, and
seemed to say :

" Speak the truth."

" I don't know," said Yevsey, dropping his head,

108

and for the first time feeling that he used the phrase very often.

" So ?" said the Smokestack. " So ?"

" I don't know anything," said Yevsey, disappointed with himself. Suddenly he grew bold. " I see this and that ; but what it is, what for, why, I cannot understand. And there must be another life."

" Another ?" repeated the Smokestack, screwing up his eyes.

" Yes. It would be impossible otherwise."

The Smokestack smiled quietly. He hit his knife on the table, and shouted to the waiter :

" A bottle of beer. So it can't be otherwise ? That's curious. Yes—we'll see who will do whom."

" Do, please, let me live with you," Yevsey repeated.

" Well, we'll live together. All right."

" I'll come to you to-day."

" Come on."

The Smokestack began to drink his beer in silence.

When they returned to the office, they found Dorimedont Lukin there, who hastened up to Yevsey. His bandages had loosened, the one eye visible was suffused with blood.

" Did you hear about Rayisa ?" he inquired gravely.

" Yes, I did."

" She did it out of—— It was drink that did it, upon my word," whispered the spy, putting his uninjured hand to his breast.

" I won't go back there any more," said Yevsey.

" What then ? Where will you go ?

" I am going to live with Kapiton Ivanovich."

" Um-m-m !"

Dorimedont suddenly became embarrassed, and looked around.

109

THE SPY

" Take care ! He's not in his right senses. They keep him here from pity. He's even a dangerous man. Be careful with him. Keep mum about all you know."

Yevsey thought the spy would fly into a passion. He was surprised at his whispering, and listened attentively to what he said.

" I am going to leave the city. Good-bye. I am going to tell my chief about you, and when he needs a new man, he will take you, rest assured. Move your bed and whatever there is in my rooms to your new quarters. Take the things to-day, do you hear ? I'll go from there this evening to a hotel. Here are five rubles for you. They'll be useful to you. Now, keep quiet, do you understand ?"

He continued to whisper long and rapidly, his eyes running about suspiciously on all sides, and when the door opened he started from his chair as if to run away. The smell of an ointment emanated from him. He seemed to have grown less bulky and lower in stature, and to have lost his importance.

" Good-bye," he said, placing his hand on Yevsey's shoulder. " Live carefully, don't trust people, especially women. Know the value of money. Buy with silver, save gold, don't scorn copper, defend yourself with iron—a Cossack saying. I am a Cossack, you know."

It was hard and tiresome for Yevsey to listen to his softened voice. He did not believe one word of the spy's, and, as always, feared him. Klimkov felt relieved when he walked away, and went eagerly to his work, trying to use it as a shield against the recollection of Rayisa and all other troublesome thoughts. Something turned and bestirred itself within him that day. He felt he was standing on the eve of another life, and

gazed after the Smokestack from the corners of his eyes.
The old man bent over his table in a cloud of grey
smoke. Yevsey involuntarily thought :

"How everything happens at once. There she cut
her throat, and now maybe I will—— "

He could not picture to himself what might be ; in
fact, he did not understand what he wanted, and impatiently awaited the evening, working quickly in an
endeavour to shorten the time.

In the evening, as he walked along the street at the
Smokestack's side, he remarked that almost everybody
noticed the old man, some even stopping to look at him.
He walked not rapidly, but in long strides, swinging his
body and thrusting his head forward like a crane. He
held his hands behind his back, and his open jacket,
spreading wide, flapped against his sides like broken
wings. In Klimkov's eyes the attention the old man
attracted seemed to sever him from the rest of the
world.

"What is your name ?"

" Yevsey."

" John is a good name," observed the old man,
arranging his crumpled hat with his long hand. " I
had a son named John."

" Where is he ?"

" That doesn't concern you," answered the old man
calmly. After taking several steps he added in the
same tone, " If I say ' had,' that means I have him no
longer, no longer." He stuck out his lower lip and
pinched it with his little finger. " We shall see who
will do whom." Now he inclined his head on one side,
and looked into Klimkov's eyes. " To-day a friend
will come to me," he said solemnly, shaking his finger.
" I have a certain friend. What we speak about and

what we do does not concern you. What you know I do not know, and what you do I do not want to know. The same applies to you. Absolutely."

Yevsey nodded his head.

" You must make this a general rule. Apply it to everybody. No one knows anything about you. That's the way it should be. And you do not know anything about others. The path of human destruction is knowledge sown by the devil. Happiness is ignorance. That's plain."

Yevsey listened attentively, looking into his face. The old man observed his regard, and grumbled :

" There's something human in you. I notice it." He stopped unexpectedly, then went on : " But there's something human even in a dog."

They climbed a narrow wooden stairway, with several windings, to a stifling garret, dark and smelling of dust. At the Smokestack's request Yevsey held up burning matches while he fumbled a long time over opening the door. As Yevsey held up the matches, which scorched his fingers, a new hope flickered in his breast.

At last the old man opened the door, covered with torn oilcloth and ragged felt, and they entered a long, narrow white room, with a ceiling resembling the roof of a tomb. Opposite the door a wide window gleamed dimly. In the corner to the right of the entrance stood a little stove, which was scarcely noticeable. The bed extended along the left wall, and opposite sprawled a sunken red sofa. The room smelled strongly of camphor and dried herbs. The old man opened the window, and heaved a noisy breath.

" It's good to have pure air. You will sleep on the sofa. What is your name ? I've forgotten—Aleksey ?"

112

THE SPY

" Yevsey."

" Oh yes." He raised the lamp, and pointed to the wall. " There's my son John."

A portrait made in thin pencil strokes, and set in a narrow white frame, hung inconspicuously upon the wall. It was a young but stern face, with a large forehead, a sharp nose, and stubbornly compressed lips. The lamp shook in the old man's hands, the shade knocked against the chimney, filling the room with a gentle whining sound.

" John," he repeated, setting the lamp back on the table. " A man's name means a great deal."

He thrust his head through the window, breathed in the cold air noisily, and without turning to Yevsey, asked him to prepare the samovar.

When Yevsey was busying himself around the oven, a hunchbacked man entered, removed his straw hat in silence, and fanned his face with it.

" It's close, even though it's autumn already," he said, in a beautiful chest voice.

" Aha, you here !" said the Smokestack.

They began to converse in low tones while standing at the window. Yevsey, realizing that they were speaking about him, strained his ears to catch what they were saying. But he could not distinguish any words.

The three then seated themselves at the table, and the Smokestack began to pour the tea. Yevsey from time to time stole a look at the guest. His face, shaven like the Smokestack's, was bluish, with a huge thin-lipped mouth and dark eyes sunk in two hollows under a high, smooth forehead. His head, bald to the crown, was angular and large. He kept drumming quietly on the table with his long fingers.

THE SPY

" Well, read," said the Smokestack.

" From the beginning ?"

" Yes."

The hunchback pulled out a package of papers from his coat-pocket and opened it. " I'll skip the titles. This is the way I've done it." He coughed, and, half closing his eyes, began to read. " ' We people, known to nobody and already arrived at a ripe age, now fall slavishly at your feet with this distressing statement of grievances, which wells from the very depths of our hearts, our hearts shattered by life, but not robbed of sacred faith in the grace and wisdom of Your Majesty.' Well, is it good ?"

" Continue," said the Smokestack.

" ' For you are the father of the Russian people, the source of good counsel, and the only power on earth capable——' "

" Better say, ' the only power on earth endowed with authority,' " suggested the Smokestack.

" Wait, wait. ' The only power capable of restoring and maintaining order, justice——' Here we must put in a third word for the sake of symmetry, but I don't know what word."

" Be more careful in your choice of words," said the Smokestack sternly, but not aloud. " Remember that they convey a different meaning to every man."

The hunchback looked at him, and adjusted his glasses.

" Yes, that will come later. ' Great Russia is falling into ruin. Evil is rampant in our country, and horror prevails. People are oppressed by want. The heart has become perverted with envy. The patient and gentle Russian is perishing, and a heartless tribe, ferocious with greed, is being born, a race of wolves, cruel animals of prey. Faith is dissolved, and outside her fortress the people stand perturbed. Persons of depraved minds aim at the defenceless, take them captive with satanic shrewdness, and entice them on to the road of crime against all thy laws, Master of our lives !' "

" ' Master ' ? That's for a bishop," grumbled the Smokestack.

" Don't you like it ?"

" No ; we must do it differently."

" How ?"

" We must tell him directly that a general revolt against life is stirring among the people, and that ' therefore Thou, who art called by God——' "

The hunchback shook his head disapprovingly.

" We may point out. We have no right to advise."

" Who is our enemy, and what is his name ? Atheist, Socialist, and Revolutionist, a trinity. The destroyer of the family, the robber of our children, the forerunner of Antichrist."

" You and I don't believe in the Antichrist," said the hunchback quietly.

" That doesn't matter. We are speaking of the masses. They believe in the Antichrist. And we must point out the root of the main evil where we see it. In the doctrine of destruction——"

" He knows it himself."

" How should he ? Who would tell him the truth ? Nobody cast the noose of insanity around his children. And on what are their teachings based ? On general poverty and discontent with poverty. And we ought to say to him straight out : ' Thou art the father, and thou art rich. Then give the riches thou hast accumulated to thy people. Thus thou wilt cut off the root of

THE SPY

the evil, and everything will have been saved by thy hand.' "

The hunchback drew up his shoulders, and spread his mouth into a wide, thin crack.

" They'll send us to the mines for that."

Then he looked into Yevsey's face and at the master.

Klimkov listened to the reading and the conversation as to a fairy-tale, and felt that all the words entered his head and fixed themselves for ever in his memory. With parted lips and protruding eyes, he looked now at one, now at the other, and did not drop his gaze even when the dark look of the hunchback fastened upon his face. He was fascinated by the proceedings.

" Anyway," said the hunchback, " this is inconvenient."

" What is it, Klimkov ?" asked the Smokestack glumly.

Yevsey's throat grew dry, and he did not answer at once.

" I am listening."

Suddenly he realized by their faces that they did not believe him, that they were afraid of him. He rose from the table, and said, getting his words mixed :

" I won't say anything to a soul—I need it myself. Please let me listen—why, I myself said to you, Kapiton Ivanovich, that things ought to be different."

" You see ?" said the Smokestack crossly, pointing at Yevsey. " You see, Anton ; what does it mean ? Still a boy, a little boy—yet he, too, says things should be different. That's where they get their strength from."

" Yes, yes," said the hunchback.

Yevsey grew timid, and dropped back on his chair.

THE SPY

The Smokestack, moving his eyelids sternly, bent toward him.

" I will tell you—we are writing a letter to the Czar. We ask him to take more rigorous measures against those who are under supervision for political infidelity. Do you understand ?"

" I understand."

" Those people," the hunchback began to say clearly and slowly, " are agents of foreign Governments, chiefly of England. They receive huge salaries for stirring up the Russian people to revolt, and for weakening the power of the Government. The Englishmen do it so that we should not take India from them."

They spoke to Yevsey by turns. When one had finished, the other took up the word. He listened attentively, trying to remember their strange, eloquent flow of language. Finally, however, he tired from the unusual exertion of his brain. It seemed to him he would soon understand something huge, which would illuminate the whole of life and all people, their entire misfortune and their malicious irritation. It was inexpressibly pleasant for him to recognize that two wise men spoke to him as to an adult, and he was powerfully gripped by a feeling of gratitude and respect for these men, poorly dressed and so preoccupied with deliberations upon the construction of a new life. But now, his head grown heavy, as if filled with lead, he involuntarily closed his eyes, oppressed by a painful sensation of fulness in his breast.

" Go and lie down and sleep," said the Smokestack.

Klimkov rose obediently, undressed, and lay down on the sofa.

The autumn night breathed warm, fragrant moisture

in at the window. Thousands and thousands of bright stars quivered in the dark sky, flying up higher and higher. The fire of the lamp flickered and twisted itself upward. The two men, bending toward each other, read and spoke gravely and quietly. Everything round about was mysterious, awe-inspiring. It lifted Yevsey upward pleasantly, to something new, to something good.

CHAPTER XII

WHEN Yevsey had been living with Kapiton Ivanovich only a few days, he began to feel he was of some consequence. Formerly he had talked quietly and respectfully with the gendarmes who served in the chancery. Now, however, he called the old man Butenko to him in a stern voice, in order to administer a rebuke.

"Look, flies in my inkstand! How can I write with flies in my ink?"

The grey soldier, covered with crosses and medals, entered into his usual nonchalant, many-worded explanation:

"There are, all in all, thirty-four inkstands here, and there are thousands of flies. All the flies want to drink. That's why they crawl into the inkstands. What are they to do?"

"Wash it, and put in fresh ink," ordered Klimkov. Then he walked into the dressing-room, where he stationed himself before the looking-glass, and carefully regarded his thin face, grey and angular, with its sharp little nose and narrow lips. He searched for signs of a moustache, looked into his watery and uncertain eyes.

"I must get my hair cut," he decided, after failing to smooth the thin, light tufts of hair on his head. "And I ought to wear starched collars; my neck is too thin."

119

THE SPY

The very same evening he got his hair cut, bought two collars, and felt himself still more a man.

The Smokestack was attentive and kind in his behaviour toward Yevsey, but often a smile of derision gleamed in his eyes, which somewhat disconcerted and awed the young fellow. Whenever the hunchback came, the old man's face assumed a preoccupied expression, and his voice sounded stern. He cut short almost everything the other man said with an objection :

" It's not that—it's not so—no, you're no wiser than I am—your brain is like a poor gun, it scatters the thought on all sides. You ought to shoot so that the whole charge goes in the same direction."

The hunchback shook his head sadly, and answered in a thick voice :

" Wait. Good work cannot be done in a day. You must keep at it."

" Time flies ; the enemy grows."

" By the way, I noticed a man the other day," said the hunchback, " who took lodgings not far from my place. He was tall, had a pointed beard, and screwed-up eyes, and walked quickly. I asked the dvornik where he was working. He told me the man had come to look for a position. I immediately wrote a letter to the Department of Safety. You see ?"

The Smokestack interrupted his talk with a wide sweep of his arm.

" That's not important. The house is damp, that's why there are cockroaches in it. You won't get rid of them that way. The house must be made dry."

Another time, in the course of the evening the Smokestack said :

" I am a soldier. I commanded half a company, and I understand life. It is necessary for everybody to be

120

thoroughly familiar with the laws and regulations. Such knowledge produces unanimity. What hinders knowledge of the law ? Poverty and stupidity ; stupidity in itself being a result of poverty. Why doesn't he fight poverty ? In want is the root of human folly and of hostility to him, the Czar."

Yevsey greedily swallowed the old man's words, and believed them. The root of all human misfortune is poverty. That was clear and simple. Hence come envy, malice, cruelty. Hence also greed, and the fear of life common to all people, the apprehension of one another. The Smokestack's plan was also simple. The Czar was rich, the people poor ; then let the Czar give the people his riches, and all would be contented and good.

Yevsey's attitude toward people changed. He remained as obliging as before, but became more self-assertive, and began to look upon others condescendingly, with the eyes of a man who understands the secret of life, and can point out where the road lies to peace and calm.

He felt the need for boasting of his knowledge, so once, when lunching in the café with Yakov Zarubin, he proudly expounded everything he had heard from the old man and his hunchback friend.

Zarubin's narrow eyes flashed. He fidgeted in his seat, and for some reason rumpled his hair by thrusting the fingers of both hands through it.

" That's true, by golly !" he exclaimed, in an undertone. " Devil knows, really true ! He has thousands of millions, and we are perishing here. Who taught you all that ?"

" Nobody," said Yevsey firmly. " I thought it out myself."

" No, tell me the truth.   Where did you hear it ?"

" I tell you, I came to the conclusion myself."

Yakov looked at him with satisfaction.

" If that's so," he said, " you haven't a bad head. But you're lying."

Yevsey felt affronted.

" It's all the same to me whether you believe me or not.   It's the worse for you if you don't."

" For me ?" asked Yakov, and for some reason burst out laughing merrily, and vigorously rubbed his hands.

Two days later the assistant captain Komov and a grey-eyed gentleman with a round, close-cropped head and a bored, yellow face, came up to Yevsey's table.

" Klimkov, betake yourself to the Department of Safety," said the Captain clearly and ominously.   " Is your desk locked ?"

" No."

Yevsey rose, but his legs trembled, and he dropped into his chair again.   The crop-haired man drew nearer.

"Permit me," he said dryly, then pulled out the table drawer and took out the papers.

Weak and uncomprehending, Klimkov recovered his senses in a half-dark room at a desk covered with green felt.   A wave of anguish rose and fell in his breast.   The floor heaved and billowed under his feet, and the walls of the room, filled, as it were, with a green dusk, turned around steadily.   Over the table rose a man's white face framed in a thick black beard and spotted by gleaming blue eye-glasses.   Yevsey kept his eyes fastened on the glass of the spectacles, on the blue bottomless darkness, which drew him like a magnet, and seemed to suck the blood from his veins.   Without waiting for a question, Klimkov quietly told about the Smokestack and his

hunchbacked friend. He had understood their talks well, and now spoke connectedly in great detail. He seemed to be removing a thin layer of skin from his heart.

A high voice, which cut the ear, interrupted him.

" So ? So these jackasses say the Emperor the Czar is the fault of everything ?"

" Yes !'

The man with the blue glasses slowly stretched out his hand, put the telephone receiver to his ear, and asked in a sportive tone :

" Belkin, that you ? Yes ? See to it, old fellow, that search is made to-night in the rooms of two scoundrels. Arrest them. Eh—eh—a clerk in the Chancery Department, Kapiton Reüsov. Eh—eh— and a functionary of the Court of Exchequer—Anton Driagin—what ? Well, yes, of course."

Yevsey seized the edge of the table with his hand, feeling a dull pain in his eyes.

" So, my friend," said the man with the black beard, throwing himself back on the arm-chair. He smoothed his beard with both hands, played with his pencil, flung it on the table, and thrust his hands into his trousers pockets. He was silent for a painfully long time, then he asked sternly, emphasizing each word :

" What am I to do with you now ?"

" Forgive me," came from Yevsey, in a whisper.

" Klimkov ?" mused the black-bearded man, ignoring Yevsey's reply. " Seems to me I heard the name somewhere."

" Forgive me," repeated Yevsey.

" Do you feel yourself very guilty ?"

" Very."

" That's good. What do you feel guilty of ?"

Klimkov was silent. He felt as if the black-bearded

man sitting so comfortably and calmly in his chair would never let him leave the room.

" You don't know ?   Think !"

Klimkov drew more air into his lungs, and began to tell of Rayisa and how she had suffocated the old man.

" Lukin ?" the man with the blue goggles queried, yawning indifferently.   " Aha ! that's why your name is familiar to me."

He walked over to Yevsey, lifted his chin with his finger, and looked into his face for a few seconds. Then he rang.

A heavy tramp was heard, and a big pock-marked fellow with huge wrists appeared at the door, and looked at Yevsey.   He had a terrifying way of spreading his red fingers like claws.

" Take him, Semyonov."

" To the corner cell ?" asked the fellow, in a hollow voice.

" Yes."

" Come," said Semyonov.

Klimkov wanted to drop on his knees.   He was already bending his legs, when the fellow seized him under the arm, and pulled him through the long corridor down the stone stairway.

" What's the matter, brat ?   Frightened ?" he said, pushing Yevsey through a small door.   " Such a spider, no face, no skin, yet a rebel."

His words completely crushed Yevsey.   He walked forward with outstretched hands, and bumped against the wall.   When he heard the heavy clang of the iron door behind him, he squatted on the floor, putting his hands about his knees and raising his knees to his drooping head.   A heavy silence descended upon him. It seemed to him he would die instantly.   Suddenly he jumped from the floor, and ran about the room like a mouse. His groping hands felt the palette covered with a rough blanket, a table, a chair. He ran to the door, touched it, noticed in the wall opposite a little square window, and rushed toward the window. It was below the level of the ground. The area between the ground and the outer wall was laid over with horizontal bars, through which the snow sifted with a soft swish, creeping down the dirty panes. Klimkov turned noiselessly toward the door, and leaned his forehead upon it.

" Forgive me. Let me out," he whispered in his anguish.

Then he dropped on the floor again, and lost consciousness, drowned in a wave of despair.

CHAPTER XIII

THE days and nights dragged along in black and grey stripes, slowly poisoning Yevsey's soul, biting into it and enfeebling it. They crept by in dumb stillness, filled with ominous threats and forebodings. They said nothing of when they would end their slow, racking course. In Yevsey's soul everything grew silent and numb. He did not dare, was unable to, think; and when he paced his cage, he tried to make his steps inaudible.

On the tenth day he was again set before the man in the blue glasses. The man who had brought him there the first time was also present.

" Not very pleasant—eh, Klimkov ? " the dark man asked, smacking his thick red lower lip. His high voice made an odd splashing sound, as if he were laughing inside himself. The reflection of the electric light upon the blue glass of his spectacles sent strong rays into Yevsey's empty breast and filled him with slavish readiness to do everything necessary to end these slimy days which sank into darkness and threatened madness.

" Let me go," he said quietly.

" Yes, I will, and more besides. I will take you into the service. Now you will yourself put people into the place from which you have just been taken—into the same place and into other cosy little rooms." He laughed, smacking his lip. Klimkov bowed. " The late Lukin interceded for you ; and in memory of his honest service I will give you a position. You will receive twenty-five rubles a month to begin with."

His words entered Yevsey's breast and memory, and disposed themselves in a row, as if a commanding hand had written them there. He bowed again.

" This man, Piotr Petrovich, will be your chief and teacher. You must do everything he tells you. Do you understand ?" He turned to the other man. " So it's decided—he will live with you."

" Very well," came the response, with unexpected loudness. " That will be more convenient for me."

" All right."

The dark man, turning again to Yevsey, began to speak to him in a softened voice, telling him something soothing and promising. Yevsey tried to take in his words, and followed the heavy movement of the red lip under the moustache without winking.

" Remember, you will now guard the sacred person of the Czar from attempts upon his life and upon his sacred power. You understand ?"

" I thank you humbly," said Yevsey quietly.

Piotr Petrovich pushed his hat up on his forehead.

" I will explain everything to him," he interjected hastily. " It is time for me to go."

" Go, go. Well, Klimkov, off with you. Serve well, brother, and you will be satisfied. You will be happy. All the same, don't forget that you took part in the murder of the second-hand book-dealer Raspopov. You confessed to it yourself, and I took your testimony down in writing. Do you understand ? Well, so long."

Philip Philippovich nodded his head, and his stiff beard, which seemed to be cut from wood, moved in unison with it. Then he held out to Yevsey a white bloated hand with a number of gold rings on the short fingers.

Yevsey closed his eyes and started.

"What a scared fellow you are, brother!" Philip Philippovich ejaculated in a thin voice, and laughed a glassy laugh. "Now you have nothing and nobody to fear. You are now the servant of the Czar, and ought to be self-assured and bold. You stand on firm ground. Do you comprehend?"

When Yevsey walked out into the street, he could not catch his breath. He staggered, and almost fell. Piotr, raising the collar of his overcoat, looked around and waved to a cab.

"We will ride home—to my house," he said, in a low tone.

Yevsey looked at him from the corners of his eyes, and almost uttered a cry. Piotr's smooth-shaven face had suddenly grown a small light moustache.

"Well, why are you gaping at me in that fashion?" he asked gruffly, in annoyance.

Yevsey dropped his head, trying, in spite of his wish to do so, not to look into the face of the new master of his destiny. Piotr did not speak to him throughout the ride, but kept counting something on his fingers, bending them one after the other, and knitting his brows and biting his lips. Occasionally he called out angrily to the driver:

"Hurry up!"

It was cold; sleet was falling, and plashing sounds floated in the air. It seemed to Yevsey that the cab was quickly rolling down a steep mountain into a black, dirty ravine.

They stopped at a large, three-storied house. Most

of the windows in three rows were dark and blind. Only a few gleamed with a sickly yellow from the lights within. Streams of water poured from the roof, sobbing.

" Go up the steps," commanded Piotr, who was now sans moustache.

They ascended the steps, and walked through a long corridor, past a number of white doors. Yevsey thought the place was a prison, but the thick odour of fried onion and blacking did not accord with his conception of a prison. Piotr quickly opened one of the white doors, turned on two electric lights, and carefully scrutinized all the corners of the room.

" If anybody asks you who you ɾe," he said dryly and quickly, while removing his hat and overcoat, " say you are my cousin. You came from Tzarskoe Seloe to look for a position. Remember—don't make a mistake."

Piotr's face wore a preoccupied expression, his eyes were cheerless, his speech abrupt, his thin lips twitched. He rang, and thrust his head out of the door.

" Ivan, bring in the samovar," he called.

Yevsey, standing in a corner of the room, looked around dismally, dully waiting for something.

" Take off your coat, and sit down. You will have the next room to yourself," said the spy, quickly unfolding a card-table. He took from his pocket a notebook and a pack of cards, which he laid out for four hands.

" You understand, of course," he went on, without looking at Klimkov—" you understand that ours is a secret business. We must keep under cover, or else they'll kill us as they killed Lukin."

" Was he killed ?" asked Yevsey quietly.

" Yes," said Piotr unconcernedly. He wiped his forehead and examined the cards. " Deal one thousand two hundred and fourteenth—I have the ace, seven of hearts, queen of clubs." He made a note in his book, and without raising his head continued to speak to himself.

When he calculated the cards, he mumbled indistinctly with a preoccupied air ; but when he instructed Yevsey, he spoke dryly, clearly, and rapidly. " Revolutionists are enemies of the Czar and God—ten of diamonds—three—Jack of spades—they are bought by the Germans in order to bring ruin upon Russia. We Russians have begun to do everything ourselves, and for the Germans—king, five and nine—the devil ! The sixteenth coincidence !"

Piotr Petrovich suddenly grew jolly; his eyes gleamed, and his face assumed a sleek, satisfied expression.

" What was I saying ?" he asked Yevsey, looking up at him.

" The Germans."

" Oh yes ! The Germans are greedy ; they are enemies of the Russian people; they want to conquer us. They want us to buy all our goods from them, and give them our bread. The Germans have no bread—queen of diamonds—all right—two of hearts, ten of clubs, ten——" Screwing up his eyes, he looked up at the ceiling, sighed, and shuffled the cards. " In general, all foreigners envious of the wealth and power of Russia —one thousand two hundred and fifteenth deal—want to create a revolt in our country, dethrone the Czar, and—three aces—h'm !—and place their own officials everywhere, their own rulers over us in order to rob us and ruin us. You don't want this to happen, do you ?"

" I don't," said Yevsey, who understood nothing, and

followed the quick movements of the card-player's fingers with a dull look.

"Of course, nobody wants it," remarked Piotr pensively. He laid out the cards again, and stroked his cheeks meditatively. "You are a Russian, and you cannot want that—that—this should happen—therefore you ought to fight the revolutionaries, agents of the foreigners, and defend the liberty of Russia, the power and life of the Czar. That's all. Did you understand?"

"I did."

"Afterward you will see the way it must be done. The only thing I'll tell you beforehand is, don't dawdle. Carry out all orders precisely. We fellows ought to have eyes at the back as well as in front. If you haven't, you'll get it good and hard on all sides—ace of spades, seven of diamonds, ten of clubs."

There was a knock at the door.

"Open the door."

A red, curly-haired man entered, carrying a samovar on a tray.

"Ivan, this is my cousin. He will live here with me. Get the next room ready for him."

"Yes, sir. Mr. Chizhov was here."

"Drunk?"

"A little. He wanted to come in."

"Make tea, Yevsey," said the spy, after the servant had left the room. "Get yourself a glass, and drink some tea. What salary did you get in the Police Department?"

"Nine rubles a month."

"You have no money now?"

"No."

"You've got to have some, and you must order a

suit for yourself. One suit won't do. You must notice everybody, but nobody must notice you."

He again mumbled calculations of the cards. Yevsey, while noiselessly serving the tea, tried to straighten out the strange impressions of the day. But he was not successful. He felt sick. He was chilled through and through, and his hands shook. He wanted to stretch himself out in a corner, close his eyes, and lie motionless for a long time. Words and phrases repeated themselves disconnectedly in his head.

" What are you guilty of, then ?" Philip Philippovich asked, in a thin voice.

" They killed Dorimedont Lukin," the spy announced dryly, then exclaimed joyfully : " The sixteenth coincidence !"

" You will choke yourself," said Rayisa, in an even voice.

There was a powerful rap on the door. Piotr raised his head.

" Is it you, Sasha ?"

" Well, open the door," an angry voice answered.

When Yevsey opened the door, a tall man loomed before him, swaying on long legs. The ends of his black moustache reached to the bottom of his chin. The hair of it must have been stiff and hard as a horse's, for each one stuck out by itself. When he removed his hat, he displayed a bald skull. He flung the hat on the bed, and rubbed his face vigorously with both hands.

" Why are you throwing your wet hat on my bed ?" observed Piotr.

" The devil take your bed !" said the guest through his nose.

" Yevsey, hang up the overcoat."

THE SPY

The visitor seated himself, stretching out his long legs and lighting a cigarette.

" What's that—Yevsey ?"

" My cousin. Will you have some tea ?"

" We're all akin in our natural skin. Have you got any whisky ?"

Piotr told Klimkov to order a bottle of whisky and some refreshments. Yevsey obeyed, then seated himself at the table, putting the samovar between his face and the visitor's, so as not to be seen by him.

" How's business, you card-sharper ?" he asked, nodding his head at the cards.

Piotr suddenly half raised himself from the chair, and said animatedly :

" I have found out the secret ! I have found out the secret !"

" You have found it out ?" queried the visitor. " Fool !" he exclaimed, drawling the word and shaking his head.

Piotr seized the notebook, and rapping his fingers on it, continued in a hot whisper :

" Wait, Sasha. I have had the sixteenth coincidence already. You know the significance of that ? And I made only one thousand two hundred and fourteen deals. Now the cards keep repeating themselves oftener and oftener. I must make two thousand seven hundred and four deals. You understand ? Fifty-two times fifty-two. Then make all the deals over again thirteen times, according to the number of cards in each colour. Thirty-five thousand one hundred and fifty-two times. And repeat these deals four times according to the number of colours. One hundred and forty thousand six hundred and eight times."

" Fool !" the visitor again drawled through his nose, shaking his head and curling his lips in a sneer.

" Why, Sasha, why ?   Explain !" Piotr cried softly. " Why, then I'll know all the deals possible in a game. Think of it !   I'll look at my cards "—he held the book nearer to his face and began to read quickly— " ace of spades, seven of diamonds, ten of clubs. So of the other players one has king of hearts, five and ten of diamonds, and the other, ace, seven of hearts, queen of clubs, and the third has queen of diamonds, two of hearts, and ten of clubs."

His hands trembled, sweat glistened on his temples, his face became young, good, and kind.

Klimkov, peering from behind the samovar, saw on Sasha's face large dim eyes with red veins on the whites, a coarse, big nose, which seemed to be swollen, and a net of pimples spread on the yellow skin of his forehead from temple to temple, like the band worn by the dead. He radiated an acrid, unpleasant odour. The man recalled something painful to Yevsey.

Piotr pressed the book to his breast, and waved his hand in the air.

" I shall then be able to play without losing once," he whispered ecstatically.   " Hundreds of thousands, millions, will be lost to me, and there won't be any sharp practice, any jugglery in it, a matter of my knowledge— that's all.   Everything strictly within the law."

He struck his chest so severe a blow with his fist that he began to cough.   Then he dropped on his chair, and laughed quietly.

" Why don't they bring the whisky ?" growled Sasha, throwing the stump of his cigarette on the floor.

" Yevsey, go, tell——" Piotr began quickly, but at

that instant there was a knock at the door. " Are you drinking again ?" Piotr asked, smiling.

Sasha stretched out his hand for the bottle.

" Not yet, but I shall be in a second."

" It's bad for you with your sickness."

" Whisky is bad for healthy people, too — whisky and the imagination. You, for instance, will soon be an idiot."

" I won't. Don't be uneasy."

" You will. I know mathematics. I see you are a blockhead."

" Everyone has his own mathematics," replied Piotr, upset.

" Shut up !" said Sasha, who slowly sipped the glass of whisky, and smelt a piece of bread. Having drained the first glass, he immediately filled another for himself.

" To-day," he began, bending his head and resting his hands on his knees, " I spoke to the general again. I made a proposition to him. I said : ' Now give me means, and I'll unearth people. I will open a literary club, and trap the very best scamps for you, all of them.' He puffed his cheeks, and stuck out his belly, and said— the jackass !—' I know better what has to be done, and how it has to be done.' He knows everything. But he doesn't know that his mistress danced naked before Von Rutzen, or that his daughter had an abortion." He drained the second glass of whisky, and filled a third. "Everybody's a blackguard and a skunk. It's impossible to live ! Once Moses ordered twenty-three thousand syphilitics to be killed. At that time there weren't many people, mark you. If I had the power I would destroy a million."

" Yourself first ?" suggested Piotr, smiling.

Sasha sniffed without answering, as if in a delirium.

" All those liberals, generals, revolutionists, dissolute women—I'd make a large pyre of them and burn them. I would drench the earth with blood, manure it with the ashes of the corpses. There would be a rich crop. Satiated muzhiks would elect satiated officials. Man is an animal, and he needs rich pastures, fertile fields. The cities ought to be destroyed, and everything superficial, everything that hinders me and you from living simply as the sheep and fowls—to the devil with it all ! "

His viscid, rank smelling words fairly glued themselves to Yevsey's heart. It was difficult and dangerous to listen to them.

" Suddenly they will summon me and ask me what he said. Maybe he's speaking on purpose to trap me. Then they'll seize me." He trembled, and moved uneasily in his chair. " May I go ? " he requested of Piotr quietly.

" Where ? "

" To my room."

" Oh yes, go along."

" Got frightened, the donkey ! " remarked Sasha, without lifting his head.

" Go on, go on," repeated Piotr.

Klimkov undressed noiselessly, without making a light. He groped for the bed in the dark, and rolled himself up closely in the cold, damp sheet. He wanted to see nothing, to hear nothing ; he wanted to squeeze himself into a little unnoticeable lump. The snuffled words of Sasha clung in his memory. Yevsey thought he smelt his odour and saw the red band on the yellow forehead. As a matter of fact, the irritated exclamations came in to him through the door.

" I am a muzhik myself ; I know what's necessary."

136

Without wishing to do so, Yevsey listened intently. He racked his brain to recall the person of whom this sick man, so full of rancour, reminded him, though he actually dreaded lest he should remember.

It was dark and cold. Behind the black panes rocked the dull reflections of the light, disappearing and re-appearing. A thin scraping sound was audible. The wind-swept rain knocked upon the panes in heavy drops.

"Shall I enter a monastery?" Klimkov mused mournfully, and suddenly he remembered God, whose name he had seldom heard in his life in the city. He had not thought of Him the whole time. In his heart, always full of fear and insult, there had been no place for hope in the mercy of Heaven. But now it unexpectedly appeared, and suffused his breast with warmth, extinguishing his heavy, dull despair. He jumped from bed, kneeled on the floor, and firmly pressed his hands to his bosom. He turned his face to the dark corner of the room, closed his eyes, and waited without uttering words, listening to the beating of his heart. But he was exceedingly tired. The cold pricked his skin with thousands of sharp needles. He shivered, and lay down again in bed, and fell asleep.

CHAPTER XIV

WHEN Yevsey awoke, he saw that in the corner to which he had directed his mute prayer there were no ikons, but two pictures on the wall, one representing a hunter with a green feather in his hat kissing a stout girl, the other a fair-haired woman with naked bosom, holding a flower in her hand.

He sighed as he looked around his room without interest. When he had washed and dressed he seated himself at the window. The middle of the street upon which he looked, the pavements, and the houses were all dirty. The horses plodded along shaking their heads, damp drivers sat on the box-seats, also shaking as if they had come unscrewed. The people, as always, were hurrying somewhere. To-day, when splashed with mud, they seemed less dangerous than usual.

Yevsey was hungry. But he did not know whether he had the right to ask for tea and bread, and remained motionless as a stone until he heard a knock on the wall, upon which he went to the door of Piotr's room.

" Have you had tea yet ?" asked the spy, who was still lying in bed.

" No."

" Ask for it."

Piotr stuck his bare feet out of the bed, and looked at his fingers as he stretched them.

" We'll drink tea, and then you'll go with me," he said, yawning. " I'll show you a man, and you will follow him. You must go wherever he goes, you understand ? Note the time he enters a house and how long he stays there. If he leaves the house, or meets another man on the way, notice the appearance of that man, and then—well, you won't understand everything at the very first." Piotr looked at Klimkov, whistled quietly, and turning aside, continued lazily : " Last night Sasha babbled about various things here— he upbraided everybody—don't think of saying anything about it. Take care. He's a sick man, and drinks, but he's a power. *You* can't hurt *him*, but *he'll* eat *you* up alive. Remember that. Why, brother, he was a student once himself, and he knows their business to a ' t.' He was even put in prison for a political offence. And now he gets a hundred rubles a month, and not only Philip Philippovich, but even the general, calls on him for advice. Yes, indeed." Piotr drew his flabby face, crumpled with sleep, in a frown ; his grey eyes lowered with dissatisfaction. He dressed while he spoke in a bored, grumbling voice. " Our work is not a joke. If you catch people by their throats in a trice, then, of course—but first you must tramp about a hundred versts for each one, and sometimes more. You must know where each man was at a given time, with whom he was—in fact, you have to know everything—everything."

The evening before, notwithstanding the agitations of the day, Klimkov had found Piotr an interesting, clever person. Now, however, seeing that he spoke with an effort, that he moved about reluctantly, and that everything dropped from his hands, Yevsey felt bolder in his presence.

" Must we walk the streets the whole day long ?" he plucked up the courage to ask.

"Sometimes you have a night's outing too, in the cold, thirty degrees Centigrade. A very evil demon invented our trade."

" And when they all will have been caught ?"

" Who ?"

" The unfaithful ones—the enemies."

" Say revolutionists, or political offenders. You and I won't catch every one of them. They all seem to be born twins."

At tea Piotr opened his book. On looking into it, he suddenly grew animated. He jumped from his chair, quickly laid out the cards, and began to calculate— " One thousand two hundred and sixteenth deal. I have three of spades, seven of hearts, ace of diamonds."

Before leaving the house, he put on a black overcoat and an imitation sheepskin cap, and stuck a portfolio in his hand, making himself look like an official.

" Don't walk alongside me in the street," he said sternly, " and don't speak to me. I will enter a certain house ; you go into the dvornik's lodging, tell him you have to wait for Timofoyev. I'll soon—— "

Fearing he would lose Piotr in the crowd, Yevsey walked behind him without removing his eyes from his figure. But all of a sudden Piotr disappeared. Klimkov was at a loss. He rushed forward, then stopped, and pressed himself against a lamp-post. Opposite him rose a large house with gratings over the dark windows of the first story. Through the narrow entrance he saw a bleak, gloomy yard, paved with large stones. Klimkov was afraid to enter. He looked all around him, uneasily shifting from one foot to the other.

A man with a reddish little beard now walked out

with hasty steps.   He wore a sort of sleeveless jacket,
and a cap with a peak pulled down on his forehead.   He
winked his grey eyes at Yevsey, and said in a low tone :
   " Come here.   Why didn't you go to the dvornik ?"
   " I lost you," Yevsey admitted.
   " Lost ?   Look out !   You might get reprimanded
for that.   Listen.   Three doors away from here is the
Zemstvo Board building.   A man will soon leave the
place who works there.   His name is Dmitry Ilyich
Kurnosov.   Remember.   You are to follow him.   You
understand ?   Come, and I will show him to you."

   Several minutes later Klimkov, like a little dog, was
quickly following a man in a worn overcoat and a
crumpled black hat.   The man was large and strong.
He walked rapidly, swung a cane, and rapped it on the
asphalt vigorously.   Black hair, with a sprinkling of
grey, fell from under his hat on his ears and the back of
his neck.

   Yevsey was suddenly overcome by a feeling of pity,
which was a rare thing with him.   It imperiously demanded action.   Perspiring from agitation, he darted
across the street in short steps, ran forward, recrossed
the street, and met the man breast to breast.   Before
him flashed a dark-bearded face, with meeting brows,
a smile reflected in blue eyes, and a broad forehead
seamed with wrinkles.   The man's lips moved.   He
was evidently singing or speaking to himself.

   Klimkov stopped and wiped the perspiration from
his face with his hands.   Then he followed the man
with bent head and eyes cast to the ground, raising them
only now and then in order not to lose the object of his
observation from sight.

   " Not young," he thought.   " A poor man, apparently.   It all comes from poverty and from fear, too."

THE SPY

He remembered the Smokestack, and trembled.

"He'll kill me," he thought. Then he grew sorry for the Smokestack.

The buildings looked down upon him with dim, tired eyes. The noise of the street crept into his ears insistently; the cold liquid mud squirted and splashed. Klimkov was overcome by a sense of gloomy monotony. He recalled Rayisa, and felt drawn to move aside, away from the street.

The man he was tracking stopped at the steps of a house, pushed the bell-button, raised his hat, fanned his face with it, and flung it back on his head, leaving bare part of a bald skull. Yevsey stationed himself five steps away at the curb. He looked pityingly into the man's face, and felt the need to tell him something. The man observed him, frowned, and turned away. Yevsey, disconcerted, dropped his head, and sat down on the curb.

"If he only had insulted me," he thought. "But this way, without any provocation, it's not good, it's not good."

"From the Department of Safety?" he heard a low, hissing voice.

The question was asked by a tall reddish muzhik with a dirty apron, and a broom in his hands.

"Yes," responded Yevsey, and the very same instant thought: "I ought not to have told him."

"A new one again?" remarked the janitor. "You are all after Kurnosov?"

"Yes."

"Ah? Tell the officers that this morning a guest came to him from the railroad-station with trunks—three trunks. He hasn't registered yet with the police. He has twenty-four hours' time. A little sort of a

142

pretty fellow with a small moustache. He wears clean clothes." The dvornik ran the broom over the pavement several times, and sprinkled Yevsey's shoes and trousers with mud. Presently he stopped to remark : " You can be seen here. They aren't fools, either ; they notice your kind. You ought to stand at the gates."

Yevsey obediently stepped to the gates. Suddenly he noticed Yakov Zarubin on the other side of the street, wearing a new overcoat and gloves, and carrying a cane. The black chimney-pot was tilted on his head, and as he walked along the pavement he smiled and ogled like a street girl confident of her beauty.

" Good-morning," he said, looking around. " I came to replace you. Go to Somov's café on Lebed Street ; ask for Nikolay Pavlov there."

" Are you in the Department of Safety, too ?" asked Yevsey.

" I got there ten days before you. Why ?"

Yevsey looked at him—at his beaming, swart countenance.

" Was it you who told about me ?"

" And didn't you betray the Smokestack ?"

After thinking a while, Yevsey answered glumly :

" I did it after you had betrayed me. You were the only one I told."

" And you were the only one the Smokestack told. Ugh !" Yakov laughed, and gave Yevsey a poke on the shoulder. " Go quick, you cooked chicken !" He walked by Yevsey's side, swinging his cane. " This is a good position. I understand that much. You can live like a lord, walk about, and look at everything. You see this suit ? Now the girls show me especial attention."

Soon he took leave of Yevsey, and turned back quickly. Klimkov, following him with an inimical glance, fell to thinking. He considered Yakov a dissolute, empty fellow, whom he placed lower than himself, and it was offensive to see him so well satisfied and so elegantly dressed.

"He informed against me. If I told about the Smokestack, it was out of fear. But why did he do it ?" He made mental threats against Yakov. "Wait ; we will see who's the better man."

When he asked at the café for Nikolay Pavlov, he was shown a stairway, which he ascended. At the top he heard Piotr's voice on the other side of the door.

"There are fifty-two cards to a pack. In the city in my district there are thousands of people, and I know a few hundreds of them, maybe. I know who lives with whom, and what and where each of them works. People change, but cards remain one and the same."

Besides Sasha, there was another man in the room with Piotr—a tall, well-built person, who stood at the window reading a paper, and did not move when Yevsey entered.

"What a stupid mug !" were the words with which Sasha met Yevsey, fixing an evil look upon his face. "It must be made up. Do you hear, Maklakov ?"

The man reading the paper turned his head, and looked at Yevsey with large bright eyes.

"Yes," he said.

Piotr, who seemed to be excited, and had dishevelled hair, asked Yevsey what he had seen. The remnants of dinner stood on the table ; the odour of grease and *Sauerkraut* titillated Yevsey's nostrils, and gave him a keen appetite. He stood before Piotr, who was cleaning his teeth with a goose-quill, and in a dispassionate voice repeated the information the dvornik had given him. At the first words of the report Maklakov put his hands and the paper behind his back and inclined his head. He listened attentively, twirling his moustache, which, like the hair on his head, was a peculiar light shade—a sort of silver with a tinge of yellow. The clean, serious face, with the knit brows and the calm eyes ; the confident pose of his powerful body, clad in a close-fitting, well-made, sober suit ; the strong bass voice—all this distinguished Maklakov advantageously from Piotr and Sasha.

" Did the dvornik himself carry the trunks in ?" he asked Yevsey.

" He didn't say."

" That means he did not carry them in. He would have told you whether they were heavy or light. They carried them in themselves. Evidently that's the way it was."

" The printing-office ?" asked Sasha.

" Literature, the current number."

" Well, we must have a search made," said Sasha gruffly, and uttered an ugly oath, shaking his fist.

" I must find the printing-press. Get me type, boys, and I'll fix up a printing-press myself. I'll find donkeys. We'll give them all that's necessary. Then we'll arrest them, and we'll have lots of money."

" Not a bad scheme !" exclaimed Piotr.

Maklakov looked at Yevsey, and asked :

" Have you had your dinner yet ?"

" No."

" Take your dinner," said Piotr, with a nod towards the table. " Be quick about it."

" Why treat him to remnants ?" asked Maklakov

calmly. Then he stepped to the door, opened it, and called out : " Dinner, please."

" You try," Sasha snuffled to Piotr, " to persuade that idiot Afanasov to give us the printing-press they seized last year."

" Very well, I'll try," Piotr assented meditatively.

Maklakov did not look at them, but silently twisted his moustache. Dinner was served. A round, pock-marked, modest-looking man made his appearance in the room at the same time as the waiter. He smiled at everyone benevolently, and shook Yevsey's hand vigorously.

" My name is Solovyov," he said to him. " Have you heard the news, friends ? This evening there will be a banquet of the revolutionists at Chistov's hall. Three of our fellows will go there as butlers, among others you, Piotr."

" I again ?" shouted Piotr, and his face became covered with red blotches. His anger made him look older. " The third time in two months that I have had to play lackey ! Excuse me ! I don't want to."

" Don't address me on the subject," said Solovyov affably.

" What does it mean ? Why do they choose just me to be a servant ?"

" You look like one," said Sasha, with a smile.

" There will be three," Solovyov repeated, sighing. " What do you say to having some beer ? All right ?"

Piotr opened the door, and shouted in an irritated voice :

" Half a dozen of beer," and he went to the window, clenching his fists and cracking his knuckles.

" There, you see, Maklakov ?" said Sasha. " Among

us no one wants to work seriously, with enthusiasm.
But the revolutionists are pushing right on—banquets,
meetings, a shower of literature, open propaganda in
the factories !"

Maklakov maintained silence, and did not look at
Sasha. The rotund Solovyov then took up the word,
smiling amiably.

" I caught a girl to-day at the railroad-station with
books. I had already noticed her in a villa in the
summer. 'Well,' thought I, ' amuse yourself, my
dear.' To-day, as I was sauntering in the station with
no people to track, I was looking about, and there I saw
her marching along, carrying a handbag. I went up
to her, and respectfully proposed that she should have
two words with me. I noticed she started and paled,
and hid the bag behind her back. ' Ah,' thinks I, ' my
dear little stupid, you've got yourself into it.' Well, I
immediately took her to the police-station ; they
opened her luggage, and there was the last issue of
Emancipation, and a whole lot more of their noxious
trash. I took the girl to the Department of Safety.
What else was I to do ? If you can't get Krushin pike,
you must eat flounders. In the carriage she kept her
little face turned away from me. I could see her
cheeks burned, and there were tears in her eyes. But
she kept mum. I asked her : ' Are you comfortable,
madam ?' Not a word in reply."

Solovyov chuckled softly. Trembling rays of
wrinkles covered his face.

" Who is she ?" asked Maklakov.

" Dr. Melikhov's daughter."

" Ah," drawled Sasha, " I know him."

" A respectable man. He has the orders of Vladimir
and Anna," remarked Solovyov.

" I know him," repeated Sasha. " A charlatan, like all the rest. He tried to cure me."

" God alone can cure you now," said Solovyov in his affable tone. " You are ruining your health quickly."

" Go to the devil !" roared Sasha.

Maklakov asked, without turning his gaze from the window :

" Did the girl cry ?"

" No. But she didn't exactly rejoice. You know it's always unpleasant to me to take girls, because, in the first place, I have a daughter myself."

" What are you waiting for, Maklakov ?" demanded Sasha testily.

" Until he finishes eating his dinner. I have time."

" Eat faster, you !" Sasha bawled at Klimkov.

" Yes, yes, hurry," Piotr observed dryly.

As he ate his dinner, Klimkov listened to the talk attentively, and observed the people while he himself remained unnoticed. He noted with satisfaction that all of them except Sasha did not seem bad, not worse or more horrible than others. He was seized with a desire to ingratiate himself with them—make himself useful to them. He put down the knife and fork, and quickly wiped his lips with the soiled napkin.

" I have done."

The door was flung open, and a loose-limbed fellow, his dress in disorder, his body bent and stooping, darted into the room, and hissed :

" Ssh ! Ssh !"

He thrust his head into the corridor, listened, then carefully closed the door. " Doesn't it lock ? Where's the key?" He looked around, and drew a deep breath. "Thank God!" he exclaimed.

"Eh, you dunce," sneered Sasha. "Well, what is it? Do they want to thrash you again?"

The man ran up to him. Panting, and wiping the sweat from his face, he began to mutter in a low voice:

"They did, of course. They wanted to kill me with a hammer. Two followed me from the prison. I was there on business. As I walked out, they were standing at the gate—two of them—and one of them had a hammer in his pocket."

"Maybe it was a revolver," suggested Solovyov, stretching his neck.

"A hammer."

"Did you see it?" inquired Sasha sarcastically.

"Ah, don't I know? They agreed to do for me with a hammer, without making any noise. One——"

He adjusted his necktie, buttoned his coat, searched for something in his pockets, and smoothed his curly head, which was covered with sweat. His hands incessantly flashed about his body; they seemed ready to break off at any moment. His bony grey face was dank with perspiration, his dark eyes rolled from side to side, now screwed up, now opened wide. Suddenly they became fixed. With unfeigned horror depicted in them, they rested upon Yevsey's face, as the man backed to the door.

"Who's that? Who's that?" he demanded hoarsely.

Maklakov went up to him, and took his hand.

"Calm yourself, Yelizar. He's one of our own—a new one."

"Do you know him?"

" Jackass !" came Sasha's exasperated voice. " You ought to see a doctor."

" Have you ever been pushed under a tram-car ? Not yet ? Then wait before you call names."

" Just look, Maklakov," began Sasha, but the man continued in extreme excitement :

" Have you ever been beaten at night by unknown people ? Do you understand ? Unknown people ! There are hundreds of thousands such people unknown to me in the city—hundreds of thousands. They are everywhere, and I am a single one. I am always among them, do you understand ?"

Now Solovyov began to speak in his soft, reassuring voice, which was drowned, however, by the new burst of words coming from the shattered man, who carried in himself a whirlwind of fear. Klimkov immediately grew dizzy, overwhelmed by the alarming whisper of his talk, blinded by the motion of his broken body, and the darting of his cowardly hands. He expected that now something huge and black would tear its way through the door, would fill the room, and crush everybody.

" It's time for us to go," said Maklakov, touching his shoulder.

When they were sitting in the cab, Yevsey sullenly remarked :

" I am not fit for this work."

" Why ?" asked Maklakov.

" I am timid."

" That'll pass away."

" Nothing will pass away."

" Everything," rejoined Maklakov calmly.

It was cold and dark, and sleet was falling. The reflections of the lights lay upon the mud in golden patches, which the people and horses tramped upon and extinguished. The two men were silent for a long time. Yevsey, his brain empty, looked into space, and felt that Maklakov was watching his face, in wait for something.

" You'll get used to it," Maklakov went on, " but if you have another position, leave it at once. Have you ?"

" No."

" Is it long since you've been in the Department of Safety ?"

" Yesterday."

" That accounts for it."

" Now, where am I to go ?" inquired Yevsey quietly.

Maklakov, instead of replying to the question, asked :

" Have you relatives ?"

" No ; I have no one."

The spy leaned over, though without saying anything. His eyes were half shut. As he drew his breath through his nose, the thin hair of his moustache quivered. The thick sounds of a bell floated in the air, soft and warm, and the pensive song of copper crept mournfully over the roofs of the houses without rising under the heavy cloud that covered the city with a solid dark canopy.

" To-morrow is Sunday," said Maklakov in a low tone. " Do you go to church ?"

" No."

" Why not ?"

" I don't know. It is so. It's close there."

" I do. I love the morning service. The choristers sing, and the sun looks through the windows. That is always good."

THE SPY

Maklakov's simple words emboldened Yevsey. He felt a desire to speak of himself.

"It is nice to sing," he began. "When I was a little boy, I sang in the church in our village. When I sang I didn't know where I was. It was just the same as if I didn't exist."

"Here we are," said Maklakov.

Yevsey sighed, and looked sadly at the long structure of the railway-station, which all of a sudden loomed up before them and barred the way.

They went to the platform, where a large public had already gathered, and leaned up against the wall. Maklakov dropped his lids over his eyes, and seemed to be falling off into a doze. The spurs of the gendarmes began to jingle, a well-shaped woman with dark eyes and a swarthy face laughed in a resonant young voice.

"Remember the woman there who is laughing and the man beside her," said Maklakov in a distinct whisper. "Her name is Sarra Lurye, an accoucheure. She lives in the Sadovoy, No. 7. She was in prison and in exile—a very clever woman. The old man is also a former exile—a journalist."

Suddenly Maklakov seemed to become frightened. He pulled his hat down over his face with a quick movement of his hand, and continued in a still lower voice :

"The tall man in the black suit and the shaggy hat, red-haired, do you see him ?"

Yevsey nodded his head.

"He's the author Mironov. He has been in prison four times already in different cities. Do you read books ?"

"No."

THE SPY

"A pity. He writes interestingly."

The black iron worm with a horn on its head and three fiery eyes uttered a scream, and glided into the station, the metal of its huge body rumbling. It stopped, and hissed spitefully, filling the air with its thick white breath. The hot steamy odour struck Yevsey in the face. The black bustling figures of people quickly darted before his eyes, seeming strangely small in contrast with the overwhelming size of the train.

It was the first time that Yevsey had seen the mass of iron at such close range. It seemed alive, and endowed with feeling. It attracted his attention powerfully, at the same time arousing a hostile, painful premonition. The large red wheels turned, the steel lever glittered, rising and falling like a gigantic knife. Maklakov uttered a subdued exclamation.

"What is it?" asked Yevsey.

"Nothing," answered the spy, vexed. His cheeks reddened, and he bit his lips. By his look Yevsey guessed that he was following the author, who was walking along without haste, twirling his moustache. He was accompanied by an elderly, thick-set man, with an unbuttoned coat and a summer hat on a large head. This man laughed aloud, and exclaimed, as he raised his bearded red face :

"You understand ? I rode and rode———"

The author lifted his head, and bowed to somebody. His head was smoothly shorn, his forehead lofty. He had high cheek-bones, a broad nose, and narrow eyes. Klimkov found his face coarse and disagreeable. There was something military and harsh in it, due to his large red moustache.

"Come," said Maklakov. "They will probably go

together. You must be very careful. The man who just arrived is an experienced man."

In the street they took a cab again.

"Follow that carriage," Maklakov said angrily to the driver. He was silent for a long time, sitting with bent back and swaying body. "Last year, in the summer," he finally muttered, "I was in his house making a search."

"The writer's house?" asked Yevsey.

"Yes. Drive on farther," Maklakov ordered quickly, noticing that the cab in front had stopped. "Quick!"

A minute later he jumped from the cab, and thrust some money into the driver's hand.

"Wait," he said to Yevsey, and disappeared in the damp darkness. Yevsey heard his voice. "Excuse me, is this Yakovlev's house?"

Someone answered in a hollow voice:

"This is Pertzev's."

"And which is Yakovlev's?"

"I don't know."

"Pardon me."

Yevsey leaned against the fence, counting Maklakov's tardy steps.

"It's a simple thing—just to follow people," he thought.

The spy came up to him, and said in a satisfied tone:

"We have nothing to do here. To-morrow morning you will put on a different suit, and we'll keep an eye on this house."

They walked down the street. The sound of Maklakov's talk kept knocking at Klimkov's ears like the rumble of a drum.

"Remember the faces, the dress, and the gait of the

people that pass this house. There are no two people
alike. Each one has something peculiar to himself.
You must learn at once to seize upon this peculiar
something in a person—in his eyes, in his voice, in the
way in which he holds out his hands when he walks,
in the manner in which he lifts his hat in greeting.
Our work, above all, demands a good memory."

Yevsey felt that the spy talked with concealed
enmity toward him, which aggrieved him.

"You have an exceedingly marked face, especially
your eyes. That won't do. You mustn't go about
without a mask, without the dress peculiar to a certain
occupation. Your figure, you in general, resemble a
hawker of dry goods. So you ought to carry about a
box of stuffs—pins, needles, tape, ribbon, and all sorts
of trifles. I will see that you get such a box. Then
you can go into the kitchens and get acquainted with
the servants." Maklakov was silent, removed his
beard, fixed his hat, and began to walk more slowly.
"Servants are always ready to do something unpleasant for the masters. It's easy to get something
out of them, especially the women—cooks, nurses,
chamber-maids. They like to gossip. However, I'm
chilled through," he ended in a different voice. "Let's
go to a café."

"I have no money."

"That's all right."

In the café he said to the owner in a stern voice :

"Give me a glass of cognac—a large one—and two
beers. Will you have some cognac ?"

"No, I don't drink," answered Yevsey, embarrassed.

"That's good."

The spy looked carefully into Klimkov's face,
smoothed his moustache, closed his eyes for a minute,

155

and stretched his whole body, so that his bones cracked.
When he had drunk the cognac, he remarked in an
undertone :

" It's good you are such a taciturn fellow. What do
you think about, eh ?"

Yevsey dropped his head, and did not answer at
once :

" About everything, about myself."

" But what in particular ?"

Maklakov's eyes gleamed softly.

" I think, perhaps, it would be better for me to enter
a monastery," Yevsey answered sincerely.

" Why ?"

" Just so."

" Do you believe in God ?"

After a moment's thought Yevsey said, as if excusing
himself :

" I do. Only I am not for God, but for myself.
What am I to God ?"

" Well, let's drink."

Klimkov bravely gulped down a glass of beer. It
was cold and bitter, and sent a shiver through his
body. He licked his lips with his tongue, and suddenly
asked :

" Do they beat you often ?"

" Me ? Who ?" the spy exclaimed, amazed and
offended.

" Not you, but all the spies in general."

" You must say ' agents,' not ' spies,' " Maklakov
corrected him, smiling. " They get beaten—yes, they
get beaten. I have never been beaten."

He became lost in reflection. His shoulders drooped,
and a shadow crept over his white face.

" Ours is a dog's life. People look upon us in

an ugly enough light." Suddenly his face broke into a smile, and he bent toward Yevsey. "Only once in five years did I see a man—human conduct towards me. It was in Mironov's house. I came to him with gendarmes in the uniform of a sergeant-inspector. I was not well at the time. I had fever, and was scarcely able to stand on my feet. He received us civilly with a smile. He wore a slightly embarrassed air. Such a large man, with long hands and a moustache like a cat's. He walked with us from room to room, addressed us all with the respectful plural ' you,' and if he came in contact with any of us, he excused himself. We all felt awkward in his presence—the Colonel, the procurator, and we small fry. Everybody knew the man ; his pictures appeared in the newspapers. They say he's even known abroad. And here we were paying him a night visit ! We felt sort of abashed. I noticed him look at me. Then he walked up closer to me, and said : ' You ought to sit down. You look as if you were feeling ill. Sit down.' His words upset me. I sat down, and I thought to myself : ' Go away from me.' And he said : ' Will you take a powder ?' All of us were silent. I saw that no one looked at me or him." Maklakov laughed quietly. " He gave me quinine in a capsule, and I chewed it. I began to feel an insufferable bitterness in my mouth and a turmoil in my soul. I felt I should drop if I tried to stand. Then the Colonel interfered, and ordered me to be taken to the police-office. The search just then happened to end. The procurator excused himself to Mironov, and said : ' I must arrest you.' ' Well, what of it ?' he said. ' Arrest me. Everyone does what he can.' He said it so simply with a smile."

Yevsey liked the story. It touched his heart softly,

THE SPY

as if embracing it with a caress. The desire awoke in
him again to make himself useful to Maklakov.

" He's a good man," he thought.

The spy sighed. He called for another glass of
cognac, and sipped it slowly. He seemed suddenly to
grow thin, and he dropped his head on the table.

Yevsey wanted to speak, to ask questions. Various
words darted about in disorder in his brain, for some
reason failing to arrange themselves in intelligible and
clear language. Finally, after many efforts, Yevsey
found what he wanted to ask.

" He, too, is in the service of our enemies ?"

" Who ?" asked the spy, scarcely raising his head.

" The writer."

" What enemies ? What do you mean ?" The spy's
voice was mocking, and his lips curled in aversion.
Yevsey grew confused, and Maklakov, without awaiting his answer, arose, and tossed a silver coin on the
table.

" Score it up," he said to someone.

He put on his hat, and without a word to Klimkov
walked to the door. Yevsey followed on tiptoe, not
daring to put on his hat.

" Be at the place at nine o'clock to-morrow. You
will be relieved at twelve," said Maklakov in the street.
He thrust his hands in his coat-pockets, and disappeared.

" He didn't say ' good-bye,' " thought Yevsey,
aggrieved, walking along the deserted street.

When he entered within the circles of light thrown by
the street-lamps, he slackened his pace, and instinctively hastened over the parts enveloped in obscurity.
He felt ill. Darkness surrounded him on all sides. It
was cold. The gluey, bitter taste of beer penetrated

from his mouth into his chest, and his heart beat
unevenly. Languid thoughts stirred in his head like
heavy flakes of autumn snow.

" There, I've served a day. What are they all—these
different days ? If only somebody liked me."

At night Yevsey dreamed that his cousin Yashka
seated himself on his chest, seized him by the throat,
and choked him. He awoke, and heard Piotr's angry
dry thin voice in the other room :

" I spit upon the Czar's empire and all this
humbuggery !"

A woman laughed, and someone's thin voice sounded.

" Hush, hush, don't bawl !"

" I have no time to calculate who is right and who is
wrong. I am not a fool ; I am young, and I ought to
live. This rapscallion reads me lectures about autocracy, and I fuss about for three hours as a waiter, near
every sort of scamp. My feet ache, my back pains from
the bows. If the autocracy is dear to you, then don't
be stingy with your money. But I won't sell my pride
to the autocracy for a mere penny. To the devil with
it !"

Yevsey looked drowsily through the window, his
gaze losing itself in the sleepy depth of the autumn
morning. Blinded, he quietly flung himself back in
bed, and again fell asleep.

Several hours later he was sitting on the curb opposite
Pertzev's house. He walked back and forth a long
time, counted the windows in the house, measured its
width with his steps, studied in all its details the grey
front, flabby with old age, and finally grew tired. But
he had not much time to rest. The writer himself came
out of the door with an overcoat flung over his
shoulders, no overshoes on his feet, his hat on one side

of his head.   He walked across the street straight up to Yevsey.

" He will give me a slap in the face," thought Yevsey, looking at the sullen face and the lowering red brows. He tried to rise and go away, but was unable to move, chained to the spot by fear.

" Why are you sitting here?" he heard an angry voice.

" Nothing."

" Get away from here."

" I can't."

" Here's a letter.   Go.   Give it to him who sent you here."

" I can't."

" Why not?"

The large blue eyes commanded.   Yevsey had not the power to disobey the look.   Turning his face aside, he mumbled:

"I—I—I have no permission—to take anything from you—or to converse with you.   I am going away."

" Yes, go away," the author commanded, and for some reason smiled a morose smile.

Klimkov took the grey envelope, and walked away without asking himself where he was going.   He held the envelope in his right hand on a level with his breast, as if it were something murderous, threatening unknown misfortune.   His fingers ached as from cold.

" What is going to happen to me?" knocked importunately at his brain.

Suddenly he noticed the envelope was not sealed. This amazed him.   He stopped, looked around, and quickly removed the letter.

" Take this dunce away from me.—MINOROV," he read.

He heaved a sigh of relief.

" I must give this to Maklakov. He will scold me. Maybe I ought to turn back. But it's not necessary. Somebody else will come soon, anyway."

Though his fear had disappeared, Yevsey felt sad from the realization of his unfitness for the position, and he felt heavy at the thought that he had again failed to suit the spy, whom he liked so much.

He found Maklakov at dinner in the company of a little squint-eyed man dressed in black.

" Let me introduce you. Klimkov—Krasavin."

Yevsey put his hand in his pocket to get out the letter, and said in an embarrassed tone :

" This is the way it happened——"

Maklakov held up his hand.

" You will tell me later. Sit down, and have your dinner."

His face was weary, his eyes dim, his light, straight hair dishevelled.

"Evidently he got drunk yesterday," thought Yevsey.

" No, Timofey Vasilyevich," the squint-eyed man said coldly and solemnly ; " you are not right. There's something pleasant in every line of work if you love it."

Maklakov looked at him, and drank a large glass of whisky in one gulp.

" They are people, we are people ; that doesn't signify anything. One says this, another says that, and I do just as I please."

The squint-eyed man noticed that Yevsey was looking at his eyeballs as they rolled apart, and he put on a pair of glasses with tortoise-shell rims. His movements were soft and alert, like a black cat's. His teeth were small and sharp, his nose straight and thin. When he spoke his rosy ears moved. His crooked fingers kept quickly rolling a crumb of bread into little pellets, which he placed on the edge of his plate.

" An assistant ?" he asked, nodding his head toward Yevsey.

" Yes."

" How's business, young man ?"

" I only began yesterday."

" Oh, oh !" Krasavin nodded his head. Pinching his thin dark moustache, he began to speak fluently. " Of course, Timofey Vasilyevich, you can't step on the tail of life's destiny. According to God's law, children grow old, people die. Only all this doesn't concern you and me. We received our appointed task. We were told to catch the people who infringe on law and order. That's all. It's hard business; it's a clever business. To use a figure of speech, it is a kind of hunt."

Maklakov rose from the table, and walked into a corner, from where he beckoned to Yevsey.

" Well, what is it ?"

Yevsey gave him the note. The spy read it, looked into Klimkov's face in astonishment, and read it again.

" From whom is this ?" he asked in a low voice.

Yevsey answered in an embarrassed whisper :

" He himself gave it to me. He came out into the street."

In the expectation of a rebuke, or even a blow, he bent his neck. But, hearing a low laugh, he cautiously raised his head, and saw the spy looking at the envelope with a broad smile on his face and a merry gleam in his eyes.

"Oh, you strange fellow," said Maklakov. "Now keep quiet about this, you droll creature."

"Can I congratulate you on a successful piece of work?" asked Krasavin.

"You can—yes," Maklakov said aloud, walking up to him.

"That's good, young man," remarked Krasavin encouragingly. His pupils, with green sparks flashing in them, turned inward to the bridge of his nose, and his nostrils quivered and expanded.

"But the Japs licked us after all, Gavrilo," Maklakov exclaimed merrily, rubbing his hands.

"I cannot in the least comprehend your joy in this event," said Krasavin, wagging his ears. "Although it was instructive, as many say, still, so much Russian blood was shed, and the insufficiency of our strength was made so apparent."

"And who is to blame?"

"The Japs. What do they want? Every country ought to live within itself."

They started a discussion, to which Yevsey, rejoiced over Maklakov's attitude, did not pay any attention. He looked into the spy's face, and thought it would be well to live with him instead of Piotr, who scolded at the authorities, and maybe would be arrested as they had arrested the Smokestack.

Krasavin left. Maklakov took out the letter, read it once more, and burst into a laugh, looking at Yevsey.

"Now, don't say a word about it to anybody. Do you understand? He came out himself?"

"Yes, he came out and said, 'Get away from here.'" Yevsey smiled guiltily.

"You see, another one in his place would have

stroked you with a cat's paw." Screwing up his eyes, the spy looked through the window, and said slowly : " Yes, you ought to take to peddling wares. I told you so. To-day you are free. I have no more commissions for you. Be off with you. Have a good time. I'll try one of these days to fix you up differently. Good-bye."

Maklakov held out his hand. Yevsey touched it gratefully, and walked away happy.

CHAPTER XV

A FEW weeks later Klimkov began to feel freer and more at ease. Every morning, warmly and comfortably dressed, with a box of small wares on his breast, he went to receive orders either at one of the cafés where the spies gathered or at a police office, or at the lodging of one of the spies. The directions given him were simple and distinct.

" Go to such and such a house ; get acquainted with the servants ; find out how the masters live."

If he succeeded in penetrating to the kitchen of the given house, he would first try to bribe the servants by the cheap price of the goods and by little presents. Then he would carefully question them about what he had been ordered to learn. When he felt that the information gathered was insufficient, he filled up the deficiency from his own head, thinking it out according to the plan draughted for him by the old, fat, and sensual Solovyov.

" These men in whom we are interested," Solovyov once said in a smug, honey-sweet voice, " all have the same habits. They do not believe in God, they do not go to church, they dress poorly, but they are civil in their manners. They read many books, sit up late at night, often have gatherings of guests in their lodgings, but drink very little wine, and do not play cards.

THE SPY

They speak about foreign countries, about systems of government, working men's Socialism, and full liberty for the people; also about the poor masses, declaring it is necessary to stir them up to revolt against our Czar, to kill off the entire administration, take possession of the highest offices, and by means of Socialism again introduce serfdom, in which they will have complete liberty." The warm voice of the spy broke off. He coughed, and heaved a sentimental sigh. "Liberty —everybody likes and wants to have liberty. But if you give me liberty, maybe I'll become the first villain in the world. That's it. It is impossible to give even a child full liberty. The Church Fathers, God's saints, even they were subject to the temptations of the flesh, and they sinned in the very highest. People's lives are held together, not by liberty, but by fear. Submission to law is essential to man. But the revolutionists reject law. They form two parties. One wants to make quick work with the Ministers and the faithful subjects of the Czar by means of bombs, etc. The other party is willing to wait a little; first they'll have a general uprising, then they'll kill off everybody at once." Solovyov raised his eyes pensively, and paused an instant. "It is difficult for us to comprehend their politics. Maybe they really understand something. But for us, everything they propose is an obnoxious delusion. We fulfill the will of the Czar, the anointed sovereign of God. And he is responsible for us before God, so we ought to do what he bids us. In order to gain the confidence of the revolutionists, you must complain: ' Life is very hard for the poor; the police insult them, and there's no sort of law.' Although they are people of villainous intent, yet they are credulous, and you can always catch them with that bait. Behave cannily towards their servants ; for their servants aren't stupid, either. Whenever necessary, reduce the price of your goods, so that they will get used to you and value you. But guard against exciting suspicion. They will begin to think, ' What is it ? He sells very cheap, and asks prying questions.' The best thing for you to do is to strike up friendships. Take a little dainty, hot, full-breasted thing, and you get all sorts of good information from her. She will sew shirts for you, and invite you to spend the night with her, and she will find out whatever you order her to. You know—a tiny, soft little mouse. You can stretch your arm a long distance, through a woman."

This round man, hairy-handed, thick-lipped, and pock-marked, spoke about women more frequently than the others. He would lower his soft voice to a whisper, his neck would perspire, his feet would shuffle uneasily, and his eyes, minus eyebrows and eyelashes, would fill with warm, oily moisture. Yevsey, with his sharp scent, observed that Solovyov always smelt of hot, greasy, decayed meat.

In the chancery the spies had been spoken of as people who know everything, hold everything in their hands, and have friends and helpers everywhere. Though they could seize all the dangerous people at once, they were not doing so simply because they did not wish to deprive themselves of a position. On entering the Department of Safety, everyone swore an oath to pity nobody—neither father, mother, nor brother—nor to speak a word to one another about the sacred and awful business which they vowed they would serve all their lives.

Consequently Yevsey had expected to find sullen personalities. He had pictured them as speaking little, in words unintelligible to simple people, as possessing the miraculous perspicacity of a sorcerer, able to read man's thoughts and divine all the secrets of his life.

Now, from his sharp observation of them, he clearly saw they were not unusual, nor for him either worse or more dangerous than others. In fact, they seemed to live in a more comradely fashion than was common. They frankly spoke of their mistakes and failures, even laughed over them. All, without exception, were equally fervent in swearing at their superiors, though with varying degrees of malice.

Conscious of a close bond uniting them, they were solicitous for one another. When it happened that someone was late for a meeting, or failed to appear at all, there was a general sense of uneasiness about the absentee, and Yevsey, Zarubin, or someone of the numerous group of " novices," or " assistants," was sent to look for the lost man at another gathering-place.

A stranger, observing them, would have been instantly struck by the lack of greed for money among the majority, and the readiness to share money with comrades who had gambled it away or squandered it in some other fashion. They all loved games of hazard, took a childish interest in card tricks, and envied the cleverness of the card-sharper.

They spoke to one another with ecstasy and acute envy of the revelries of the officials, described in detail the lewd women known to them, and hotly discussed their various relations with them. Most of them were unmarried, almost all were young, and for every one of them a woman was something in the nature of whisky—to give him ease and lull him to sleep.

Woman brought them relief from the anxiety of their dog's work. Their discussions roused in Yevsey a sharp, intoxicating curiosity, sometimes incredulity and nausea. They all drank a lot, mixing wine with beer, and beer with cognac, in an effort to get drunk as quickly as possible.

Only a few of them put hot enthusiasm, the passion of the hunter, into their work. These boasted of their skill, swelling with pride as they described themselves as heroes. The majority, however, did their work wearily, with an air of being bored.

Their talks about the people whom they hunted down like beasts were seldom marked by the fierce hatred that boiled in Sasha's conversation like a seething hot-spring. One who was different from the rest was Melnikov, a heavy, hairy man with a thick, bellowing voice, who walked with oddly bent neck and spoke little. His dark eyes were always straining, as if in constant search. The man seemed to Yevsey ever to be thinking of something terrible. Krasavin and Solovyov also contrasted with the others, the one by his cold malice, the other by the complacent satisfaction with which he spoke about fights, bloodshed, and women.

Among the youth, the most noticeable was Yakov Zarubin, who was constantly fidgeting about, and constantly running up to the others with questions. When he listened to the conversations about the revolutionists, he knitted his brows in anger, and jotted down notes in his little notebook. He tried to be of service to all the important spies, though it was evident that no one liked him, and that his book was regarded with suspicion.

The larger number spoke indifferently about the

revolutionists, sometimes denouncing them as incomprehensible men of whom they were sick, sometimes referring to them in fun as to amusing cranks. Occasionally, too, they spoke in anger as one speaks of a child who deserves punishment for impudence. Yevsey began to imagine that all the revolutionists were empty people, who were not serious, and did not themselves know what they wanted, but merely brought disturbance and disorder into life.

Once Yevsey asked Piotr:

" There, you said the revolutionists are being bribed by the Germans, and now they say differently."

" What do you mean by ' differently'?" Piotr demanded angrily.

" That they are poor and stupid, and nobody says anything about the Germans."

" Go to the devil! Isn't it all the same to you? Do what you are told. Your colour is the diamond, and you go with diamonds."

Matters of business were discussed in a lazy, unwilling way, and, " You don't understand anything, brother," was a common rejoinder of one spy to another.

" And you?" would be the counter-retort.

" I keep quiet."

Klimkov tried to keep as far away as possible from Sasha. The ominous face of the sick man frightened him, and the smell of iodoform and the snuffling, cantankerous voice disgusted him.

" Villains!" cried Sasha, swearing at the officials. " They are given millions, and toss us pennies. They squander hundreds of thousands on women and on various genteel folk, who, they want us to believe, work for the good of society. But it's not the gentry that make revolutions—you must know that, idiots—the revolution grows underneath, in the ground, among the people. Give me five millions, and in one month I'll lift the revolution up above-ground into the street. I'll carry it out of the dark corners into the light of day, then—choke it!"

Sasha always contrived horrible schemes for the extermination of the noxious people. While devising them he stamped his feet, extended his trembling arms, and tore the air with his yellow fingers, while his face turned leaden, his red eyes grew strangely dim, and the spittle spurted from his mouth.

All, it was evident, looked upon him with aversion and feared him, though they were anxious to conceal the repulsion produced by his disease. Maklakov alone calmly avoided close intercourse with the sick man. He did not even give him his hand in greeting. Sasha, in his turn, who ridiculed everybody, who swore at all his comrades, setting them down as fools, plainly put Maklakov in a category by himself. He was always serious in his intercourse with this spy, and apparently spoke to him with greater will than to the rest. He did not abuse him even behind his back.

Once, when Maklakov had walked out without, as usual, taking leave of him, he cried:

" The nobleman is squeamish. He doesn't want to come near me. He has the right to be, the devil take him! His ancestors lived in lofty rooms; they breathed rarefied air, ate wholesome food, wore clean undergarments—he, too, for that matter. But I am a muzhik. I was born and brought up like an animal, in filth, among lice, on coarse black bread made of unbolted meal. His blood is better than mine—yes, indeed, both the blood and the brain, and the brain is the soul." After a pause he added in a lower voice, gloomily, without ridicule : " Idiots and impostors speak of the equality of man. The aristocrat preaches equality because he is an impudent scoundrel, and can't do anything himself. So, of course, he says : ' You are just as good a man as I am. Act so that I shall be able to live better.' This is the theory of equality."

Sasha's talks did not evoke a response from the other spies. They failed to be moved by his excitement, and listened to his growling in indifferent silence. He received sulky support, however, from one—the large Melnikov, who acted as a detective among working men.

" Yes," Melnikov would say, " they are all deceivers," and nod his dark, unkempt head in confirmation while vigorously clenching his hairy fist.

" They ought to be killed, as the muzhiks kill horse-thieves," screamed Sasha.

" To kill may be a little too much, but sometimes it would be delicious to give a gentleman a box on the ear," said Chashin, a celebrated billiard-player, curly-haired, thin, and sharp-nosed. " Let's take this example. About a week ago I was playing in Kononov's hotel with a gentleman. I saw his face was familiar to me, but all chickens have feathers. He stared at me in his turn. ' Well,' thinks I, ' look. I don't change colour.' I fixed him for three rubles and half a dozen beers, and while we were drinking he suddenly rose, and said : ' I recognize you. You are a spy. When I was in the University,' said he, ' thanks to you,' he said, ' I had to stick in prison four months. You are,' he said, ' a scoundrel.' At first I was frightened, but soon the insult gnawed at my heart. ' You sat in prison not at all thanks to me, but to your politics. And your politics do not concern me personally. But let me tell you that on your account I had to run about day and night hunting you in all sorts of weather. I had to stick in the hospital thirteen days.' That's the truth. The idea, of him jumping on me ! The pig, he had eaten himself fat as a priest, wore a gold watch, and had a diamond pin stuck in his tie !"

Akim Grokhotov, a handsome fellow, with a face mobile as an actor's, observed :

" I know men like that, too. When they are young, they walk on their heads ; when the serious years come, they stay at home peacefully with their wives, and for the sake of a livelihood are even ready to enter our Department of Safety. The law of Nature."

" Among them are some who can't do anything besides revolutionary work. Those are the most dangerous," said Melnikov.

" Yes, yes," shot from Krasavin, who greedily rolled his oblique eyes.

Once Piotr lost a great deal in cards. He asked in a wearied, exasperated tone :

" When will this dog's life of ours end ?"

Solovyov looked at him, and chewed his thick lips.

" We are not called upon to judge of such matters. Our business is simple. All we have to do is to take note of a certain face pointed out by the officials, or to find it ourselves, gather information, make observations, give a report to the authorities, and let them do as they please. For all we care, they may flay people alive. Politics do not concern us. Once there was an agent in our department, Grisha Sokovnin, who also thought about such things, and ended his life in a prison hospital, where he died of consumption."

Oftenest the conversation took some such course as the following :

Viekov, a wig-maker, always gaily and fashionably dressed, a modest, quiet person, announced :

" Three fellows were arrested yesterday."

" Great news !" someone responded indifferently.

But Viekov, whether or no, would tell his comrades all he knew. A spark of quiet stubbornness flared up in his small eyes, and his voice sounded inquisitive.

" The gentlemen revolutionists, it seems, are again hatching plots on Nikitskaya Street—great goings-on."

" Fools ! All the dvorniks there are old hands in the service."

" Much help they are, the dvorniks !"

" H'm, yes, indeed."

" However," said Viekov cautiously, " a dvornik can be bribed."

" And you, too. Every man can be bribed—a mere matter of price."

" Did you hear, boys, Siekachev won seven hundred rubles in cards yesterday ?"

" How he packs the cards !"

" Yes, yes. He's no sharper, but a young wizard."

Viekov looked around, smiled in embarrassment, then silently and carefully smoothed his clothes.

" A new proclamation has appeared," he announced another time.

" There are lots of proclamations. The devil knows which of them is new."

" There's a great deal of evil in them."

THE SPY

" Did you read it ?"

" No. Philip Philippovich says there's a new one, and he's mad."

" The authorities are always mad. Such is the law of Nature," remarked Grokhotov with a smile.

" Who reads those proclamations ?"

" They're read all right—very much so."

" Well, what of it ? I have read them, too, yet I didn't turn black. I remained what I was, a red-haired fellow. It's not a matter of proclamations, it's a matter of bombs."

" Of course."

" A proclamation doesn't explode."

Evidently, however, the spies did not like to speak of bombs, for each time they were mentioned all made a strenuous effort to change the subject.

" Forty thousand dollars' worth of gold articles were stolen in Kazan."

" There's something for you !"

" Forty thousand ! Whew !"

" Did they catch the thieves ?" someone asked in great excitement.

" They'll get caught," prophesied another sorrow-fully.

" Well, before that happens they'll have a good time."

A mist of envy enveloped the spies, who sank into dreams of revelries, of big stakes, and costly women.

Melnikov was more interested than the others in the course of the war. Often he asked Maklakov, who read the newspapers carefully :

" Are they still licking us ?"

" They are."

" But what's the cause ?" Melnikov exclaimed in

perplexity, rolling his eyes. " Aren't there people enough, or what ?"

" Not enough sense," Maklakov retorted dryly.

" The working men are dissatisfied. They do not understand. They say the generals have been bribed."

" That's certainly true," Krasavin broke in. " None of them are Russians." He muttered an ugly oath. " What's our blood to them ?"

" Blood is cheap," said Solovyov, and smiled strangely.

As a rule the spies spoke of the war unwillingly, as if constrained in one another's presence, and afraid of uttering some dangerous word. On the day of a defeat they all drank more whisky than usual, and having got drunk, quarrelled over trifles.

On such days Yevsey, trying to avoid possible brawls, made his escape unnoticed to his empty room, and there thought about the life of the spies. All of them—and there were many, their numbers constantly increasing—all of them seemed unhappy to Klimkov. They were all solitary, and he pitied them with his colourless pity. Nevertheless he liked to be among them and listen to their talk.

At the meetings Sasha boiled over and swore.

" Monstrosities ! You understand nothing. You can't understand the significance of the business. Monstrosities !"

In answer some smiled deprecatingly, others maintained sullen silence.

" For forty rubles a month you can't be expected to understand very much," one would sometimes mutter.

" You ought to be wiped off the face of the earth," shrieked Sasha.

Klimkov began to dislike Sasha more and more,

THE SPY

strengthened in his ill-will by the fact that nobody else cared for the diseased man.

Many of the spies were actually sick from the constant dread of attacks and death. Fear drove some, as it had Yelizar Titov, into an insane asylum.

" I was playing in the club yesterday," said Piotr in a disconcerted tone, " when I felt something pressing on the nape of my neck, and a cold shiver running up and down my backbone. I looked around. There in the corner stood a tall man looking at me as if he were measuring me inch by inch. I could not play. I rose from the table, and I saw him move. I backed out, and ran down the stairs into the yard and out into the street. I took a cab, sat in it sidewise, and looked back. Suddenly the man appeared from somewhere in front of me, and crossed the street under the horse's very nose. Maybe it wasn't he. But in such a case you can't think. How I yelled! He stopped, and I jumped out of the cab, and off I went at a gallop, the cabmen after me. Well, how I did run, the devil take it !"

" Such things happen," said Grokhotov, smiling. " I once hid myself for a similar reason in the yard. But it was still more horrible there, so I climbed up to a roof, and sat there behind the chimney until daybreak. A man must guard himself against another man. Such is the law of Nature."

Krasavin once entered pale and sweating, with staring eyes.

" They were following me," he announced gloomily, pressing his temples.

" Who ?"

" They."

Solovyov endeavoured to calm him.

" Lots of people walk the streets, Gavrilo. What's that to you ?"

" I could tell by the way they walked they were after me."

For more than two weeks Yevsey did not see Krasavin

The spies treated Klimkov good-naturedly, and their occasional laughter at his expense did not offend him, for when he was grieved over his mistakes they comforted him.

" You'll get used to the work."

He was puzzled as to when the spies did their work, and tried to unriddle the problem. They seemed to pass the greater part of their time in the cafés, sending novices and such insignificant fellows as himself out for observations.

He knew that, beside all the spies with whom he was acquainted, there were still others, desperate, fearless men, who mingled with the revolutionists, and were known by the name of provocators. There were only a few such men, but these few did most of the work, and directed it entirely. The authorities prized them very highly, while the street spies, envious of them, were unanimous in their dislike of the provocators because of their haughtiness.

Once in the street Grokhotov pointed out a provocator to Yevsey.

" Look, Klimkov, quick !"

A tall, sturdy man was walking along the pavement. His fair hair, combed back, fell down beautifully from under his hat to his shoulders. His face was large and handsome, his moustache luxuriant. His soberly-clad person produced the impression of that of an important, well-fed gentleman of the nobility.

" You see what a fellow ?" said Grokhotov with pride. " Fine, isn't he ? Our guard. He handed over twenty makers of bombs. He made the bombs with them himself. They wanted to blow up a Minister. He taught them, then delivered them up. Clever piece of business, wasn't it ?"

" Yes," said Yevsey, amazed at the man's stately appearance, so unlike that of the busy bustling street spies.

" That's the kind they are, the real ones," said Grokhotov. " Why, he would do for a Minister ; he has the face and figure for it. And we—what are we ? Poverty-stricken dependents upon a hungry nobleman."

Yevsey sighed. The magnificent spy aroused his envy.

Ready to serve anybody and everybody for a good look or a kind word, he ran about the city obediently, searched, questioned, and informed. If he succeeded in pleasing, he rejoiced sincerely, and grew in his own estimation. He worked much, made himself very tired, and had no time to think.

Maklakov, reserved and serious, seemed better and purer to Yevsey than any person he had met up to that time. He always wanted to ask him about something, and tell him about himself—such an attractive and engaging face did this young spy have.

Once Yevsey actually put a question to him :

" Timofey Vasilyevich, how much do the revolutionists receive a month ?"

A light shadow passed over Maklakov's bright eyes.

" You are talking nonsense," he answered, not in a loud voice, but angrily.

The days passed quickly, in a constant stir, one just

like the other. At times Yevsey felt they would file on in the same way far into the future—vari-coloured, boisterous, filled with the talk now become familiar to him, and with the running about to which he had already grown accustomed. This thought enwrapped his heart with cold tedium, his body in enfeebling languor. Everything within and without became empty. Klimkov seemed to be sliding down into a bottomless pit.

CHAPTER XVI

In the middle of the winter everything suddenly trembled and shook. People anxiously opened their eyes, gesticulated, disputed furiously, and swore. As though severely wounded and blinded by a blow, they all stampeded to one place.

It began in this way. One evening, on reaching the Department of Safety to hand in a hurried report of his investigations, Klimkov found something unusual and incomprehensible in the place. The officials, agents, and clerks appeared to have put on new faces. All seemed strangely unlike themselves. They wore an air of astonishment and rejoicing. They spoke now in very low tones and mysteriously, now aloud and angrily. There was a senseless running from room to room, a listening to one another's words, a suspicious screwing-up of anxious eyes, a shaking of heads and sighing, a sudden cessation of talk, and an equally sudden burst of disputing. A whirlwind of fear and perplexity swept the room in broad circles. Playing with these people's impotence, it drove them about like dust, first blowing them into a pile, then scattering them on all sides. Klimkov, stationed in a corner, looked with vacant eyes upon this state of consternation, and listened to the conversation with strained attention.

THE SPY

He saw Melnikov, with his powerful neck bent and his head stuck forward, place his hairy hands on different persons' shoulders, and demand in his low, hollow voice :

" Why did the people do it ? "

" What of it ? The people must live. Hundreds were killed, eh ? Wounded ! " shouted Solovyov.

From somewhere came the repulsive voice of Sasha, cutting the ear.

" The priest ought to have been caught. That before everything else. The idiots ! "

Krasavin walked about with his hands folded behind his back, biting his lips and rolling his eyes in every direction.

Quiet Viekov took up his stand beside Yevsey, and picked at the buttons of his vest.

" So this is the point we've reached, " he said. " My God ! Bloodshed ! What do you think, eh ? "

" What happened ? " Yevsey asked.

Viekov looked around warily, took Klimkov by the hand, and whispered :

" This morning the people in St. Petersburg, with a priest and sacred banners, marched to the Czar Emperor. You understand ? But they were not admitted. The soldiers were stationed about, and blood was spilled. "

A handsome, staid gentleman, Leontyev, ran past them, glanced back at Viekov through his pince-nez, and asked :

" Where is Philip Philippovich ? " But he disappeared without waiting for the information he wanted, and Viekov ran after him.

Yevsey closed his eyes for a minute, in order to try in the darkness to get at the meaning of what had been told him. He could easily represent to himself a mass of people walking through the streets in a sacred procession, but since he could not understand why the soldiers had shot at them, he was sceptical about the affair. However, the general agitation seized him, too, and he felt disturbed and ill at ease. He wanted to bustle about with the spies, but, unable to make up his mind to approach those he knew, he merely retreated still farther into his corner.

Many persons passed by him, all of whom, he fancied, were quickly searching for a little cosy corner where they might stand to collect their thoughts.

Maklakov appeared. He remained near the door, with his hands thrust into his pockets, and looked sideways at everybody. Melnikov approached him.

" Did they do it on account of the war ?"

" I don't know."

" For what else ? If it was really the people. But maybe it was simply some mistake. Eh ? What did they ask for, do you know ?"

" A constitution," replied Maklakov.

The sullen spy shook his head.

" I don't believe it."

" As you please."

Then Melnikov turned heavily, like a bear, and walked away grumbling :

" No one understands anything. They stir about, make a big noise——"

Yevsey went up to Maklakov, who looked at him.

" What is it ?"

" I have a report."

Maklakov waived him aside.

" Who wants to bother about reports to-day ?"

Yevsey drew still nearer, and asked :

" Timofey Vasilyevich, what does ' constitution ' mean ?"

" A different order of life," answered the spy in a low voice.

Solovyov, perspiring and red, came running up.

" Have you heard whether they are going to send us to St. Petersburg ?"

" No, I haven't."

" I think they probably will.   Such an event !   Why, it's a revolt, a real revolt."

" To-morrow we will know."

" How much blood has been shed !   What is it ?"

Maklakov's eyes ran about uneasily.   To-day his shoulders seemed more stooping than ever, and the ends of his moustache dropped downward.

Something seemed to be revolving in Yevsey's brain, and Maklakov's grim words kept repeating themselves.

" A different order of life—different."

They gripped at his heart, arousing a sharp desire to extract their meaning.   But everything around him turned and darted hither and thither.   Melnikov's angry, resonant voice sounded sickeningly :

" The thing is, to know what people did it.   The working people are one thing, simply residents another. This differentiation must be made."

And Krasavin spoke distinctly :

" If even the people begin to revolt against the Czar, then there are no people any more, only rebels."

" Wait, and suppose there's deception here."

" Hey, you old devil," whispered Zarubin, hastening up to Yevsey.   " I've struck a vein of business.   Come on, I'll tell you."

Klimkov followed him in silence for a space, then stopped.

" Where shall I go ?"

" To a beer saloon. You understand ? There's a girl there—Margarita. She has an acquaintance, a milliner. At the milliner's lodging they read books on Saturdays—students and various other people like that. So I'm going to cut them up. Ugh !"

" I won't go," said Yevsey.

" Oh, you ! Ugh !"

The long ribbon of strange impressions quickly enmeshed Yevsey's heart, hindering him from an understanding of what was happening. He walked off home unobserved, carrying away with him the premonition of impending misfortune—a misfortune that already lay in hiding, and was stretching out irresistible arms to clutch him. It filled his heart with new fear and grief. In expectation of this misfortune he endeavoured to walk in the obscurity close against the houses. He recalled the agitated faces and excited voices, the disconnected talk about death, about blood, about the huge graves into which dozens of bodies had been flung like rubbish.

At home he stood at the window a long time looking at the yellow light of the street-lamp. The pedestrians quickly walked into the circle of its light, then plunged into the darkness again. So in Yevsey's head a faint timid light was casting a pale illumination upon a narrow circle, into which ignorant, cautious grey thoughts, helplessly holding on to one another like blind people, were slowly creeping. Small and lame, they gathered into a shy group driven into one place like a swarm of mosquitoes. But suddenly, loosing hold of the bond uniting them, they disappeared without leaving a trace, and his soul, devoid of them, remained like a desert illuminated by a solitary ray from a sorrowful moon.

THE SPY

The days passed as in a delirium, filled with terrible tales of the fierce destruction of people. For Yevsey these days crawled slowly over the earth like black eyeless monsters, swollen with the blood they had devoured. They crawled with their huge jaws wide open, poisoning the air with their stifling, salty odour. People ran and fell, shouted and wept, mingling their tears with their blood. And the blind monster destroyed them, crushed old and young, women and children. They were pushed forward to their destruction by the ruler of their life, fear—fear leaden-grey as a storm-cloud, powerful as the current of a broad stream.

Though the thing had happened far away, in a strange city, Yevsey knew that fear was alive everywhere. He felt it all over round about him.

No one understood the event, no one was able to explain it. It stood before the people like a huge riddle and frightened them. The spies stuck in their meeting-places from morning until night, and did much reading of newspapers and drinking of whisky. They also crowded into the Department of Safety, where they disputed, and pressed close against one another. They were impatiently awaiting something.

"Can anybody explain the truth?" Melnikov kept asking.

One evening a few weeks after the event they assembled in the Department of Safety. Sasha said sharply:

"Stop this nonsensical talk! It's a scheme of the Japs. The Japs gave eighteen million rubles to Father Gapon to stir the people up to revolt. You understand? The people were made drunk on the road to the palace; the revolutionists had ordered a

186

few wine-shops to be broken into. You understand?"
He let his red eyes rove about the company as if seeking
those of his listeners who disagreed with him. "They
thought the Czar, loving the people, would come out
to them. And at that time it was decided to kill him.
Is it clear to you?"

"Yes, it's clear," shouted Yakov Zarubin, and began
to jot something down in his notebook.

"Jackass!" shouted Sasha in a surly voice. "I'm
not asking you. Melnikov, do you understand?"

Melnikov was sitting in a corner, clutching his head
with both hands, and swaying to and fro as if he had
the toothache. Without changing his position he
answered:

"A deception!" His voice struck the floor dully,
as if something soft, yet heavy, had fallen.

"Yes, a deception," repeated Sasha, and began
again to speak quickly and fluently. Sometimes he
carefully touched his forehead, then looked at his
fingers, and wiped them on his knee. Yevsey had the
sensation that even his words reeked with a putrid
odour. He listened, wrinkling his forehead painfully.
He understood everything the spy said, but he felt that
his speech did not efface—in fact, could not efface—from
his mind the black picture of the bloody holiday.

All were silent, now and then shaking their heads,
and refraining from looking at one another. It was
quiet and gloomy. Sasha's words floated a long time
over his auditors' heads, touching nobody.

"If it was known that the people had been deceived,
then why were they killed?" the unexpected question
suddenly burst from Melnikov.

"Fool!" screamed Sasha. "Suppose you had been
told that I was your wife's paramour, and you got

187

drunk and came at me with a knife, what should I do ?
Should I tell you ' Strike !' even though you had been
duped, and I was not guilty ?''

Melnikov started to his feet, stretched himself, and
bawled :

" Don't bark, you dog !"

A tremor ran through Yevsey at his words, and
Viekov, thin and nerveless, who sat beside him, whispered in fright :

" O God ! Hold him !"

Sasha clenched his teeth, thrust one hand into his
pocket, and drew back. All the spies—there were
many in the room—sat silent and motionless, and
waited, watching Sasha's hand. Melnikov waved his
hat, and walked slowly to the door.

" I'm not afraid of your pistol."

He slammed the door after him noisily. Viekov
went to lock it, and said as he returned to his place :

" What a dangerous man !"

" So," continued Sasha, pulling a revolver from his
pocket and examining it, " to-morrow morning you are
each of you to get down to business, do you hear ?
And bear in mind that now you will all have more to do
than before. Part of us will have to go to St. Petersburg. That's number one. Secondly, this is the very
time that you'll have to keep your eyes and ears particularly wide open, because people will begin to
babble all sorts of nonsense in regard to this affair.
The revolutionists will not be so careful now, you
understand ?"

Handsome Grokhotov drew a loud breath, and said :

" We understand, never mind ! If it's true that the
Japs gave such large sums of money, that explains it,
of course.'"

THE SPY

"Without any explanation, it's very hard," said someone.

"Ye-e-e-s.'

"People cry, 'What does it mean?' And they give you poisonous talk, and you don't know how to answer back."

"The people are very much interested in this revolt."

All these remarks were made in an indolent, bloodless fashion, and with an air of constraint.

"Well, now you know what you are about, and how you should reply to the fools," said Sasha angrily. "And if some donkey should begin to bray, take him by the neck, whistle for a policeman, and off with him to the police-station. There they have instructions as to what's to be done with such people. Ho, Viekov, or somebody, ring the bell, and order some seltzer."

Yakov Zarubin rushed to the bell.

Sasha looked at him, and said, showing his teeth:

"I say, pup, don't be mad with me for having cut you off."

"I'm not mad, Aleksandr Nikitich."

"Ye-e-s," Grokhotov drawled pensively. "Still they are a power, after all! Consider what they accomplished—raised a hundred thousand people."

"Stupidity is light; it's easy to raise," Sasha interrupted him. "They had the means to raise a hundred thousand people—they had the money. Just you give me such a sum of money, and I'll show you how to make history." Sasha uttered an ugly oath, lifted himself slightly from the sofa, stretched out the thin yellow hand which held the revolver, screwed up his eyes, and aiming at the ceiling, cried through his teeth in a yearning whine: " I would show you !"

189

THE SPY

All these things—Sasha's words and gestures, his eyes and his smiles—were familiar to Yevsey, but now they seemed impotent, useless, as infrequent drops of rain in extinguishing a conflagration. They did not extinguish fear, and were powerless to stop the quiet growth of a premonition of misfortune.

At this time a new view of the life of the people unconsciously developed in Yevsey's mind. He learned that on the one hand some people might gather in the streets by the tens of thousands in order to go to the rich and powerful Czar and ask him for help, while others might kill these tens of thousands for doing so. He recalled everything the Smokestack had said about the poverty of the people and the wealth of the Czar, and was convinced that both sides acted in the manner they did from fear.

Nevertheless the people astonished him by their desperate bravery, and aroused in him a feeling with which he had hitherto been unfamiliar.

Now as before, when walking the streets with the box of goods on his breast, he carefully stepped aside for the passers-by, either taking to the middle of the street or pressing against the walls of the houses. However, he began to look into the people's faces more attentively, with a feeling akin to respect, and his fear of them seemed to have diminished slightly. Men's faces had suddenly changed, acquiring more variety and significance of expression. All began to talk with one another more willingly and simply, and to walk the streets more briskly, with a firmer tread.

CHAPTER XVII

YEVSEY often entered a house occupied by a physician and a journalist upon whom he was assigned to spy. The physician employed a wet-nurse named Masha, a full, round little woman with merry, sky-blue eyes, who was always neat and clean, and wore a white or blue sarafan with a string of beads around her bare neck. Her full-breasted figure gave the impression of a luscious, healthy creature, and won the fancy of Yevsey, who imagined that a strong savoury odour, as of hot rye-bread, emanated from her. She was an affectionate little person. He loved to question her about the village, and hear her replies in a rapid sing-song. He soon came to know all her relatives—where each one lived, what was the occupation of each, and what the wages.

He paid her one of his visits five days after Sasha had explained the cause of the uprising. He found her sitting on the bed in the cook's room adjoining the kitchen. Her face was swollen, her eyes were red, and her lower lip stuck out comically.

"Good-morning," she said sullenly. "We don't want anything. Go. We don't want anything."

"Did the master insult you?" Yevsey asked. Though he knew the master had not insulted her, he regarded it as his professional duty to ask just such questions. His next duty was to sigh and add : " That's the way they always are. You've got to work for them your whole life long."

Anfisa Petrovna, the cook, a thin, ill-tempered body, suddenly cried out :

" Her brother-in-law was killed, and her sister was knouted. She had to be taken to the hospital."

" In St. Petersburg ?" Yevsey inquired quietly.

" Yes."

Masha drew a deep breath, and groaned, holding her head in her hands.

" What for ?" asked Yevsey.

" Who knows them ? A curse upon them !" shrieked the cook, rattling the dishes in her exasperation. " Why did they kill all those people ? That's what I would like to know."

" It wasn't his fault," Masha sobbed. " I know him. O God ! he was a book-binder, a peaceful fellow. He didn't drink. He made forty rubles a month. O God ! they beat Tania, and she's soon to have a child. It will be her second child. ' If it's a boy,' she said, ' I'll christen him Foma, in honour of my husband's friend.' And she wanted the friend to be the child's godfather, too. But they put a bullet through his leg, and broke his head open, the cursed monsters ! May they have neither sleep nor rest ! May they be torn with anguish and with shame ! May they choke in blood, the infernal devils !"

Her words and tears flowed in tempestuous streams. Dishevelled and pitiful, she screamed in desperate rage, and scratched her shoulders and her breast with her nails. Then she flung herself on the bed, and buried her head in the pillow, moaning and trembling convulsively.

THE SPY

"Her uncle sent her a letter from there," said the cook, running about in the kitchen from the table to the stove and back again. "You ought to see what he writes! The whole street is reading the letter. Nobody can understand it. The people marched with ikons, with their holy man; they had priests. Everything was done in a Christian fashion. They went to the Czar to tell him : ' Father, our Emperor, reduce the number of officials a little. We cannot live with so many officers and such burdensome taxes on our shoulders. We haven't enough to pay their salaries, and they take such liberties with us—the extremest of liberties. They squeeze everything out of us they want.' Everything was honest and open. They had been preparing for this a long time—a whole month. The police knew of it, yet no one interfered. They went out, and marched along the streets, when suddenly off go the soldiers, shooting at them! The soldiers surrounded them on all sides, and fired at them; hacked them and trampled them down with their horses—everybody, even the little children! They kept up the massacre for two days. Think of it! What does it mean? That the people are not wanted any more? That they have decided to exterminate them?"

Anfisa's cutting, unpleasant voice sank into a whisper, above which could now be heard the sputtering of the butter on the stove, the angry gurgle of the boiling water in the kettle, the dull roaring of the fire, and Masha's groans. Yevsey felt obliged to answer the sharp questions of the cook, and he wanted to soothe Masha. He coughed carefully, and said, without looking at anybody :

"They say the Japs arranged the affair."

193

THE SPY

" S-s-s-o ?" the cook cried ironically. " The Japs, the Japs, of course ! We know the Japs. They keep to themselves ; they stick in their own home. Our master explained to us who they are. You just tell my brother about the Japs. He knows all about them, too. It was scoundrels, not Japs !"

From what Melnikov had said, Yevsey knew that the cook's brother, Matvey Zimin, worked in a furniture factory, and read prohibited books. Now, all of a sudden, he was seized with the desire to tell her that the police knew about Zimin's infidelity to the Czar. But at that minute Masha jumped down from the bed, and cried out, while arranging her hair :

" Of course, they have no way of justifying themselves, so they hit upon the Japs as an excuse."

" The blackguards !" drawled the cook. " Yesterday, in the market, somebody also made a speech about the Japs. Evidently he had been bribed to justify the officials. One old man was listening, and then you should have heard what he said about the generals, about the Ministers, and even about the Czar himself. How he could do it without putting the least check upon himself—— No, you can't fool the people. They'll catch the truth, no matter into what corner you drive it."

Klimkov looked at the floor, and was silent. The desire to tell the cook that watch was being kept upon her brother now left him. He involuntarily thought that every person killed had relatives who were now just as puzzled as Masha and Anfisa, and asked one another " Why ?" He realized that they were crying and grieving in dark perplexity, with hatred secretly springing up in their hearts—hatred of the murderers

194

and of those who endeavoured to justify the crime. He sighed and said :

" A horrible deed has been done." At the same time he thought : " But I, too, am compelled to protect the officials."

Masha giving the door to the kitchen a push with her foot, Yevsey remained alone with the cook, who looked at the door sidewise, and grumbled :

" The woman is killing herself. Even her milk is spoiled. This is the third day she hasn't given nourishment. Look here, Thursday next week is her birthday, and I'll celebrate my birthday then, too. Suppose you come here as a guest, and make her a present, say, of a good string of beads. You must comfort a person some way or other."

" Very well ; I'll come."

" All right."

Klimkov walked off slowly, revolving in his mind what the woman had said to him. The cook's talk was too noisy, too forward, instantly creating the impression that she did not speak her own sentiments, but echoed those of another. As for Masha, her grief did not touch him. He had no relatives ; moreover, he rarely experienced pity for people. Nevertheless, he felt that the general revolt everywhere noticeable was reflected in the outcries of these women, and—the main thing—that such talk was unusual, inhumanly brave. Yevsey had his own explanation of the event : fear pushed people one against the other. Then those who were armed and had lost their senses exterminated those who were unarmed and foolish. But this explanation did not stand firm in Yevsey's mind, and failed to calm his soul. He clearly realized from what he had seen and heard that the people were beginning to free themselves from the thraldom of fear, and were insistently and fearlessly seeking the guilty, whom they found and judged. Everywhere large quantities of leaflets appeared, in which the revolutionists described the bloody days in St. Petersburg, and cursed the Czar, and urged the people not to believe in the administration. Yevsey read a few such leaflets. Though their language was unintelligible to him, he scented something dangerous in them—something that irresistibly made its way into his heart and filled him with fresh alarm. He resolved not to read any leaflets again.

Strict orders were given to find the printing-office in which the leaflets were printed, and to catch the persons who distributed them. Sasha swore, and even gave Viekov a slap in the face for something he had done. Philip Philippovich invited the agents to come to him in the evenings, in order to deliver speeches to them. He usually sat in the middle of the room behind his desk, resting the lower half of his arms upon it, and keeping his long fingers engaged in quietly toying with the pencils, pens, and papers. The various gems on his hands sparkled in different colours. From under his black beard gleamed a large yellow medal. He moved his short neck slowly, and his blue spectacles rested in turn upon the faces of all present, who meekly and silently sat against the wall. He scarcely ever rose from his arm-chair. Nothing but his fingers and his neck moved. His heavy face, bloated and white, looked like a face in a portrait ; the hairs of his beard seemed glued together. When silent, he was calm and staid, but the instant he spoke in his thin voice, which screeched like an iron saw while being filed, everything about him—the black frock-coat, and the order, the gems, and the beard—seemed to be stuck upon somebody else. Sometimes Yevsey fancied that an artificial puppet sat in front of him, inside of which was hidden a little shrivelled-up fellow, resembling a little red devil. If someone were to shout at the puppet, he imagined, the little devil would be frightened, and would jump out with a squeak and leap through the window.

Nevertheless, Yevsey was afraid of Philip Philippovich. In order not to attract to himself the gobbling look of his blue glasses, he sat as far as possible from him, trying the entire time not to move.

" Gentlemen "—the thin voice trembled in the air ; it drove against Yevsey's breast unpleasantly and coldly, like a gleaming steel rod—" gentlemen, you must listen to me carefully. You must remember my words. In these days every one of you should put your entire mind, your entire soul, into the war with the secret and cunning enemy. You should listen to your orders and fulfil them strictly, though you may act on your own initiative, too. In the secret war for the life of your mother Russia, you must know, all means are permissible. The revolutionists are not squeamish as to the means they employ ; they do not stop at murder. Remember how many of your comrades have perished at their hands. I do not tell you to kill—no, of course not. I cannot advise such measures. To kill a man requires no cleverness. Any fool can kill. Yet the law is with you. You go against the lawless. It would be criminal to be merciful toward them. They must be rooted out like noxious weeds. I say, you must for yourselves find out what is the best way to stifle the rising revolution. It isn't I who demand this of you ; it is the Czar and the country." After a pause,

197

during which he examined his rings, he went on:
" You, gentlemen, have too little energy, too little love
for your honest calling. For instance, you have let the
old revolutionist Saydakov slip. I now know that he
lived in our city for three and a half months. Secondly,
up to this time you have failed to find the printing-
office."

" Without provocation it is hard," someone ventured
in an offended tone.

" Don't interrupt, if you please. I myself know
what is hard, and what is easy. Up to this time you
have not been able to gather serious evidence against
a whole lot of people known for their seditious ten-
dencies, and you cannot give me any grounds for their
arrest."

" Arrest them without grounds," said Piotr with a
laugh.

" What is the object of your facetiousness ? I am
speaking seriously. If you were to arrest them without
grounds, we should simply have to let them go again.
That's all. And to you personally, Piotr Petrovich, I
want to remark that you promised something a long
time ago. Do you remember ? You likewise, Krasavin. You said you had succeeded in becoming acquainted with a man who might lead you to the
Terrorists. Well, and what has come of it ?"

" He turned out to be a cheat. You just wait. I'll
do my business," Krasavin answered calmly.

" I have no doubt of it whatsoever, but I beg all of
you to understand that we must work more energeti-
cally ; we must hurry matters up."

Philip Philippovich discoursed a long time—sometimes a whole hour—without taking breath, calmly, in
the same level tone. The only words that varied the

monotonous flow were "You must." The "you" came out resonantly like a long-drawn hammer-blow, the "must" in a drawled hiss. He embraced everybody with his glassy blue stare. His words fairly choked Yevsey.

Once at the end of a meeting, when Sasha and Yevsey were the only ones who remained with Philip Philippovich, Yevsey heard the following colloquy:

PHILIP PHILIPPOVICH (glumly, dejectedly). "What idiots they are, though!"

SASHA (snuffling). "Aha!"

PHILIP PHILIPPOVICH. "Yes, yes, what *can* they do?"

SASHA. "It seems that now you are going to learn the value of decent people."

PHILIP PHILIPPOVICH. "Well, give them to me—give them to me."

SASHA. "Ah, they cost dear!"

Klimkov was neither surprised nor offended. This was not the first time he had heard the authorities swear at their subordinates. He counted it in the regular order of life.

The spies after the meetings spoke to one another thus:

"Um, yes, a converted Jew, and just look at him!"

"They say he got a rise of six hundred rubles on the first of January."

"The value of our labour is growing."

Sometimes a handsome, richly-dressed gentleman by the name of Leontyev addressed the spies in place of Philip Philippovich. He did not remain seated, but walked up and down the room holding his hands in his pockets, politely stepping out of everybody's way. His smooth face, always drawn in a frown, was cold and repellent ; his thin lips moved reluctantly, and his eyes were veiled.

Another man named Yasnogursky came from St. Petersburg for the same purpose. He was a low, broad-shouldered, bald man with an order on his breast. He had a large mouth, a wizened face, heavy eyes, like two little stones, and long hands. He spoke in a loud voice, smacking his lips, and pouring out streams of strong oaths. One sentence of his particularly impressed itself on Yevsey's memory :

" They say to the people, ' You can arrange another, an easy life for yourselves.' They lie, my children. The Emperor, our Czar, and our Holy Church arrange life, while the people can change nothing—nothing."

All the speakers said the same thing. The political agents must serve more zealously, must work more, must be cleverer, because the revolutionists were growing more and more powerful. Sometimes they told about the Czars—how good and wise they were, how the foreigners feared them and envied them because they had liberated various nations from the foreign yoke. They had freed the Bulgarians and the Servians from the oppression of the Turkish Sultan, the Khivans, the Bokharans, and the Turkomans from the Persian Shah, and the Manchurians from the Chinese Emperor. As a result, the Germans and the English, along with the Japanese, who were bribed by them, were dissatisfied. They would like to get the nations Russia had liberated into their own power. But they knew the Czar would not permit this, and that was why they hated him, why they wished him all evil, and endeavoured to bring about the revolution in Russia.

Yevsey listened to these speeches with interest, waiting for the moment when the speakers would begin to tell about the Russian people, and explain why all of them were unpleasant and cruel ; why they loved to torture one another, and lived such a restless, uncomfortable life. He wanted to hear what the cause was of such poverty, of the universal fear, and the angry groans heard on all sides. But of such things no one spoke.

After one of the meetings Viekov said to Yevsey as the two were walking in the street :

" So it means that they are getting into power. Did you hear ? It's impossible to understand what it signifies. Just see : here you have secret people who live hidden, and suddenly they cause general alarm, and shake everything up. It's very hard to comprehend. From where, I'd like to know, do they get their power ?"

Melnikov, now even more morose and taciturn, grown thin and all dishevelled, once hit his fist on his knee, and shouted :

" I want to know where the truth is !"

" What's the matter ?" asked Maklakov angrily.

" What's the matter ? This is the matter. I understand it this way. One class of officials has grown weak—our class. Now another class gets the power over the people—that's all."

" And the result is—fiddlesticks !" said Maklakov, laughing.

Melnikov looked at him, and sighed :

" Don't lie, Timofey Vasilyevich. You lie out and out. You are a wise man, and you lie. I understand."

Thoughts instinctively arose in the dark depths of Yevsey's soul. He did not realize how they formed themselves, did not feel their secret growth. They appeared suddenly, in perfect array, and frightened him by their unexpected apparition. He endeavoured to hide them, to extinguish them for a time, but unsuccessfully. They quietly flashed up again, and shone more clearly, though their light only cast life into still greater obscurity. The frequent conversations about the revolutionists became interwoven in his brain, creating an insensible sediment in his mind, a thin strata of fresh soil for the growth of puny thoughts. These thoughts disquieted him, and drew him gently to something unknown.

CHAPTER XVIII

WHILE on his way to Masha to take part in her birthday celebration, the thought occurred to Yevsey :

" I am going to get acquainted with the joiner to-day. He's a revolutionist."

Yevsey was the first guest to arrive. He gave Masha a string of blue beads, and Anfisa a shell comb. In return for the gifts, with which both were greatly pleased, they treated him to tea and nalivka (a sort of wine made of berries with whisky or water). Masha, prettily arching her full white neck, looked into his face with a kind smile. Her glance softly caressed his heart, enlivened and emboldened him. Anfisa poured out the tea, and said, winking her eyes :

" Well, merchant, you are our generous donor. When shall we celebrate your wedding ?"

Yevsey, trying not to show his embarrassment, said quietly and confidingly :

" I cannot decide to get married. It's very hard."

" Hard ? Oh, you modest man ! Marya, do you hear ? He says it's hard to get married."

Masha smiled in answer to the cook's loud laugh, looking at Klimkov from the corner of her eyes.

" Maybe by ' hard ' he has his own meaning."

" Yes, I have my own meaning," said Yevsey, raising his head. " You see, I am thinking of the fact that it is hard to find a person with whom you can live soul to soul, so that the one would not fear the other. It is hard to find a person whom you could believe in."

Masha sat beside him. He glanced sidewise at her neck and breast, and sighed.

" Suppose I were to tell them where I work ?"

He started, frightened by the desire, and with a quick effort he suppressed it.

" If a man does not understand life," he continued, raising his voice, " it's better for him to remain alone."

" For one person to live all alone is hard too," said Masha, pouring out another glass of nalivka for him. " Drink."

Yevsey longed to speak much and openly. He observed that the women listened to him willingly, and this, in conjunction with the two glasses of wine, aroused him. But the journalist's servant-girl Liza, who came in at that moment, also excited, at once usurped the attention of Anfisa and Masha. She was bony, and had a cast in one eye. Her hair was handsomely dressed, and she was cleverly gowned. With her sprightly manner she seemed a good, forward, little girl.

" My good people invited guests for to-day, and did not want to let me go," she said, sitting down.

" ' Well,' said I, ' you can do as you please.' And I went off. Let them bother themselves."

" Many guests ?" Klimkov asked wearily, remembering his duty.

" A good many. But what sort of guests ! Not one of them ever sticks a sixpence into your hand. On New Year's all I got was two rubles and thirty kopeks."

" So they're not rich ?" asked Yevsey.

"Oh, rich! No! Not one of them has a whole overshoe."

"Who are they? What's their business?"

"Different things. Some write for the newspapers, another is simply a student. Oh, what a good fellow one of them is! He has black eyebrows, and curly hair, and a cute little moustache, white, even teeth— a lively, jolly fellow. He came from Siberia not long ago. He keeps talking about hunting."

Yevsey looked at Liza, and bent his head. He wanted to say "Stop!" to her. Instead, he apatheti- cally asked: "I suppose he must have been exiled."

"Who can tell? Maybe. My master and mistress were exiles, too. The sergeant told me so."

"Yes, who nowadays hasn't been an exile?" ex- claimed the cook. "I lived at Popov's, an engineer, a rich man. He had his own house and horses, and was getting ready to marry. Suddenly the gendarmes came at night, seized him, and broke up everything, and then he was sent off to Siberia."

"I don't condemn my people," Liza interrupted— "not a bit of it. They are good folks. They don't scold. They're not grasping. Altogether, they're not like other people. And they're very interesting. They know everything and speak about everything."

Yevsey looked at Masha's ruddy face, and thought:

"I'd better go; I'll ask her about her master next time. But I can't make up my mind to go. If only she had kept quiet, the silly!"

"Our people understand everything too," Masha announced with pride.

"When that affair happened, that revolt in St. Petersburg," Liza began with animation, "they stayed up nights at a time talking."

" Why, our people were in your house then," observed the nurse.

" Yes, indeed, there were lots of people at the house. They talked, and wrote complaints. One of them even began to cry. Upon my word !"

" There's enough to cry about," sighed the cook.

" He clutched his head, and sobbed. ' Unhappy Russia !' he said, ' unhappy people that we are !' They gave him water, and even I got sorry for everybody, and began to cry."

Masha looked around frightened.

" God, when I think of my sister !" She rose and went into the cook's room. The women looked after her sympathetically.

Klimkov sighed with relief. Against his will he asked Liza wearily, and with an effort :

" To whom did they write complaints ?"

" I don't know," answered Liza.

" Marya went off to cry," remarked the cook.

The door opened, and the cook's brother entered coughing.

" It's chilly," he said, untwisting the scarf from his neck.

" Here, take a drink—quick !"

" Yes, indeed. And here's health to you."

He was a thin person, who moved about freely and deliberately. The gravity of his voice did not accord very well with his small light beard and his sharp, somewhat bald skull. His face was small, thin, insignificant, his eyes large and hazel.

" A revolutionist," was Yevsey's mental observation as he silently pressed the joiner's hand. " Time for me to be going," he announced unexpectedly to everybody.

" Where to ? " cried Anfisa, unceremoniously seizing his hand. " Now, you merchant, don't break up our company. Look, Matvey, what a present he gave me."

Zimin looked at Yevsey, and said thoughtfully :

" Yesterday they got another order in our factory for fifteen thousand rubles. A drawing-room, a cabinet, a bedroom, and a salon—four rooms. All the orders came from the military. They stole a whole lot of money, and now they want to live after the latest fashion."

" There you are ! " Yevsey exclaimed mentally, vexed and heated. " Begins the minute he comes in. Oh, Lord ! "

He felt a painful ache in his chest, as if something inside him had been torn. Without thinking of what his question would lead to, he quickly asked the joiner :

" Are there any revolutionists in the factory ? "

As if touched to the quick, Zimin quickly turned to him, and looked into his eyes. The cook frowned, and said in a voice dissatisfied, but not loud :

" They say revolutionists are everywhere nowadays."

" From smartness or stupidity ? " asked Liza.

Unable to withstand the hard, searching look of the joiner, Klimkov slowly bowed his head, though he followed the working man with a sidelong glance.

" Why does that interest you ? " Zimin inquired politely, but sternly.

" I have no interest in it," Yevsey answered lazily.

" Ah ! Then why do you ask ? "

" Just so," said Yevsey; and in a few seconds added ; " Out of politeness."

The joiner smiled.

It seemed to Yevsey that three pairs of eyes were looking at him suspiciously and severely. He felt awkward, and something bitter nipped his throat. Masha came out of the cook's room, smiling guiltily. When she looked at the others' faces, the smile disappeared.

" What's the matter ?"

" It's the wine," flashed through Yevsey's mind. He rose to his feet, shook himself, and said : " Don't think I asked for no reason at all. I asked because I wanted to tell her long ago—your sister—about you."

Zimin also rose. His face gathered in wrinkles, and turned yellow.

" What can you tell her about me ?" he asked with calm dignity.

Masha's quiet whisper reached Yevsey's ear: "What's up between them ?"

" Wait," said Anfisa.

" I know," said Yevsey. He had the sensation that he was being swung up from the floor into the air, light as a feather. He seemed to see everything, observe everything with marvellous plainness. " I know you're being followed— followed by the agents of the Department of Safety ; I know you're a revolutionist."

The cook shook in her chair, crying out in astonishment and fright :

" Matvey, what does this mean ?"

" Excuse me," said Zimin, passing his hand reassuringly before her face. " This is a serious matter." Then he said to Yevsey in a decided, stern tone : " Young man, put your overcoat on. You must go home. And I, too, must go. Put your overcoat on."

Yevsey smiled. He still felt empty and light. It was a pleasant sensation, but his eyes were dim, and the caustic, tickling taste in his mouth came back again. He scarcely realized how he walked away, but he did not forget that all were silent, and no one said good-bye to him.

In the street Zimin nudged his shoulder, and said not aloud, but emphatically :

" I beg you not to come to my sister any more."

" Why ? Did I offend you ?" asked Yevsey.

" No, not in the least."

" Why, then ?"

" Who are you ?"

" A peddler."

" Then how do you know what I am, and that I am being followed ?"

" An acquaintance told me."

" A spy ?"

" Yes."

" So ? And you are a spy, too ?"

" No," said Yevsey. But looking into Zimin's lean, pale face, he remembered the calm, dull sound of his voice, and without an effort corrected himself : " Yes, I, too."

They walked a few steps in silence.

" Well, go," said Zimin, suddenly halting. His voice sounded subdued and sorrowful. He shook his head strangely. " Go away."

Yevsey leaned his back against the enclosure, and gazed at the man, blinking his eyes. Zimin, too, looked at Yevsey, shaking his right hand.

" Why ?" said Yevsey in perplexity. " Didn't I tell you the truth—that you are being tracked ?"

" Well ?"

" And you are angry ?"

Zimin bent towards him, and poured a wave of hissing words upon Klimkov.

" Yes, go to the devil ! I know without you that

they are tracking me. What's the matter? Is business going badly among you? Did you think you'd buy me, and betray people behind my back? Or did you want to throw a sop to your conscience? Go to hell! I say, go, or else I'll give you a black eye."

Yevsey started from his leaning posture, and walked off.

" Vermin !" he heard breathed behind him contemptuously.

Klimkov stopped, turned around, and for the first time swore at anybody with the whole power of his voice.

" Vermin yourself! You—cur !"

Zimin did not reply. His steps were inaudible. Somewhere Yevsey heard the snow crunching under the runners of a cab and the grinding of iron on stone.

" He went back there," thought Klimkov, walking slowly along the pavement. " He will tell. Masha will curse me." He spat out, then hummed :

" Oh, garden, garden mine !" He stopped at a lamp-post, feeling he had to calm himself.

" Here I am, and I can sing if I want to. If a policeman hears it, and asks, ' What are you bawling there ?' I'll show him my ticket from the Department of Safety. ' Oh, excuse me !' he'll say. But if the joiner should sing, he'll be hustled off to the station-house, and they'll give him a cudgelling. ' Don't disturb the peace !' " Klimkov smiled, and peered into the darkness. " Well, brother, won't you strike up a song ?"

However, this failed to calm him as he had expected. His heart was sad, and a bitter soapy saliva seemed to be glued in his mouth, making tears well up in his eyes.

> " Oh ga-a-a-arden, ga-a-a-arden mine !
> Green is this garden of mine."

He sang with the full power of his lungs, shutting his eyes tight. This did not help either. The dry, prickly tears trickled through his lids, and chilled his cheeks.

" Ky-a-b !" Klimkov called in a low voice, still trying to put on a bold front. But when he had seated himself in the sleigh, his body grew faint, as if a great many tightly-drawn fibres had suddenly burst within him. His head drooped, and swaying from side to side in his seat, he mumbled : " A fine insult—very strong—thank you ! Oh, you good people, wise people——"

This complaining was pleasant. It filled his heart with drunken sweetness. Yevsey had often felt this sweetness in his childhood. It set him in a martyr-like attitude toward people, and made him more significant to himself.

211

CHAPTER XIX

In the morning Yevsey lay in bed frowning up at the ceiling.

"Put my foot into it!" he thought dismally, as the recollection of what had happened the day before came back to him. "No, I oughtn't to track people, but track myself." The ideas seemed strange to him. "How's that, though? Am I rascally toward myself?"

He remembered the melancholy hazel eyes of the joiner, the expression of dignity on his thin face, and his assured voice as he said: "It's chilly." Suddenly Yevsey was perplexed to feel within himself something alien, something ready to struggle with him. He rose to his feet, took in as much air as he could, and for a long time stood without emitting breath, as if to stifle inside himself that which was alien and which hindered him.

"I must stop all this. What do I want it for?" he urged himself. Nevertheless ease did not return. He began to dress lazily, compelling himself to think about the task of the day.

Now he seldom went about with goods, because there was much other work to be done. This day, for instance, he was to go to a factory suburb to observe the working men, with the object of discovering the persons who distributed proclamations.

212

THE SPY

He smeared his hands with soot and oil, then washed them with soap, after which an oily film was left, such as on the hands of metal workers. This was not essential. But Klimkov liked to dye his tufty hair, and colour his brows and moustache. Such proceedings made his work more interesting, and heightened its gravity.

The handsome Grokhotov had been very assiduous in teaching Yevsey the art of disguising his face and figure. Grokhotov was sincerely attracted by the work. He possessed a large supply of beards, moustaches, and wigs of all colours, and could paste scars and warts on the face. Sometimes he would display his arts of mimicry to his comrades. Suddenly, right in everybody's presence, he would give his face, voice, and figure a striking resemblance to one of the officials. Or he would cackle like a goose, roar like a lion, bark like a dog, or meow like a cat. His astonished audience praised him generously, and held their sides with laughter, while he, smiling sedately, declared modestly :

"Just the A B C. Wait until I've been at it a year ; then I'll go on the stage. I'll hit off all the celebrities, and I'll imitate every animal on earth."

Melnikov would look at him with contempt, and spit. Once he even shouted :

"Hey, you clown, show us a louse !"

"The louse is a mute insect," remarked the spy.

"Well, then, profit by its example. Eat and keep quiet."

While dressing Klimkov remembered this interchange of words, which in turn recalled Anatol.

"There," he thought, "Anatol would have made a good spy. But Zimin wouldn't do at all. His eyes are in the way. You can recognize him by the eyes at

213

once. He certainly wants to take Masha as his mistress."

Yevsey stopped at the door, his heart unpleasantly gripped by this conjecture. But the next instant he waved his hand carelessly.

" To the devil with all of them ! What do I care !"

This thought, which had calmed him before, now irritated a sore spot in his feelings.

The sun was shining, water flowed from the roofs, babbling and washing away the dirty reddish snow. The people walked quickly and merrily. The good chimes of the Lenten bells floated lengthily in the warm moist atmosphere, mingling in a broad ribbon of soft sounds, which waved in the air, and floated away from the city into the pale-bluish distance.

" Now to go off somewhere, to walk in the fields, in the deserts," thought Yevsey, as he entered the narrow streets of the factory suburb.

Round about him rose the red filthy walls, supporting themselves one against the other. The sky over them was besmirched with smoke, the air was steeped in the stifling odour of warm oil. White teeth gleamed angrily in the dirty faces of the working men. All the surroundings were unlovely, and the eyes quickly wearied in looking upon the smoked stone cages in which the men worked.

At noon Klimkov, exhausted and feeling insulted by everything he saw, entered a tavern, where he ordered dinner to be brought to him at a small table next to a window. He reluctantly listened to the people's conversation. There were not many, but all were working men, who lazily cast short words at one another as they ate and drank. The only lively sound was of a young, incessant voice which reached him from a corner.

" Now think, where does wealth come from ?"

The person who spoke was a broad-shouldered, curly-haired fellow. Yevsey looked at him in vexation, and turned away. He frequently heard talks about wealth, which always inspired him with a sense of bored perplexity. He felt they were dictated only by envy and greed. He knew that just such talks were accounted noxious, and he forcibly compelled himself to listen to them, though to-day he wanted to traverse the broad light streets of the city.

" You work cheaply, and you buy dearly. Isn't it so ?" cried the curly-headed fellow. " All wealth is accumulated from the money by which we are underpaid for our work. Let's take an example."

" Everybody's greedy," thought Yevsey. " How Masha snatched the beads yesterday ! All are scoundrels. And the reason Zimin did not strike me was because he was afraid I would call the police. Ha ! They drove me out, but they kept my presents. If they thought me a dirty fellow, they should have returned my presents, the skunks !"

Filling himself with the pleasant bitterness that comes from censuring people, he was carried away by it, and no longer heard or saw anything. Suddenly, however, a merry voice fell upon his ear.

" What, Yevsey Klimkov ?"

He raised his head hastily, and wanted to rise, but was unable to do so. He saw standing before him the curly-headed orator, whom, however, he did not recognize.

" You don't know me ? Yakov, your cousin."

He laughed, held out his hand to Yevsey, and seated himself opposite him at the table. His laughter enveloped Klimkov in a warm cloud of reminiscences--

THE SPY

of the church, the quiet ravine, the fire, and the talks
of the blacksmith. Silent, smiling in embarrassment,
he carefully pressed his cousin's hand.

" I didn't recognize you."

"Of course not!" exclaimed Yakov. " Your memory
gets weak in the city. Various things creep upon you
from all sides, so no place is left for the old. How are
you getting along ?"

" So, so."

" Out of work ?"

" Yes."

Klimkov answered unwillingly. He wanted to learn
whether this meeting might be dangerous for him.
But Yakov spoke for both. He rapidly gave an
account of the village, as if it were absolutely necessary
for him to get through with it as quickly as possible.
In two minutes he had told Yevsey that his father had
become blind, that his mother was always sick, and that
he had been living in the city three years working in
the factory.

" There you've got the whole story."

Yakov was even more thickly besmudged with soot
and oil than most of the men. Though his clothes were
torn, he seemed to be rich. He was outspoken and free
in his demeanour. Klimkov looked at him with
pleasure, and recalled without malice how this strong
fellow had beaten him.

" Is he a revolutionist, too ?" he asked himself
timidly.

" Well, how are you getting along ?" said Yakov.
His broad round face, glossy and smiling good-
naturedly, called for frankness in return, which
Klimkov, however, did not want to give. He felt
the new and alien thing that he had found in his soul

216

in the morning growing in him. In the desire to evade Yakov's questions he himself began to question him.

" And how are you ?"

" Work is hard, and life is easy. I like the city very much. It's a smart thing, the city is. And how simple, how intelligible things are here ! It's true that work for us fellows is, you may say, humiliating. There's so much work, and so little time to live. Your whole day, your whole life, goes to your employer. You can keep only minutes for yourself. There's no time to read a book. I'd like to go to the theatre, but when should I sleep ? Do you read books ?"

" I ? No."

" Well, yes, you have no time. Isn't it so ? Though I get to read things, after all. Such books as you get here ! You start one, and you just sink away as if a dear girl and you were embracing. Honest ! How do you get along with girls ? Lucky ?"

" So, so," said Yevsey.

" They love me ! The girls here, too—ah, God, what a life ! Do you go to the theatre ?"

" I've been."

" I love the theatre. I snatch up everything as if I were going to leave to-morrow, or die. Really, I like to hear music, everything ; the zoological garden—that's a nice place, too."

The red of excitement broke through the black layer of dirt on Yakov's cheeks. His eyes burned eagerly. He smacked his lips, as if he were sucking in something refreshing and vivifying.

Quiet envy stirred in Yevsey—envy of this healthy body with its keen appetites. He stubbornly recalled how Yakov had pummelled his sides with his powerful

THE SPY

fists, and something sad softly hindered him from doing violence to himself. Quick, joyous speech came from Yakov without cease ; the ringing, exulting words and exclamations fluttered around Yevsey like swallows. He drank in his spring-like talk, involuntarily smiling. He seemed to himself to be splitting in two, torn by the desire to listen and the awkward, almost shameful feeling that possessed him. Though he wished to speak in his turn, he feared he might betray himself. His shirt-collar pressed his neck. He turned his head round, and suddenly saw Grokhotov on the street at the window. Over the spy's left shoulder and arm hung torn breeches, dirty shirts, and jackets. He gave Yevsey a scarcely perceptible wink as he shouted in a sour voice :

" I sell and buy old clothes."

" It's time for me to be going," said Yevsey, jumping to his feet.

" You are free on Sundays, aren't you ? Oh yes, you're out of work. Well, then, let's go to the zoological garden. Come to me. No, I'd better go to you. Where do you live ?"

Yevsey was silent. He did not want to tell him where he lodged

" What's the matter ? Do you live with a girl ? That doesn't matter. You'll introduce me to her. That's all. What are you ashamed of ? Is that it ?"

" You see, I don't live alone."

" Well, yes."

" But I don't live with a girl. I live with an old man."

Yakov guffawed.

" How funny you are ! The devil knows what you mean. Well, we don't want an old man, of course.

I live with two comrades. It's not convenient for anyone to call on me either. Come, let's agree on a place where we can meet."

They decided on a meeting-place, and left the café. Yakov on taking leave gave his cousin an affectionate and vigorous handshake, and Yevsey left him as precipitately as if he feared his cousin would return to take it back. On his way he reflected dismally :

" I cannot go on the side of the city where the railway-station is because I'll meet Zimin there, and they'll beat me. Here, the toughest place, the place they call a hot-bed of revolutionists, Yakov will be in my way. I can't do a thing. I can't turn anywhere."

A feeling of spiteful irritation glided over his soul like a grey shadow.

" I sell old clothes," sang Grokhotov behind his back, then whispered : " Buy a shirt from me, Klimkov."

Yevsey turned around, took some rag in his hand, and examined it silently, while the spy, praising the wares aloud, managed to get in a whisper : " See here, you just hit it. That curly-headed fellow, I had my eyes on him. He's a Socialist. Hold on to him. You can hook a great many with him. He's a young fellow, a simple sort of fellow, do you hear ? " He tore the rag from Yevsey's hand, and shouted in an offended tone : " Five kopeks for such a garment as this ? You're making sport of me, friend. Why should you insult me ? Go your way, go !" And shouting his wares, Grokhotov strode down the street.

" There, I myself am going to be under surveillance," thought Yevsey, looking at Grokhotov's back.

When a spy with little experience became acquainted with a working man, he was obliged to report the fact immediately to the spy above him. The latter either gave him as an assistant a spy with more experience, or he himself went among the working men, upon which the other spies would say of him enviously :

" He ' noosed ' himself into the provocatorship."

The rôle of provocator was considered dangerous, so by way of compensation the officers at once gave money rewards for the handing over of a group of people. All the spies not only gladly " noosed " themselves, but sometimes also even tripped one another up in the endeavour to snatch away the lucky chance. In this way the entire business was not infrequently spoiled. More than once it happened that a spy had already got inside a circle of working men, when suddenly, in some secret manner, they learned of his profession, whereupon they would beat him if he had not succeeded in time in slipping away from the circle. This was called " snapping the noose."

It was hard for Klimkov to believe that Yakov was a Socialist, though at the same time he wanted to believe it. The envy his cousin aroused was transformed again into irritation against him for having put himself in his way. Yevsey now also recalled the blows his cousin had bestowed upon him.

In the evening, with downcast eyes, he informed Piotr of his acquaintance.

" Well, what of it ?" asked Piotr angrily.

" Nothing."

" You don't know what you must do ? Then what the devil is the use of teaching you fellows ?" Piotr hastened off, crumpled, lean, with dark stains under his eyes.

" Evidently he's lost again at cards," thought Yevsey gloomily.

CHAPTER XX

THE next day Sasha learned of Yevsey's success. He questioned him in detail. After reflecting a while he smiled his putrid smile, and gave Klimkov instructions.

"Wait a little. Then you'll tell him in a careful way that you have got a position as clerk in a printing-office—do you hear? Ask as few questions as possible; let them speak for themselves. Very likely they'll ask you whether you can't get them type. Tell them you can, but learn to say it simply, so that they should see it's all the same to you whether you get it or don't get it. Don't ask what for. Behave like a little fool, as you actually are. Only I want you to know that if you botch this matter it will be bad for you. After every meeting report to me what you have heard."

In intercourse with Sasha, Yevsey felt like a little dog on a strap. He looked at the spy's pimply yellow face, and thought of nothing but the moment when he would be permitted to depart from the cloud of disgusting odours, which nauseated him and ate into the skin of his face and hands.

He went to meet Yakov as empty as a pipe. But when he saw his cousin with a cigarette between his teeth, and his hat cocked to one side, he gave him a pleasant smile, while something unpleasant stirred within him.

"How's business?" shouted Yakov merrily.

221

" So, so."

" Got a job ?"

" Yes." The next instant Yevsey thought : " I said it too soon."

" What ?"

" Clerk in a printing-office."

Yakov whistled.

" Capital ! What do you get ?"

" Twenty-five."

" In a printing-office ? Indeed !" said Yakov thoughtfully, then suddenly became animated. " What do you say ? I'll take you to pay a visit this evening. Good company, coz. Two girls—one a milliner, the other a spool-girl in a thread-factory. There'll be a locksmith there too, a young fellow. He sings and plays the guitar. Two more, also good people. All people are good, only they have no time to pay attention to themselves."

Yakov spoke quickly, and his eyes smiled joyously at everything he saw. He stopped in front of the shop-windows, and examined their contents with the gaze of a man to whom all articles are pleasant and everything is interesting.

" Look, what a dress ! Ha ! If you were to put such a thing on our Olga, she'd get tangled up in it. Books—that little one there, yellow, you see it ? I've read it. ' Primitive Man.' Interesting. Read it, and you'll see how people grew up. Books are very interesting. They at once open up for you all the cunning of life. Those thick books are awkward to read. By the time you get to the middle you forget what happened at the beginning, and at the end you forget the beginning also. The devil take them ! Why don't they write shorter books ?"

The next minute he pointed out a gun, and cried ecstatically :

" Revolvers, eh ? Just like toys."

Giving himself over to Yakov's mood, Yevsey looked at the various articles with the wandering look of empty eyes, and smiled, astounded, as if for the first time seeing the pretty alluring multitude of brilliant materials and vari-coloured books, the blinding gleam of colours and metals. He was pleased to hear the young voice still in the state of change ; the rapid talk steeped in the joy of life was agreeable to him. It lightly penetrated the dark void of Klimkov's soul, and allowed him to forget himself for a moment.

" You're a jolly fellow," he said approvingly.

" Very. I learned to dance from the Cossacks. A score of Cossacks are stationed in our factory. Did you hear that the men in our factory wanted to rise ? You didn't ? How's that ? The newspapers wrote about it. Yes, so I learned to dance from the Cossacks. Wait ; you'll see. Nobody can beat me."

" Why did they want to rise ?" asked Yevsey, provoked by the simplicity with which Yakov spoke of a revolt.

" Why ? They wrong us working men. What, then, are we to do ?"

" And you would have done it, too ?"

" What ? Rebel ? Of course. What else ? Our people are good ; they're solid."

" And how about the Cossacks ?"

" The Cossacks ? So, so. They are people, too. At first they thought they would officer it over us, but then they said : ' Comrades, give us leaflets.' "

Yakov suddenly broke off and looked into Yevsey's

face. For a minute he walked in silence with knit brows.

The mention of the leaflets recalled his duty to Yevsey. He wrinkled his forehead painfully. Wishing to push something away from himself and his cousin, he said quietly :

" I read these leaflets."

" Well ?" asked Yakov, slackening his gait.

" I don't understand them. What are they for ?"

" You read some more."

" I don't want to."

" Why not ?"

" It's so."

" They're not interesting to you ?"

" No, they're not."

For a while they walked in silence. Yakov sniffed meditatively, and gave a hasty look into his cousin's face. Yevsey felt he had not succeeded in keeping off the unpleasant and dangerous theme.

" There, leaflets, they're a precious matter. It's necessary for us to read them. All the slaves of labour ought to read them," Yakov began heartily, but in a modulated voice. " We, cousin, are slaves, chained to everlasting work. They have made us captives of capitalists, and we live poor in body and in soul. Isn't it so ? Now the leaflets eat at our chains the way rust eats iron, and they liberate our human minds."

Klimkov walked more quickly. He did not want to hear the smooth talk. The desire even darted through his mind to say :

" Don't speak to me about such things, please."

But Yakov himself interrupted his speech.

" There's the zoo !"

THE SPY

They drank a bottle of beer in the bar, and listened to the playing of a military band.

" Good ?" Yakov asked, nudging Yevsey's side with his elbow. On the cessation of the playing Yakov sighed. " That was ' Faust ' they played. An opera. I saw it three times. Beautiful, very ! The story is stupid, but the music is good, and the songs, too. Come, let's look at the monkeys." On the way to the monkey-house he told Yevsey the story of Faust and the devil Mephistopheles. He even attempted to sing something, but not succeeding, he burst out laughing. " I can't," he declared. " It's hard. Besides, I've forgotten it. Do you know, the singer who plays the Devil gets a thousand rubles every time he sings. The devil take him ! let him get ten thousand rubles, because it's good. When it's good, I don't grudge anybody anything. I'd give my life ; there, take it, eat ! Isn't it so ?"

" Yes," replied Yevsey, looking around.

Yakov's account of the opera—the pretty women's faces, the laughter and talk of the crowds of people in holiday attire, and over all the spring sky bathed in sunlight—all this intoxicated Klimkov and expanded his heart

" What a young fellow he is !" he thought in amazement, as he looked at Yakov. " So brave ! And he knows everything. Yet he's the same age as I am."

Now it seemed to Yevsey that his cousin was leading him somewhere far off, and was quickly opening up before him a long row of little doors, behind each of which the sound and the light grew pleasanter and pleasanter. He looked around, absorbing the new impressions, and at times opening his eyes wide in anxiety. It seemed to him that the familiar face of a spy was darting about in the crowd.

The two youths stood before the monkey-cage. Yakov, with a kind smile in his eyes, said :

" I love these wise animals. In fact, I love every living thing. Just look ! Wherein are they less than human beings ? Isn't it so ? Eyes, chins, how bright all their features are, eh ? Their hands——" He suddenly broke off to listen to something. " Wait a minute ; there go our folks." He disappeared, and in a minute returned leading a girl and a young man up to Yevsey. The young man wore a sleeveless jacket. Yakov cried out joyously :

" You said you weren't coming here, you deceivers. Well, all right. This is my cousin, Yevsey Klimkov. I told you about him. This is Olga—Olga Konstantinova, and this is Aleksey Stepanovich Makarov."

Klimkov bowed clumsily, and silently pressed the hands of his new acquaintances.

" There, he's going to ' noose ' me in," he thought. " It's better for me to go away."

But he did not go away, though he looked around again, fearful lest he might see one of the spies. He saw none, however.

" He's not a very free sort of a fellow," said Yakov to the girl. " He's not my sort, sinner that I am. He's a quiet fellow."

" You needn't feel constrained with us. We are simple people," said Olga.

She was taller than Yevsey by a whole head, and her size was heightened by her luxuriant glossy hair, which she wore combed high. Her grey-blue eyes smiled serenely in a pale oval face.

The expression of the man in the sleeveless jacket

was intelligent and kind. His eyes were screwed up, and his ears large. His motions were slow. In walking he moved his apparently powerful body with a peculiar sort of unconcern.

" Are we going to wander about here long like unrepentant sinners ?" he asked in a soft bass.

" What else should we do ?" asked Yakov.

" Let's sit down somewhere."

Olga bent her head to look into Klimkov's face.

" Have you ever been here before ?"

" No. This is the first time."

" Do you find it interesting ?"

" Yes, I like it."

He walked at her side trying for some reason to lift his feet higher, by which walking became awkward. They sat down at a table, and called for beer. Yakov made jokes, while Makarov whistled softly and regarded the public with his screwed-up eyes.

" Have you any companions ?" asked Olga.

" No, not one."

" That's what I thought at once. I thought you were a solitary person," she said, smiling. " Lonely people have a peculiar gait. Altogether, there's something noticeable about them. How old are you ?"

" I'll soon be nineteen."

" Look, there's a spy !" Makarov exclaimed quietly.

Yevsey jumped to his feet, but quickly resumed his seat, and looked at Olga to see if she had observed his involuntary movement of alarm. He could not make out, however. She was silently and attentively examining Melnikov's dark figure, which slowly moved through the passage-way between the tables as if with an effort. Melnikov walked with bent neck and eyes fastened on the ground. His arms hung at his side as if dislocated.

" He walks like Judas to the aspen-tree," said Yakov in a subdued voice.

" He must be drunk," observed Makarov.

" No, he's always like that," was on the tip of Yevsey's tongue. He fidgeted in his chair.

Melnikov pushed himself through the crowd like a black stone, and was soon lost in its gaily-coloured stream.

" Did you notice how he walked ?" Olga asked Klimkov.

Yevsey nodded his head.

" Of course, he's a mean man, but he must be unhappy and lonely."

Yevsey raised his head, and looked at her attentively, with expectation.

" Do you know, I think that for a weak man loneliness is the most horrible thing. It can drive him to anything."

" Yes," said Klimkov in a whisper, comprehending something. He looked into the girl's face gratefully, and repeated in a louder tone, " Yes."

" I knew him four years ago," Makarov recounted. Makarov's face seemed suddenly to have lengthened and dried up. His bones became visible, his eyes opened and darkened and looked firmly into the distance. " He delivered up one student, who gave us books to read, and a working man, Tikhonov. The student was exiled ; Tikhonov stayed in prison about a year, then died of typhus."

" Are you afraid of spies ?" Olga suddenly asked Klimkov.

" Why ?" Yevsey returned dully.

" You started so when you saw him."

Yevsey, rubbing his throat vigorously, answered without looking at her :

" That was—because I know him, too."

" Aha !" Makarov drawled, smiling.

" Ah, and such a quiet fellow !" exclaimed Yakov.

All now moved more closely around Klimkov, as if desiring to hide him from somebody's eyes. He did not understand their exclamations, nor their movements and kind looks. He endeavoured to keep quiet, fearing that against his will he would say words that would at once destroy the anxious yet pleasant half-dream of these minutes.

The fresh spring evening approached quietly and benignly, softening sounds and colours. There was a red flush in the sky, and the brass instruments sang a soft, pensive strain.

" Well," said Makarov, " are we going to stay here, or are we going home ?"

" What will they give here ?" asked Olga.

" Chorus-singing, tight-rope dancing, and all sorts of similar nonsense."

They decided to go home. On the way Olga asked Klimkov :

" Have you ever been in prison ?"

" Yes," he answered, but in an instant added : " Not for long."

They took the tramway to their place of destination. Yevsey found himself in a little room with blue paper on the walls. It was close and stifling, now merry, now gloomy. Makarov played the guitar, and sang songs which Yevsey had never before heard. Yakov boldly discussed everything in the world, laughing at the rich and swearing at the officials. Then he danced,

THE SPY

filling the whole room with the tread of his feet and the cries and the whistling that accompanied the dances. The guitar tinkled the measure of the dance, and Makarov encouraged Yakov with popular sayings and shouts.

" Go ahead, Yasha ! Heigho !

> " Who with merriment is blessed,
> Frightens sorrow from his breast."

Olga looked on serenely and contentedly.

" Good, isn't it ?" she asked Klimkov occasionally, smiling at him.

Drunk with a quiet joy unknown to him, Klimkov smiled in response. He forgot about himself, and felt the unrelenting, inner pricks only rarely, for a few seconds at a time. Before his consciousness was able to transform them into clear thought, they disappeared, without recalling his life to him.

It was not until he had reached his home that he remembered his work, his obligation to deliver these merry people into the hands of the gendarmes. On recalling this duty, he was seized with cold anguish. He stopped in the middle of the room, his brain a void. Breathing became difficult, and he passed his dry tongue over his lips. He drew off his clothes quickly, and, clad in nothing but his underwear, seated himself at the window. After several minutes of numbness, he thought :

" I will tell them—her—Olga."

But that very minute he heard in his memory the angry and contemptuous shouts of the joiner, " Vermin !" Klimkov shook his head in repudiation of the idea. " I'll write to her. ' Take care,' I'll say —and I'll write about myself."

This thought cheered him. The next minute, however, he reasoned :

" They'll find my letter when they make the search. They'll recognize my handwriting, and then I'm ruined."

Someone within him commanded imperiously :

" You can't do anything of yourself. Do that which you have been bidden to do."

He sat at the window almost until daybreak. It seemed to him that his entire body shrivelled up and collapsed within him like a rubber ball from which the air is expelled. Within grief relentlessly sucked at his heart ; without the darkness pressed upon him, full of faces lying in wait. Amid them, like a red ball, lowered the sinister face of Sasha. Klimkov crouched on his seat, unable to think. Finally, he rose cautiously, and quietly hid himself under the blanket of the bed.

CHAPTER XXI

LIFE, like a horse that has stood idle too long, began to caper strangely, refusing to surrender to the will of those who wanted to control it—who wanted to control it just as senselessly, just as cruelly as before.

Every evening the people connected with the Department of Safety, who were utterly at a loss, spoke more and more alarmingly of the increasing signs of universal excitement—of the secret league of peasants, who had resolved to take the land by force from the landowners; of the gatherings of working men, who began to censure the administration openly; of the power of the revolutionists, which clearly was growing from day to day. Philip Philippovich, without abating, continued to goad the agents of the Department of Safety with his sharp-edged voice, which irritated the ears. He overwhelmed everybody with reproaches for inactivity, and Yasnogursky, smacking his lips, made tragic appeals to the agents while pressing his hand to his bosom.

" My children, exert yourselves. Remember that service in behalf of the Czar is not wasted."

But when Krasavin inquired gloomily, " What are we to do ?" he merely waved his hand, and stood for a long time with his deep black mouth gaping strangely, unable to find a reply.

" Catch them !" he finally shouted.

Yevsey, who listened to everything, heard the dapper Leontyev cough dryly, and say to Sasha :

" Apparently our old methods of war upon the rebels are no good in these days of universal madness."

" Ye-e-e-es, you can't put out fire with spittle," hissed Sasha, a smile distorting his face.

Everybody was vexed, and complained and shouted. Sasha drew up his long legs, and cried in mocking derision :

" Aha ! the gentlemen revolutionists are getting the better of us, eh ?"

He laughed, and his laugh irritated everybody. Yevsey felt that this man was not afraid of anything, and he endeavoured not to hear his talk.

The spies kept about the streets day and night, and every evening brought long reports of their observations. They spoke to one another mournfully :

" Is this the way to work nowadays ? Dear me !"

Apparently, no one knew a means by which the elemental growth of the popular revolt could be restrained.

" They will comb our curls," said Piotr, cracking his knuckles.

" They'll take us off the list if we remain alive," Solovyov chimed in dismally.

" If only they would give us a pension ! But they won't."

" A noose round our necks, not a pension," said Melnikov sombrely.

The spies were all exhausted and confused ; all trembled in fear of the morrow. Both they and the officials seemed to have faded. These people, who but a short time ago had been terrible in Yevsey's eyes, who had appeared to him to be the powerful and invincible masters of life, now ran from one corner of the Department of Safety to another, and fluttered about in the streets like last year's dried leaves.

He observed with amazement that there were other people, cheerful, simple, and trusting, who were able to walk into the future, carelessly stepping over every obstacle and snare in their way, every one of whom was good in his own fashion, and every one of whom clearly hinted at the possibility of something better than himself. Yevsey compared them with the spies, who unwillingly, with clandestine tread, crept along the streets and into houses, and secretly spirited away these people at night, in order to seclude them in prisons. He clearly realized that the spies did not understand the aim of their work, did not believe that it was needful for life, and did not think or reason when, instinctively, according to their habit, they went about half-sick, half-drunk, driven by different fears.

He liked the tranquil talk of Olga, her greyish-blue eyes, and that live strong pity for people which sounded in the girl's every word. He liked the noisy, jesting, somewhat boastful talker Yakov, the careless Aleksey, good-naturedly ready to give away his last shirt and penny to anyone who asked for them. He met an increasing number of people new to him, in each of whom he perceived faith in the victory of his dream. And Yevsey, involuntarily, insensibly, yielded to this faith.

Observing the quick crumbling of that power which he had hitherto submissively served, Yevsey began to seek a way by which it would be possible for him to circumvent and escape the necessity of betrayal. He reasoned thus :

"If I go to them, then it will be impossible for me not to deliver them up. To hand them over to another agent is still worse. I must tell them. Now that they are becoming more powerful, it will be better for me to be with them."

So, yielding to the attraction exerted upon him by persons new to him, he visited Yakov more frequently, and became more insistent in endeavouring to meet Olga. After each visit he reported in a quiet voice to Sasha every detail of his intercourse with them—what they said, what they read, and what they wanted to do. He enjoyed telling of them—in fact, repeated their talk with secret satisfaction.

"Oh, a funeral," snuffled Sasha, angrily and sarcastically fixing Klimkov with his dim eyes. "You must push them on yourself if they are inattentive. You must get in a hint that you can furnish them with type, fix up a printing-office. Is it possible you can't do that ?"

Yevsey was silent.

"I am asking you, idiot, can you do it ? Well ?"

"I can."

"Why don't you speak out ? Suggest it to them to-morrow—do you hear ?"

"Very well."

It was easy for Klimkov to fulfil Sasha's order. In reporting about his cousin's circle, he had not ventured to tell Sasha that both Olga and Yakov had already asked him twice whether he could obtain type for them. Each time he had managed to get away without answering.

The next evening he went to Olga, carrying in his

breast the dark feeling of emptiness he always experienced in moments of nervous tension. The resolution to fulfil the task was put into him by a stranger's will; he did not have to think about it himself. This resolution spread within him, and crowded out all fear, all inconvenient sympathy.

But when the tall figure of Olga stood before him in the small, dimly-lighted room, and behind her he saw her large shadow on the wall, which moved to meet him, Klimkov lost courage, grew confused, and stood in the doorway without speaking.

" I've just returned from the factory," said Olga, pressing his hand. " We had another meeting to-day. What's the matter with you ? Are you tired ? Are you sick ? Come in ; sit down. Let's have some tea—yes ?"

She turned the light in the lamp higher, and looked at Klimkov with a smile. While getting the dishes ready, she continued :

" I like to drink tea with you alone. I myself and all the comrades, we talk a great deal. We must talk so much we scarcely have time to think. That's absurd and bad, but it's true. So now it's pleasant to see a taciturn, thinking man. Will you have a glass of milk ? It will do you good. You are growing very thin, it seems to me."

Klimkov took the glass she offered him, and slowly sipped the watery, unsavoury milk. He wanted to get through with the business at once.

" This is it. You said you need type."

" I did. I know you'll give it to us."

She said these words simply, with a confidence not to be shaken. They were like a blow to Yevsey. He flung himself on the back of the chair astonished.

" Why do you know ?" he asked dully after a pause.

" When I asked you, you said neither yes nor no. So I thought you would certainly say yes."

Yevsey did not understand. He tried not to meet her look.

" Why ?" he queried again.

" It must be because I consider you a good man. I trust you."

" You mustn't trust," said Yevsey.

" Well, enough nonsense—you must."

" And suppose you've been mistaken ?"

She shrugged her shoulders.

" Well, what of it ?" After a pause she added calmly : " Not to believe a man means not to respect him. It means to think him beforehand a liar, an ugly person. Is that possible ?"

" That's what is necessary," mumbled Yevsey.

" What ?"

" I can furnish the type." He sighed. The task was accomplished. He was silent for several minutes, sitting with his head bowed, his hands pressed tight between his knees, while he listened suspiciously to the rapid beating of his heart.

Olga leaned her elbows on the table, and in a low voice told him when and where the promised type must be brought. He made a mental note of her words, and repeated them to himself, desiring by this repetition to hinder the growth of the painful feeling in his empty breast. Now that he had fulfilled his duty, a stifling nausea slowly arose from the depths of his soul, and that feeling of an alien inside himself, of a constantly widening cleft in his being, came over him in a tormenting wave.

" You notice," the girl said quietly, " how rapidly

the people are changing, how faith in other persons is growing, how quickly one gets to know the other, how everybody seeks friends and finds them. All have become simpler, more trusting, more willing to open up their souls. See how good it is."

Her words trembled before him like moths, each with its own character. Simple, kind, joyous, they all seemed fairly to smile. Unable to make up his mind to look Olga in the face, Klimkov took to watching her shadow on the wall over her shoulders, and drew upon it her blue eyes, the medium-sized mouth with the pale lips, her face somewhat weary and serious, but soft and kind.

" Shall I tell her now that all this is a falsity—that she will be ruined ?"

He answered himself.

" They'll drive me out. They'll swear at me, and drive me out."

" Do you know Zimin, the joiner ?" he suddenly asked.

" No, why ?"

Yevsey sighed painfully.

" Just so. He's a good man, too—a Socialist."

" We are many," observed Olga with assurance.

" If she knew the joiner," Klimkov thought slowly, " I would tell her to ask him about me. Then——."

The chair seemed to be giving way beneath him ; his nausea, he thought, would immediately seize him by the throat. He coughed, and examined the clean little room, which, small and poor though it was, once more gripped at his heart .The moon looked into the room, round as Yakov's face, and the light in the lamp seemed irritatingly superfluous.

" More and more people come into being who realize

that they are called upon by destiny to order life differently—upon truth and intellect," said Olga dreamily and simply.

Yevsey, yielding more and more to the power of the triumphant feeling that the girl and the quiet contracted room inspired in him, thought :

" I'll put out the light, fall on my knees before her, embrace her feet, and tell her everything— and she will give me a kick."

But the fear of ill-treatment did not deter him. He raised himself heavily from his chair, and put out his hand to the lamp. Then his hand dropped lazily, drowsily, his legs shook. He started.

" What are you doing ?" demanded Olga.

He tried to answer, but a soft gurgle came instead of words. He dropped to his knees, and seized her dress with trembling hands. She pressed one hot hand against his forehead, and with the other grasped his shoulder, at the same time hiding her legs under the table with a powerful movement.

" No, no ; get up !" she exclaimed sternly. " Ah me, how dreadful this is ! My dear, I understand ; you are worn out. I am sorry for you ; you are an honourable man. I cannot— why, you don't ask for charity—then get up."

The warmth of her strong body roused in him a sharp sensual desire, and he mistook the push of her hand as an encouraging caress.

" She's not a saint," darted through his mind, and he embraced the girl's knees more vigorously.

" I tell you, get up !" she exclaimed in a muffled voice, no longer persuasively, but in a commanding tone.

He rose without having succeeded in saying anything. The girl had confused his desires, his words, and feelings.

She had put into his breast something insulting and stinging.

"Understand——" he mumbled, spreading out his hands.

"Yes, yes, I understand. My God, always this on the road!" she exclaimed. Looking into his face, she went on harshly : "I am sick of it. I am insulted. I can't be only a woman to everybody. Oh, God! How pitiful you all are, after all!"

She went to the window, and the table now separated her from Yevsey. A dim, cold perplexity took hold of his heart, an insulting shame quietly burned him.

"I tell you what, don't come to me—I beg of you. I'll feel awkward in your presence, and you, too—please."

Yevsey took up his hat, flung his coat over his shoulders, and walked away with bowed head. Several minutes later he was sitting on a bench at the gate of a house mumbling, as if drunk :

"The baggage!" But he had to strain himself to bring out the epithet. It was not genuine. He ransacked all the shameful names for a woman, all ugly oaths, and poured them over the tall, shapely figure of Olga, desiring to sully every bit of her with mud, to darken her from head to foot, in order not to see her face and eyes. But oaths did not cling to her. She stood before his eyes, stretching out her hands, pushing him away, serene and white. Her image robbed his oaths of their force, and though Yevsey persistently roused anger within himself, he felt only shame.

He looked for a long time at the round, solitary ball of the moon, which moved in the sky in bounds, as if leaping like a large, bright rubber ball; and he heard the quiet sound of its motion, resembling the beatings of a heart.

He did not love this pale melancholy disc, which always seemed to watch him with cold obstinacy in the heavy moments of his life. It was late, but the city was not yet asleep. From all sides floated sounds.

"Formerly the nights were quieter," thought Klimkov. He rose, and walked away, without putting his arms into the sleeves of his coat, his hat pushed back on his neck.

"Well, all right, wait," he thought, doing violence to himself. Finally he decided : "I'll deliver them over, and as a reward I'll ask to be transferred to another city. That's all."

He reluctantly surrendered himself to the desire to revenge himself upon Olga, and strengthened the feeling with a supreme effort. Nevertheless it continued to cover his heart with a thin film, and was constantly breaking down, so that he had to fortify it again. Beneath this desire unexpectedly appeared another, not strong, but restless. He wanted to see the girl once more, wanted to listen in silence to her talk, to sit with her in her room. He quenched the longing with thoughts that designedly lowered Olga.

"If I had a lot of money, you would dance naked before me. I knew your lewd set." But to himself he said obdurately : "You won't sully her ; you won't attain it."

He wanted this or the other, but neither this nor the other was attainable. In calmer moments he realized this truth, which fairly crushed him, and plunged him into a heavy sleep troubled by nightmares.

CHAPTER XXII

BUT Yevsey pursued his work precisely. He gave Makarov a few heavy bundles of type in three instalments, and cleverly found out from him where the printing-press would be established. This elicited public commendation from Sasha.

" Good boy ! Now we have six in our hands—that's not so bad, Klimkov. You will receive a reward."

Yevsey treated his praise indifferently. When Sasha was gone, the sharp face of Maklakov, which had grown thin, leaped into his eyes. The spy, sitting in a dark corner of the room on a sofa, looked into Yevsey's face, twirling his moustache, frowning, and vexed. Something in his look provoked Yevsey, who turned aside.

" Klimkov, come here," the spy called out.

Klimkov turned back, and seated himself next to Maklakov.

" Is it true that you delivered up your brother ?" asked Maklakov in a low voice.

" My cousin."

" You're not sorry ?"

" No." Yevsey quietly and angrily repeated the phrase that the officials often uttered. " For us, as for soldiers, there is neither mother, nor father, nor brother, only enemies of the Czar and our country."

"Well, of course," said Maklakov, and smiled. After a pause he added : " Really, you are a ' good boy !' "

By his voice and smile Klimkov understood that the spy was making sport of him. He felt offended.

"Maybe I am sorry."

"Yes ?"

"But if I have to serve honestly and faithfully——"

"Of course. I'm not disputing with you, you queer fellow."

Then Maklakov lighted a cigarette, and asked Yevsey :

"Why are you sitting here ?"

"Oh, for no reason. I have nothing to do."

Maklakov slapped him on his knee, and suddenly said :

"You're a poor unfortunate brother, little man."

Yevsey rose.

"Timofey Vasilyevich," he began in a trembling voice.

"Well, what is it ?"

"Tell me——"

"Tell you what ?"

"I don't know."

"Well, I don't either."

Klimkov mumbled :

"I am sorry for my cousin—and there's a girl there, too. They are all better than we, by God they are. Really and truly they're better."

Maklakov also rose to his feet, stretched himself, and stepping to the door, uttered coldly :

"Go to the devil !"

Yevsey remained alone.

"Well, there!" thought he ; "there's another fellow—

all alike. First they draw me on, then they push me away."

The vengeful feeling toward Olga awoke in him, and blended with his sense of ill-will toward all people, which found ample nourishment in his soul, powerless to resist because of the poison of many insults. Yevsey vigorously set to work to enmesh himself in a net of new moods, and he served now with a dull zeal hitherto unknown to him.

Gradually the night came upon which it had been decided to arrest Olga, Yakov, and all implicated in the affair of the printing-press whom Yevsey had succeeded in tracking. He knew that the printing-office was located in the wing of a house set in a garden, and occupied by a large, red-bearded man named Kostya and his wife, a stout, pock-marked woman. He also knew that Olga was the servant of these two people. Kostya's head was close-cropped, and his wife had a grey face and restless eyes. Upon Yevsey both produced the impression of witless persons, or persons who have lain in a hospital a long time.

" What fearful people they are !" he remarked to Yakov when he pointed them out one evening during a party at Makarov's lodging.

Yakov loved to boast of his acquaintances. He proudly shook his curly head, and explained with an air of importance :

" It's from their hard life. They work in cellars at night, where it is damp and the air is close. They get their rest in prison. Both of them are fugitives, who live on other people's passports. Such a life turns everybody inside out and upside down. They're jolly people, too. When Kostya begins to tell about his life, you would think it is nothing but tears ; but he talks so that when he is done your sides ache from laughing. You can't trap such people very easily."

Klimkov decided to get a last look at Olga. He learned through what street the prisoners would be led, and went to meet them, trying to persuade himself that all this did not touch him. All the time he was thinking about the girl.

" She'll certainly be frightened. She'll cry."

He walked, as always, keeping in the shade. He tried once or twice to whistle carelessly, but never succeeded in checking the steady streams of recollection about Olga. He saw her calm face, her trusting eyes, listened to her somewhat broken voice, and remembered her words :

" It's no use for you to talk so badly about people, Klimkov. Why, have you nothing to reproach yourself with ? Suppose everybody were to say what you say, ' It's hard for me to live, because everybody is so mean,' why, that would be ridiculous. Can't you see ? Value yourself highly, but do not lower others. What right have you to do that ?"

When listening to Olga, Yevsey had always felt that she spoke the truth. Now, too, he had no cause to doubt it. But he was filled with the sheer desire to see her frightened, pitiful, and in tears.

From afar the wheels of an equipage began to rumble ; the horses' shoes clattered. Klimkov pressed himself against the gate of a house, and waited. The carriage rolled by him. He looked at it unconcernedly, saw two gloomy faces— the grey beard of the driver, and the large moustache of the sergeant at his side.

" That's all," thought he; " and I didn't get a chance to see her."

But another carriage came rolling from the end of the

street, and passed him quickly. Yevsey listened to the cut of the whip on the horse's body, and its tired snorting. The sounds seemed to hang motionless in the air. He thought they would hang there for ever.

Olga, with her head wrapped in a kerchief, was sitting at the side of a young gendarme. On the coach-box beside the driver rose the figure of the policeman. A familiar face darted by, white and good. Yevsey understood more than saw that Olga was perfectly calm, was not in the least frightened. For some reason he suddenly grew glad, and said to himself, as if retorting to an unpleasant interlocutor :

" She won't cry, not she !"

Closing his eyes and smiling, he stood a while longer. Then he heard steps and the jingling of spurs, and he comprehended that the men prisoners were being led along the street. He tore himself from the place, and, trying to make his footsteps inaudible, quickly ran down the street and turned the first corner. He kept up the same rapid pace almost the entire way to his home, at which he arrived exhausted and covered with sweat.

The evening of the next day, Philip Philippovich, casting his glassy stare upon Yevsey, said ceremoniously, in a thinner voice than usual :

" I congratulate you, Klimkov, on your fine achievement. I hope it will be the first link in a long chain of successes."

Klimkov shifted from one foot to the other, and quietly spread out his arms, as if desiring to free himself from the invisible chain.

There were a few spies in the room. They listened in silence to the sawlike voice, and looked at Yevsey, who, without seeing them, felt their glances upon his skin. He felt awkward and annoyed.

When Philip Philippovich had finished talking, Yevsey quietly asked him for a transfer to another city.

" That's nonsense, brother," said Philip Philippovich dryly. " It's a shame to be a coward, especially at this time. What's the matter ? Your first success ! yet you want to be running off. I myself know when a transfer is necessary. Go."

" There, they've rewarded me," thought Klimkov dismally, and with a sense of hurt. But he was mistaken. The reward came from Sasha.

" Hey, you mushroom, you !" he called to him ; " there, take this."

Touching Yevsey's hand with his dark yellow hand, he thrust a piece of paper into his grasp, and walked away.

Yakov Zarubin leaped up to Yevsey.

" How much ?"

" Twenty-five rubles," said Klimkov, unfolding the bill with reluctant fingers.

" How many people were there ?"

" Seven."

" Seven ? Ugh !"

Zarubin raised his eyes to the ceiling, and mumbled :

" Twice—no, three times seven is twenty-one. Four into seven—three and a half per person."

He whistled softly, and, looking round, announced :

" Sasha got a hundred and fifty, and his bill of expenses in the affair was sixty-three rubles. They cheat us fools. Well, what now, Yevsey ? Give us a treat. For luck !"

" Come," said Klimkov, looking askance at the money. He could not make up his mind to put it in his pocket.

CHAPTER XXIII

On the way Zarubin said in a business-like way :

" After all, your people seem to have been trash."

" Why ?" asked Klimkov, offended. He sighed, and said in a lower voice : " Not trash a bit."

" They gave little for them—very little. Ugh ! I know how such things are done. You can't fool me, not a bit. Krasavin once caught a single revolutionist, and he got a hundred rubles. Do you hear ? And they sent him another hundred from St. Petersburg. Solovyov got seventy-five for an illegal lady. You see ? And Maklakov, ugh ! Of course, he catches advocates, professors, writers, who have a special price. They are not dangerous, but I suppose it must be hard to catch them."

Zarubin spoke without ceasing. Klimkov was satisfied with his tattle, which kept him from thinking of the oppressive something that lay in his breast like a cold stone.

The two youths entered a public-house. Zarubin, in the confident voice of a habitué, asked the tall, thin, one-eyed housekeeper :

" Is Lydia well ? And Kapa ? There, Yevsey, you will get acquainted with Kapa. She's a girl, I tell you— a monster ! She'll teach you what you wouldn't learn in a hundred years without her. Well, give us lemon-

ade and cognac. First of all, Yevsey, we must take a
bit of cognac with lemonade. That's a sort of cham-
pagne. It lifts you up into the air at once. All
right ?"

" All the same to me."

The house, apparently, was an expensive one. The
windows were hung with sumptuous curtains. The
furniture seemed unusual to Yevsey, the prettily
dressed girls proud and inaccessible. All this dis-
tracted him. He squeezed himself into a corner,
stepping aside to let the girls pass, who went by him as
if they did not notice him. Their clothes grazed his
legs. The half-dressed bodies, painted and already
sweaty, lazily glided by in turn, bppressively. Their
eyes, set in pencilled lids, turned in their orbits. The
eyes were all large, though dead and uniform, notwithstanding their various colours.

" Students ?" asked a reddish girl of her companion,
a stout brunette with a high, bare bosom and a blue
ribbon about her neck. The one who whispered in her
ear made a grimace at Yevsey. He turned away from
her, and asked Zarubin in annoyance :

" Do they know who we are ?"

" Yes, of course. That's why they take only half
the price for entrance, and discount twenty-five per
cent. from the bill."

Yevsey emptied two beakers of the sparkling
beverage. Though it did not make him merrier, everything around him, nevertheless, assumed a more
uniform, less irritating, aspect. Two girls seated themselves at their table, Lydia and Kapitolina, the one tall
and strong, the other broad and heavy. Lydia's head
was absurdly small in proportion to her body ; her
forehead, too, was small ; her chin was sharp and

prominent, her mouth round, her teeth little and fine, like a fish's, and her eyes dark and cunning. Kapitolina seemed put together from a number of balls of various sizes. Her protruding eyes were also like balls, and dull as a blind person's.

Little black Zarubin was restless as a fly. He smelt at everything, turned his head from side to side, moved his legs up and down and sideways, and his thin, dark hands flew over the table to seize everything and feel everything. Yevsey suddenly began to feel a heavy, dull irritation rising in him against Zarubin.

"The skunk!" he thought. "He brought me a monster for my money, and chose a pretty one for himself."

But Yevsey knew that his annoyance at Zarubin had a deeper-seated cause than this. He filled a large glass of cognac, swallowed it, and opened his burned mouth and rolled his eyes.

"Capital!" shouted Yakov.

The girls laughed, and for a minute Yevsey was deaf and blind, as if he had fallen fast asleep.

"This Lydia, Yevsey, my true friend, is a wise girl—oh, so wise!" Zarubin waked him, pulling his sleeve. "Whenever I merit the attention of the officials, I will take her away from here, will marry her, and will establish her in my business. Yes, Lydia darling? Ugh!"

"We'll see," replied the girl languidly, looking sidewise at his oily eyes.

"Why are you silent, friend Yevsey?" asked Kapitolina, slapping Yevsey's shoulder with her heavy hand.

"She addresses everybody by the first name," Yakov remarked.

"All the same to me," said Yevsey, without looking at the girl, and moving away from her. "Only tell her that I don't like her, and she should go away."

For a few seconds all kept silent.

"To the devil with you!" said Kapitolina thickly and calmly. Propping herself on the table with her hands, she slowly lifted her heavy body from the chair. Yevsey was annoyed because she was not offended. He looked at her, and said :

"A species of elephant."

"How impolite!" shouted Lydia compassionately.

"Ugh! Yes, Yevsey. That's impolite, brother. Kapitolina Nikolayevna is an excellent girl. All connoiseurs value her."

"To me it's all the same," said Yevsey. "I want beer."

"Hey, there, beer!" shouted Zarubin. "Kapa dear, be so kind as to see we get beer."

The stout girl turned and left, scraping her feet. Zarubin, bending over to Yevsey, began insinuatingly and didactically :

"You see, Yevsey, of course this is an establishment of such a kind, and so on ; but still, the girls are human beings like you and me. Why should you insult them uselessly? Ugh! They're not all here of their own accord."

"Stop!" said Klimkov.

He wanted everything around him to be quiet. He wanted the girls to cease floating in the air, like melancholy drifts of spring clouds torn by the wind. He wanted the shaven pianist with the dark blue face, like that of a drowned person, to stop rapping his fingers on

251

the yellow teeth of the piano, which resembled the jaw of a huge monster—a monster that roared and shrieked loud laughter. He wanted the curtains of the windows to cease flapping so strangely, as if someone's unseen and spiteful hand were pulling at them from the street. Olga, dressed in white, should station herself at the door. Then he would rise, walk round the room, and would strike everybody in the face with all his might. Let Olga see that they were all repulsive to him, and that she wasn't right, and understood nothing.

The complaining words of Zarubin settled themselves obstinately in his ears :

" We came here to make merry, but you at once begin a scandal."

Yevsey, his whole body swaying, gave a dull glance into Yakov's face, and suddenly said to himself with cold precision :

" On account of that—sneak, I fell into this pit of an infernal life—all on account of him !"

He took a full bottle of beer into his hands, filled a glass for himself, drank it out, and, without letting go of it, rose from his seat.

" The money is mine, not yours, you skunk !"

" What of it ? We are comrades !"

Zarubin's black head, cropped and prickly, fell back. Yevsey saw the sharp, gleaming little eyes on the swarthy face, saw the set teeth.

" You wait. Sit down."

Klimkov waved the bottle, and hit him in the face, aiming at his eyes. The ruddy blood gleamed oily and moist, awakening a ferocious joy in Klimkov. He swung his hand once again, pouring the beer over himself. Everybody began to cry, " Oh, oh !" to

THE SPY

scream and rock. Somebody's nails drove themselves into Klimkov's face. He was seized by the arms and legs, lifted from the floor, and carried off. Somebody spat warm, sticky saliva into his face, squeezed his throat, and tore his hair.

He came to his senses in the police-station, all in tatters, scratched, and wet. He at once remembered everything.

" What will happen now ?" was his first thought, though unaccompanied by alarm.

A police officer whom he knew advised him to wash his face and ride home.

" Are they going to try me ?"

" I don't know," said the police officer, who sighed, and added enviously : " Hardly. Your department is a power. It is permitted everything. So they'll take care of you."

Yevsey smiled.

After several days of a sort of even, indistinct life without impressions and excitement, Yevsey was summoned to the presence of Philip Philippovich, who shouted shrilly a long time.

" You idiot ! you ought to set other people an example of good conduct. You ought not to make scandals. Please remember that. If I learn anything of the same kind about you, I'll place you under arrest for a month. Do you hear ?"

Klimkov was frightened. He shrank within himself, and began to live quietly, silently, unobserved, trying to exhaust himself as much as possible in order to escape thought.

When he met Yakov Zarubin, he saw a small red scar over his right eye, which new feature on the mobile face was pleasant to him. The consciousness that he had found the courage and the power to strike a person raised him in his own eyes.

"Why did you do it to me?" asked Yakov.

"Did I?" said Yevsey. "I was drunk."

"Oh, you devil! You know what a face means in our service. We can't afford to spoil it."

Zarubin demanded to be treated to a good dinner from Yevsey.

CHAPTER XXIV

KLIMKOV did not succeed in hiding himself from the power of hostile thoughts. They appeared again.

The news spread among the spies that some of the Ministers had also been bribed by the enemies of the Czar and Russia. They had formed a cabal to take his power from him, and replace the existing good Russian order of life by another order borrowed from foreign governments, which, of course, would be pernicious to the Russian people. Now these Ministers issued a manifesto, in which they announced that, with the will and consent of the Czar, freedom would soon be given to the people to assemble wherever they pleased, to speak about whatever interested them, and to write and publish everything they needed to in newspapers. Moreover, they would even be granted the liberty not to believe in God.

The authorities, dismal and demoralized, again began to rush about anxiously. They again spoke kindly to the spies, and though they did not demand anything of the agents, nor advise them what to do, it was apparent that preparations were being made for the disclosure of something significant and important. For whole hours Philip Philippovich would consult secretly with Krasavin, Sasha, Solovyov, and other experienced agents, after which they all went about gloomy and preoccupied, and gave brief, unintelligible responses to the questions of their comrades.

Once the voice of Sasha, virulent and breaking with excitement, leaked through the door standing slightly ajar between the outer office and the cabinet of Philip Philippovich.

" It's not about the constitution, not about politics, that we ought to speak to them. We must tell them that the new order would destroy them—the quiet among them would die of starvation, the more forward would rot in prison. What sort of men have we in our service ? Hybrids, degenerates, the physically sick, stupid animals."

" You talk God knows what," Philip Philippovich piped aloud.

The mournful voice of Yasnogursky was heard next.

" What a scheme you have ! My good man, I can't understand what you're driving at."

Piotr, Grokhotov, Yevsey, and two new spies were sitting in the office. One of the novices was a reddish, hook-nosed man, with large freckles on his face and gold glasses, the other shaven, bald, and red-cheeked, with a broad nose and a purple birthmark on his neck near his left ear. They listened attentively to Sasha's talk, glancing at each other sideways. All kept silent. Piotr rose a number of times, and walked to the door. Finally he coughed aloud near it, upon which an invisible hand immediately closed it. The bald spy carefully felt his nose with his thick fingers, and asked quietly :

" Who was it he called hybrids ?"

At first nobody responded, then Grokhotov, sighing humbly, said :

" He calls everybody hybrids."

THE SPY

" A smart beast !" exclaimed Piotr, smiling dreamily. " Rotten to the core, but just see how his power keeps rising ! That's what education will do for you."

The bald-headed spy looked at everybody with his mole eyes, and again asked hesitatingly :

" What does he mean—eh, eh—does he mean us ?"

" Politics," said Grokhotov. " Politics is a wise business. It's not squeamish."

" If I had received an education, I, too, would have turned up trumps," declared Piotr.

The red-headed spy carelessly swung himself on his chair, his mouth frequently gaping in a wide yawn.

Sasha emerged from the cabinet, livid and dishevelled. He stopped at the door, and looked at everybody.

" Eavesdropping, eh ?" he asked sarcastically.

The rest of the spies dropped into the office one by one, wearily and dismally, flinging various remarks at one another. Maklakov came in an ill humour. The look in his eyes was sharp and insulting. He passed quickly into the cabinet, and banged the door behind him.

" Tables are going to be turned," Sasha said to Piotr. " We'll be the secret society, and they'll remain patent fools. That's what's going to happen. Hey !" he shouted, " no one is to leave the office. There's going to be a meeting."

All grew still. Yasnogursky came out from the cabinet with a broad smile widening his large mouth. His protuberant, fleshy ears reached to the back of his neck. All sleek and slippery, he produced the impression of a large piece of soap. He walked among the crowd of spies pressing their hands, and kindly and humbly nodding his head. Suddenly he walked off into a corner, and began to address the agents in a lachrymose voice :

" Good servants of the Czar, it is with a heart penetrated by grief that I address myself to you—to you, men without fear, men without reproach, true children of the Czar, your father, and of the true Orthodox Church, your mother—to you I speak."

" Look at him howling !" somebody whispered near Yevsey, who thought he heard Yasnogursky utter an ugly oath.

" You already know of the fresh cunning of the enemy, of the new and baneful plot. You read the proclamation of Minister Bulygin, in which it is said that our Czar wishes to renounce the power entrusted to him by our Lord God over Russia and the Russian people. All this, dear comrades and brothers, is the infernal game of people who have delivered over their souls to foreign capitalists. It is a new attempt to ruin our sacred Russia. What do they want to attain with the Duma they have promised ? What do they want to attain by this very constitution and liberty ?"

The spies moved closer together.

" In the name of the Father, Son, and Holy Ghost, let us examine the snares of the devils in the light of truth. Let us look at them with our simple Russian mind, and we'll see how they scatter like dust before our eyes. Just look ! They want to deprive the Czar of his Divine power, his liberty to rule the country according to the dictates from on high. They want to arrange popular elections, so that the people should send their representatives to the Czar, who would promulgate laws abridging his power. They hope that our people, ignorant and drunk, will permit themselves to be bought with wine and money, and will bring into the Czar's palace those who are pointed out to them by the traitors, Liberals, and revolutionists. And whom will they point out ? Jews, Poles, Armenians, Germans, and other strangers, enemies of Russia."

Klimkov observed that Sasha, standing at the back of Yasnogursky, smiled sardonically like the devil. He inclined his head to keep the sick spy from noticing him.

" This band of venal swindlers will surround the bright throne of our Czar, and will close his wise eyes to the destiny of our country. They will deliver Russia over into the hands of strangers and foreigners. The Jews will establish their government in Russia, the Poles their government, the Armenians and the Georgians theirs, the Letts theirs, and other paupers whom Russia took under the shelter of her powerful hand theirs. They will establish their governments, and when we Russians remain alone—then—then—it means——"

Sasha, standing at Yasnogursky's side, began to whisper into his ear. The old man waved him off in annoyance, and said aloud :

" Then the Germans and the English will rush upon us, and will clutch us in their greedy paws. The destruction of Russia is threatening us, dear comrades, my friends. Have a care !"

The last words of his speech were uttered in a shout ; then he lapsed into silence lasting about a minute, after which he raised his hand over his head, and resumed his discourse :

" But our Czar has friends. They watch over his power and over his glory like faithful dogs unbought. They have organized a society for war upon the dastardly conspiracies of the revolutionists, upon the constitution, and every abomination destructive to us, the true Russian people. Counts and princes celebrated for their services to the Czar in Russia are entering this organization, governors submissive to the will of the Czar and faithful to the covenant of our sacred past. Perhaps even the very highest——"

Sasha again stopped Yasnogursky. The old man listened to him, grew red, waved his hands, and suddenly shouted :

"Well, speak. What does it mean ? What right have you—I don't want to——"

He gave an odd little leap, and, pushing the crowd of spies apart, walked away. Sasha now took his place, and stood there tall and stooping, with head thrust forward. Looking around with his red eyes, and rubbing his hands, he asked sharply :

"Well, did you understand ?"

"We did—we did," several voices sounded sullenly and half-heartedly.

"Of course !" exclaimed Sasha in derision. Then he began to speak, pronouncing every word with the precision of a hammer-blow. His voice rang with malice.

"Let those also listen who are wiser. Let them explain my words to the fools. The revolutionists, the Liberals, our Russian gentry in general, have conquered. Do you understand ? The administration has resolved to yield to their demands ; it wants to give them a constitution. What does a constitution mean to you ? Starvation, death, because you are idlers and do-nothings ; you are no good for any sort of work. It means prison for the most of you, because most of you have merited it ; for a few others it means the hospital, the insane asylum, because there are a whole

lot of half-witted men, physically sick, among you.
The new order of life, if established, will make quick
work of you all. The Police Department will be
destroyed, the Department of Safety will be shut down ;
you will be turned out into the street. Do you
understand ?"

All were silent, as if turned to stone.

" Then I would go away somewhere," Klimkov
thought.

" I think it's plain," said Sasha, after a period of
silence. As he again embraced his audience in his
look, the red band on his forehead seemed to have
spread over his whole face, and his face to become
covered with a leaden blue.

" You ought to realize that this change is not
advantageous to you, that you don't want it. Therefore you must fight against it now. Isn't that so ?
For whom, in whose interest, are you going to fight ?
For your own selves, for your interests, for your right
to live as you have lived up to this time. Is what I say
clear ? What can we do ? Let everyone think about
this question."

A heavy noise suddenly arose in the close room, as if
a huge sick breast were sighing and rattling. Some of
the spies walked away silently and sullenly with
drooping heads. One man grumbled in vexation :

" They tell us this and they tell us that. Why don't
they increase our salaries instead ?"

" They keep frightening us—always frightening us."

In the corner near Sasha about a dozen men had
gathered. Yevsey quietly moved up to the group, and
heard the enraptured voice of Piotr.

" That's the way to speak ! Twice two are four,
and all are aces."

THE SPY

" No, I'm not satisfied," said Solovyov sweetly, with a prying note in his voice. " Think ! What does it mean to think ? Everyone may think in his own way. You should tell me what to do."

" You *have* been told !" put in Krasavin roughly and sharply.

" *I* don't understand," Maklakov declared calmly.

" You ?" shouted Sasha. " You lie ! You do understand !"

" No."

" And I say you do ; but you're a coward, you're a nobleman—and—and—and I know you."

" Maybe," said Maklakov. " But do you know what you want ?" He spoke in so cold a tone, and put so much significance into his voice, that Yevsey trembled, and thought :

" Will Sasha strike him ?"

Sasha, however, merely repeated the question in a screeching voice :

" I ? Do I know what I want ?"

" Yes."

" I will tell you." Sasha raised his voice threateningly. " I am soon going to die. I have nobody to fear. I am a stranger to life. I live with hatred of good people before whom you in your thoughts crouch on your knees. Don't you know ? You lie. You are a slave—a slave in your soul ; a lackey, though you are a nobleman—and I am a muzhik, a perspicacious muzhik. Even though I attended the University, nothing has corrupted me."

Yevsey felt that Sasha's words crawled in his heart like spiders, enmeshing him in gluey threads, squeezing him, tying him up, and drawing him to Sasha. He pressed through to the front, and stood alongside the combatants, trying to see the faces of both at the same time.

"I know my enemy. It's you, the gentry. You are gentlemen, even as spies. You are abhorrent everywhere, everywhere execrable, men and women, writers and spies. But I know a means for having done with you gentlemen, the gentry. I know a way. I see what ought to be done with you, how to destroy you."

"That's the very point that's interesting, not your hysterics," said Maklakov, thrusting his hands in his pockets.

"Yes, it's interesting to you? Very well, I'll tell you."

Sasha evidently wanted to sit down, for he vacillated like a pendulum. He looked around as he spoke without pause, and growing breathless from his quick utterance.

"Who orders life? The gentry. Who spoiled the pretty animal man? Who made him a dirty beast, a sick beast? You, the gentry. Hence all this, the whole of life, ought to be turned against you. So we must open all the ulcers of life, and drown you in the stream of abomination that will flow from them, in the vomit of the people you have poisoned. A curse on you! The time of your execution and destruction has come. All those who have been mutilated by you are rising against you, and they'll choke you, crush you —you understand? Yes, that's how it will be—nay, it already is. In some cities they have already tried to find out how firmly the heads of the gentlemen are fixed on their shoulders. You know that, don't you?"

Sasha staggered back, and leaned against the wall,

stretching his arms forward, and choking and gasping over a broken laugh. Maklakov glanced at the men standing around him, and asked, also with a laugh:

" Did you understand what he said ?"

" One can say whatever he pleases," replied Solovyov ; but the next instant added hastily, " in one's own company. The most interesting thing would be to find out for certain whether a secret society has actually been organized in St. Petersburg, and for what purpose."

" That's what we want to know," said Krasavin in a tone of demand, " and what sort of people are in it, too."

" In reality, brothers, the revolution has been transferred to other quarters," exclaimed Piotr merrily and animatedly.

" If there really are princes in that society," Solovyov meditated dreamily, " then our business ought to improve."

" You have twenty thousand in the bank, anyway, old devil."

" And maybe thirty. Count again," said Solovyov in an offended tone, and stepped aside.

Sasha coughed dully and hoarsely, while Maklakov regarded him with a scowl. Yevsey gradually freed himself from the thin shackles of the attraction that the sick spy had unexpectedly begun to exert upon him. His talk, which at first had seized Klimkov, now dissolved and disappeared from his soul like dust under rain.

" What are you looking at me for ?" shouted Sasha at Maklakov.

Maklakov turned and walked away without answering. Yevsey involuntarily followed him.

"Did you understand anything?" Maklakov suddenly inquired of Yevsey.

"I don't like it."

"No? Why?"

"He's always rancorous, and there's rancour enough without him."

"Yes, so there is," said Maklakov, nodding his head. "There's rancour enough."

"And it's impossible to understand anything," Klimkov continued, looking around cautiously. "Everybody speaks differently——"

The words had scarcely left his mouth when he grew alarmed, and glanced sidewise at Maklakov's face. The spy pensively brushed the dust from his hat with his handkerchief, apparently oblivious of the dangerous words.

"Well, good-bye," he said, holding out his hand to Yevsey, who wanted to accompany him. But the spy put on his hat, and twirling his moustache, walked out without so much as looking at him.

CHAPTER XXV

SOMETHING strange, like a dream, grew in the city, rushing onward with irresistible rapidity. People lost their fear completely. On the faces which only a short time ago had been flat and humble an expression of conscious power and preoccupation now appeared sharply and clearly. All recalled builders preparing to pull down an old structure, and busily considering the best way of beginning the work.

Almost every day the working men in the factory suburb openly arranged meetings, at which known revolutionists appeared, who in the very presence of the police and officials of the Department of Safety sharply censured the order of life, and pointed out that the manifesto of the Minister convoking the Duma was an attempt of the administration to pacify the people, who were stirred up by misfortune, in order to deceive them in the end, as always. The speakers urged their listeners not to believe anybody except their own reason.

Once, when a rebel orator shouted, " The people alone are the true and legal masters of life ; to them belong the whole earth and all freedom," a triumphant roar came in reply : " True, brother !"

Yevsey, deafened by the shouts, turned away, and met Melnikov, who had been standing behind him.

His eyes burned, he was black and dishevelled. He flapped his arms, as a crow flaps its wings, and bawled :

" Tr-r-rue !"

Klimkov pulled the skirt of his coat in amazement, and whispered in a low voice :

" What ails you ? The speaker is a Socialist. He's under surveillance."

Melnikov blinked his eyes, and asked :

" He ?" Without awaiting a reply, he shouted again : " Hurray ! true !" Then to Yevsey, very angrily : " Get out ! It's all the same who speaks the truth."

Yevsey smiled timidly at the new speeches. He looked around helplessly for some person in the crowd with whom he might speak openly ; but on finding a pleasant face that inspired confidence, he sighed and thought :

" I'll begin to talk with him, and he'll at once understand that I'm a spy."

He frequently heard the revolutionists speak of the necessity of arranging another life upon earth. Dreams of his childhood returned, broadened and filled him with content. He believed in the hot, fearless words. But the faith grew feebly and lazily upon the shaky, slimy soil of his soul, choked with impressions, poisoned by fear, and exhausted by violence. His faith was like a child suffering with rachitis, bow-legged, with large eyes always gazing into the distance.

Yevsey admired the beautiful growth of the rebellion, but he lacked the power to fall in love with it. He believed words ; he did not believe people. The dreams stirring his heart died the instant they touched it. A timorous spectator, he walked along the shore of a stream without the desire to plunge into its soul-refreshing waves. At the same time, he longed wistfully for someone to triumph, for someone to make life calm and pleasing, and point out a comfortable place in it where he might find repose.

At first he could not comprehend why both the revolutionists and the officers of the spies censured the administration, why both asserted that someone wanted to deceive the people. When the people themselves, however, came out into the street, and began to speak, Yevsey stopped to think about this question.

The spies walked about slowly, indolently; they all grew strange to one another, maintaining sullen silence, and looking into the eyes of their comrades suspiciously, as if expecting something dangerous from one another. The officials ceased to talk, and sank into the background. They gave out no plans of action, and said nothing new.

"Has nothing been heard in regard to this St. Petersburg league of princes?" Krasavin asked almost every day.

Once Piotr joyously announced:

"Boys, Sasha has been summoned to St. Petersburg. He'll fix up a game there, you'll see."

Viakhirev, the hook-nosed, reddish spy, remarked lazily:

"The League of Russian People has been permitted to organize fighting bands to kill the revolutionists. I'll go there; I'm a good shot."

"A pistol is a fine thing," said someone. "You shoot, and then run away."

"How simply they speak about everything!" thought Yevsey. He involuntarily recalled other conversations—Olga and Makarov—which he impatiently pushed away from himself.

Sasha returned from St. Petersburg, as it were, stronger. Concentrated green sparks gleamed in his dim eyes. His voice had become deeper, his entire body seemed to have straightened and grown sounder.

" What are we going to do ?" asked Piotr.

" You'll soon find out," answered Sasha, showing his teeth.

Autumn came, as always, quiet and melancholy. But the people did not remark its advent. Yesterday bold and noisy, to-day they came out into the streets still bolder, still more confident, and upheld Yevsey's faith in their victory, in the nearness of a calm, peaceful, comfortable life.

Then came the fabulously terrible and marvellous days, when all the people ceased to work, and the customary life, that for so long had held oppressive sway —oppressive in its cruelty and aimless play—suddenly ceased, as if crushed by a giant embrace. The people refused the city, their ruler, bread, fire, and water ; and for a number of nights it stood in darkness, hungry, thirsty, sullen and affronted. During those dark, insulting nights, the working people walked through the streets with song, childish joy shining in their eyes. For the first time they clearly saw their power, and themselves were amazed at its significance. They understood their might in life, and good-naturedly exulted, looking at the blinded houses, the motionless dead machines, the dumbfounded police, the closed, ever-hungry jaws of the shops and restaurants, the frightened faces, the humble figures of those persons who had never learned to work, but only to eat much, and who therefore considered themselves the best blood in the city. Their power over people had been torn from their impotent hands in these days, yet their cruelty and cunning remained. Klimkov looked at the people accustomed to command now silently submitting to the will of the hungry, poor, and unwashed. He understood that it had become a shame for the lords to live. So, trying to cover up their shame, they smiled approvingly upon the working people, and lied to them. They were afraid of the workers. In spite of the lords, however, it seemed to Yevsey that the past would not return. He felt that new masters had arisen, and if they had been able all of a sudden to stop the course of life, then they would now be able to arrange it differently, more freely, and more easily for themselves and for all.

The old, the cruel, and the malicious abandoned the city. It melted away in the darkness. The people perceptibly grew better, and though the city remained without illumination, yet the nights were stirring, merry as the days.

Everywhere crowds of people gathered and spoke animatedly in free, bold, human speech, of the approaching days of the triumph of truth. They believed in it hotly. The unbelievers were silent, but looked into the new faces, impressing the new speech upon their minds.

Often Klimkov observed the spies in the crowds of people. Not wishing to be seen by them, he walked away. He met Melnikov more frequently than the others. This man roused his particular interest. A dense crowd of people always gathered around him, and his thick voice flowed from the centre of the group like a dark stream.

" There, you see ! The people wanted it, and everything is up. If the people want it, they will take everything into their own hands. They're a power, the people are. Remember this—don't let what you have obtained slip from your grasp. Take care ! More than everything, guard against the cunning of various gentlemen. Away with them. Drive them off ! If they dispute, beat them to death."

When Klimkov heard this, he thought :

" For such talk people used to be put in prison. What numbers have been put in prison ! And now they speak that way themselves."

He wandered about in the crowd alone from morning until late at night. Sometimes he had an irresistible yearning to speak ; but as soon as he felt the desire coming upon him, he immediately walked off into empty by-streets and dark corners.

" If I speak, they'll recognize me," he thought with importunate dread. And he comforted himself by reflecting : " No hurry ! I'll have time enough yet to speak."

One night, while walking along the street, he saw Maklakov hidden in a gateway, looking up to a lighted window on the opposite side of the street like a hungry dog waiting for a sop.

" Keeps at his work," thought Yevsey ; then said to Maklakov : " Do you want me to take your place, Timofey Vasilyevich ?"

" You—me, Yevsey ?" exclaimed the spy in a subdued voice ; and Klimkov felt that something was wrong, for it was the first time that the spy had ever addressed him by the first name. Moreover, Maklakov's voice was not his own. " No, go," he said.

The spy, always so smooth and decorous, now had a shabby appearance. His hair, as a rule carefully and prettily combed behind his ears, lay in disorder over his forehead and temples. He smelt of whisky.

" Good-bye," said Yevsey, raising his hat and walking off slowly. He had taken only a few steps, however, when he heard a call behind him :

" Listen !"

Yevsey turned back to Maklakov noiselessly, and stood beside him.

" Let's walk together."

" He must be very drunk," thought Yevsey.

" Do you know who lives in that house ?" asked Maklakov, looking back.

" No."

" Mironov, the writer. Do you remember him ?"

" I do."

" Well, I should think you would. He made you out a fool so simply."

" Yes," agreed Yevsey.

They walked slowly with noiseless tread. The narrow street was quiet, deserted, and cold.

" Let's go back," continued Maklakov. Then he adjusted his hat on his head, buttoned his overcoat, and declared thoughtfully : " Brother, I am going away—to Argentine. That's in America."

Klimkov heard something hopeless, dismal, in his words, and he, too, began to feel gloomy and awkward.

" Why—so far ?"

" I must."

Maklakov again stopped opposite the illuminated window and looked up to it silently. Like a huge solitary eye on the black face of the house, it cast a peaceful beam of light into the darkness—a small island amid black and heavy waters.

" That's his window—Mironov's," said Maklakov

THE SPY

quietly. " That's the way he sits at night all by himself and writes. Come."

Some people advanced toward them singing softly :

" It comes ! it comes ! the last decisive fight !"

" We ought to cross to the other side," Yevsey proposed in a whisper.

" Are you afraid ?" asked Maklakov, though he was the first to step from the pavement to cross the frozen dirt of the middle of the street. " No reason to be afraid. These fellows, with their songs of war and all such things, are peaceful people. The wild beasts are not among *them*—no. It would be good to sit down now in some warm place in a café, but everything is closed, brother."

" Come home," Klimkov suggested.

" Home ? No, thank you. You can go if you want to."

Yevsey remained, submissively yielding to the sad foreboding of something inevitable. From the other side of the street came the sound of the people's talk.

" Misha, is it possible you don't believe ?" one asked in a ringing, joyous voice.

A soft bass answered :

" I do believe, but I say it won't happen so soon."

" Listen ! What a devil of a spy are you, eh ?" Maklakov suddenly demanded, nudging Yevsey with his elbow. " I've been watching you a long time. Your face always looks as if you had just taken an emetic."

Yevsey grew glad at the possibility of speaking about himself openly.

" I am going away, Timofey Vasilyevich," he quickly mumbled. " On the day that everything is arranged, I am going away. I'll gradually settle

273

myself in business, and I'm going to live quietly by myself——"

" Wait ! As soon as what is arranged ?"

" Why, all this about the new life—when the people start out all for themselves."

" Eh, eh," drawled the spy, waving his hand and smiling. His smile robbed Yevsey of the desire to speak about himself.

They walked in silence again, and turned again. Both were gloomy.

" There, now," Maklakov exclaimed with unexpected roughness and acerbity, as they once more approached the author's house. " I'm really going away for ever entirely from Russia. Do you understand ? And I must hand over some papers to this—this author. You see this package ?"

He waved a white parcel before Yevsey's face, and continued quickly, in a low growl : " I won't go to him myself. This is the second day I've been on the watch for him, waiting for him to come out. But he's ill, and he won't come out. I would have given it to him in the street. I can't send it by mail. His letters are opened and stolen in the post-office, and given over to the Department of Safety. And it's absolutely impossible for me to go to him myself. Do you understand ?"

The spy, pressing the package to his breast, bent his head to look into Yevsey's eyes.

" My life is in this package. I have written about myself—my story—who I am, and why. I want him to read it—he loves people."

Taking Yevsey's shoulder in a vigorous clutch, the spy shook him, and commanded :

" You go and give it to him into his own hands—go,

tell him that one——" Maklakov broke off, and continued after a pause. " Tell him that a certain agent of the Department of Safety sent him these papers, and begs him most humbly—tell him that way, ' begs him most humbly '—to read them. I'll wait here for you in the street. Go. But look out, don't tell him I'm here. If he asks, tell him I've escaped, and gone to the Argentine. Repeat what I've told you."

" Gone to the Argentine."

" And don't forget, ' begs most humbly.' "

" No, I won't."

" Go on, quick !"

Giving Klimkov a gentle shove on the back, he escorted him to the door of the house, walked away, and stopped to observe him.

Yevsey, agitated and seized with a fine tremor, lost consciousness of his own personality, crushed by the commanding words of Maklakov. He pushed the electric button, and felt ready to crawl through the door in the desire to hide himself from the spy as quickly as possible. He struck it with his knee, and it opened. A dark figure loomed in the light ; a voice asked testily :

" What do you want ?"

" The writer, Mr. Mironov—himself in person. I have been told to deliver a package into his own hands. Please, quick !" said Yevsey, involuntarily imitating the rapid and incoherent talk of Maklakov. Everything became confused in his brain. But the words of the spy lay there, white and cold as dead bones. And when a somewhat dull voice reached him, " What can I do for you, young man ?" Yevsey said in an apathetic voice, like an automaton : " A certain agent of the Department of Safety sent you these papers, and begs you most humbly to read them. He has gone to the Argentine." The strange name embarrassed Yevsey, and he added in a lower voice : " The Argentine, which is in America."

" Yes, but where are the papers ?"

The voice sounded kind. Yevsey raised his head, and recognized the soldierly face with the reddish moustache. He pulled the package from his pocket, and handed it to him.

" Sit down."

Klimkov seated himself, keeping his head bowed. The sound of the tearing of the wrapping made him start. Without raising his head, he looked at the writer warily from under lowered lids. Mironov stood before him looking at the package, his moustache quivering.

" You say he's gone off ?"

" Yes."

" And you yourself are also an agent ?"

" Yes," said Yevsey quietly, and thought : " Now he'll scold me."

" Your face seems familiar to me."

Yevsey tried not to look at him, but he felt the writer was smiling.

" Yes, I suppose it is familiar to you," said Yevsey, sighing.

" Have you, too, been tracking me ?"

" Once. You saw me from the window. You came out into the street and gave me a letter."

" Yes, yes ; I remember. The devil ! So that was you ? Well, excuse me, my dear man. I think I must have offended you, eh ?"

Yevsey rose from the chair, looked into his laughing face incredulously, and glanced around.

" That's nothing," he said.

He felt unbearably awkward as he listened to the somewhat rude yet kindly voice. He was afraid that, after all, the writer would abuse him and drive him out.

" There, you see how strangely we meet this time, eh ?"

" Nothing else ?" asked Yevsey, confused.

" Nothing else. But I believe you are tired. Sit down. Rest."

" I must be going."

" Very well. As you please. Well, thank you. Good-bye."

He extended his large hand with reddish hairs on the fingers. Yevsey touched it cautiously.

" Permit me also to tell you my life," he requested unexpectedly to himself. When he had distinctly uttered these words, he instantly thought : " This is the very man to whom I ought to speak, if Timofey Vasilyevich himself, such a wise person, and better than everybody, respects him." Recalling Maklakov, Yevsey looked at the window, and for a moment grew anxious.

" No matter," he said to himself. " It's not the first time he's had to freeze."

" Well, why not ? Tell me, if you want to. Won't you take off your overcoat ? And perhaps you will have a glass of tea. It's cold."

Yevsey wanted to smile, but he restrained himself. In a few minutes, his eyes half closed, he monotonously and minutely told the writer about the village, about Yakov, and about the blacksmith. He spoke in the same voice in which he reported his observations in the Department of Safety.

THE SPY

The writer, whom Yevsey observed from under his lashes, was sitting on a broad heavy taborette, his elbows on the table, over which he bent, twirling his moustache with a quick movement of his fingers. His eyes gazed sharply and seriously into the distance above Klimkov's head.

" He doesn't hear me," thought Yevsey, and raised his voice a little, continuing to examine the room without himself being observed, and jealously watching the face of the author.

The room was dark and gloomy. The shelves, crammed with books, which increased the thickness of the walls, apparently did not admit the sounds from the street into this little room. Between the shelves the glass of the windows glistened dully, scaled by the cold darkness of the night, and the white narrow stain of the door obtruded itself on the eye. In the middle of the room was a table, whose covering of grey cloth seemed to lend a dark grey tone to everything around it.

Yevsey was ensconced in a corner of a chair covered with smooth leather. For some reason he propped his head hard against its high back, then slid down a little. The flames of the candles disturbed him ; the yellow tongues, slowly inclining toward each other, seemed to be holding a conversation. They trembled, and straightened themselves out, struggling upward. Behind the author, over the sofa, hung a large portrait, from which a yellow face with a sharp little beard looked out sternly.

The author began to twirl his moustache more slowly, but his look, as before, travelled beyond the confines of the room. All this disturbed Yevsey, breaking the thread of his recollections. He bethought himself of closing his eyes. When he did so, and darkness closely enveloped him, he sighed lightly. Suddenly he beheld himself divided in two—the man who had lived, and the other being who was able to tell about the first as about a stranger. His speech flowed on more easily, his voice grew stronger, and the events of his life drew themselves connectedly one after the other, unrolling easily like a ball of grey thread. They freed the little feeble soul from the dirty and cumbersome rags of its experiences. It was pleasant to Yevsey to tell about himself. He listened to his own voice with quiet astonishment. He spoke truthfully, and clearly saw that he had not been guilty of anything, for he had lived all his days, not as he had wanted to, but as he had been compelled to do ; and he had been compelled to do what was unpleasant and unnecessary to him. Filled with a sense of sincere self-pity, he was almost ready to weep and to fall in love with himself.

Whenever the author asked him a question which Yevsey did not understand, he would say, without opening his eyes, sternly and quietly :

" Wait ; I'm telling it in order."

He spoke without tiring, but when he came to the moment of his meeting with Maklakov, he suddenly stopped as before a pit. He opened his eyes, and saw at the window the dull look of the autumn morning, the cold grey depth of the sky. Heaving a deep sigh, he straightened himself up. He felt washed within, unusually light, unpleasantly empty. His heart was ready submissively to receive new orders, fresh violence.

The author rose noisily from his seat, tall and strong. He pressed his hands together, cracking his fingers disagreeably.

" What do you think of doing now ?" he asked,

as he turned to the window without looking at Klimkov.

Yevsey also rose, and repeated with assurance what he had told Maklakov.

" As soon as the new life is arranged, I'll quietly go into some business. I'll go to another city. I've saved about one hundred and fifty rubles."

The author turned to him slowly.

" What ?" he said. " You have no other desire whatsoever ?"

Klimkov thought, and answered :

" No."

" And you believe in the new life ? You think it will come to pass ?"

" Of course. How else ? If all the people want it. Why shouldn't it come to pass ?"

" I'm not saying anything."

Mironov, keeping silent, turned to the window again, and straightened out his moustache with both his hands. Yevsey stood motionless, awaiting something, and listening to the emptiness in his breast.

" Tell me," said the writer softly and slowly, " aren't you sorry for those people, that girl, your cousin, and his comrade ?"

Klimkov bowed his head, and drew the skirts of his coat together.

" You found out that they were right, didn't you ?"

" At first I was sorry for them. I must have been ashamed, I suppose. But now I'm not sorry any more."

" No ? Why not ?"

Klimkov did not answer at once. At the end of a few moments he said in a low voice :

" Well, they are good people, and they attained to what they wanted."

THE SPY

" And didn't it occur to you that you were in a bad business ?"

Yevsey sighed.

" Why, I don't like it. I do what I'm told to do."

The author stepped up to him, then turned aside. Klimkov saw the door through which he had entered, saw it because the author's glance was turned to it.

" I ought to go," he thought.

" Do you want to ask me anything ?" inquired the author.

" No ; I am going."

" Good-bye." And the host moved to let him pass. Yevsey, walking on tiptoe, went into the antechamber, where he began to put on his overcoat. From the door of the room he heard a question :

" Listen ; why did you tell me about yourself ?'

Squeezing his hat in his hands, Yevsey thought, and answered :

" Just so. Timofey Vasilyevich respects you very much, the one who sent me."

The writer smiled.

" Aha ! Is that all ?"

" Why *did* I tell him ?" Klimkov suddenly wondered. Blinking his eyes, he looked fixedly into the author's face.

" Well, good-bye," said his host, rubbing his hands. He moved away from his visitor.

Yevsey nodded to him politely.

" Good-bye."

When he came out of the house, he looked around, and immediately observed the black figure of a man at the end of the street in the grey twilight of the morning. The man was quietly striding along the pavement holding his head bent.

281

"He's waiting," Klimkov thought. He shrank back. "He'll scold me. He'll say I was too long."

The spy must have heard the resonant sound of steps on the frozen paving in the stillness of the morning. He raised his head, and fairly ran to meet Yevsey.

"Did you give it to him? Yes?"

"I did."

"Why were you so long? Did he speak to you? What did he ask?"

Maklakov shivered. His cheeks were blue, his nose red. He seized the lapels of Yevsey's overcoat, and instantly released him, blew on his fingers, as if he had burned them, and began to tramp his feet on the ground. Thus, chilled through and through, and pitiful, he was not awe-inspiring.

"I, too, told him all my life," Yevsey declared aloud. It was pleasant to tell Maklakov about it.

"Well, didn't he ask about me?"

"He asked whether you had gone away."

"What did you say?"

"I said you had."

"Yes. Nothing else?"

"Nothing."

"Well, let's go. I'm frozen, brother. Maklakov darted forward, thrusting his hands in his overcoat pockets, and hunching his back. "So you told him your life?"

"The whole of it, completely, to the very moment of my last meeting with you," answered Yevsey, again experiencing a pleasant sensation, which raised him to the same level as the spy whom he respected.

"What did he say to you, then?"

For some reason confused and embarrassed, Klimkov waited before he replied.

" He didn't say anything."

Maklakov stopped, seized him by the sleeve, and asked in a stern, though quiet, tone :

" Did you give him my papers ? "

" Search me, Timofey Vasilyevich," Yevsey cried sincerely.

" I won't," said Maklakov, after reflecting. " Well, now good-bye. I'll disappear this very day. Take my advice. I'm giving it because I pity you. Get out of this service, and be quick about it. It's not for you, you know it yourself. Go away now. Now is the time to leave. You see what days these are. The dead are coming to life ; people trust one another : they can forgive much in a period like this—they can forgive everything, I think. And, above all, avoid Sasha. He's sick and insane. He's made you deliver up your cousin ; he—he ought to be killed, like a mangy dog. Well, good-bye, brother." He seized Yevsey's hand in his cold fingers, and pressed it firmly. " So you gave him my papers ? " he asked once more. " You're sure of it, are you ? "

" I did—by God ! The moment I caught sight of him I at once remembered him."

" All right. I believe you. Don't speak about me there for a few days, I beg you."

" I'm not going there. On the twentieth I'll call for my salary."

" Tell them then. By that time I'll be far away. Good-bye."

He turned the corner quickly. Yevsey looked after him, thinking suspiciously :

" He's going off. Probably he did something against the authorities, and got frightened. How he looks, just as if he had had a beating."

He grew sorry for himself at the thought that he would never again see Maklakov. Nevertheless, it was agreeable to recall how weak, chilled through, and troubled the spy had looked—the spy who had always borne himself so calmly and firmly.

He spoke boldly even with the officers of the Department of Safety, spoke to them as if he were their equal. But apparently he was all the time afraid of the author who was under surveillance. " And here am I, a little man," thought Yevsey, as he strode down the street—" a little man, afraid of everybody, yet the author didn't frighten me. I was drinking tea at his house, while Maklakov was shivering on the street." Klimkov, content with himself, smiled. " He couldn't say anything, the author couldn't." Yevsey was suddenly seized with a mingled feeling of sadness and insult. He slackened his pace, and sank into reflections as to why this was. He sought the cause of the grief that unexpectedly rose within him.

" Why did I speak to him ?" he thought again on the way. " Instead, I should have told it, that time, to Olga."

The city awoke, and Yevsey wanted to sleep. He felt uneasiness, discomfort in his breast again. His heart was like a little room from which all the furniture had been removed, and is left bare and empty, with green stains of dampness on the torn wall-paper, which shows the dumb patterns made by the chinks in the plastering.

He wanted to sleep, but it was pleasant to go home, and he walked with reluctant steps.

CHAPTER XXVI

ABOUT midday Yevsey was awakened by Viekov, dressed in an overcoat and hat. He looked downcast. He shook the back of the bed, and said in a muffled voice, monotonously :

" Hey, Klimkov! get up. They are summoning everybody to the office. Hey, Klimkov! they have proclaimed the constitution. They are summoning all the agents from their lodgings. Philip Philippovich gave the order. Do you hear, Klimkov ?"

His words fell like large drops of rain, full of sadness. His face was drawn, as with the toothache. His eyes blinked frequently, as if he were about to cry.

" What is it ?" asked Yevsey, jumping out of bed.

Viekov pursed his lips dismally.

" Is it possible to understand ? They said yesterday the Czar would give a full constitution, and to-day here's the manifesto : he's actually giving it. Our Department is like an asylum for the insane; that Sasha is such a coarse creature—astonishing. He keeps shouting, ' Strike ! slash !' and so forth. Why, look here : I wouldn't make up my mind to kill a man even for five hundred rubles. Yet he proposes we should kill for forty rubles a month. Why, it's savagery even to listen to such talk." Viekov puffed his cheeks, and sighed in weariness of spirit as he paced up and down the room. "It's horrible. Dress quickly. We must go."

Pulling on his trousers, Klimkov asked musingly :

" Whom do they want us to kill ?"

" The revolutionists. Although what revolutionists are there now ? According to the Czar's ukase, you'd suppose the revolution was ended. They tell us we should gather the people in the streets, march with flags, and sing, ' God save the Czar !' Well, why not sing, if liberty has been granted ? But, then, they say that while doing this we should shout, ' Down with the constitution !' and so forth. I can't for the life of me understand. That's going against the manifesto and the will of the Czar Emperor. There are many besides me who don't understand it. I'm not the only one."

His voice sounded protesting and insulted ; his legs knocked together. He seemed as soft as if his bones had been removed from his body.

" I'm not going there," said Klimkov.

" What do you mean ?"

" Just that. First I'll walk the streets, and see what they're going to do."

Viekov sighed again, and whistled.

" Yes, of course. You're a single man. But when you have a family—that is, a woman who demands this, that, the fifth thing, and the tenth thing—then you'll go where you don't want to—yes, you will. The need of livelihood compels a man to dance a tight-rope. When I see tricks on a tight-rope, my head begins to turn, and I feel a pain in the lower part of my chest. But I think to myself : ' If it would be necessary for your livelihood, then you, too, Ivan Petrovich Viekov, would dance a tight-rope.' Yes, indeed. A poor man must live by doing things that wring his heart, and whether he

286

wants to or not. Such is the law of Nature, as Grokhotov says."

Viekov swung himself about the room, knocking against the table and the chairs, mumbling and swelling his rosy cheeks. His little face was puffed like a bladder. His insignificant eyes disappeared, and the little red nose hid itself between his cheeks. His sorrowful voice, his dejected figure, his hopeless words, annoyed Klimkov, who said unamiably :

" Soon everything will be arranged differently. So there's no use complaining now."

" But in our place they don't · want a different arrangement," exclaimed Viekov, gesticulating, and stopping in front of Yevsey. " You understand ?"

Yevsey, disturbed, turned on the chair, desiring to express a thought in his mind ; but he was unable to find words, and began to lace his shoes, sniffling.

" Sasha shouts, ' Beat them. Show them what liberty is. So that they may,' he says, ' get frightened of it.' Viakhirev displays revolvers. ' I'll shoot,' he says, ' straight into the eyes.' Krasavin is gathering a gang of some sort of people, and also speaks about knives, and hacking people down, and all such things. Chasin is preparing to kill a certain student because he took his mistress from him. Some other new fellow has come. He's one-eyed, and smiles all over, and his teeth are knocked out in front. A very terrible face. Sheer savagery, all this."

Viekov lowered his voice to a whisper, and said mysteriously :

" Everyone ought to protect his means of a livelihood. That's understood—but preferably without murder, because, if we start to kill, then we in turn will be killed too."

THE SPY

Viekov shuddered.   He turned his head toward the window, and listened to something.   Then he raised his hand, and his face turned pale.

" What's the matter ?" asked Yevsey.

A resonant noise broke against the windows with soft uneven blows, as if to open them cautiously and pour itself into the room.   Yevsey rose to his feet with a look of inquiry and alarm at Viekov, while Viekov, standing at some distance from the window, stretched his hand out in order to open it, apparently taking care not to be seen from the street.   At the same moment a broad stream of sounds broke in, surrounded the spies, passed out at the door, and floated into the corridor, powerful, exulting, sturdy.

" They are rejoicing," said Viekov quietly, starting.

" Look out and see what it is," said Yevsey, hurriedly throwing an overcoat on.

But Viekov was already looking out, and he began to report what he saw, every minute quickly turning his head from the window to Yevsey.   He spoke rapidly and brokenly.

" The people are marching—red flags—a great many people—countless—of various stations—all mixed up in one crowd—an officer even—and Father Uspensky—without hats—Melnikov with a flag—our Melnikov—look !"

Yevsey ran to the casement, looked down, and there saw a thick mass of people filling the entire street.   Before his eyes gleamed a compact mass of faces, which shone like the stars in the Milky Way.   Over the heads of the throng waved the flags resembling red birds.   Klimkov was deafened by the seething noise.   In the first row he saw the tall bearded figure of Melnikov, who held the short pole of the standard in both hands, and waved it.

288

THE SPY

At times the cloth of the flag enveloped his head like a
red turban. From under his hat escaped dark strands
of hair, which fell on his forehead and cheeks, and
mingled with his beard. He was shaggy as a beast.
Evidently he was shouting, for his mouth stood wide
open.

"Where are they going?" mumbled Klimkov,
turning to his comrade.

"They are rejoicing," Viekov repeated, and looked
out into the street, leaning his forehead against the
glass.

Both men were silent, attentively watching the
motley stream of people. With acute hearing, they
caught the loud surging of different exclamations in
the deep sea of the din.

Viekov shook his head.

"What a power, eh? The people were living their
lives separately, and now suddenly they all move
together—what a phenomenon!"

"They've grown wise, it means. They are becoming
masters of life," said Yevsey with a smile. At that
moment he actually believed so.

"And our Melnikov, did you see him?"

"He always stood up for the people," Yevsey explained didactically. He left the window, feeling himself near his aim, bold and new.

"Now everything will go well. No one wants
another to order him about. Everyone wants to live
according to his needs, quietly, peacefully, with things
arranged in a good system," he said gravely, examining
his sharp face in the mirror. He liked his face to-day.
It was calm, almost cheerful. Wishing to strengthen
the new and pleasant feeling of satisfaction with himself, he reflected as to how he might raise himself in the

eyes of his comrade. So he announced with an air of mystery: " Do you know Maklakov has escaped to America ?"

" So ?" the spy rejoined indifferently. " What of it ? He's a single man."

" Why did I tell him ?" Yevsey reproached himself. A feeling of slight alarm and enmity came over him.

" Don't speak of this to anybody, please," he begged Viekov.

" About Maklakov ? Very well ; I have to go to the office. Aren't you going ?"

" No. But we can go out together."

On the street Viekov remarked in dismal irritation, speaking in a subdued voice :

" Stupid people, after all. They ought not to be going about with flags and songs. Now they have once begun to feel themselves in power they ought to ask the authorities straightway to abolish all sorts of politics ; to transform everybody into people, both us and the revolutionists ; to distribute awards to whom they are due, both on our side and theirs, and to make a strict announcement : ' All politics strictly prohibited.' We've had enough of hide-and-seek !"

Viekov suddenly disappeared around the corner without taking leave of Klimkov. Yevsey walked like a man who to-day has no reason to hasten.

" I have one hundred and fifty rubles," he thought. " I have an inclination for business, and I know about it to some extent. In business a man is free. Soon I'll receive twenty-five rubles more."

The people moved about in the street excitedly ; all spoke loud, all faces smiled joyously, and the gloomy autumn evening recalled a bright Easter day. Songs started up, now near by, now at the end of the street

curtained by a grey cloud.   These loud shouts quenched
the singing.

" Long live liberty !"

From everywhere came laughter and the sound of
kindly voices. This pleased Klimkov. He politely
stepped aside for those who came his way, looking at
them approvingly with a light smile of satisfaction, and
continued to picture his future in warm colours.

Two people darted from around the corner, laughing
quietly. One of them jostled Yevsey, but immediately
pulled off his hat, and exclaimed :

" Oh, I beg your pardon."

" Don't mention it," answered Klimkov affably.

Before Yevsey stood Grokhotov, cleanly shaven,
looking as if he had been smeared with ointment. He
beamed all over, and his small soft eyes frolicked,
running from side to side.

" Well, Yevsey, I nearly got myself into a mess. If
it hadn't been for my talent—are you acquainted ?
This is Pantaleyev, one of our men."   Grokhotov lost
his breath, and spoke in a quick whisper, hurriedly
wiping the sweat from his face. " You know I was
walking along the boulevard, when I saw a crowd with
an orator in the centre. Well, I went up and listened.
He spoke so—you know—without any restraint at all.
So I thought I'd ask who that wise fellow was. I
inquired of the man standing next to me. ' His face
is familiar to me,' says I. ' Do you know his name ?'
' His name is Zimin.'   The words were scarcely out of
his mouth when two fellows grabbed hold of me under
my arm. ' People, he's a spy !' I couldn't get in a
word before I found myself in the middle of the crowd,
and such a press around me—and everybody's eyes like
awls. ' I'm done for,' thinks I."

THE SPY

" Zimin ?" asked Yevsey, disturbed, looking behind him and beginning to walk more rapidly.

Grokhotov raised his head to the sky, crossed himself, and continued still more hurriedly :

" Well, the Lord inspired me with an idea. I recovered my presence of mind at once, and shouted out : ' People, it's a mistake, absolutely. I'm no spy, but a well-known mimic of celebrated personages and of animal sounds. Wouldn't you please give me a trial ? The men who had seized me shouted : ' No, he lies ; we know him !' But I had already made a face like the Chief of Police, and called out in his voice : ' Who gave you per-r-r-rmission to hold this meeting ?' And, Lord ! I hear them laughing already. Well, then I began, I tell you, to imitate everything I know—the Governor, the Archpresbyter Izverzhensky, a saw, a little pig, a fly. They roared with laughter. They roared so that the earth trembled under my feet, so help me, God ! Even the men holding me had to laugh —a curse on them !—and let me go. They began to clap and applaud. Upon my word, here is Pantaleyev ; he can testify ; he saw everything."

" True," said Pantaleyev in a hoarse voice. He was a dumpy person with eyeglasses, and wore a sleeveless jacket.

" Yes, brother, they applauded," exclaimed Grokhotov in ecstasy. " Now, of course, I know myself—an artist ; that's me. No doubt of it now. I may say I owe my life to my art. What else ? It's very simple. A crowd cannot be taken in by a mere joke."

" The people have begun to be trusting," remarked Pantaleyev pensively and strangely. " Their hearts have greatly softened."

" That's true. See what they're doing, eh ?"

Grokhotov exclaimed quietly. Then he added in a whisper : " Everything is above-board now. Everywhere the persons under surveillance, our old acquaintances, are in the very first rank. What does it mean, eh ?"

" Is the joiner's name Zimin ?" Yevsey asked again.

" Matvey Zimin, case of propaganda work in the furniture factory of Knop," replied Pantaleyev with stern emphasis.

" He ought to be in prison," said Yevsey, dissatisfied.

Grokhotov whistled merrily.

" In prison ? Don't you know they let everybody out of prison ?"

" Who ?"

" The people."

Yevsey walked a few steps in silence.

" Did they permit them ?"

" Why, yes."

" Why did they do it ?"

" That's what I say, too. They oughtn't to have permitted them," said Pantaleyev. His glasses moved on his broad nose. " What a situation ! The authorities do not think about the people at all."

" Did they release everybody ?" asked Klimkov.

" Everybody." Pantaleyev's hoarse voice was stern, his nostrils dilated. " And there have already been a number of unpleasant encounters. Chasin, for instance, had to threaten to fire his revolver because he was hit in the eye. He was quietly standing off on one side, when suddenly a lady comes up, and cries out, ' Here's a spy !' Inasmuch as Chasin cannot imitate animals, he had to defend himself with a weapon, which isn't possible for everybody either. Not everybody carries a revolver about with him."

" It's been decided to give all of us revolvers."

" Even so no good will come of it. I know positively that a revolver begs of itself to be used. It sets your hand itching."

" Good-bye," said Yevsey. " I'm going home."

He walked through small by-streets. When he saw people coming his way he crossed to the other side, and tried to hide in the shade. The premonition rose and stubbornly grew that he would meet Yakov, Olga, or somebody else of that company.

" The city is large ; there are many people," he comforted himself. Nevertheless, each time he heard steps in front his heart sank painfully, and his legs trembled, losing their strength.

" They let them go," he thought in dismal annoyance. " They didn't say anything, and let them go. And how about me ? It isn't a matter of indifference to me where they are. Of course not !"

It was already dark. A solitary lamp was burning in front of the gates of the police-station. Just as Yevsey approached it he heard someone say in a muffled voice :

" Here, this way, then to the back courtyard."

Yevsey stopped, and peered in alarm into the darkness. The gates were closed, but a dark man stood at the wicket set in one of the heavy swinging doors, apparently awaiting him.

" Hurry up !" the man commanded in a dissatisfied tone.

Klimkov stopped, crept through the wicket, and went along the dark vaulted corridor under the building to a light feebly flickering in the depths of the court, where he heard the scraping of feet on the stone, subdued voices, and the familiar repulsive snuffling.

THE SPY

Klimkov stopped, listened, quietly turned, and walked back to the gate, raising his shoulders, so as to conceal his face in the collar of his overcoat. He had already reached the wicket, and was about to push it, when it opened of itself, and a man darted through, stumbling and clutching at Yevsey.

" The devil ! Who's that ?"

" I."

" Who ?"

" Yevsey Klimkov."

" Aha ! Well, show me the way. Why are you standing there ? Don't you recognize me ?"

Yevsey looked at the hooked nose, the curls behind the ears, the protruding narrow forehead.

" I do. Viakhirev," he said with a sigh.

" Yes. Come on."

Klimkov returned in silence to the courtyard, where his eyes now distinguished many obscure figures looming in the darkness in uneven hillocks, slowly shifting from place to place, like large black fish in dark cold water. The satiated voice of Solovyov resounded sweetishly :

" That doesn't suit me. But catch a girl for me, a little girl, a dainty little girl. I'll knout her for you."

" Always joking, the old devil!" mumbled Viakhirev. " A fitting time for it."

" I can't give beatings, but I like to give lashings. I remember how I used to flog my nephew—ah-h !"

From a corner flowed the voice of Sasha, falling incessantly like water dripping from roofs on a rainy day, monotonous as the sound of chants recited in church.

" Every time you meet those fellows with red flags,

beat them. First beat the men carrying the flags; the rest will take to flight."

" And if they don't ?"

" You will have revolvers. So that if you see people known to you by their participation in secret societies—these people upon whom you spied in your time—who were released from the prisons to-day by the insubordination of the unbridled mob—kill them outright !"

" That's reasonable," said somebody, whose voice resembled Pantaleyev's. " Either we or they."

" Of course. How else ?"

" The people have got their liberty, but what are *we* to do ?" cried Viakhirev sharply.

Yevsey walked into a corner, where he leaned against a pile of wood, and looked and listened in perplexity.

" A body, a little body, a tiny wee little calf—meat !" The senseless words of Solovyov spread out like a thick oily spot.

The dark heavy walls of unequal height surrounded the court sternly. Overhead slowly floated the clouds. On the walls gleamed the square windows, scattered and dim. Klimkov saw a low porch in one corner of the court, upon which Sasha was standing, his overcoat buttoned to the top, his collar raised, and a low cap thrust on the back of his head. Above him swung a small lamp, whose feeble flame trembled and smoked as if endeavouring to consume itself as quickly as possible. Behind Sasha's back was the black stain of the door. A few dark people sat on the steps of the porch at his feet. One, a tall grey person, stood in the doorway.

" You must understand that you are given the

liberty to make war upon the revolutionists," said Sasha, putting his hands behind his back.

The air hummed with the scraping of soles on the flagging, with dry metallic raps, and at times with subdued voices uttering exclamations and officious advice.

" Look out ! Be more careful !"

" We're not allowed to load the revolvers."

The vaguely outlined figures in the dark strangely resembled one another—quiet black people scattered over the yard. They stood in compact groups, and listened to the viscid voice of Sasha, rocking and swinging on their feet, as if swayed by powerful puffs of wind. Sasha's talk drowned all sounds, filling Klimkov's breast with a dreary, cold and acute hatred of the spy.

" You are given the right to proceed against the rebels in open fight. Upon you lies the duty to defend the deceived Czar with all possible means. And know that generous rewards await you. Who has not yet received a revolver ? Come up here."

Several muffled voices called out :

" I—me—I."

Some persons moved to the porch. Sasha stepped aside, and the grey man squatted down on his heels.

" Mayn't I have two ?" asked a lugubrious voice.

" What for ?"

" For a comrade."

" Go along !"

The voices of the spies whom Yevsey knew sounded louder, braver, and jollier than before.

" I'm not going to do any beating."

" We've heard that," the hoarse voice of Pantaleyev sounded rudely.

THE SPY

" Silence !"

Someone smacking his lips greedily complained :

" I haven't enough cartridges. We ought to get a whole boxful."

" I set things going in two station-houses to-day," said Sasha. " I'm tired."

" It'll be interesting to-morrow."

" Well, yes."

The words and the sounds flashed up before Yevsey's mind like large sparks illuminating the morrow. They slowly dried up and consumed the hope of a placid life soon to come. He felt with his whole being that out of the darkness surrounding him, from these people about him, advanced a power inimical to his dreams and aims. This power would seize him again, would put him on the old road, would bring him back to the old terror. Hatred of Sasha seethed in his heart—the live, tenacious, yet pliant hatred of the weak, the implacable, sharp, revengeful feeling of a slave who has once been tortured by hope of liberty. He stood there thinking of nothing, in the quick realization that his hopes must inevitably die. He looked at Sasha, half closing his eyes, and strained his ears to catch the spy's every word.

The men hurriedly departed from the yard in twos and threes, disappearing under the broad archway that yawned in the wall. The light over the head of the spy trembled, turned blue, and went out. Sasha seemed to jump from the porch into a pit, from which he snuffled angrily :

" To-day seven men of my division of the Safety Department did not show up. Why ? Many seem to think that a holiday is here. I won't tolerate stupidity, nor laziness either. I want you to know it. I am now going to introduce strict regulations. I am not Philip Philippovich. Who said that Melnikov is going about with a red flag ? Who ?"

" I saw him."

" With a flag ?"

" Yes. Marching and bawling ' Liberty !' "

" Is it you talking, Viakhirev ?"

" Yes, I."

Now that the tall body of Sasha had disappeared and mingled with the dark mass of people at the platform, it seemed to Yevsey that he grew in size and spread over the court like a stifling cloud, which imperceptibly floated toward him in the darkness. Yevsey came out of his leaning posture, and walked toward the exit, stepping as on ice, as if fearing he would sink through a hole. But the penetrating voice of Sasha overtook him, pouring a painful cold on the back of his neck.

" Well, that fool will be the first to slash. I know him." Sasha laughed a thin, howling laugh. " I have a slogan for him : ' Strike on behalf of the people.' And who said that Maklakov dropped the service ?"

" He knows everything, the vile skunk !" Yevsey said to himself with a calm that surprised him.

" I said it. I heard it from Viekov, and he got it from Klimkov."

" Viekov, Klimkov, Grokhotov—all trash. I'll step on the tails of all of them. Parasites, hybrids, lazy good-for-nothings ! Is any one of them here ?"

" Klimkov must be here," answered Viakhirev.

Sasha shouted :

" Klimkov !"

Yevsey extended his arm before him and walked faster. His legs bent under him. He heard Krasavin say :

" Gone, apparently. You ought not to shout family names."

" Don't talk to me. I'll soon destroy all family names and similar stupidities."

" It's you that I'm going to destroy." Yevsey made the mental threat, gnashing his teeth until they pained him.

But when he had left the gate behind him he was seized by the debilitating consciousness of his impotence and nothingness. It was a long time since he had experienced these feelings with such crushing distinctness. He was frightened by their load, and succumbed to their pressure.

" Maybe it will still be warded off." He tried to embolden himself. " Maybe he won't succeed."

But Yevsey did not believe his own thoughts. Without a will of his own he regarded everybody else as equally devoid of will, and he knew that Sasha could easily compel all whom he wanted to compel to submit to his domination.

CHAPTER XXVII

THE next day Yevsey resolved not to leave the house for a long time. He lay in bed looking at the ceiling. The leaden face of Sasha, with the dim eyes and the band of red pimples on the forehead, floated before him. To-day this face recalled his childhood and the sinister disc of the moon in the mist over the marsh.

As he lay there, empty, languid, and cold, he gave himself over to grief at his shattered dreams—the dreams that Sasha so easily crushed. His hatred of the spy deepening, he felt himself capable of biting him with his teeth, of gouging out his eyes.

It occurred to him that some of his comrades might come to fetch him, and he hurriedly left the house, and ran down several streets. Tiring almost immediately, he stopped and waited for a car. People passed by in a continuous stream. He scented something new in them to-day, and did violence to himself in examining them closely. Soon he realized that this new thing was the old fear so well known to him. It was the old dread and perplexity. People looked around distrustfully, suspiciously, no longer with the kind expression their eyes had recently worn. Their voices sounded lower, and betrayed anger, resentment, sorrow. Their talk was of the horrible.

Two persons stationed themselves near Yevsey.

THE SPY

One of them, a stout shaven man, asked of the other, who had a large black beard :

" How many were killed ?"

" Five. Sixteen wounded."

" Did the Cossacks shoot ?"

" Yes. A boy was killed, a student at the high school."

Yevsey looked at them, and inquired dryly :

" What for ?"

The man with the black beard shrugged his shoulders, and answered reluctantly in a low voice :

" They say the Cossacks were drunk."

" Sasha arranged that," thought Yevsey.

" And on the Spassky Bridge the mob beat a student, and threw him into the river," announced the shaven man, drawing a deep breath.

" What mob ?" Yevsey asked again.

" I don't know. Some sort of patriots."

The black-bearded man explained :

" Since this morning tramps waving tricoloured flags and carrying portraits of the Czar have been marching the streets, and beating the decently clad people."

" Sasha !" Yevsey repeated to himself.

" They say it was organized by the police and the Department of Safety."

" Of course !" burst from Klimkov. But the next instant he compressed his lips tightly, and glanced sidewise at the black-bearded man. He resolved to go away. But just then the car came along, and as the two men prepared to board it, he thought :

" I must get on too, or else they'll guess I'm a spy. What would they think of a man who waited for a car with them, and then didn't take it ?"

THE SPY

The passengers in the car seemed calmer to Yevsey than the pedestrians on the street.

" After all, it's some sort of concealment, though only behind glass," was his explanation of the difference, as he listened to the animated conversation in the car.

A tall man with a bony face said plaintively, spreading his hands :

" I, too, love and respect the Czar; I'm heartily thankful to him for the manifesto. I'm ready to shout ' Hurrah !' as much as you please, and offer up prayers of gratitude. But to smash windows from patriotism and break bones— what's that ?"

" Barbarism, beastliness in these days," said a stout lady. " Oh, those people, how horribly cruel they are !'

From a corner came a firm, assured voice :

" All the work of the police, no doubt of it !"

" But what for ?"

All were silent for a minute.

" I know," thought Klimkov.

From the corner came the same assured voice :

" They're preparing a counter-revolution in Russian fashion. You just take a close look at those in command of the patriotic demonstrators—disguised police, agents of the Department of Safety."

Yevsey heard these words with joy, and furtively regarded the young face. It was dry and clean, with a cartilaginous nose, a small moustache, and a tuft of light hair on a determined chin. The youth sat leaning against the back of his seat in a corner of the car, one leg crossed over the other. He looked at the passengers in the car with a wise glance from his blue eyes, and spoke like a man who masters his words and thoughts, and believes in their power.

303

THE SPY

Dressed in a short, warm jacket and tall boots, he resembled a working man, but his white hands and the thin horizontal lines on his forehead betrayed him.

" Disguised," thought Yevsey. " Well, let him be disguised. What difference does it make to me ?"

He began to follow the loud, firm talk of the fair-haired youth with the greatest attention, looking at his wise, transparent blue eyes, and agreeing with him. But suddenly he shuddered, seized with a sharp premonition. On the platform of the car, at the conductor's side, he saw through the window a pair of narrow drooping shoulders, and the back of a black, protruding head. The car jolted, and the familiar figure swayed.

" Yakov Zarubin !"

Klimkov, utterly dismayed, turned his look again upon the blue-eyed youth. He had removed his hat, and he smoothed his wavy hair as he said :

" As long as our administration has the soldiers in its hands, the police, and the spies, it will not yield the people and society their rights without a fight, without bloodshed. We must remember that."

" It isn't true, my dear sir," cried the bony-faced man. " The Czar granted a full constitution. He granted it, yes, so how dare you——"

" But who is arranging the street massacres ? And who's shouting, ' Down with the constitution ' ?" the young man asked coldly. " You had better take a look at the defenders of the old system. There they go !"

At that instant the car came to a standstill with a creak, and when the irritating noise of its movement had subsided the passengers could hear loud, turbulent shouts.

THE SPY

" God save the Czar !"

" Hurrah !"

A pack of boys came running from around the corner in front of the car, and scattered noisily over the street, as if dropped from above. A crowd of people waving three-coloured flags over their heads pushed after them like a black wedge in hurried disorder. Alarming shouts filled the air.

" Hurrah !"

" Stop, boys !"

" Down with the Constitution !"

" We don't want——"

" God save the Czar !"

" Hurrah !"

The people shoved past one another, gesticulated wildly, and threw their hats in the air. In front of all, with his head hanging low like a bull, walked Melnikov, holding a heavy pole from which the national flag floated. His eyes were fastened on the ground. He lifted his feet high, and apparently was tramping the ground with great force, for at each step his body quivered and his head shook. His heavy bellow could be heard above the chaos of thinner shouts.

" We don't want deceit——"

Behind, a crowd of ragged people, dark and grey, pushed down the street, jumping, and twisting their necks. They raised their heads, hands, and arms, looked up to the windows of the houses, jumped on the pavements to knock off the hats of passers-by, ran up to Melnikov again, shouted and whistled, and seized one another, rolling into a heap. Melnikov, waving the flag, clanged like a huge bell.

" Down with the traitors ! Down with the impostors ! Stop !"

305

" Drunk or what ?" thought Klimkov coldly.

" Halt !" Raising his head and the flag on high, the spy commanded : " Sing !"

From his broad mouth gushed a savage mournful note :

" Go-o-od——"

But at that moment excited shouts clashed in the air, disordered and rapacious, like a flock of hungry birds. They overbore the voice of the spy, and hid it in their hasty greedy mass.

" Hurrah for the Emperor ! Hats off ! True orthodox people—we want the old ! Down with treachery !"

It was quiet in the car.   All stood with their hats off, silent, pale, observing the crowd that encircled them like a wavy dirty ring. But the disguised man did not remove his hat. Yevsey looked at his stern face, and thought : " Putting on airs." And he turned his eyes on the street with a wry smile on his face. He felt very distinctly the nothingness of these restless, jumping people. He clearly understood that dark terror was whipping them from within, was pushing and carrying them from side to side. They were fighting, intoxicating themselves with loud shouts in the desire to prove to themselves that they were afraid of nothing. They ran around the car like a pack of hounds just released from the leash, full of senseless joy, without having had time to free themselves from the customary fear. Apparently they could not make up their minds to traverse the broad bright street. They were unable to gather themselves into one body. They tossed about, roared, and glared around alarmingly, waiting for something.

Near the car stood a little thin, sharp-bearded muzhik

in a torn hat and short fur coat. He held his eyes
closed and his face raised on high. His hungry mouth
gaped, displaying his yellow teeth, as he shouted in a
thin voice :

" Do-o-o-wn ! We don't want——"

Tears of fear and excitement ran down his cheeks.
His forehead glistened with sweat. Ceasing to shout,
he bent his neck and looked around distrustfully. Then
he raised his shoulders, and, closing his eyes again,
yelled once more as if he were being beaten.

" E-e-e-nough !"

" That's the way I would have become, too,"
thought Yevsey to himself. Though the muzhik cut a
droll figure, Yevsey was sorry for him and for himself.

He saw the familiar faces of the dvornik, always
grim ; the large-whiskered visage of the church watchman, Klimych, pious and sullen ; the hungry eyes of the
young hooligans ; the astonished expression of timorous
muzhiks, and a few creatures who pushed everyone,
gave everyone orders, and filled the will-less blind bodies
with their will, with their sick ferocity. Yevsey well
understood that all these petty people, like himself,
lived in the close captivity of fear, with no power to
tear themselves from its clutches. A powerful person
might gain mastery over them ; in obedience to the
will of a still more powerful person they would overthrow the old temple of fear in exchange for a new
one. Now, separated by the windows from the mob, he
looked at it from aside and above, and his eyes were
able to embrace much. Everything was clear to him
ad nauseam. Anguish and wrath sucked at his
heart.

Little Yakov Zarubin was twisting and turning in
the middle of the crowd like an eel. Now he ran up to

THE SPY

Melnikov, pulled his sleeve, and said something to him, nodding his head in the direction of the car.

Klimkov quickly glanced around at the man in the hat, who had already risen, and was walking to the door, his head lifted high and a frown on his brow. Yevsey stepped after him, but Melnikov jumped to the platform, and blocked the doorway with his large body.

" Hats off !" he bawled.

The man faced about abruptly, and walked to the other exit. There he was met by Zarubin, who shouted in a loud voice :

" Here, this man in a hat ! I know him ! He makes bombs ! Take care, boys !"

A revolver gleamed in Zarubin's hand. He swung it as if it were a stone, and thrust it forward. People from the street clambered to the platform, and the passengers, pressing to the exits, met them face to face. The lady screeched :

" Take off your hat ! Why, man !"

All screamed, roared, and pressed one another. Their eyes, staring insanely, fastened upon the man in the hat.

" I'm going to shoot ! Get away !" the man shouted aloud, advancing upon Zarubin. The spy retreated, but he was pushed in the back, and fell to his knees. Supporting himself on the floor with one hand, he stretched out the other. A shot rang out, then another. The windows rattled. For a second all the cries congealed. Then the firm voice said contemptuously :

" Vile curs !"

The air and the windows quivered with a third shot, and Zarubin uttered a loud cry :

" Ugh !" His head struck the floor, as if he were making an obeisance at somebody's feet. The car became emptier and quieter. Klimkov, ensconced in a corner, shrivelled up on his seat, and thought listlessly :

" I might have been killed."

The thought darted by, and disappeared without rousing in the darkness of his soul either fear or joy. He looked around wearily. The man in the hat stood on the platform of the car. Melnikov advanced toward him, past Yevsey, and Zarubin lay motionless, face downward.

" I will shoot you down—every one of you ! Get away from here !" the loud dry cry was heard from the platform.

But Melnikov stepped across the body of Yakov, seized the fair-haired youth by the waist, and threw him into the street.

" Beat him down !" he shouted bluntly in a savage voice.

Three revolver shots followed in quick succession. The deaf blows clapped. Someone howled in a long-drawn plaintive cry like an infant :

" Oh, oh, my leg !"

Another man shouted hoarsely with an effort :

" Ah, ah ! Hit him on the head ! Hey, hey !"

And a thin hysterical voice pealed in ecstasy :

" Tear him to pieces, my dear people. Choke him ! Enough ! Their time is past ! Now we'll give it to them. Now our turn has come——"

All the cries were suddenly covered by a loud ejaculation full of mournful disdain.

" Idiots !"

Yevsey reeled from weakness in his legs. He walked to the platform, from which he saw a dark heap of people. With bent backs, swinging their arms and legs, groaning with the strain of excitement, uttering tired hoarse articulations, they stirred busily in the street, like large shaggy worms, as they dragged over the stones the body of the fair-haired youth, already crushed and torn. They kicked at it, trampled on its face and chest, pulled its hair, its legs and arms, and simultaneously tore it in different directions. Half bare, covered with blood, it flapped against the stones, soft as dough, with each blow losing more and more semblance to a human figure. These people worked over it industriously. The little lean muzhik, trying to crush its skull, stepped on it with one foot, and sang out :

" Aha ! Our time has come, too."

The work was accomplished. One after the other they left the middle of the street for the pavement. A pock-marked fellow wiped his hands on his short sheepskin overcoat, and asked with the air of a manager or superintendent :

" Who took his pistol ?"

Now the voices sounded weary, reluctant. But on the pavement a laugh was heard coming from a small group of people standing next to the lamp-post. An offended voice was discussing hotly :

" You lie ! I was the first. The second he fell I gave him one on the jaw with my boot."

" Cabman Mikhailov pounced on him first, then I."

" Mikhailov got a bullet in his leg."

" If it didn't hit the bone it's all right."

These people, after tasting blood, had apparently grown bolder. They looked around on all sides with unsatiated eyes, with greed, and assured expectation.

In the middle of the street lay a formless dark heap, from which blood was oozing into the hollows between the stones.

" That's the way——" Yevsey thought, looking at the red streaks on the pavement. In the dark red mist trembling before his eyes appeared the hairy face of Melnikov. His voice was tired and muffled.

" There, they've killed him !"

" Yes, how quickly !"

" They killed another one this morning."

" What for ?"

" He was speaking. He was standing on the kerb addressing the people. Chasin fired into his stomach."

" What for ?" Yevsey repeated.

" Those speakers are deceivers—a spurious manifesto. There's no such thing—all a bluff !"

" Sasha thought that all out," said Yevsey quietly, with conviction.

Melnikov shook his head, and looked at his large hands.

" Somebody always deceives," he mumbled in a drunken voice.

He entered the car, and raised Zarubin lightly, placing him on the bench face up.

" He's dead. There's where it hit him——"

Yevsey sought the scar on Zarubin's face that the blow of the bottle had left. He did not find it. Now over the right eye was a little red hole from which Klimkov could not tear his eyes. It absorbed his entire attention, and aroused sharp pity for Yakov.

" Have you a pistol ?" asked Melnikov.

" No."

" There, take Yakov's."

" I don't want to. I don't need it."

" Now everybody needs a pistol," said Melnikov simply, and slipped the revolver into Yevsey's overcoat

311

pocket. " Yes, there was a Yakov ; now there is no Yakov."

" It was I who marked him for death," thought Yevsey, looking at his comrade's face.

Zarubin's brows were sternly drawn. A look of serious preoccupation gleamed and died away in his dim eyes. His little black moustache bristled on his raised lip. He appeared to be annoyed. His half-open mouth seemed ready to pour forth a rapid torrent of irritated talk.

" Come," said Melnikov.

" And he—how about them ?" asked Yevsey, tearing his eyes from Zarubin.

" The police will take them away. It's against the law to remove the killed. Let's go somewhere and shake ourselves up. I haven't had a bite to-day. I can't eat—the third day without food. No sleep either." He sighed painfully, and concluded with sombre *sang froid :* " I should have been killed in Yakov's place."

" Sasha will ruin all," said Yevsey through his teeth. " He'll ruin us all."

" Blindness of the soul."

They walked along the street without observing anything, and each spoke that with which his own mind was occupied. Both were like drunken men.

" Where's the truth ?" asked Melnikov, putting his hand forward, as if to test the air.

" There, you see, two have been killed," said Yevsey, making an effort to catch an elusive thought.

" To-day I should think many have been killed. All are blind."

" Why did Sasha arrange this ?"

" I don't love him either."

312

THE SPY

" He's the one who ought to be killed," exclaimed Yevsey, with bitter vengefulness.

Melnikov was silent for a long time. Then he suddenly shook his fist in the air, and said resolutely :

" Enough ! I've taken sins enough upon myself. On the other side of the Volga I have an uncle, a very old man. He is all I have in this world. I'll go to him. He keeps an apiary. When he was young he was tried for forgery." After another pause of silence the spy laughed quietly.

" What's the matter ?" asked Yevsey, annoyed.

" I'm forgetting everything. My uncle has now been dead for three years."

They reached a café known to them. Yevsey stopped at the door, and looked meditatively at the illuminated windows.

" People again," he muttered, dissatisfied. " I don't want to go in there."

" Let's go in. It's all the same," said Melnikov, taking him by the arm and making him follow him. " It will be wearying for me to be here alone. Besides, I've become fearful. I'm not afraid of being killed if I'm recognized as a spy. It's just a general feeling of dread."

The two men did not enter the room in which their comrades were wont to gather, but took seats in a corner of the common hall, where there were a number of persons, none of whom were drunk, though the talk was noisy and evinced unusual excitement. Klimkov by habit began to listen to the conversation, while the thought of Sasha clung to him, and quietly unfolded itself in his head stupefied by the impressions of the last days, but freshened by the constant influx of poignant hatred and fear of the spy.

THE SPY

He recalled the sullen face of the dead Zarubin, the mauled body of the fair-haired man. He looked in perplexity at the noisy public, blinking as if half asleep. All was incoherent, as in a nightmare. Melnikov drank tea with no appetite, keeping silent, and from time to time stretching himself.

Not far from them at a table sat three men, apparently clerks, with the speech characteristic of the class. They were young and fashionably dressed, with a display of gay necktie. One of them, a curly-headed youth with a tanned face, spoke excitedly, his dark eyes flashing.

" They utilize the ferocity of hungry, ragged rowdies, by which they want to prove to us that liberty is impossible because there are many barbarians such as these. However—permit me—savages did not show themselves yesterday. There have always been such, and justice has always been able to cope with them ; they could be held under fear of the law. Then, why are they permitted to perpetrate every sort of outrage and bestiality to-day ?" He looked around the hall with the air of a victor, and answered his question with hot conviction. " Because they want to point out to us, ' You are for freedom, ladies and gentlemen : well, here you have it. Freedom for you means murder, robbery, and all kinds of mob violence.' "

" Do you hear ?" demanded Yevsey triumphantly. " Isn't that Sasha's scheme ?" The hot voice of the orator roused in his soul the quiet smouldering hope, " Maybe Sasha won't conquer."

Melnikov looked at him sullenly, without replying.

The curly-headed man rose from the chair, and continued, waving a glass of wine in his hand :

" It's not true, and I protest. Honest people want

THE SPY

liberty, not in order to crush one another, but in order to be protected against the prevailing violence of our lawless life. Liberty is the Goddess of Reason. They have drunk enough of our blood. I protest. Long live Liberty!"

The public raised a cheer, and sprang to their feet.

Melnikov looked at the curly-headed orator, and muttered:

"What a fool!"

"He speaks truly," rejoined Yevsey angrily.

"How do you know?" asked the spy indifferently, and began to drink the beer in slow gulps.

Yevsey wanted to tell this heavy man that he himself was a fool, a blind beast, whom the cunning and cruel masters of his life had taught to hunt people down. But Melnikov raised his head, and, looking into Klimkov's face with dark eyes terribly widened, said in a loud whisper:

"I'm afraid for this reason, you know: when I was in prison an incident happened there——"

"Hold on," said Yevsey; "I want to listen."

A thin voice, which drilled the ear, pierced triumphantly through the soft mass of sounds.

"Did you hear? He says a goddess, yet we Russian people have only one goddess, the Holy Mother of God, the Virgin Mary. That's how those curly-headed youngsters speak!"

"Out with him!"

"Silence!"

"No, if you please. If there's liberty, everyone has a right——"

"You see? The curly-headed youngsters walk the streets, beat the people who rise up to maintain the Czar's truth against treachery, while we Russians, the true Orthodox, don't dare even to speak. Is this liberty?"

"They'll fight," said Klimkov, starting to tremble. "Somebody will be killed. I'm going."

"What a peculiar fellow you are! Well, let's go. The devil take them! What are they to you?"

Melnikov flung the money on the table, and moved toward the exit, his head bowed low, as if to conceal his conspicuous face. On the street in the dark and the cold, he began to speak in a subdued voice :

"When I was in prison—it was on account of a certain foreman who was strangled in our factory—I was hauled up, too. They told me I would get hard labour. Everybody said it—first the coroner, then the gendarmes joined in. I got frightened. I was still young, and I didn't take to the idea of hard labour. I used to cry." He coughed a hollow cough, and slackened his pace. "Once the assistant overseer of the prison, Aleksey Maksimych, a good little old man, came in to me. He loved me. He grieved for me all the time. ' Ah,' says he, ' Liapin '—my real name is Liapin—' Ah,' says he, ' brother, I'm sorry for you. You are such an unfortunate fellow——"

Melnikov's speech unfolded itself like a soft band upon which Klimkov quietly let himself down, as upon a narrow path leading down into the darkness, into something terrible and awesomely interesting.

"He comes, and says he : ' Liapin, I want to save you for a good life. Yours is a hard-labour case, but you can escape it. The only thing you need to do is to execute a man. He was sentenced for political assassination. He will be hanged according to law in the presence of a priest, will be given a cross to kiss, so that you needn't be uneasy about it.' I say : ' Why not ?

THE SPY

If with the consent of the authorities, and if I'm to be pardoned, I'll hang him. Only I can't——' 'We'll teach you,' says he. 'We have a man who knows how, only he's stricken with paralysis, and can't do it himself.' Well, for a whole evening they taught me. It was in a deep dungeon. We stuffed a sack with rags, tied it with a string, so as to make a neck. Then I pulled it up on a hook. I learned how to do the business. Early in the morning they gave me half a bottle to drink, led me out into the yard with soldiers carrying guns. I see a gallows has been erected, and various officers before it. They are all muffled up and shrivelled. It was autumn then, too—November. I ascended the scaffolding, and the boards shook, creaked under my feet like teeth. This made me feel uncomfortable, and I said : 'Give me more whisky. I'm afraid.' Then they brought him——"

Melnikov again began to cough dully, and clutched at his throat. Yevsey pressed up to him, trying to keep step with him. He kept his eyes fastened on the ground, not daring to look either to the front or the side.

" I see a young, powerful fellow. He stands firm, and all the time keeps stroking his head from his forehead back to his neck. I began to put the face-cloth on him. I must have pulled or pinched him in some way, and he tells me quietly, without anger : ' Be more careful, brother.' Yes. The priest gave him the cross, and he says : ' Don't disturb yourself. I'm not a believer.' His face was so—as if he knew everything that would be after death, and now and to-morrow and always—knew it for certain. Somehow I strangled him, shaking all over. My hands grew numb, my legs would not hold me. I felt horrible on account of him :

he was so calm about it all—stood a master over death."

Melnikov was silent, looked around, and began to walk more quickly.

" Well ?" asked Yevsey in a whisper.

" Well, I strangled him. That's all. Only ever since, when I see or hear that a man has been killed, I recollect him—always. In my opinion he was the only man who knew the truth. That was why he was not afraid. And the main thing is, he knew what would be to-morrow, which no one knows. I tell you what, Yevsey : come to me to sleep, eh ? Come, please."

" All right," said Yevsey quietly.

He was glad of the offer. He could not walk to his room alone—along the streets in the darkness. He felt a tightness in his breast and a heavy pressure on his bones, as if he were creeping underground, and the earth were squeezing his back, his chest, his sides, and his head, while in front of him gaped a deep pit, which he could not escape, into which he must soon descend— a silent bottomless abyss, down which he would drop endlessly.

" That's good," said Melnikov. " I should feel bored alone."

" If you would kill Sasha——" Yevsey advised him sadly.

" There you are !" Melnikov fended off the idea. " What do you think—that I love to kill ? They asked me twice again to hang people, a woman and a student. I declined. I might have had two to remember instead of one. The killed appear again. They come back."

" Often ?"

" Sometimes, sometimes not. But often it's every night. How can you defend yourself against them ?

THE SPY

I can't pray to God. I've forgotten my prayers. Have you ?"

" I remember mine."

They entered a court, and were long in penetrating to its depths, stumbling as they walked over boards, stones, and rubbish. Then they descended a flight of steps, which Klimkov, feeling the walls with his hands, thought would never come to an end. When he found himself at last in the lodging of the spy, and had examined it in the light of the lamp, he was amazed to see the mass of gay pictures and paper flowers with which the walls were almost entirely covered. Melnikov at once became a stranger in this comfortable little room, with a broad bed in a corner behind white curtains.

" All this was contrived by the woman with whom I lived," said Melnikov, beginning to undress. " She ran away, the hussy ! A gendarme, a quartermaster, decoyed her. I can't understand it. He's a grey-haired widower, while she's young and greedy for a man. Nevertheless, she went away—the third one that's left me already. Come, let's go to bed."

They lay side by side in the same bed, which rocked under Yevsey like waves, and all the time descended lower and lower. His heart sank with it. The spy's words laid themselves heavily upon his breast.

" One was Olga."

" What !"

" Olga. Why ?"

" Nothing."

" A little one—thin and jolly. She used to hide my hat, or something else, and I would say : ' Olga, where's my hat ?' And she would say : ' Look for it. You're a spy.' She liked to joke, but she was a loose woman.

319

I hardly had my head turned before she was with somebody else. I was afraid to beat her. She was frail. Still, I pulled her hair. You've got to do something."

" Lord !" quietly exclaimed Klimkov. " What am I going to do ?"

His comrade was silent for a while, then said dully and slowly :

" That's the way I howl, too, sometimes."

Klimkov buried his head in the pillow, compressing his lips tightly, to restrain the stubborn need to utter cries and complaints.

CHAPTER XXVIII

YEVSEY awoke with a certain secret resolution, which held his bosom as with a broad invisible belt. It stifled him. The ends of this band, he felt, were held by some insistent being, who obstinately led him on to something inescapable. He hearkened to this desire, and tested it carefully with an awkward, timorous thought. At the same time he did not want it to define itself.

Melnikov, dressed and washed, but uncombed, was sitting at the table next to the samovar, munching his bread lazily like an ox.

" You sleep well," he said. " I drowsed a little, then I awoke, while it was still night, and suddenly I saw a body beside me. I remembered that Tania wasn't here, but I had forgotten about you. Then it seemed to me that that person was lying there. He came and lay down—wanted to warm himself."" Melnikov laughed a stupid laugh, which apparently embarrassed him the next instant. " However, it's not a joke. I lighted a match, and looked at you. It's my idea you're not well. Your face is blue like——" He broke off with a cough, but Yevsey guessed the unspoken word, and thought gloomily :

" Rayisa, too, said I should hang myself."

The thought frightened him, clearly alluding to

something he did not want to remember. Then he tried insistently to evoke some desire which might help him to befool himself, to conceal the unavoidable, that which had already been determined.

" What time is it ?" he asked.

" Eleven."

" Early still."

" Early," confirmed the host, and both were silent. Then Melnikov proposed :

" Let's live together, eh ?"

" I don't know."

" What ?"

" What will happen," said Yevsey, after reflecting a moment.

" Nothing will happen. You're a quiet fellow. You speak little, neither do I like to speak always. If it's tiresome I speak, or else I keep quiet all the time. When you ask about something, one says one thing, another says another thing, and a third still another. Well, the devil take you, think I. You have a whole lot of words, but none that are true."

" Yes," said Yevsey, for the sake of answering.

" Something must be done," he thought in self-defence. Suddenly he resolved : " At first I will— Sasha——" But he did not wish to represent to himself what would be afterwards. " Where are we going to go ?" he inquired of Melnikov.

" To the office," Melnikov replied with unconcern.

" I don't want to," declared Yevsey dryly and firmly.

Melnikov combed his beard for a time in silence. Then he shoved the dishes from him, and placing his elbows on the table, said meditatively in a subdued voice :

THE SPY

" Our service has become hard. All have begun to rebel, but who are the real rebels here ? Make it out if you can."

" I know who's the first scoundrel and skunk," muttered Klimkov.

" Sasha, you mean ?" inquired Melnikov.

Yevsey gave no reply. He was quietly beginning to devise a plan of action. Melnikov started to dress, sniffing loudly.

" So we're going to live together ?"

" Yes."

" Are you going to bring your things to-day ?"

" I don't know."

" Will you sleep here to-night ?"

After some reflection Yevsey said :

" Yes."

When the spy had gone Klimkov jumped to his feet, and looked around frightened, quivering under the stinging blows of suspicion.

" He locked me in, and went to tell Sasha. They'll come soon to seize me. I must escape through the window."

He rushed to the door. It was not locked. He calmed himself, and said with heat, as if convincing somebody :

" Well, is it possible to live this way ? You don't believe anybody—there is nobody——"

He sat long behind the table without moving, straining his mind, employing all his cunning to lay a snare for the enemy without endangering himself. Finally he hit upon a plan. He must in some way lure Sasha from the office to the street, and walk with him. When they met a large crowd of people he would shout :

THE SPY

"This is a spy; beat him." And probably the same thing would happen as had happened to Zarubin and the fair-haired young man. If the people would not turn upon Sasha as seriously as they had yesterday with the disguised revolutionist, Yevsey would set them an example. He would fire first, as Zarubin had. But *he* would *hit* Sasha. He would aim at his stomach.

Klimkov felt himself strong and brave, and hurried himself. He wanted to do the thing at once. But the recollection of Zarubin hindered him, knotting up the poverty-stricken simplicity of his contrivance. He involuntarily repeated his notion. "It was I who marked him for death."

He did not reproach, he did not blame himself. Yet he felt that a certain thread bound him to the little black spy, and he must do something to break the thread.

"I didn't say good-bye to him—and where shall I find him now?"

On putting on his overcoat he was pleased to feel the revolver in his pocket. Responding to a fresh influx of power and resolution, he walked out into the street with a firm tread.

But the nearer he got to the Department of Safety the more did his bold mood melt and fade away. The feeling of power became dissipated, and when he saw the narrow dull alley, at the end of which was the dusky, three-storied building, he suddenly felt an invincible desire to find Zarubin and take leave of him.

"I insulted him," he explained his desire to himself, embarrassed and quickly turning aside from his aim. "I must find him."

At the same time he vaguely felt he could not escape from that which seized his heart and pressed him, drew him on after itself, and silently indicated the one issue from the terrible entanglement.

The problem of the day, the resolve to destroy Sasha, did not hinder the growth of the dark and evil power which filled his heart, while the sudden wish to find the body of the little spy instantly became an insurmountable obstacle to the carrying out of his plan.

He fed this desire artificially in the fear that it, too, would disappear. He rode about in cabs to police stations for a number of hours, taking the utmost pains in his inquiries regarding Zarubin. When at last he found out where the body was it was too late to visit it, and he returned home secretly pleased that the day had come to an end.

Melnikov did not put in an appearance at his lodging. Yevsey lay alone the whole night, trying not to stir. At each movement of his the canopy over the bed rocked. An odour of dampness was wafted in his face, the bed creaked a tune ; he felt stifled, nauseated, and timorous. Taking advantage of the stillness, the mice ran about, and the rustling sounds they made tore the thin net of Yevsey's thoughts of Zarubin and Sasha. The interruptions displayed to him the dead, calm emptiness of his environment, with which the emptiness of his soul insistently desired to blend.

CHAPTER XXIX

EARLY in the morning he was already standing in the corner of a large yard at a yellow hovel with a cross over the roof. A grey, humpbacked watchman said, as he opened the door :

" There are two of them here. One was recognized, the other not. The unidentified one will soon be taken to the grave."

Then Yevsey saw the sullen face of Zarubin. The only change it had undergone was that it had grown a little blue. The small wound in place of the scar had been washed, and had turned black. The little alert body was naked and clean. It lay face upward, stretched like a cord, with the tanned hands folded over the bosom, as if Zarubin were sullenly asking :

" Well, what ?"

Beside him lay the other dark body, all rent, swollen, with red, blue, and yellow stains. Someone had covered its face with blue and white flowers. But under them Yevsey could see the bones of the skull, a tuft of hair glued together with blood and the torn shell of the ear.

Leaning his back against the wall, the old man said :

" This one cannot be recognized. He has almost no head. Yet he was recognized. Two ladies came yesterday with these flowers and covered up this

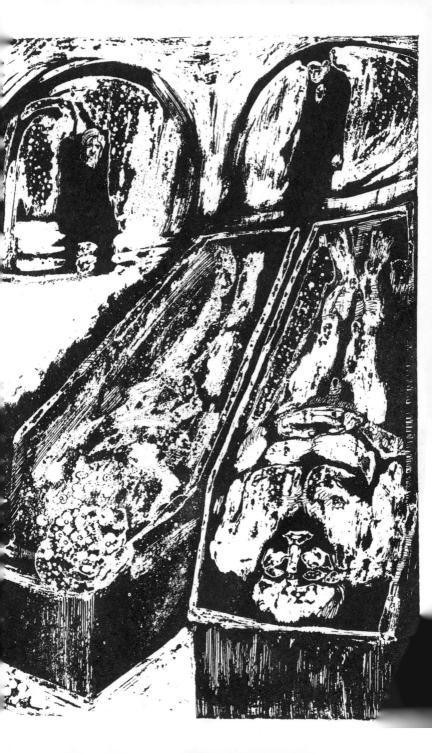

human outrage. As for the other one, he's remained unidentified."

" I know who he is," said Yevsey firmly. " He's Yakov Zarubin. He served in the Department of Safety."

The watchman looked at him, and shook his head in negation.

" No, it's not he. The police told us he was Zarubin, and our office inquired of the Department of Safety, but it appeared it wasn't he."

" But I know," Yevsey exclaimed quietly, in an offended tone.

" In the Department of Safety they said, ' We don't know such a person. A man by that name never served here.' "

" It's not true," exclaimed Yevsey, grieved and dumbfounded.

Two young fellows came in from the court, one of whom asked the watchman :

" Which is the unidentified man ?"

The humpback pointed his finger at Zarubin, and said to Yevsey :

" You see ?"

Klimkov walked out into the court, thrust a coin into the watchman's hand, and repeated with impotent stubbornness :

" It's Zarubin, I tell you."

" As you please," said the old man, shrugging his hump. " But if it is so, others would have recognized him. An agent came here yesterday in search of someone who had been killed. He didn't recognize your man either, though why shouldn't he admit it if he did ?"

" What agent ?"

" A stout man, bald, with an amiable voice."

" Solovyov," guessed Yevsey, observing dully that Zarubin's body was being laid in a white, unpainted coffin.

" It doesn't go in," mumbled one of the fellows.

" Bend his legs, the devil !"

" The lid won't close."

" Sideways ; put him in sideways, eh ?"

" Don't make such a fuss, boys," said the old man calmly.

The fellow who held the head of the body snuffled, and said :

" It's a spy, Uncle Fiodor."

" A dead man is nobody," observed the humpback didactically, walking up to them. The fellows were silent, but went on trying to squeeze the springy, tawny body into the narrow, short coffin.

" You fools, get another coffin," said the humpback angrily.

" It's all the same," said one, and the other added grimly : " He's not a great gentleman."

Yevsey left the court carrying in his soul a bitter humiliating feeling of insult on Zarubin's behalf. Behind him he clearly heard the humpback say to the men as they bore off the body :

" Something wrong there, too. He came here, and says, ' I know him.' Maybe he knows all about this affair."

The two men answered almost simultaneously :

" Seems to be a spy, too."

" What's the difference to us ?"

Klimkov quickly jumped into a cab, and shouted to the driver :

" Hurry up !"

THE SPY

" Where to ?"

Yevsey answered quietly after a pause :

" Straight ahead."

The insulting thoughts dully knocked in his head.

" They bury him like a dog—no one wants him—and me, too——"

The streets came to meet him. The houses rocked and swayed, the windows gleamed. People walked noisily, and everything was alien.

" To-day I'm going to make an end of Sasha. I'll go there at once and shoot him." In a moment he was already compelled to persuade himself : " It's got to be done. As for me, nothing matters to me any more."

Dismissing the cabman, he walked into a restaurant, to which Sasha came less frequently than to the others. He stopped in front of the door of the room where the spies gathered.

" The instant I see him I'll shoot him," he said to himself.

He knocked at the door tremulously, and felt the revolver in his hand. His soul was congealed in cold expectation.

" Who's there ?" asked someone on the other side of the door.

" I."

The door was opened a little. In the chink flashed the eyes and the reddish little nose of Solovyov.

" Ah-h-h !" he drawled in amazement. " There was a rumour that you had been killed."

" No, I have not been killed," Klimkov responded sullenly, removing his coat.

" I see. Lock the door. They say you went with Melnikov——"

Solovyov was masticating slowly a piece of ham,

THE SPY

which interfered with his articulation. His greasy lips smacked slowly, and let out the unconcerned words: " So it isn't true that you went with Melnikov ?"

" Why isn't it true ?"

" Why, here you are alive, and he's in bad shape. I saw him yesterday."

" Where ?"

The spy named the hospital from which Yevsey had just come.

" Why is he there ?" Klimkov inquired apathetically.

" This is it : a Cossack struck him a sabre blow on the head, and the horses trampled on him. It's not known how it happened, or why. He's unconscious. The physicians say he won't recover."

Solovyov poured some sort of green whisky into a glass, held it up to the light, and examined it with screwed-up eyes. After which he drank it, and asked :

" Where are you hiding yourself ?"

" I'm not hiding."

" You *have* been hiding, all the same."

A plate fell to the floor in the corridor. Yevsey started. He remembered he had forgotten to remove the revolver from his overcoat pocket. He rose to his feet.

" Sasha is raging at you."

Before Yevsey's eyes swam the sinister red disc of the moon, surrounded by a cloud of ill-smelling lilac-coloured mist. He recalled the snuffling, ever-commanding voice, the yellow fingers of the bony hands.

" Won't he come here ?"

" I don't know. Why ?"

Solovyov's face wore a sleek expression. Apparently

330

THE SPY

he was very well satisfied with something. In his voice
sounded the careless affability of an aristocrat. All
this was repulsive to Yevsey. Incoherent thoughts
darted through his mind, one breaking the other off.

" You are all rascals—sorry for Melnikov—so this
fat fellow didn't want to recognize Yakov—why ?"

" Did you see Zarubin ?"

" Who's that ?" asked Solovyov, raising his brows.

" You know. He lay in the hospital there. You
saw him."

" Yes, yes, yes. Of course I saw him."

" Why didn't you say there that you knew him ?"
Yevsey demanded sternly.

The old spy reared his bald head, and exclaimed in
astonishment, with a sarcastic expression

" W-w-w-hat ?"

Yevsey repeated the question, but this time in a
milder tone.

" That's not your business, my dear fellow. I want
you to know that. But I'm sorry for your stupidity,
so I'll tell you, we have no need for fools ; we don't
know them, we don't comprehend them, we don't
recognize them. You are to understand that, now
and for ever, for all your life. Remember what I say,
and tie your tongue with a string."

The little eyes of Solovyov sparkled cold as two
silver coins ; his voice bespoke evil and cruelty. He
shook his short thick fingers at Yevsey. His greedy,
bluish lips were drawn sullenly. But he was not
horrible.

" It's all the same," thought Yevsey. " They are
all one gang ; they all ought to be——"

He darted to his overcoat, snatched the revolver
from the pocket, aimed at Solovyov, and shouted dully :

331

THE SPY

" Well !"

The old man crawled from his chair, and grovelled on the floor, looking like a large heap of dirt. He seized the leg of the table with one hand, and stretched the other toward Yevsey.

" Don't—you mustn't," he muttered in a loud whisper. " My dear sir, don't touch me."

Klimkov pressed the trigger more tightly, more tightly. His head chilled with the effort, his hair shook.

" I will go away—I'm going to get married to-morrow—I'll go away—for always—I'll never——"
His heavy, cowardly words rustled and crept in the air. Grease glistened on his chin, and the napkin over his bosom shook.

The revolver did not go off. Yevsey's finger pained, and horror took powerful possession of him from head to foot, impeding his breath.

" I can give you money," Solovyov whispered more quickly. " I will tell nothing—I will keep quiet—always—I understand——"

Klimkov raised his hand, and flung the revolver at the spy. Then he caught up his overcoat and ran off. Two feeble shouts overtook him :

" Ow ! ow !"

CHAPTER XXX

THE shrieks stuck to Yevsey, to the back of his neck, like leeches. They filled him with the power of insane horror, and drove him on, on, and on. Behind him a crowd of people were gathering, it seemed to him, noiselessly, their feet never touching the ground. They ran after him, stretching out scores of long, clutching hands, which reached his neck and touched his hair. They played with him, mocked at him, disappearing and reappearing. He took cabs, rode for a while, jumped out, ran along the streets, and rode again. For the crowd was near him all the time, unseen, yet by this the more horrible.

He felt more at ease when he saw before him the dark-patterned wall of bare boughs which stretched to meet him. He dived into the thicket of trees which stood upon the ground firmly, and walked in amid them, strangely moving his hands behind his back, as if to draw the trees together more compactly behind him. He descended into a ravine, seated himself on the cold soil, and rose again. Then he walked the length of the ravine, breathing heavily, perspiring, drunk with fear. Soon he saw an opening between the trees. He listened carefully, noiselessly advanced a few steps further, and looked. In front of him stretched the embankment of a railroad, beyond which rose more trees. These were small and far between. Through the network of their branches shone the grey roof of a building.

He walked back quickly up the bed of the ravine to where the woods were thicker and darker.

" They'll catch me "—the cold certainty pushed him on—" they'll catch me—they must be looking for me already—they're running."

A soft ringing sound strayed through the woods. It came from near by, and shook the thin branches, which swayed in the dusk of the ravine, filling the air with their rustle. Under his feet crackled thin ice, which covered the grey, dried-out little pits of the bed of a stream with white skin.

Klimkov sat down, bent over, and put a piece of ice in his mouth. The next instant he jumped to his feet, and clambered up the steep slope of the ravine. Here he removed his belt and braces, and began to tie them together, at the same time carefully examining the branches over his head.

" I needn't take my overcoat off," he reflected without self-pity. " The heavier the quicker."

He was in a hurry; his fingers trembled, and his shoulders involuntarily rose as if to conceal his neck. In his head a timorous thought kept knocking.

" I shan't have time. I'll be too late."

A train passed along the edge of the woods. The trees hummed in displeasure and the ground quivered. The white vapour threaded its way between the branches. It stole through the air and melted away, as though to get a look at this man and then disappear from his eyes.

334

Titmice came flying and whistling boldly. They gleamed in the dark nets of the branches, and their quick flight hastened the movements of Yevsey's cold and disobedient fingers.

He made a slipknot in the strap, threw it over a branch, and tugged at it. It was firm. Then, just as hurriedly, he began to make a slipknot in his braces, which he had twisted into a rope. When everything was ready, he heaved a sigh.

" Now I ought to say my prayers."

But the prayers did not come to him. He thought for a few seconds. The words flashed up, but were instantly extinguished, without forming themselves into a prayer.

" Rayisa knew my fate," he recalled unexpectedly.

Thrusting his head into the noose, he said quietly, simply, and without a quiver in his breast :

" In the name of the Father, and of the Son, and of the Holy Ghost——"

He pushed the ground with his feet, and jumped into the air, doubling his legs under him. There was a painful tug at his ears ; a strange inward blow hit his head, and stunned him. He fell. His whole body struck the hard earth, turned over, and rolled down the slope. His arms caught in the roots of trees, his head knocked against their trunks. He lost consciousness.

When he recovered his senses, he found himself sitting at the bottom of the ravine, the torn braces dangling over his breast. His trousers were torn, his scratched, blood-stained knees looked through the cloth pitifully. His body was a mass of pain, especially his neck, and the cold seemed to be flaying his skin. Throwing himself on his back, Yevsey looked up the incline. There, under a white birch-branch, the strap swung in the air like a thin serpent, and lured him to itself.

" I can't," he said to himself in despair—" I can't—nothing—I don't know how."

He began to cry thin tears of impotence and anger. He lay with his back on the ground, and through his tears saw over him the one-toned, dim sky, streaked by the dry designs of the dark branches.

He lay for a long time muffled in his overcoat, suffering from cold and pain. Without his willing it, his strange, senseless life passed before him like a chain of smoke-dark rings. It passed by him impetuously. It trampled pitilessly upon his half-dead soul, crushing it finally with heavy blows, which prevented one spark of hope from glimmering in his heart. It pressed him to the ground.

A dismal chord hummed and trembled brokenly in his breast. Its lugubrious song spread through his bones. His little dry body, quivering with a sickly tremor, shrivelled up in the cold of the twilight into a shelterless heap, pressed itself more and more closely to the ground, so firm and so powerful.

Trains passed the woods several times, filling it with a creaking and rumbling, with clouds of steam and rays of light. The rays glided by the trunks of the trees, as if feeling them, as if desiring to find some-body there. Then they hastily disappeared, quick, trembling, and cold.

When they found Yevsey and touched him, he raised himself to his feet with difficulty, and plunged into the obscurity of the woods in pursuit of them. He stopped at the edge, and leaned against a tree, waiting and listening to the distant angry hum of the city. It was already evening; the sky had grown purple. Over the city quietly flared a dim red. The lights were being kindled to meet the night.

From a distance sprang up a howling noise and a drone. The rails began to sing and ring. A train was passing over them, its red eyes twinkling in the twilight. And the dusk quickly sailed after it, growing ever thicker and darker. Yevsey went to the embankment as fast as he could, sank on his knees, then laid his side across the track, with his back to the train, and his neck upon the rail. He enveloped his head closely in the skirts of his overcoat.

For some seconds it was pleasant to feel the burning contact of the iron. It appeased the pain in his neck; but the rail trembled and sang louder, more alarmingly. It filled his whole body with an aching groan. The earth, too, now quivered with a fine tremor, as if swimming away from under his body and pushing him from itself.

The train rolled heavily and slowly, but the clang of its couplings, the even raps of the wheels upon the joinings of the rails were already deafening. Its snorting breath pushed Klimkov in the back. Everything round about him and with him shook in tempestuous agitation, and tore him from the ground.

He could wait no longer. He jumped to his feet, ran along the rails, and shouted in a high screech:

" I am guilty—I will everything—I will, I will !"

Along the smoothly polished metal of the rails darted reddish rays of light, outstripping Klimkov. They glared more and more fiercely. Now glowing strips to each side of him ran impetuously into the distance, directing his course.

337

" I will——" he yelled, waving his hands.

Something hard and wide struck his back. He fell across the sleepers between the red lines of rail, and the harsh iron rumble crushed his feeble screams.

This book, designed by
William B. Taylor
is a production of
Edito-Service S.A., Geneva

Printed in France

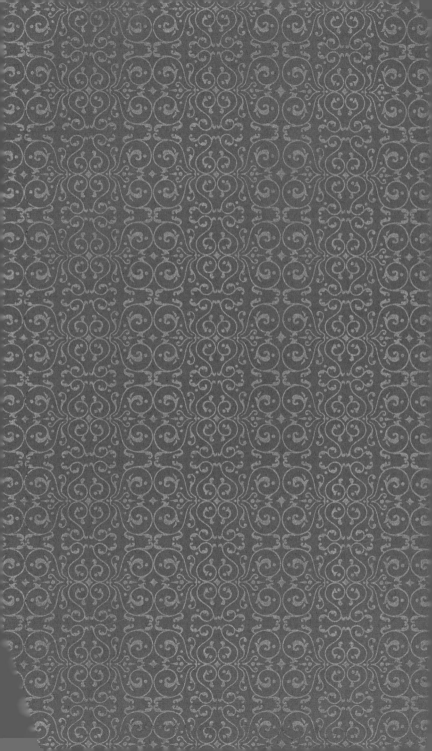